Wishing On a Star

Wishing On a Star Copyright © 2021 by Cion C. Lee.
All Rights Reserved. This book or any portion cannot be

reproduced in any form unless granted written

permission by the publisher, except for the use of brief quotations in book review.

This book is a work of fiction. All settings, characters,names,events,real people, living or dead, are in place to give the book a sense of reality. Any similarities to real life such as characters, places, names, or descriptions are entirely coincidental or a product of the author's imagination.

Chapter 1

January 2, 2020

It was indeed a new year. Star felt content as she stood in the middle of her three bedroom home that she'd poured her blood, sweat, and tears into getting. She never thought New Orleans would be the place she'd be laying down roots in because she'd gone out of her way to run away from this city. But between family, friends, and her love for this place she could never stay away completely. She'd visit as much as she could. Considering she was 35 minutes away in Slidell it wasn't hard. Still, visiting didn't equate to living and owning a home here. She finally felt complete.

"Mommy our room is so big!"

Star couldn't help the smile that spread across her face as her identical twin girls ran into the living room area. Their long curly ponytails bounced with excitement as they jumped all over the place. So far the best part of the new house had been seeing how much it made them happy. Ever since they'd entered the world on September 20, 2013, Star's sole purpose had been to keep a smile on their faces. She had fallen on some hard times, but her daughters never knew a thing.

"Y'all don't have to share a room anymore,no." Star said, even though she knew it was no use. Her babies were velcroed together. Seeing how hard they went for each other made her heart warm. God forbid something happened to her she was certain they'd hold eachother down.

"Me and my Twinkie want to share a room, mommy!" True shouted.

"Alright girl, don't go getting all excited." Star laughed. "What about you Tahiry? You don't want your own room?"

"I'm scared to be in the room by myself. I wanna be with my sister." She hunched her shoulders. To say they were so close they were like night and day. True was outspoken and sassy while Tahiry was shy and sweet. Star had the best of both worlds.

"This is the last box, sis." Star's brother, Diamond, announced as he entered the house. He helped her move today with the help of some movers that he'd hired and his brother Zane. They weren't blood like Star and Diamond, but they'd grown up in the same household together.

Their mom, Teoine, went to prison when they were both really young, which left Diamond and Star separated. Diamond was left with his mom's best friend, Zora, while Star was left with her mom's sister, Fee. Both environments weren't the best for either child, but Diamond wasn't subjected to verbal and physical abuse daily like Star. He also got to grow up with Zora's kids who fully accepted him as their brother. Star had always envied that because most of Fee's kids gave her hell. One would think it shouldn't have been like that because she was with family and they were her *blood* cousins, but it was her truth. She ended up leaving that hell hole before she even graduated high school because her cousin Devlin sexually assaulted her. No, he never got to touch her, but she wasn't going to give him the chance. She thought things could only get better after leaving. In some ways they did, and in some ways they didn't.

"Thank y'all so much." Star said graciously. "And thanks for paying to get my stuff moved Dia-"

"Thank me one more time," Diamond threatened. "I told you it's nothing. I'm just happy to have you and my nieces back home. Y'all wanna go get something to eat?"

"I don't knowww,"Star dragged. "I really should start unpacking, and I need to finish up this boo-"

"Star y'all gotta eat. Neyow's it is." Diamond said with finality. Sometimes Star would forget she was the oldest by two years at 25 with the way he constantly took charge. He'd grown up to be a good man.

"Yes! I like that restaurant,uncle!" True clapped before jumping into Diamond's arms.

"Yea? What do you like eating from there, True?" He grinned.

"Osh-sters!" She said "Oysters" the best way she could with her two missing front teeth.

"And what you want, Ri?" He asked Tahiry who was looking up at them while clutching her favorite Trollz Build-a-Bear.

"Strawberry cheesecake." She answered clearly.

"Damn these children got some elite tastebuds. I wasn't eating shit but noodles and pig lips when I was five." Zane chuckled.

"Language, Zane." Star pursed her lips. Everytime he came around her kids he had a potty mouth.

"Shit, my bad." He apologized.

"Another bad word." Tahiry sighed heavily, making everybody laugh.

The thought of moving back to New Orleans permanently used to scare Star shitless, but looking around at all the love in the room she knew she'd made the right decision.

January 3, 2020

"Mommy can I stay at home with you?" Tahiry whined as they walked to the car.

"No baby, you can't miss the first day of school." Star yawned as she hit the locks to her 2019 black Honda Civic. She knew they were tired because she was tired. Moving the day before their first day of school probably wasn't the best idea, but it was done now. They were only going to kindergarten so they'd be fine. Hell they even had an hour of nap time.

"Mommy I wanted to wear my hair hanging." True complained.

"Maybe next week, True." She lied. Her girls had way too much hair for her to just allow it to hang. They also had 4b hair textures like her which meant it was hard to maintain. So ponytails were the go to hairstyle for them unless it was a special occasion.

On the way to their school Star blasted some of their favorite songs to get them pumped up for their first day at their new school. When she looked back and saw them singing along and jamming she knew it was working.

When she walked the girls into their classroom at Ursuline Academy she felt grateful that she could afford to send them to a great school to earn the best education. Ursiline was one of the top rated all girls elementary through high school in New Orleans. The only thing that had her skeptical about the school at first was the assumption that it was predominately white. When she visited at the beginning of December she saw that wasn't the case. The school was diverse from the faculty to the scholars. Her girls would fit in great here.

"Good evening Ms. Francois! I've been waiting for you!" The teacher walked over eagerly to shake Star's hand.

"You have?" Star smiled. It was the first day back after winter break, so she was certain that her girls weren't the only newbies.

"Yes! When the Dean told me I would have Thee Starlah Francois' daughters in my class I felt honored. We have so many of your books here in our library. Wishing on a Star is my son Timmy's favorite book. It helped him stop wetting the bed."

Star cheesed from ear to ear. It amazed her how she never revealed her face as the author behind her children's books, yet she was still recognized by her name. She did have a unique one, so she couldn't say it surprised her.

"Thank you so much. I'm honored." She touched her heart.

"The honor is all mine, Ms.Francois. Your daughters will be in great hands. I promise."

"That's great to know, Mrs. Towner. And please, call me Star."

"Okay, well call me Pat." She giggled, as her white skin turned bright red. She was having a fangirl moment for sure, but she couldn't help herself. She'd been reading Star's books to her kids and pupils for the past two and a half years. The books were so well written for kids and they always had a valuable message that wasn't hard to miss.

"Will do,"Star nodded, before looking down at her girls. "Behave yourself, ladies. And give mommy a kiss."

She knelt down and kissed their little faces. Unlike most parents, she never did the most when she dropped her kids off at school on the first day. They had begun going to daycare when they were only three months old because she had to get a job. Then when January hit she enrolled in school at Southern University. When she moved to Baton Rouge life got ten times harder. She received a lot of government help that kept her afloat, so she didn't have to maintain a full time job. But it was still hard being a full time student and mother. There was no off button for either role and with no family help, she was always overwhelmed. Thankfully, she'd graduated college way back in spring of 2017, but she still appreciated her breaks as a mother. Them going to school was just that. She planned on unpacking, napping, and writing while they were here. When she picked them up she was going to check in with the Dean about after school activities.

"Come on! Come on! Smile y'all! It's the second half of the school year. Y'all almost done." Tahj pep talked to his kids as they climbed into his Acura MDX. It was funny to him how they were acting as if they were going to the electric chair when these were the best years of their lives. They had zero responsibilities and they were only in elementary school. These were the golden years of school.

"Daddy, mama ain't give us breakfast,"his Junior, Baby Tahj, snitched as soon as he climbed in the car. "I'm staying with you for the rest of the week so the chef can cook for me."

"Boy, I don't have a chef at my house 24/7,"Tahj laughed. "I only do that when y'all come over."

"Well can you move back with us daddy?" His youngest daughter at four, Tahja, asked.

Tahj didn't even know how to respond to that as guilt consumed him. He thought he was doing his kids a favor by having them all under one roof, but it gave them a false sense of reality. There was nothing normal about him playing house with both of his baby mama's and all of their kids. It was beneficial for him at the time because he was still screwing them both and he loved coming home to all of his kids. He knew how it felt to jump between two households because he'd done it for a while. It was nothing but drama and confusion. No matter what he did he could never please everybody and somebody always felt like they were getting the shorter end of the stick.

He came up with the idea of them all moving in together once his bm's, Janikka and Alyxandria, started to actually get along for the sake of the kids. At first they hated each other's guts. Nikka was his highschool girlfriend and first love. When he went away to college they decided to part ways, but they never actually stopped messing around. Lexi was supposed to be his rebound college chick, but he had fucked around and caught feelings for her. When he was away at school it was all about Lexi, but whenever he came home he was all for Nikka. Shit hit the fan when Nikka got pregnant with Baby Tahj. It was WW3 and neither one of them were trying to let Tahj go.

It's like they came to a mutual understanding by the time both of them were on their second kid with him. Neither of them were walking away and they were tired of the drama, so they just accepted that he was going to deal with both of them. So when he suggested that they move in together they agreed. The arrangement was copacetic until Lexi got pregnant for a third time. Naturally Tahj thought it was for him, but that wasn't the case this time around.

With Tahj's busy career as a sports/entertainment manager, he was always on the go, so she got lonely. Nikka was a good girl who could hold it down for him, but Lexi wasn't set up that way. She'd been a hot girl until she allowed Tahj to sit her down. She started feeling really stupid being there catering to him when he wasn't even faithful to her and Nikka. That's right, he was still out in the streets sleeping with other girls as if he wasn't already having his cake and eating it too. So she said fuck it and began doing her thing. Unfortunately she'd been caught with her hand in the cookie jar. When her son came out with blue eyes and white skin, it appeared as if the wind had been knocked out of Tahj.

Lexi couldn't even flex, she just started bawling and admitted to the affair she'd been having with a white plastic surgeon by the name of Channing. Just like that their little arrangement was dead. Nikki was happy because she thought she'd finally have Tahj to herself but she was mistaken. Tahj couldn't just live with Nikka after living with them both. That would make his kids feel like he was choosing between them, and he'd never. So he let the house go that they shared together and everybody moved into separate spaces.

He was still smashing Nikka on the regular, and she was constantly demanding things like marriage or a relationship, but he wasn't trying to hear that shit. As for Lexi, she'd married her baby daddy and she was pretending to be happy with him, but she was constantly sending Tahj pussy pictures. He wouldn't double back and fuck her ass with the next niggas dick.

"Yea, we wanna live with you!" His oldest daughter, Tazzlyn exclaimed, adding to his guilt. "Channing is nice, but he's not you daddy!"

Tahj chuckled. "I'm glad to hear that, Tazzy. But y'all do live with me. I told y'all my house is y'all house, and if y'all want to spend the night for the rest of the week y'all can."

"YAYYYY!" They all applauded, as he silently dreaded moving his schedule around to accommodate them. But putting his kids first was his number one priority. He also had the pull to move shit around in his work life.

"Now Colley, why is this lil girl not in school?" Star asked as her little cousin, Collandria, stepped into her house with her three year old daughter, Caidence, on her hip.

"Girl, she only three. She don't have to be in school."

"There's pre-school, yea, Colley."

"And that's a waste of our time and money. Ain't that right Suga?" Colley referred to her by her nickname before pecking her cheek. "Say hey girl."

"Hey Titi Star," Suga said in her adorable voice. Star's heart always swelled when she looked at Caidence because she was like a younger version of the twins with her perfect brown skin, her round nose, and her big lips. The only difference was that True had a silky hair texture much like Colley. In fact, people would always mistake those three for siblings in public. That placed all kinds of crazy ideas in Star's head because she had no idea who Caidence's daddy was, and Colley wasn't trying to share. One day Star just came out and asked if Colley had fucked her baby daddy. Colley was so offended that they didn't talk for a little while.

Star felt a little bad, but Colley could get downright grimey where men were concerned. She wasn't opposed to fucking with men that had entire families or wives. Colley could admit she had her scandalous ways, but the one person she'd never cross was Star. Star had been like the big sister she never had since they were in diapers. She could honestly say she loved Star more than she loved the majority of her *real* siblings. Most of those mutherfuckers were dead to her, but that's another story.

Seeing how mad Colley got over the accusation made Star realize that she was tripping. If she was being honest their girls probably looked like each other because their mothers were blood sisters with the same mom and dad. Teione and Fee looked just alike, and their girls resembled them both.

"Hey Suga baby,"Star poked her nose before whisking her away from Colley. "Tell your mama to put you in daycare so you can get used to school before you have to go to real school."

"I told you it's a waste of money." Colley smacked her teeth.

"Says the girl with a brand new Chanel bag on her arm. Miss me with the bs, Colley." Star rolled her eyes. Colley didn't have a day or a night job. Her job was dating men with money and making them take care of her, government assistance, and she also received money from her baby daddy. Sometimes Star would be irritated because Colley wasn't living up to her full potential, but she'd stopped preaching a long time ago. Colley was a 22 year old woman going on 23 soon, her life was hers to live. At the very least she could say she took great care of Suga. Colley had also been through a lot in her younger years, so Star would forever have a soft spot for her. She was another big reason Star had returned to New Orleans.

"Sister cousin," Colley flashed her pretty smile. Looking at her face made Star's head hurt sometimes because God really took his time with her. She was drop dead gorgeous.

"No bitch. Yo light skin ass always want something."

"How do you know I want something?" She asked innocently as her brown eyes wandered.

"Anytime you smile at me and say sister cousin you want something."

"Bitch I just need you to watch Suga while I go to Atlanta this weekend. That's it."

"That's it?!"

"C'monnnn, my daddy is working all weekend and you know Cordell then move away." She said, referring to her brother. Out of all her siblings they were the only ones who shared the same mom and dad. He was also the only one Star and Colley were close with. Those other three could go straight to hell.

"I'm working this weekend too, bitch."

"But you work from home."

"And?!"

"C'monnn. The twins are gonna be here too."

"Shitttt...I'm finna find an activity to put their asses in."

"Whatever it is, sign Suga up too."

"Oh but you would spend money on that but you can't spend it on day care?"

"Star pleaseeee," she begged. "This Atlanta Falcons player is tryna fly me out. We've only been texting and he already sent me 10k. Let me go run this bag up right quick."

Star just looked off.

"Fine. I guess she gotta come with me." Colley shrugged.

Star sucked her teeth. "You can leave her with me, Colley! Damn!"

"Thank you sister cousin," she smiled. She always got her way with Star. "Ima bring snacks and stuff when I drop her off on Friday."

Chapter 2

January 17, 2020

"I know I tell you this everytime I come in here, but I'm proud of you sis." Tahj expressed as he looked around at his younger sister's dance school. "Taija LeBlanc's Dance Academy" had been gifted to her by her husband, Supreme, last April. Between being pregnant for the second time and having a wedding last year, Taija aka Choc was finally opening the doors to her dance school for the new year. It was registration week and she'd already accepted over 100 applications. She was thrilled. She was also happy that she'd followed her first mind and hired five other dance teachers. It was looking like she'd need all the help she could get.

"And I love hearing it everytime." Choc smiled brightly. She was only a year younger than Tahj at 30, but he was her only older sibling so she loved making him proud. His opinion meant a lot to her. Honestly, his opinion meant a lot to all of their siblings. Tahj was like a father figure to them because their real one was trash.

Tahj poked her cheek. "You glowing, Choc. Let me find out you let that nigga Supreme knock you up again."

"Ouuu, I want another little cousin Titi Choc!" Tahjaria clapped her hands excitedly. She was Tahj's second oldest daughter that he'd had with Nikka.

"You better holla at one of your other aunties or uncles, Jari." Choc pursed her lips. "I don't know what your daddy is talking about but ain't no more babies coming outta me until Siraiya is at least two."

"She's almost one so that's close enough." Tahj said while holding back laughter.

"Nigga my baby barely 5 months! Cut it out."

"I'm just fucking with ya." He laughed.

"I'm not laughing though. Fill out these packets for your daughters so you can get out my face."

His laughter ceased. "You gon really make me do all this paperwork, Choc?"

"Hell yea. Ain't no special treatment round here."

"I'm saying though…you they auntie. You know everything about them."

"And? If they're going to be students at *this* dance academy then I need all their information on file. I'm running a serious institution here."

"Alright, bruh. Hand me a pen."

Since today was the last day for registration it had been Choc's busiest day thus far. She was the last one left at the school and her husband was waiting for her in the parking lot. He was ready to go but she said she'd be here until 7 on Instagram, so she wanted to stand by that. Being professional was everything to her. There was only ten minutes left, so she had begun cleaning up. In the midst of her sweeping the entrance, the front door jingled. She looked up and the first thing she saw was two dark brown girls.

"Titi babies what are y'all doing back he..."her words trailed off once she came to the realization that she'd put her foot in her mouth. She assumed two of her nieces were entering the building. Obviously it wasn't Tahjaria and Tazzlyn, but damn they had the same face, same walk, same hair, same everything. Hell they even looked like *her* when she was that little. Choc's heart momentarily stopped.

"I-I'm sorry,"Choc clutched her chest as she looked up at Star. "Your girls reminded me of my nieces. They're beautiful."

"Thank you,"Star smiled. She was totally lost when Choc first acknowledged them, but now she was trying to place her face. She looked awfully familiar. But New Orleans was small so it was possible that she'd seen her around growing up or something. "I'm Star Francois, and these are my daughters. I got your card from a lady who works in the office at their school. She said you're a former SU dancing doll and how everyone is scrambling to send their daughters here to learn from you. I went and watched some of your old footage on YouTube from your days as a doll and I was impressed. I know this is the school for my girls. I just hope I'm not too late for registration."

"Nope. Just in time. What are these beauties' names?" Choc smiled down at the twins. When they smiled back she got goosebumps. They had her little sister Tamia's smile.

"I'm True and this is my twin sister Tahiry."

Choc wasn't trying to do the most, but this couldn't have been a coincidence. These babies looked just like her damn family and had names that started with a "T." They had to belong to one of the men in her family. It was just sad she didn't know who. The only male she could positively rule out was her younger brother Tavior. She was certain that he was faithful to his girlfriend, who was also pregnant with his child. It could've been a toss up between her dad, Tahj, and her other brother Tarik. She was honestly leaning more towards her dad or Tarik because Tahj claimed all of his kids and took great care of them. Her dad was a deadbeat and Tarik ran through girls like he did underwear. He could definitely have babies out here that he didn't know about. Her dad on the other hand knew about the babies he made but he just abandoned them if they weren't for his wife, Porscha. She was the mother of Tahj and Tamia, while the rest of them were outside kids or as she would call them; bastards.

Choc's smile grew. "Twinsss? I have twins of my own! Y'all are identical aren't you?"

"Yes,"Tahiry nodded.

"And how old are you ladies? Five? Six?" Choc guessed just based on their height.

True gasped. "You're good. We are six! How'd you know?"

Choc and Star laughed.

"Lucky guess." Choc smirked. "The registration packets are he-"

"Oh I already filled them out. I had the lady from the office grab me two when she came to sign her daughters up." Star pulled the paperwork from her Coach bag and handed it to Choc.

"Ouuu, they go to Ursuline?" Choc questioned as her eyes scanned over one of the forms. "So do my nieces."

"It's only been a few weeks since they've been there, but I love it so far."

"Yea I'll probably send my daughter there too. My nieces are only in Kindergarten and they know so much."

"Will they be coming here too?"

"You know it." Choc giggled. "Their parents are happy to get rid of them for a few hours every week."

"Well hey, I ain't mad at em." Star laughed.

"That's sad," Choc said playfully. "But I'm happy to take these babies off y'all hands and teach them everything I know."

"And we're looking forward to it. Aren't we girls?"

"Yessss!" They said enthusiastically. They were both girly girls so this was a dream come true for them. They couldn't wait to put on their leotards, tutus, and tights to dance.

"I like that excitement. Something tells me we're going to get along great, girls." Choc grinned, while thinking about which one of her siblings she was going to call first to ask about these twins.

It was just Star's luck that the twins' allergies had started acting up once they got home. She blamed the bipolar weather in New Orleans. It had been warm all week and today it was freezing cold. It was a good thing that Colley seemed to never want to leave her house, because she was able to stay behind with the girls while Star ran out to get some medicine. Usually she kept what she needed in the house, but with the move things were all over the place.

She went right to a 24 hour Walmart that wasn't far from her Gretna home. While she was there she decided to rack up on some wine and snacks that she liked to have while she was writing. As she was exiting the wine aisle she ran smack dead into another cart. The little girl that sat in the cart screamed. Star gasped and apologized, but her breath was immediately taken away when she locked eyes with the man pushing the cart.

Tahj's stomach did a backflip when he locked eyes with the girl who made him fall for her in record time before ghosting his ass. She literally went poof into thin air. He was so salty that he just said fuck her and wrote her off. Now she was standing here seven years later looking more beautiful than the last time he saw her. He didn't think that was possible. She had to be a vampire or something because she didn't age one bit.

Her rich brown skin was still blemish free and radiant. Her thick, coily hair was still full, shiny, and reached her shoulders like he'd remembered. Although she was wearing sweats, he could tell that body was still banging. Star was by far the thickest girl he'd encountered and it was all natural. She was the definition of home grown. Her body was just the cherry on top though. This girl was *beautiful*. God simply was not playing fair when he'd created her. Her face still looked so innocent and angelic. The way she stared at him with her big brown eyes and the way her big lips poked out had him wanting to empty his wallet and give her everything in it. That was exactly how her ass ran off on him the last time.

"Can't speak, Star?" He finally addressed her.

Star's heart dropped. She'd really convinced herself that he wouldn't remember her. She was certain that the little Christmas break fling that they'd had in 2012 wasn't anything special to him. Sure, he'd given her a place to stay when she couldn't live with her Auntie Fee anymore and he broke her virginity, but those were things that were special to *her*. He on the other hand had a whole family that he'd neglected to tell her about. She had to find out through the girlfriend of his client. That was her first heartbreak and she still remembered it vividly. She wouldn't wish the way she felt that day on her worst enemy. That feeling stuck with her over the years and that's why she could never give any man a fair chance. She'd date her and there, and she'd even slept with three more guys, but she always held back because she had trust issues thanks to this nigga standing before her.

Sometimes she'd bitterly wish ugliness and dad weight on Tahj whenever he'd cross her mind, but her miserable thoughts had no bearing on his appearance. He looked just as good as she remembered. He had a more mature vibe about him but that was a given since he was in his early 30's now.

His 360 waves and shape up looked fresh along with his beard, like he'd just gotten out of his barbers chair. He still towered over her 5'3 frame, making her look up at him. Tahj was well over 6 ft tall and he lived in the gym, so he was cocky as fuck. In that very moment Star got a sex flashback of when he'd wrap those strong arms around her waist. Her pussy thumped at the memory.

It made no sense for this man to be this fine and handsome. She couldn't tell how he felt about her, but when his strong jaw clenched she was certain he had smoke for her. Guilt immediately crept in. Did he know?

"You just gon stare at me and not speak?" He snapped.

"H-hey Tahj." She was finally able to get out.

"You bumped our cart!" Tahjaria sassed.

Chills ran up Star's spine. It was like she was looking at her daughters. They *sounded* and everything. Lil mama had even mouthed off to her like True would've.

"I'm sorry, baby. Let me get out y'all way." Star attempted to scurry off, but Tahj wasn't letting her go that easy.

"Where are you going , furniture thief?"

When she left his property that he was allowing her to stay in she took everything out that bitch except the Christmas tree. That included the furniture he'd purchased for the place. Yea he'd only furnished the home to make her stay as comfortable as possible, but she was outta pocket for taking it all when she decided to leave. She'd played his ass like a guitar.

He thought he'd fucked her into submission as far Nikka was concerned. He knew he was wrong for not being upfront about having a baby and a baby mama that he was playing house with, but he never expected to fall for Star the way he did. His only motive was to help her out in her time of need. He knew her from his auntie's old neighborhood and he was aware of how shitty her family was. He had a big heart and for some reason it was drawn to her. Unfortunately, his dick was drawn to her as well and once he stuck it in her he really fell head over heels.

To make a long story short he wanted Star to stick around despite the fact that he was with somebody else. He thought they came to that understanding on Christmas Eve. Once Christmas came he went home to Nikka and then he went to Disney World with her and Baby Tahj. Since he'd been chatting with Star over the phone the entire time he thought they were good. So his face hit the floor when he returned to his house and saw it empty. Sure it was a long time ago, but her ass still had some explaining to do.

"How I'ma steal something that was mine?" Star twisted her neck. The other side to her he remembered finally made an appearance. She could be sweet as hell but her attitude was nothing nice.

"Yours? You bought that shit?"

"No, but you bought it for me. That's why I took it when I left. If it's a problem go contact the police."

"Girl c'mon...if I was that mad about it I would've done that years ago."

"Okay, so why bring it up?" Her face twisted up.

"Because man, you tryna walk past me like I'm a stranger. What we shared didn't mean anything to you?"

"Nope. It was nothing but a meaningless fling." She fronted, but it was pretty convincing.

"Meaningless? That's how you feel about your first?" He smirked smugly. She could cap all day, but he knew what it was. Women never forget their first time.

Star let out a light laugh. "Oh Tahj...you were *not* my first."

His heart skipped a beat as his face hardened. "What?!"

She laughed forreal this time.

That's when it dawned on him. "So you lying now? You bled all on the sheets that night. Stop playing with me."

Tahjaria gasped. "She bled? Is she hurt, daddy?"

"Yea she hurt. That's why she's lying."

"Okay Tahj," she said nonchalantly. "You got that. But that was *so* seven years ago. It was nice to catch up, but I'd like to go now. Please let my arm go."

That's when he realized he still had a hold of her. He dropped her arm before glancing down at her cart.

"You got kids?" He asked bluntly while eyeing the children's Benadryl.

"Yup. Just like you."

"Maybe we can get them together one da-"

She cut him off. "Tahj don't be ridiculous."

"I'm saying, you don't wanna catch up?"

She looked at him like he was crazy. "No. I don't. I walked away for a reason and I'm sure that reason still exists."

She wanted to say so much more, but out of respect for Tahj's daughter she wasn't going to do it. But she was sure he was still fucking with his baby mama. She was a part of the reason why she decided not to tell Tahj about the twins in the first place.

That's right, the twins were Tahj's daughters. They were more than likely conceived the very first time they had sex. Star didn't find out she was pregnant until February of 2013. She was still in high school so her first thought was to have an abortion. As soon as she found out it was two lives inside of her that was no longer an option. The thought of getting rid of one baby was hard to live with, but two? She couldn't bring herself to do that. As summer rolled around and her pregnancy started getting real, she got scared. Being a first time mother was hard enough, so the thought of doing it on her own with two babies had her shook. She didn't know if Tahj's number had changed but she was going to put it to use. That was until she saw him in the mall with Janikka and she had a small round belly. They didn't notice her, but she saw them clear as day kissing while he caressed her belly all lovingly. Suddenly not telling him seemed like the right thing to do. She could handle a lot, but him rejecting their kids wasn't one of them.

After that day she deleted all of her social media because it was easier to keep folks out of her business that way. She only got Instagram and Facebook back two years ago to promote her work. Those pages were strictly about her books. Not her personal life.

"Actually I don't know why you walked away. Let's go have dinner and talk about i-"

Star smacked her teeth and walked right around him. He was obviously still a whore. Trying to take her out to dinner while he had his daughter with him was just low. Janikka had great time if she was still with his ass.

"Star!" He called out after her. He didn't want to let her get away because there was no telling when he'd see her again. He at least wanted her number or something. He started to go after her, but he had to check himself. Maybe what they shared needed to stay in the past. She obviously wasn't trying to fuck with him and it wasn't like they had long,drawn out history with eachother. What they had was intense for sure, but it was only for a few weeks. He didn't need her in his life like he needed air. That's why he was confused about his chest hurting as he watched her fat ass twist away in her grey sweats.

"Daddy, who was that lady? Mommy know her?"

Tahj chuckled. "No baby, mommy doesn't know her."

"Oh...she was pretty or whatever."

"Lil girl you funny." Tahj laughed before kissing her cheek. "You got all the snacks y'all wanted?"

"Y'all? I got what I wanted. I didn't know I was getting stuff for other people."

"Your brothers and sisters need snacks too, Jari."

"Well I guess they can have some of my stuff..." she rolled her eyes.

Tahj laughed hysterically. His daughters were nothing nice. Thirty minutes later he had loaded the car with the grocery's. He had to rush and do that because it was freezing outside. He took a second to let his body warm up in his car before pulling off. In the midst of doing that, his phone started ringing. He looked down at the screen and answered right away.

"Wassup, Choc?"

"I think we have two new members of the family."

"Aw shit, you pregnant with twins again?" He grinned.

"What?! Boy no! Stop wishing pregnancy on me! The twins I'm speaking of are six years old and they're not mine."

When he heard the number six he paused. He'd always been good at math and some shit just wasn't adding up. He didn't even have all the details yet and the wheels in his head were already spinning.

"Twins? What are their names and who are they for?"

"Okay so boom, this woman comes into my dance school late today to register her twin daughters. I kid you not, I thought they were your daughters when they walked in. I was about to address them as Jari and Tazzy, I swear! But their names are Tahiry and True and I have no idea who they're for. My money is on your no good ass daddy or maybe Tarik…but I'm leaning more towards Tarell," she referenced their father by his first name like all his kids would do whenever discussing him.

"Choc. What's their mama name?"

"Uhhhh...I'm drawing a blank but it's a unique name for sure. Unique and pretty. She was fine as hell too...and young! I can see Tarell being all over that. She had pretty dark brown skin, gorgeous kinky hair, a perfect face, and she was thick as pancake batter. A real brickhouse. Not those slim thick bitches you mess with."

Tahj's heart was beating so fast that it was about to pop out of his chest. Choc had just described the bitch that he'd seen in Walmart from head to toe.

"Is her name Star?"

"Omg! Yes! How'd you know?! Oh shit, your mom told you about her didn't she? She always knows about the outside kids. Wait, do you think Star knows I'm Tarell's daughter? I hope she's not on no weird shit."

Tahj ignored everything she was saying because it was so off base. He wasn't going to correct her either. He needed to play this smart. The last thing he needed was

Star's trifling ass running off again. It was no telling what he'd do when he saw her again but he planned on seeing her again. That was for sure.

"Go look at her paperwork and see where she stays, Choc." He demanded calmly. He wanted to pull up on her right this second.

"First of all, that's at the school. Second of all, hell no!!! I can't give you that girl's address."

"I just want to ask her some things. Those twins are our blood."

"I mean I'm not saying a relationship shouldn't be established, but let's do it the right way. Feel free to come to the first day of dance class on Monday. We'll have a *friendly* chat with her after class."

Tahj really didn't want to wait until Monday but maybe that was best. With the way his adrenaline was pumping at the moment he'd ring that bitch's neck and not think twice about it.

"Yea, you right sis. I'll see you on Monday. Who else did you tell about this?"

"You're the first person I called. I was supposed to call hours ago but these kids had me tied up."

"Cool. Let's keep it between us for now."

"Okay. We can do that." Choc agreed, not thinking much of it. Meanwhile Tahj was plotting.

Chapter 3

January 18, 2020

"Cousin I was thinking I might as well just move here with you," Colley said as Star sat breakfast down on the table. She made waffles, scrambled eggs, and bacon. The meal was slight but Colley loved waking up to hot food, and Star would cook everyday.

"I was thinking you should stop thinking. I like having y'all here and all but don't wear out your welcome." Star rolled her eyes because she was really wishing Colley would go home already. She loved her company but she also loved her space sometimes.

"Ugh, you so mean, hoe."

"Language, Colley." She scolded while looking around at their daughters who were going in on their food while watching Peppa Pig on the tv that was across the room in the living room area. She loved that her dining and living room were conjoined. It felt really cozy.

"They ain't paying me no mind. But I'm going home today, girl. I can see you getting tired of us."

"Don't do that. Especially to my baby, Suga."

"Oh so you wanna keep her? Cause I'll go run and get her some clothes right n-"

"Bitch I then kept your child every weekend since I moved back. Go to hell."

"Well damnnnn," Colley laughed. "All you had to do was say no! Lawd."

"No is never enough with you and you know it…but ummm, I got something to tell you."

"I'm listening."

"Ok. I'ma talk in code."

"Girl, these children is not worrying about us!"

"You underestimate them too much. They listen when you least expect it."

"Yea, yea. What's tea, Star?" She pressed anxiously.

"I saw TB yesterday."

"TB…"Colley repeated, trying to figure out who she was talking about. When she solved the code, her eyes expanded. "Noooo! Where at cousin?!"

"Walmart of all places."

"Whew,"Colley breathed. "Imagine if you had the girls with you. That boy would've yoked you up. Shit probably worse."

Chills ran all over Star's body because she could definitely see him doing worse if he ever found out the truth. She couldn't even say with confidence that she didn't deserve it. He would have a right to be angry. At the time she felt like she was doing the right thing, but as the girls grew older and had questions she realized she'd made a selfish move. She couldn't handle any more heartbreak or rejection, but that didn't mean Tahj would abandon his kids. Then again maybe he would've and she was just tripping with herself. Either way, she should've put the ball in his court and she'd failed to do that. By the time she'd started feeling guilty she felt like she was in too deep to pull herself out. He was one huge reason why she avoided moving back to New Orleans for so long. Running into him was something she didn't want to deal with. That reason obviously wasn't far fetched. She hadn't been back home for a full month yet and she'd already seen his ass.

"I don't even want to think about that, girl."

"You need to. Whatchu always tell me? Put my big girl panties on? That's what you need to do asap. He deserves to know and you know it."

"I know you not talking. Because I still don't know who your bd is." She said in a hushed tone.

"And you don't need to know. He knows that she exists and that's the point I'm getting at. Don't deflect, Star. Unlike you I let that nigga know what was what, he decided not to be in her life." Colley shrugged. What was sad was that it looked like she really didn't give a fuck. She was really cold hearted with men.

"And what if TB does the same thing? We're doing just fine and we don't need any hurt in our lives."

"Star, you're making this about you. If you tell TB in private his reaction will not affect the girls. Give him a chance to take care of his responsibilities because based on Instagram he looks good at it."

"Ugh, social media has you brainwashed. I told you I don't wanna hear about that boys page."

When Star got her Instagram back she didn't look or lurk on Tahj's page. He was out of sight, out of mind for her. Most of the time that made forgetting him easy. She never had to see him. Colley would try to tell her things she saw on social media about him and she'd always kill the conversation. She didn't want to hear shit about him or his family.

"I was just saying that he takes care of all four of his kids and his baby mama's are set up nice."

"All four? He has four kids now? By two different women? See…no, he's running a circus over there and I want no parts."

She really couldn't believe it. There was really no exclusivity about being his baby mama and it hurt her to be a part of that list.

"Girl, your parts are at this table with us watching Playhouse Disney. You think ignoring what's real will make it go away? Because it won't. Prolonging the situation just makes it worse. They'll be seven this year, Star. Seven years this ma-"

"Alright," Star snapped. "You saying too much now. I get it. I need to come clean."

"Mhmm, so you want me to hit him up on the gram right now?"

"No! I can do that myself."

"When?" Colley raised an eyebrow skeptically.

"When I feel like it."

"Girlll…" Colley shook her head.

"Look, it's been approximately seven years. A few more days so I can't think of an approach, won't hurt."

"Star, this shit gon blow up in your face if you keep playing. Mark my words."

January 20, 2020

Usually the weekend flew by fast, but it dragged this time. Monday was now here and it was moving even slower than the weekend did. Tahj could barely focus on the virtual business meetings he had or any other work he had to do. All he could think about was killing Star. The few days that passed hadn't calmed him down one bit. He had only gotten more mad. He was so mad that he pulled up to Choc's dance school early.

Janikka had dropped the girls off and he was supposed to be picking them up, but he couldn't wait around for another hour and a half. He pulled into the parking lot ten minutes after Janikka had dropped the girls off, which really defeated the purpose of her bringing them. It was a good thing he arrived when he did though. He got a clear view of Star walking the twins…his twins into the school. Yea he was claiming them already because that feeling he got in his chest when he saw them couldn't be mistaken. It was the same feeling he got when he witnessed all of his kids be born. He knew he was looking at his flesh and blood.

Even if there wasn't a feeling the resemblance was uncanny. He hadn't seen them up close yet but it felt like he was watching Tazzy and Jari walk in with Star. They even had their hair styled in the same bun. Then there was the math. It all added up. From Choc he'd learned that the twins were born on September, 20th of 2013. Nine months prior to that he was fucking Star raw. This bitch had really kept this a secret. He'd done a good job at not exploding yet, but seeing his daughters made shit real. He saw red.

When Star walked back out of the school, he jumped out of his ride. She was scrolling through her phone as she walked past him, completely oblivious about his presence. She was made aware quickly as she felt her hair being yanked. It felt like someone was trying to snatch her bald and break her neck. Her natural response was to scream because clearly someone was trying to attack her. It was dark outside and the parking lot was empty. Most parents were inside watching through the glass window, sitting in the lobby, or they'd dropped their kids off and left. Star had planned to go sit in her car and write. She quickly wished she'd kept her ass inside when a strong hand clamped over her mouth. She felt herself being lifted off the ground and carried away. She was paralyzed with fear, so fighting back wasn't in her. When she got tossed in the car and came face to face with her assailant her eyes widened in horror.

"Yea bitch! I know everything and I should kill your stupid ass!"

"Tahj…" her voice cracked as tears rolled down her face. She was laying on her back in his back seat so she tried to sit up, but he viciously pushed her back down.

"Shut the fuck up. You had damn near seven years to talk. It's my turn now, you stupid ass hoe."

"Wait hold up, no-" she attempted to sit up again, but he held her down.

"Star I will knock you the fuck out. Don't play with me right now."

"So you would hit me?" She whimpered.

"Bitch I can kill your stupid ass for what you did! Fuck you!"

"Fuck me?!" She screamed through tears. "No bitch, fuck you! You acting like I'm this fucked up person for not telling you but look at how you handling me now!"

"BITCH DON'T FLIP THIS SHIT ON ME!" He barked in her face, terrifying her even more. "I just found out that I have two daughters that I don't even know about! I'm entitled to react however the fuck I want!"

Star just laid there letting the tears roll down her face.

"Yea you don't got shit to say now because you know this shit is wrong!!! What did I do that was so bad that you felt like you deserved to rob me of being a father to my daughters? And just fuck the twins, huh? I guess they didn't deserve a daddy because you were hurt."

"We didn't need you." She mumbled.

"Huh?" He leaned forward. "Say it again. I didn't hear you."

She knew she should've shut the fuck up and let him have his moment, but shutting up never came easy to her. Especially as a grown ass woman.

"I *said* we didn't need you! You was already over there playing house with another bitch and y'all ki-"

SLAP!

Star couldn't believe it! That nigga had actually popped her in the mouth. It was the type of pop her mom would give her whenever she got too mouthy. He didn't use immense strength, but it was the principle. He'd put his hands on her! Everything went blank and she just started swinging and kicking.

"You hit me!" She screamed through tears as she kicked him in his chest.

"I sure did! Cause what the fuck Janikka and my kids with her gotta do with my kids would you? Huh?!" He clamored, as he wrapped his arms around her neck. Oxygen being ripped away from her made her calm down significantly. When she stopped trying to fight him, he let her go. She started gasping dramatically.

"Man I yoked yo ass up for 10 seconds. Kill that extra shit and let's talk now."

"TALK?! You wanna talk?! Bitch I should call the police on you!"

"Alright and after that we gon still have to talk because I'm going to be in my daughters' lives! Don't think you bouta keep them away from me!"

She rubbed her aching neck. "Why would I do that?"

Tahj breathed heavily while rubbing his hands over his face. He was trying his hardest not to knock this girl out but she just kept saying the dumbest shit. He really thought she was smarter than this.

"Fuck you mean, Star? You kept them a secret all this time! They damn near grown!" He shouted in her face.

She looked off. "Okay Tahj."

"Okay?"

"Yea, okay! I hear you loud and clear. I'm not going to keep them from your crazy ass. Just know that you're dead to me after tonight."

"I don't give a fuck about you, Star! You been dead to me since 2012! I'm only concerned with Tahiry and True!"

He was speaking out of anger but those words hurt Star. She always assumed she was nothing more than a young piece of side ass for him and his words had just confirmed that. Not once did he attempt to find her after she left him and now she knew why. He never actually cared.

"Great," she sniffled before looking down.

"Star."

"What?"

"When dance class is over you gon take me in there to meet my daughters."

Her head popped up. "What?!"

"You heard me loud and clear, baby. We not bouta draw this shit out or be super dramatic about it. It is what it is. I'm their father and they need to know. We need to start building a relationship asap."

"Y-you don't want a blood test or anything?"

The look he gave her made her want to take that shit back. "Bitch you asking me to fuck you up. Just shut the fuck up."

"Alright, stop talking to me like that. I really thought that was a valid ques-"

"And you thought wrong. Who popped your cherry?"

"Really Tahj?"

"Man, just answer the question."

She sighed heavily. "You."

"And when did that happen?"

She shut her eyes. "In December of 2012."

"And when were my daughters born?"

"September 20th, 2013."

"Exactly. So who's the father of your twins?"

"You Tahj."

"And who's going to introduce me to them tonight?"

"….Me."

"That's what the fuck I thought."

───────────────

"Okay, y'all can split but can y'all do this?" Tahjaria stood up from her split and lifted her leg above her head.

"Girl that's nothing but a split standing up. We sure can do that." True retorted as she stood up to show off her leg lift. Choc stood by the front desk trying not to explode into laughter. There'd been no confirmation but she was certain that these twins belonged to the Bellamy bloodline. Tahjaria had met her match in little miss True and Choc was getting her kicks out of it. Tahiry was quiet, but she was obviously there to back her sister up because she was the first one to throw her leg over her head.

"Come do the leg lift with me, Tazzy!" Jari demanded.

Tazzy's mouth frowned up. "Girl, I don't know how to do that. Dance class is over anyway."

"Y'all need to cut it out," Choc butted in while laughing hysterically. She looked down at her watch and it was almost 7:15. Class had ended at 7. Parents had a 20 minute window to pick their kids up but Star *and* Tahj were pushing it. It was a good thing they planned on confronting Star about the twins tonight.

"Alright Choc! Bye girls! See you tomorrow!" The ballet instructor, Ms.Nadia, waved goodbye on her way towards the door. She was a former Orchesis for Grambling State University, so Choc was happy to have her teaching at her school.

"Bye Ms.Nadia!!!" Jari and True said together. During the ballet portion of class, they were in competition to impress her. Actually they were in competition for the jazz and tap dance portion too. Choc had to scold them a few times because they were doing too much. She actually wanted to laugh but she wanted her students to take her seriously. Even the ones she was related to.

When Nadia exited, Tahj and Star entered a few seconds later. Star's hair appeared to be a bit messy and her eyes were red. It almost looked like she'd had a fight. And Tahj didn't look too thrilled either. He looked straight up mad, which made Choc's antennae's go up. When her brother was upset, he was dangerous. Danger wasn't cool in her dance school and around these kids. Then the thought that should've entered her brain first ran through her head. Why the fuck were they walking in together looking pissed?

"Daddyyy! These are our friends from school! They're in first grade!" Jari said excitedly as she dragged Tahiry and True over to Tahj. His heart swelled as a mixture of emotions consumed him. His daughters already knew each other and had been playing? He felt sick.

Although Jari and Tazzy were in kindergarten they had P.E, art, lunch, and recess with the first graders. So they'd been playing with the twins since the first week of school. When they saw them today at dance class they were excited that their new friends from school were here.

"They're not your friends, Jari." Tahj said while rubbing his jaw. He was about to be straightforward but he saw no point in tiptoeing around the truth.

"Tahj…"Choc chided. She wasn't sure where he was going with this, but it was sounding like he was telling his daughters they couldn't be friends with the twins. That was petty and childish.

"But we are friends, daddy." Tazzy said.

"No, they are your big sisters." Tahj corrected.

"Tahj!" Star reproved with wide eyes. She couldn't believe he was *that* blunt about it. He didn't even let her introduce him as their dad yet.

"Waitttt…"Choc clutched her chest before looking back and forth between Star and Tahj, and then down at the twins. It finally clicked. "Girl I know you lying to me!"

Choc stepped off to the side, allowing this soap opera to unfold. This was way more than she could handle or regulate.

"How? I thought I was the oldest girl." Tazzy pointed to herself.

"Yea, I thought so too baby." Tahj sighed heavily before looking over at Star. "Yo, you wanna help me out or what?"

Star could've seriously stuck her head in the mud and died. This was so awkward and embarrassing. Then Choc, who she just learned was his sister, was watching. That made it ten times worse!

"Tahiry and True this is your dad, Tahj."

"Our dad?" Tahiry looked up at him with stars in her eyes. Sometimes she'd have dreams about having a daddy like most of her peers did, and this tall man before her looked just like the daddy she'd imagined. She was immediately under a spell and in love.

"Mama I thought you said our dad was in the army." True said while looking up at Tahj skeptically.

Choc's mouth dropped. She didn't know much about Star other than her being pretty and seemingly a good mother; now she wasn't so sure. What kind of mom would purposely keep a father out of the dad's life and then proceed to lie to the kids about his existence? That was some real bird brain shit. As a woman and mother, Choc couldn't respect it, and right there she decided she didn't care for Star at all.

"You told them what?!"

"Tahj no!" Choc screamed as she rushed over and wedged herself between him and Star. Her dumb ass didn't even attempt to run when it was obvious this nigga wanted to fuck her up.

"No, please don't fight." Tahiry begged with tears in her eyes while clutching the ballerina teddy bear she'd gotten today upon arriving to dance class.

Tahj looked at her and all the anger flushed from his body. He rushed over to her and picked her up. Star was surprised at how she wrapped her arms around him and accepted the hug. Not only was Tahiry the shy twin but she was also the standoffish one. It was True who was extra friendly with strangers, yet she was looking at Tahj like he was the judge and jury. The switch up was wild.

"Daddy?"

"Yea, Jari?" Tahj looked down while still holding on to Tahiry. He was trying to stay calm for their sake but now that he was holding her he was thinking about how much he missed out on. She was hugging him like he'd disappear at any second and True was looking at him like he was a stranger. The fucked up part about it was that he was, and it made him feel sick. He didn't know his own kids and they didn't know him.

"Since they our sisters, that mean we can play together all the time now? Even at home?" Jari asked innocently. She didn't understand the gravity of the situation. She just knew her dad told her she had two new sisters. She liked the idea of that.

A small smile broke out on his face. He could always count on his kids to make shit a little easier. "Yea baby, that's exactly what that means."

"Can they spend the night with us daddy? They can sleep in my room!!!" Tazzy excitedly volunteered. Like Jari, she didn't understand how deep this was. She'd been intrigued with the twins since day one simply because they were twins. She also loved playing with them at school. Playing with them at home would be twice as fun.

"Or mine!" Jari offered.

"I wanna go home with my mommy where I have my own room and bed." True said while pouting.

That crushed Tahj, but he brushed it off. Her mom was all she knew, so the last thing he was going to do was take it personally.

"True don't do th-"Star started to reprimand her. She wasn't crazy about the girls spending the night with him, but she didn't want to hurt Tahj's feelings. He had a lot on his shoulders right now and she was to blame.

"She good,"Tahj cut her off before kneeling down with Tahiry still in his arms. " You can have your own room at my house too. I have more than enough space for you and your sister. Y'all can even have your own rooms."

"We could have our own rooms at our mommy's house too. I like sleeping in the room with my Twinkie." She rolled her eyes.

Tahj's stomach felt all soft like a marshmallow when she referred to Tahiry as her "Twinkie." He could tell their bond was something special. That was just something else for him to be upset about missing out on all these years. But he was here now and he wasn't going anywhere. True's little attitude was slight work.

"You can share a room with Tahiry at my house, baby girl." He poked her neck. She flinched and cracked a smile. That was her tickle spot and he'd hit it on the first try.

"Okay. I wanna come. You have fast internet right?" She questioned, and she was as serious as a heart attack.

Tahj and Choc laughed. They were quickly seeing who the outspoken twin was.

"I got everything you need."

"Okay. Can my mommy come though? We have a very strict hair care routine that we can't miss before bed."

Tahj looked over at Star who was just standing there looking stupid. He was so disgusted with her, but he had to put the kids first.

"Your mom's coming. This was all her idea." Tahj said before glaring back at her. He was threatening her with his eyes to go along with this. As much as she didn't want to, she felt like she didn't have a choice. She also owed him. He missed out on years of his daughter's lives. He could have one night.

Chapter 4

Star thought she was doing something with her new house, but it didn't have shit on Tahj's nine bedroom mansion. With as many kids as he had, this much space was necessary. Now he had two more, and accommodating them was obviously light work. He'd already allowed them to pick out one of his vacant guest rooms and they chose the biggest one upstairs with a bathroom. Star low key wanted the room for herself. Six year olds didn't need to stay in something that extravagant. Tahj thought otherwise because he deemed the room as "perfect" for them and changed the bedding to a Frozen comforter set. He had an entire closet of spare sheets and comforters for his kids and that just so happened to be in there. True was quick to let him know that they were Fancy Nancy type of girls. He promised he'd let them redecorate the room from top to bottom however they saw fit. Of course that made them excited because Star didn't give them that type of freedom. They were too fickle for her to ever give them a hard core theme for their room. She'd let them do their room Fancy Nancy today and they'd want Jojo Siwa tomorrow. She didn't have time for that shit, so she went for their favorite colors instead. A purple and pink room would work for the next few years.

After the girls took baths, Star did their hair in their room while Tahjaria and Tazzlyn watched and talked. They had a million questions, but it was understandable considering the circumstances.

"Miss Star?" Jari said.

"You can call me Star, girl." She laughed. She'd noticed Tahjaria was chatty and sassy like True, but she obviously had manners. One thing Star couldn't stand was a disrespectful child.

"Okay. If Tahiry and True are our sisters, why are we just meeting them?"

Star swallowed a lump in her throat. Kids really didn't hold back.

"We lived in Slidell and we just moved back. That's probably why." True made herself smart and answered. Usually Star would get on her about that but she let her have that one because she did not have the answers.

"Slidell not that far. My granny lives out there." Tazzy said. "Y'all could've came and visited us."

"Well they're here now. Y'all can make up for lost time." Star said, as she finished off Tahiry's french braid. Every night she combed the girls hair out, moisturized it, and greased their scalps before plating it into two French braids.

"Y'all have long hair." Jari marveled in amazement.

"So do you," Star laughed.

"Ou! Can you do my hair like the twins?! I want French braids!"

"Me too!" Tazzy quickly co-signed.

"I don't know…"

"Pleaseeee!" Tazzy pleaded. "I'll sit still! I'm not tender headed like my sister Tahja."

Star bursted into laughter. "That wouldn't be a problem, sweetie. It's just I need permission to do your hai-"

"We have another sister?!" True asked, cutting Star off. The only reason she didn't correct her for her rudeness was because she was obviously excited.

"Yea. Her name is Tahja and she's four. She lives with me and my mommy." Jari reported. "I have a step daddy too. He just got us a new puppy named Snowball. Y'all should come to my house and play tomorrow."

"No! They should come to my house! I have a cat named Prissy, a fish named Nemo, and a hamster named Butterball." Tazzy divulged.

"That's nothing," Jari rolled her eyes. "Our big brother Baby Tahj has a snake and he feeds it mice!"

"And the snake lives at *my* house with our mommy." Tazzy said while rolling her neck. Right then Star had confirmation that she belonged to Janikka, while the other two girls belonged to the second baby mama who had moved on.

"No fair, mommy. We don't have any pets!" Tahiry complained.

"I'll get y'all a pet," Tahj popped into the room. Star didn't know where the hell he came from but she was glad he did. Too much was being thrown her way. She was certain these kids' mothers didn't know about the twins yet.

Play dates were far-fetched. Star didn't know anything about the other ladies yet to be sending her daughters over there. For now Tahj's house was the only place she trusted for a meet up spot.

"What y'all want?"

"A puppy!" They said together.

Star frowned. "Tahj I'm not keeping no pupp-"

"The puppy can stay here." He said sharply, shutting her up.

"Daddy can Star comb our hair like she did Tahiry and True's? I want braids!" Jari said.

"Maybe tomorrow," Tahj lied. "It's past y'all bedtime. Go to y'all rooms. I'll be in there in a minute to kiss y'all."

When they ran out, Tahj focused on Star.

"You wanna sleep in here with them?"

"Hard pass." She answered. The twins slept like wild banshees. The only people who could tolerate their wild sleeping habits were them. She hadn't slept with them since they were two, and she wasn't going to start back today.

"That's not nice, mommy." Tahiry muttered.

"It's sure not, Tahiry." Tahj backed her up just to aggravate Star.

"I don't care what's not nice. Y'all know y'all sleep wild. I'm not tryna wake up in pain tomorrow."

When she said that a dirty thought entered Tahj's mind and he was mad at himself for it. He was supposed to hate this bitch right now. But shit his dick had a mind of its own. It was hardening just thinking about how her pussy used to feel. He needed to calm himself down.

"Then let me show you where you're sleeping."

Tahj had seven rooms upstairs and the last two were downstairs in the basement that resembled a two bedroom apartment. This was where most guests chose to stay because it had privacy. His other guest room was upstairs but the twins had marked it as their territory. All the other rooms upstairs were for his kids and it showed. No adult would want to lay in those beds.

Star had to admit the basement was laid but it was also kind of creepy. It was another freezing night and it was now starting to drizzle. The private entrance to the basement and the windows just seemed like easy access for somebody to come slit her throat in her sleep. Maybe she watched too many horror movies, but she wasn't feeling it.

"You gon be alright down here?"

"Ummm, it's nothing else upstairs? It's kind of scary down here."

"All the rooms upstairs are spoken for." He said rudely.

Not feeling his attitude, Star decided it was time to do what was best.

"Tahj I'll just go home to my own bed where I can be comfortable. I'll come back tomorrow morning to get the girls ready for school."

As soon as she tried to step around him he pulled her back.

"Running away your favorite thing to do, huh?"

"When I feel disrespected, absolutely."

"Alright, well look, I don't give a fuck how you feel. That weather is nasty and your ass not going nowhere. It's really not even that serious. Just take my room, scary ass."

"Ain't nobody scared." She crossed her arms.

"Girl, take your ass back up the stairs so I can show you my room. Just don't steal none of my furniture on your way out tomorrow."

"Ha-ha, very funny," she fakely laughed as she walked ahead of him and back up the stairs. He got a glimpse of her booty in her grey yoga pants and his dick jumped. Hating her would be much easier if she wasn't fucking gorgeous with a fat ass. Him already knowing what the pussy was hitting for just made his dick harder.

"Girl what you been eating?" He asked as he boldly stared at her ass. When she looked back at him he didn't bother looking up.

"Lots of dick."

That got his attention off her ass quickly.

"Yo, you trifling."

"It should mean nothing to you. You not worried about me and haven't been since 2012." She threw his words from earlier in his face. That got a smile out of him.

"That hurt ya feelings, huh? Well I meant that shit. I was just admiring your frame. You ain't have to say that hoe shit."

"What I say shouldn't bother you."

"It bothers me because you're raising my daughters. I don't want them talking like tha-"

"Alright, let's get one thing straight," she stopped right at the entrance to the basement. "Nigga I does this mommy shit and I'm phenomenal at it. I don't even allow other people to curse around them so I would never do it myself! The way I talk around you has nothing to do with the twins, so don't try me. If you couldn't tell yet, I'm raising well mannered queens."

He could definitely tell based on the little time he'd spent around them, but he wasn't about to give her ass props. She may have been a good mom, but she'd drop the ball by leaving him out of their lives.

"A good mom wouldn't lie to their kids and say their dad is in the army when he's not."

"What can I say? I'm not perfect."

"Obviously. I haven't heard an apology from your foul ass yet." He gritted.

"You haven't given me a chance. I've just been attacked so far."

"What the fuck do you expect, Star? Real shit."

"I don't expect anything, Tahj. I was wrong and I'll own that. Right now though I just want to shower and go to bed, so please escort me to your room. And stay out of it for the night."

His face tightened. "Girl what?"

"Play dumb. I see the lil situation in your sweat pants. You better go holler at your other baby mama or one of your hoes about it, because I meant it when I said you were dead to me."

"And I meant it when I said I ain't worrying about your ass. You only here because of the twins. If it wasn't for them then I would be hollering at my other baby mama right now. Shit do you wanna holler at her? You've been having her name in your mouth more than me. You must feel threatened or something."

"Boy fuck you! Me and my fucking children don't have to stay in this dusty ass house!"

"Dusty? Girl I can fit your lil ass house in my basement. Cut it out."

He saw her house because she had to get her and the twins some clothes to spend the night at his house. Truth be told he thought her spot was really nice especially for just her and the girls, but his wounds were way too fresh to give her any sort of compliment. He wasn't sure what she was doing for a living but she was obviously doing it well. It made him feel good to know that his daughters had been straight. However, he was still mad because if he was around they would've been better.

"Okay now that you've insulted me do you feel better?"

"I'm never going to feel better because you fucked over me. But you wouldn't know how that feels."

"I wouldn't?" She crossed her arms. "That wasn't you who took my virginity and neglected to tell me you had a whole family?! You don't think that hurt me?!"

"So that's why you hid my kids, huh? Because I hurt you? Star I'm not saying I was right. Keeping it real I was wrong as fuck to even deal with you in the first place, but what the fuck that had to do with Tahiry and True?!" He banged his fist against the wall.

Star's heart dropped and she looked down before looking right back up. "I'm sorry, Tahj."

"Yea, you sorry as fuck. Come on, bruh. I'm tired and we got a lifetime to talk about this shit."

Star's stomach twisted. A lifetime meant he was never going to let this go and she would hear about it for all eternity. Maybe she deserved to constantly hear about it, but she wasn't about to just take it.

―――――――――――

"Please don't turn the lights off." True whispered. Tahj wasn't expecting to hear her voice because from where he was standing it looked like both girls were knocked out.

"Why not? Aren't you about to go to sleep?" Tahj asked, as he walked over to the bed.

"Yea, but I'm scared of the dark."

"So you sleep with the lights on at your mama's house?"

"No. I have a Lion King night light. My Uncle Diamond gave it to me. Do you have a brother like my mommy?" She yawned. She was tired but she was in an unfamiliar environment so she was fighting her sleep. Meanwhile Tahiry was next to her sleeping with her mouth wide open. She always went to sleep right away.

"I have two younger brothers and I have four younger sisters. So y'all have two new uncles and four new aunties. You already met one."

"Who?"

"Choc."

"Mrs. LeBlanc?" She asked in confusion. She'd heard other adults at the dance school refer to her as Choc, but all the students called her Mrs. LeBlanc.

"Yup. That's Titi Choc. Call her that the next time you see her." He chuckled.

"What will I call you?"

"What do you feel comfortable calling me?"

He wanted to flat out tell her to call him daddy but he wanted them to move on their own timing. Everything was happening so fast and the last thing he wanted was for them to feel overwhelmed or uncomfortable.

"My Twinkie said she wants to call you daddy like Jari and Tazzy while we were in the tub. But she didn't know if it was okay." Her shoulders slouched. His heart ached hearing that shit.

"You tell your Twinkie that she's well within her rights to call me daddy because that's what I am. Y'all are my daughters just like Jari and Tazzy. Now what do you wanna call me, slick?" He poked her neck. He'd peeped how she threw Tahiry under the bus to express her own feelings. That was some shit he would've done as a child. His Auntie Holly would always call him slick.

"I think I'ma stick with my Twinkie on this."

"You just gon keep putting everything on Tahiry, huh?" He laughed.

"She was born two minutes before me, so she's in charge." She grinned while lying through her teeth. If anything she was the bossy one.

"I'ma tell her what you said when she wakes up tomorrow." Tahj chuckled.

"I can hear." Tahiry mumbled with her eyes still closed. Tahj assumed she was great at playing possum or a really light sleeper.

Tahiry opened her eyes completely and looked directly at him. "Daddy?"

His heart pounded. He was no stranger to the d word, but that shit sent him over the moon this particular time.

"Yea baby?" He played it cool.

"Can you lay with us?"

"Ouuu! Please!" True exclaimed.

"Okay."

He couldn't say no to those adorable little faces if he wanted to. He was naturally a sucker for his daughters and now he had two more to fall victim to. It was fine because they didn't have to ever hear the word no when he was capable of giving them whatever they wanted. If the twins weren't already spoiled they would be soon under his love and care.

Star was sleeping like a baby in Tahj's California king bed. When she first laid in his mattress she melted into the sheets and fell asleep within seconds. She thought her peaceful sleep was being interrupted by a bad dream when she felt someone's weight on top of her. She opened her eyes because something this heavy had to be a real human being. She saw Tahj's eyes looking back at her in the dark.

"Tahj what the fuck are you doing?" She snapped. She tried raising up but his buff ass body wasn't affording her that luxury.

"Man my dick harder than a mutherfucker, Star." He groused directly in her ear. After the twins fell asleep, and he checked on Jari and Tazzy, he poked his head into his room door. He got a glimpse of Star drying off after she got out of the shower. His dick that had calmed down turned right back into a brick.

After talking all that shit he wasn't trying to make a move on Star. He went to his den and tried everything to get his mind off of fucking her. He even pulled up porn on the tv and jacked off like a teenager. His dick was still hard because it wanted what it wanted. He was finally about to give in to his man's request.

"What the fuck that got to do with me, Tahj? Move!"

"Come one…you gon do your baby daddy like that? Let me feel that pussy. I know it's still good."

"Tahj…"she gasped as his tongue connected with the side of her neck. She was wearing nothing but an oversized Marvel t-shirt with panties so she felt his bare dick on her ass.

"You want me to fuck you, huh? Tell me." He gripped her chin so he could flicker his tongue all over her neck. She felt all light headed as his tongue made its way to her mouth for a kiss.

"Perfect ass lips." He said after tonguing her down.

"You want me to fuck you Star?" He asked again as his hands moved down to her big booty. He gripped it before his digits moved to her ass crack. He slid her lace panties to the side and she voluntarily spread her legs. Her pussy and ass crack was sparkling with her juices. He had half a mind to stick his entire head in it.

"You ain't saying shit but this pussy telling me everything I need to know." He dipped his fingers into her pussy from behind and she lost her mind.

"Ouuuu!" She moaned, as she tooted her ass up to grant him access to her clit. He took heed and began rubbing it in a circular motion. It wasn't long before Star was cumming in his hand. Yea she'd been with three other guys after him but for the past year she'd been on a drought. Tahj could've simply licked her ttties and she would've came in her panties.

"Goddamn Star." He marveled as he gazed at her fat and juicy pussy. It was breathtaking. He said fuck it and went for what he knew.

"TAHJJJJ!" She shouted when she felt his mouth on her booty hole. His mouth showed equal love to her ass and to her pussy. She felt over stimulated as she threw her ass back at his face. When he grabbed her ass cheeks and spread them, she knew she was in trouble. He was making her sit still for the tongue lashing he was giving her.

"I'ma cum!!!! I'ma cum!!!" She screamed as her pussy convulsed. He sucked her clit and fingered her ass until she exploded in his mouth. While receiving her juices he slapped her ass cheek in appreciation.

"Pussy still tastes so good." He professed as she laid flat on her stomach like someone had beat her ass.

He spread her legs a little before forcefully thrusting into her pussy. He was trying to put a hurting on her pussy, but it backfired. He knew she'd be wet, but damn he wasn't expecting her to be this tight. She fit his dick like a personalized glove. She hadn't aged in the face or in the pussy apparently.

"I'm finna be in this fire ass pussy all night, Star. You hear me?"

"Yessss! I hear you! Oh shit!" She yelped as he pounded into her g-spot. She eagerly lifted off the bed to meet his powerful strokes.

"Who's pussy is this for babymama?" He bit his lip while pounding into her. Her fucking him back didn't knock him off his square at all. In fact, he appreciated the view of her chocolate ass clapping.

"IT'S YOURS! IT'S YOURS!"

"You gon take it away from me again?"

"No! Never again, Tahj! I swearrrrr!" She cried as she violently shook. A level ten orgasm was moving through her body.

"That bet not just be the nut talking, cause I'll really kill your ass Star." He grunted as he exploded inside of her.

She looked back at him. "I thought you was good on me?"

"I thought I was dead to you?" He retorted. "Stop saying stupid shit and come ride this dick."

He meant it when he said he was going to be up in her pussy all night. They had a lot of lost time to make up for and his dick was hard all over again. His shit was calling out for her and she was going to answer.

Chapter 5

January 21, 2020

"Star…Star…Star…"

Smack!

"STAR!"

She finally opened her eyes after getting smacked roughly on her ass. "What Tahj?!"

"These children gotta be at school by 8, yea."

"Shit!" Star hissed as she noticed the alarm clock by the bed. It was 7:20. She never overslept like this on school days, but she also never fucked all night on school days. Tahj had her schedule fucked up.

"Relax," Tahj urged. "Everybody's up and getting dressed, but True not tryna get up. I tried to wake her up multiple times. Shit I had to check and make sure she was breathing."

Star let out a little laugh as she got out of the bed. "I hate waking that girl up in the morning. You should've given her a little pop on the booty. Most of the time I threaten her. That usually gets her up and moving."

"Thanks to you I don't feel comfortable doing any of that to her." He jabbed.

Her stomach churned. He was back to looking at her like she was pure garbage. Thankfully she wasn't naive enough to think last night would change things between them. He was just a horny nigga and she was available in house pussy. Of course he was going to try her. She wanted to feel silly for giving him what he wanted, but hell she wanted it too. If she was going to get dick from anybody it may as well have been someone she already fucked. She knew what he was working with and that he knew how to work it. It was a one time thing though. It was clear he hated her so she wasn't about to be giving her body to him on a regular basis. Especially when he admitted to her face last night that he would've been with Janikka had it not been for him finding out about the twins.

"Alright," she said dryly. She would be the bigger person and let him have his little comments. "Let me go wash off and I'll go get her."

When Star walked out of the room, Tahj pulled out his phone to call Lexi. She answered right away like she always did.

"Goodmorning Tahj. Why didn't you come pick up Tahja last night? She said it's not fair that you kept her sisters and not her."

He laughed. "I know she's mad with me. I'ma pick up my baby up from school today."

Unlike the rest of her sisters, Tahja attended Kingsley House because she was only in pre-k.

"You would want to," Lexi giggled. "She's already ticked off because she can't go to Choc's dance school."

"What can I say? Choc is only taking kindergartners through fifth graders right now."

"Tahja doesn't understand that shit, Tahj."

"She'll be alright. We'll find something else to put her in. But say, I need you to meet me for breakfast at The Ruby Slipper."

"Whew, we haven't been there in a long time. Can I ask why?"

"No, you can just show up. We gotta talk."

"Boy..."she mumbled. "Alright Tahj. I'll be there. What time?"

"9, and don't be late."

"I won't be." She ended the call. Tahj went straight to Nikka's number and called her to tell her the same thing. He knew he was blindsiding everybody involved, even Star, but the shit would come as a shock no matter how he did it. At least this way he could be upfront with everybody at once. Once the initial surprise wore off he was sure everything would be just fine. The family was already blended, so he highly doubted that two more kids would be an issue.

All Star wanted was for Tahj to bring her home so she could get her day started, but he insisted on going to breakfast so they could discuss some things. She could admit they had a lot to talk about as far as the twins were concerned and co-parenting. She figured he'd wait until they were seated at The Ruby Slipper to discuss these things, but as soon as they dropped the girls off at school he was running his mouth.

"So when we gon get they last name changed? As a matter of fact, what are their full names?"

"True Star Francois and Tahiry Sky Francois."

"Oh, that's your last name." He quickly remembered.

"Yup."

"Any niggas been around them playing daddy?"

"Nope. No step daddy's yet."

"Yet? Star I will knock your lights out."

"Tahj if I ever meet my soulmate and we get married he will be the girl's step dad. That's not taking anything away from you."

"I know because I'ma take something away from you."

"And what's that?"

"Your life. You got big balls talking to me about a another nigga when I just found out about my daughters like two seconds ago. Are you alright in the head?"

"Isn't your other bm married though? Doesn't she live with her husband and your daughters? I just don't see the issue."

"Man look, fuck all that, when we getting they last names changed?"

"Ion know," she shrugged.

"Alright, I guess I gotta take control of everything since you want to act like a jackass. We'll go to the court house after breakfast."

"Tahj I have shit to do, yea."

"Oh yea? Like what? You gotta work?"

"As a matter of fact, yea, I do."

"Where you work at?"

"I'm an author. I write kids books."

"That's all you do?"

"That was my only answer soooo…"

"Alright smartass. I was just asking because you must make a nice amount of money off that."

"How you figure? With my lil ass house that can fit in your basement." She chided.

"Awwww," he laughed. "Stop holding on to shit. Wasn't that you who called my house dusty?"

"Yea because you weren't being nice."

"Keeping it real, I don't wanna be nice to your ass, but I gotta be cordial for the sake of co-parenting."

"So why would you stick your dick in me last night?" She asked bluntly. "What would make you want to fuck somebody you don't like?"

"Because my dick don't got shit to do with my feelings."

"You know what…that makes a lot of sense."

"Fuck you talking bout?"

"That's why you have so many kids now. You let your dick do the thinking instead of using your brain."

"See that's where you're wrong. I fuck with a lot of bitches that will *never* carry my kids. I know what the fuck a condom is and how to use it."

"And yet you have three baby mamas and six kids."

"For three women I actually was with and had strong feelings for at one point."

"Tahj we were never together."

"Shittt, you were staying in my house, I was taking care of you, and I was giving you raw dick. We was together in my mind."

"Nigga are *you* okay in the head? Because you were doing the same thing with Janikka and the other baby mama too. Our daughters are months apart in age, which means we were all pregnant around the same time. I *know* Janikka was pregnant with Tazzlyn because I saw you in the mall with her."

"Wait, you saw us in the mall and didn't say nothing?"

"What was I supposed to say?"

"How about 'I'm pregnant'? That would've been nice."

"Hmmmm," she pretended to think. "Me telling you I'm pregnant while you were in the middle of kissing the same baby mama you neglected to tell me about. To add insult to injury she was pregnant again. The last thing I was gonna do was walk up and play myself any further."

"Play yourself how?" He squinted. She was innocent in the situation because she really didn't know about Janikka. It wasn't like she fucked the next bitches man on purpose. So he was confused as to where she was getting at.

"Because I actually thought we had something speci-" She caught herself. She was really about to pour her guts out to a dog. "Nevermind."

"No, tell me." He insisted.

"Nah, it doesn't matter anymore. But I was going to call you about the twins before I saw you that day. And yea, I should've put my personal feelings to the side and still did that. But I was young and experiencing heartbreak for the first time. In my mind there was no way you would've wanted the twins because you already had a family. Then when I left you kinda just let me…so yea, I assumed you really didn't care."

"And you assumed wrong. I cared a whole lot, but I realized it was probably best for you if I just let you go. I had a lot going on between Nikka and Lexi. I was thinking it was a good thing you got out when you did. Of course I didn't know you were carrying my babies. I would've been stalking your ass had I known that."

"Tahj…"

"Wassup?"

"Is breakfast really necessary?" She asked as he pulled into a parking spot on Magazine street. "We've already talked about a lot."

"There's more we need to discuss," he looked at the time and it was ten minutes after nine. Lexi and Janikka were most likely inside waiting. "Come on, Star."

She breathed heavily and got out of the car. She was dressed casually in a brown Juicy Couture jogging suit with basic brown uggs and a Louis Vuitton Tote bag. She was happy she threw a semi-cute outfit in her bag last night even though she assumed she'd be coming straight home in the morning.

When Janikka walked into The Ruby Slipper the first thing she saw was Lexi sitting at a table by herself. This couldn't be a coincidence. This used to be one of their favorite places to have breakfast with Tahj. He must have invited her here today too. If this meeting was about them moving back together then the answer was hell no. She wasn't moving backwards with him and Lexi didn't deserve a second chance after betraying him.

"Hey girl," Janikka approached the table. "Tahj told you to come here?"

"Yea…he told you to come too?" She asked, not being able to hide her disappointment. She figured whatever conversation he wanted to have was geared towards *them.* Yea she had a husband, but he didn't give her the same feeling Tahj had. Outside of being a good father and provider, she and Channing had no sparks or chemistry. It just felt like she was existing in the relationship and she was miserable. With Tahj there was a lot of heartache, but at least she could say she was never bored.

"He sure did." Nikka said as she sat down. "I wonder what this is about and why he didn't tell us the other would be here."

"It probably has something to do with the kids."

"Yea, most likely," she agreed. "For a second I thought he was going to finally stop playing and make things official with us again."

"Really?' Lexi giggled.

"Yea, *really*." Nikka scoffed. "What's so funny?"

"Nothing," she laughed again. "It's just this is Tahj we're talking about."

"Okay, and I'm Nikka. His first love, the mother of his first child, and the mother of his only son. I hold a lot of weight in his life."

Lexi fought the urge to roll her eyes. Although she and Nikka had become quite cool over the years the bitch was still *always* in competition with her. She never missed a chance to remind her she was the first baby mama and had his only boy. As if that made her more important. Their kids being siblings was the *only* reason she entertained the likes of her.

"I never said you didn't. I think we'll both always be important to Tahj, but it's delusional to hold on to hope that this nigga will marry you one day. He's a 31 year old man, if he wanted to be tied down to you he would've done it by now."

"Lexi you would say that since you're on the outs now. But nobody told you to cheat on him."

Lexi laughed harder even though she felt a way. "How can I cheat on a man that was fucking with both of us plus multiple outside bitches? *You* can be loyal to a man that isn't loyal to you for the rest of your life, but I couldn't do it anymore."

Despite being read, Janikka was quick with a comeback. "If you're so over him then why do you still try to fuck him? That's right, he told me how you be sending nudes and shit."

"What can I say? The dick is great. That's why I don't blame you for still fucking him even though it's obvious he doesn't want you."

"Excuse you?"

"Nikka, I'm not coming from a catty place, I'm just being real. I removed myself from the equation and he still hasn't given you a commitment. That's why I was laughing when you said you thought he invited you here to make things official again. Tahj will never make shit official with any woman. He's not that type of man."

"You know what I think? You're unhappy in your marriage so you're trying to project that on to me and Tahj. He just asked me what kind of ring I liked last week." She lied.

Lexi saw right through it. "Alright girl. Let me know when you get that ring. I wanna be the first to see it."

"You will be." She replied. She was about to say something else but her eyes caught the entrance. It was Tahj but someone was walking in front of him. As they got closer her heart dropped to her toes. She remembered this bitches face clearly. She was the only woman other than Lexi that made her feel threatened. The fact that she was popping up years later scared the shit out of her. What was really sickening was that the bitch was still super pretty even though she was dressed down. She and Lexi were dressed to the nines with full faces of makeup on.

Star could've turned around and stabbed Tahj as he touched her lower back to guide her to a table in the cafe. She immediately recognized one of the ladies as Janikka. She hadn't seen her in years but the bitch hadn't aged much. She was still gorgeous. Funnily enough, the other baby mama resembled her. They both appeared to be mixed with their extremely light skin and their silky hair textures. They gave off Afro-Latino vibes, but Star could've been wrong.

"Good Morning y'all," Tahj greeted as he pulled out Star's chair, so she could sit. "Y'all hungry? I'm starving."

Janikka looked at him like she wanted to kill him. "Tahj seriously?! What the fuck is *she* doing here?"

"I could ask the same about you, sweetie." Star replied evenly. She had no reason to get all rowdy, but she had to let this bitch know that she wasn't the one. "He just told me we were coming to breakfast to discuss our daughters. I didn't know y'all would be here."

Tahj thought he'd be the one to reveal the news about the twins and it was the sole purpose for having a sit down breakfast. Informing them about True and Tahiry shouldn't have been a phone conversation and he wanted to beat his kids to the punch. They were sure to tell their mothers everything the moment they saw them again which would be later on today.

"Y'all what?" Lexi finally said something. She wasn't completely sure because it was so long ago, but she recalled exchanging words with a female who sounded just like this woman in front of her over Tahj's phone. She did remember that her number was saved under a star emoji.

Tahj stepped in. "Look, I called y'all here because I wanted to tell y'all in person that me and Star have twin daughters together. Jari and Tazzy have already met them."

"I know you didn't let my daughter meet your outside kids!" Nikka exploded, catching several people's attention.

The "outside children" comment made Star's blood boil. She was seconds away from reaching over the table and snatching this bitch up.

"First of all, lower your fucking voice," Tahj gritted. "Second of all, I don't have no fucking outside children. You kill me with that shit. I ain't married to no fucking body."

Nikka's face turned a deep red as embarrassment consumed her.

"Look...it is what it is,"Lexi sighed. "How old are they?"

"Six. They're in first grade." Tahj answered.

"So they're older than Jari?" Lexi asked in disbelief. She talked a lot of shit about Nikka feeling as though she was important, but she too carried a sense of pride about giving Tahj his first daughter. That piece of pride had just been snatched away from her and she was bothered.

"Yea." Tahj answered.

"Which means all three of us were carrying babies at the same time." Nikka shook her head in disgust before glaring at Tahj. "You're seriously a whore."

Tahj shrugged. "And you knew that, so I don't know why you wanna make a scene about it now. I just wanted to formally introduce y'all to Star and tell y'all about our kids in person. I figured it was best you hear it from me first, and I want the rest of my kids to meet the twins ASAP."

"I mean Jari has already met them, so it's whatever." Lexi shrugged.

"It ain't no whatever for me. Have you gotten a DNA test for these children?"

"Bitc-" Star started to go in, but Tahj put his hand on her shoulder to calm her down. That just pissed Nikka off even more.

"A dna test is not needed. I know what I did with Star and True and Tahiry look just like me and all of our kids. Obviously you have a problem with this Nikka, but my kids are going to build a relationship with their sisters. So you can be mad all you want."

Nikka continued to run her mouth. "You said they're six, right? Why is she just popping up and telling you this? It just seems awfully convenient."

"Bitch fuck you!" Star lashed. Lexi's eyes bulged because Star looked so sweet. She thought for sure Nikka would eat her alive but clearly she'd thought wrong. "I didn't find his ass and tell him shit! I was perfectly fine going through life doing this shit on my own! Unlike your pathetic ass I'm not pressed to have this nigga in my life! We both know he can probably take a shit on your face and you'd still fuck with him."

"Tahj you gon let this ugly ass bitch talk to me like this?!"

Tahj gave her a look. "Nikka you know aint shit ugly about her. Now forreal, let's order some breakfast and talk about getting the kids togeth-"

"Tahj go to hell!" Nikka jumped up. "You can do whatever with those little bastards but leave me and mine out of i- AHHHHH!" She screamed as Star snatched her up by her real hair that reached the middle of her back. Star knocked her across the head several times before Tahj pulled her off. He admittedly let her get a few licks in because he felt like Nikka deserved them. Calling his kids bastards was out of line and he wanted to put hands on her for that shit himself. Lucky for her, Star beat him to the punch.

"You let that bitch hit me, Tahj?!" She screamed in horror. Usually Tahj stepped for her, but now he was holding the next bitch back after she'd just beat Mario coins out of her head. "And you just sat there and watched Lexi?"

"Girl what the fuck you wanted me to do?" Lexi asked in confusion. Truthfully Lexi enjoyed watching her get beat up because she could never do it herself.

"Real shit Nikka, I'm good on you." Tahj claimed.

"You let a bitch attack me!"

"Fucking right I did! You don't call my kids out they fucking name! Is you crazy?!" He clamored.

"That's what they are! They some basta-"

"Cool off bitch!" Star threw the entire pitcher of orange juice at her face. Lexi winced in pain for Nikka. That was definitely going to leave a mark.

"We're calling the cops!" The manager of the restaurant announced.

Tahj immediately grabbed Star's hand and made his way towards the exit.

"I'm pressing charges!" Nikka screamed.

"And it'll be your last day in my house too bitch!" Tahj shouted back.

Nikka was rendered speechless. Tahj could definitely put her out of the house she lived in because it was in his name. She wasn't pressing charges if it meant she wouldn't have a roof over her head in the end. He was crazy if he thought she was going to let this shit go though. Star was going to have to fight her again.

———————————————

"Man that shit was crazy. I really wanted some breakfast tacos," Tahj complained when they got back in his car. Star had to do a double take to gauge his seriousness. Surely that was a joke.

"Nigga the fact that you didn't get *breakfast* is on your mind now?!"

"Yea. Shit that's one of my favorite spots. I hope they let me come back after today."

Star inhaled deeply to contain her anger.

"Tahj take me home."

"What? We finna go to the courthouse."

"TAKE ME HOME RIGHT FUCKING NOW!!!" She screamed at the top of her lungs.

Tahj openly stared at her blankly before focusing back on the road.

"Ok so we're gonna go to the courthouse like I said and then I'll bring yo stupid ass home."

"Bitch you stupid! Did you really think that Love and Hip Hop ass sit down was the way to go?!"

"I didn't know shit would pop off like that, Star. Fuck, what you want me to do?"

"Use your brain! Why wouldn't a bitch you're still fucking be mad about something like this?"

"Me fucking her has nothing to do with it though. It's about my kids."

"What I'm tryna stress to you is that her feelings are still involved, so of course she was going to take that hard. Then you was on some sneaky, surprise shit."

"If I was straight up none of y'all would've wanted to come."

"And you can see why. Got me acting all ghetto and shit."

"Oh so you was acting, huh?"

"Boy I can't wait to get from 'round you."

"And I can't wait to drop you off. Cause you coming for me like I told Nikka to do allat."

"The point is still going over your empty ass head, so let's just dead the convo."

"Agreed. Can I pick the twins up from school today?"

"Yes, that's fine. I'll give you their dance clothes when you drop me off at my house."

"Cool. I'ma take them to my sister's house after they get out of dance class."

"Why?" She questioned with a stank face.

"Whatchu mean why? They need to meet my fucking family don't you think?"

"Yea in due time…but it's too soon for them to be spending the night with a sister that I don't even know. That's how shit happens and I'm not havi-"

"Woah, I don't know where you going with this, but stop. Cause nobody said shit about the twins spending a night anywhere. I'm flying out to L.A early tomorrow so everybody was going back to their mama house, including the twins. My sister's Tatiana and Tamia are cooking dinner so all my siblings can meet the twins. That's all it is. But you have to come to terms with the fact that my siblings will be involved in the twins' life like they are with all their nieces and nephews. Shit I do a lot for their kids too. That's how my family is. So it's in your best interest to get to know them too."

"I guess I won't be getting to know them tonight since I wasn't invited to dinner."

"Man loo-" He started to explain, but his phone interrupted them. "Hold on, this Tamia right here."

He accepted the call and since his phone was connected to the car's Bluetooth, Star was able to hear Tamia through the speakers.

"Wassup Mia?" Tahj greeted her.

"Nothing much. About to clean up my house for tonight."

"Damn you cleaning up for six year olds now?"

"Sure am. They won't be going back to they maw telling her my house is dirty. You know kids that age can be messy. I know I was."

He laughed. "You sure was. Used to tell everybody business. Nobody in the family wanted you to come to their house. But say, you mind if Star rolls with me tonight? It's only right y'all get acquainted with her too. She'll be the person y'all gotta go through for the twins since I travel a lot."

"Ugh, Tahj I told you I'm cool on forming relationships with your baby mamas. Star's not exempt from that, no."

Ouch. That was like a kick to Star's stomach.

"C'mon bruh, you being petty. I aint say be besties with her. I said meet her for the twi-"

"No, I'm moving how I should've moved with Nikka and Lexi. They felt like we owed them something because we were nice to them and they were screwing you. I don't need another bitch feeling entitled. There won't be any drama with this bm because we'll have little to no interaction with her. As far as the kids go you're the daddy, so I'll always go through you. With her it'll be hi and bye. Shit she's lucky we're giving her that."

"We?"

"Yup, cause me and my sisters feel the same way."

"And all y'all tripping. Being childish for no reason, bruh."

"For no reason? That wasn't her who hid kids for six years? Them children almost in middle school now. Nah, she's the childish one. And your nasty ass probably got more kids out there. Our parents should've named you Tarell Junior."

"Tamia it's a lot y'all don't kno-"

"Tahj it's fine." Star spoke loud and clear so Tamia could hear her. "I don't need a relationship with them bitches."

"Awww fuck…"Tahj threw his head back. He wished he would've waited until Star was out of the car to ask Tamia that question. But he really thought she'd automatically say yes. Star had never done them anything. His sisters felt violated on his behalf though. They had also had unpleasant experiences with Nikka and Lexi, so they weren't trying to be cool with a third baby mama. Star didn't care about any of that shit though. She just heard a bitch that she didn't know speaking on her so she was going to check it.

"Bitch?! Girl who you calling a bitch?!" Tamia clamored.

"Anybody that got my name in their mouth and don't know me! That's who!"

"See Tahj, this is exactly why I'm good on *all* of your baby mamas. Bitches is disrespectful!"

"Tell me about it! Y'all sitting around talking about me like I did y'all something!"

"Girl them my nieces, so you did do me something!"

"Bitch keep talking and you'll never meet your nieces."

"Star." Tahj scolded.

"Nah, it's cool. Just keep that stupid hoe away from me." Tamia ended the call.

"I can't believe this shit." Tahj uttered. "All that for what?!"

"Ask your sister that shit, not me!"

"Man I wasn't even talking to you, Star. I was just thinking out loud."

"I don't care. I'm not tryna be chummy with your family anyway." She fronted. Really her feelings were hurt, but what was new?

"It's not about being chummy. It's about a healthy environment for the twins, and we then already got off on the wrong foot."

"Who you telling? Cause I highkey don't want my daughters around your sisters if they can't respect their mom."

Tahj breathed heavily. "They'll respect you, Star. I'll make sure of it. I promise. And as much as they might not care for you they'd never talk down on you in front of the twins. They're not like that."

"I don't know what they're like, but I'll take your word for it for now. If my daughters even hint at the fact that they were uncomfortable they'll never see them again. I swear."

Chapter 6

January 24, 2020

"Mommy look at my Titi's! They so pretty!" True raved while showing her a picture of Tahj's sister on her iPad for the millionth time. Even Star had to admit that those hoes looked like they came straight from somebody's beauty magazine. Their melanin was popping, they had the prettiest faces, thick ass hair, and nice bodies. Even the two lightest ones' skin was toasty and warm. It was no wonder the twins were so pretty, they had bomb ass genes from both sides.

"How many times you gon show me that picture lil girl?" Star asked as she pulled Tahiry's dance tights over her behind. She was hoping she would successfully dodge Choc when she dropped the girls off to dance practice like she'd done the previous days that week. She had a petty moment and considered pulling the girls out of that dance school but she'd already paid tuition and they loved going there, so she had to hold her pettiness.

"Mommy my uncles are famous! They in the group N.O.L.A!" True went on, ignoring Star's comment only to volunteer more information she'd already told her. Star didn't live under a rock so she knew who the singing group N.O.L.A was. Two of the members with two of Tahj's sisters. Noel was with Tamia and they had a two year old daughter. Tatiana was with Ant and they had a two year old son. The twins had met them all and they wouldn't stop talking about it.

"Them my uncles too." Tahiry said. "Mama, our daddy brothers have a Granny. I saw a picture of it."

"You mean a *Grammy*, Tahiry. Y'all told me that already." Star mumbled. Tahj's younger brothers were music producers that he just so happened to manage. They were signed to the same record label as N.O.L.A called Hustler Musik. The CEO of that same record label was Choc's husband, so they were sitting on a whole lotta money over there. This whole time the twins' daddy side of the family was famous and she didn't even know. It didn't make any difference to her though. They weren't her family and they had no interest in knowing her. Therefore she had no interest in knowing them.

At first she found herself immaturely wanting the twins to dislike Tahj's family so she could have a reason to keep them away, but after one visit they loved those damn people. Just yesterday night Star overheard True and Tahiry talking to their Auntie Talea through the iPad. They were acting like they'd known these people their entire lives. She wanted to hate, but she secretly found it endearing. She just wished they'd stop telling her the same stories over and over again.

"Mommy, my brother sent me a picture of his snake last night! He said he's going to bring it by my daddy house so I can play with it!" True disclosed. Although Star was happy to finally hear something new come from her mouth, she frowned.

"Girl you not playing with no damn snake."

"But my brother said his snake is nice and doesn't bite."

"I'm not bouta play with you, True." Star brushed her off.

"Mommyyyy," Tahiry whined.

"Girl stop that whining," Star chastised, as she tied a pink ribbon around her bun. "What do you want?"

"I want to go by my daddyyyy."

"Tahiry I told you he's in L.A. He's going to call y'all tonight like he's being doing all wee-"

"But is he going to come back?" She asked in a panicked tone. Star's heart dropped from guilt weighing on her. Her poor baby.

"Of course he's coming back. Let me call him right now." She grabbed her phone and FaceTimed Tahj. He accepted the call right away despite being at lunch with his newest client who played for the Lakers.

"Wassup Star?"

She handed the phone directly to Tahiry. As soon as she saw his face the waterworks started. Star rolled her eyes at the dramatics because it was never that serious. It was serious enough to pull at Tahj's heart strings though.

"Tahiry, what's wrong? Why you crying? Star, why is my baby crying?!"

Star's head jerked back because he was acting like he had smoke with her or something.

"I wanna come by youuuuu." She cried. "Why you left us?"

"Baby girl, I'll be back on Monday. I promise. Y'all can come spend the night with me and I'll take y'all to school."

Tahiry's head dropped because she didn't like that answer. Monday was too far away in her mind. She handed her mom back the phone and ran off.

"Tahiry!" Star called after her before focusing on Tahj. "That girl is dramatic when she doesn't get her way."

"She must get that shit from you."

"She might." She tittered.

"But man, she making me feel guilty."

"She'll be fine. You gotta work."

"Yeah I guess. But say, I'ma send you some money so you can take them toy shopping when they get out of dance class."

"YAYYYY!" True jumped up and clapped.

"Is that my other twin?"

True poked her head in the camera. "Yea daddy, it's me!"

"Why you didn't say hi?"

"Because I was letting my Twinkie have her moment. Her was sad."

"She was sad." Star corrected her.

"Yea, she was sad." She fixed it. "Toy shopping is going to make her happy. Daddy when you come back are we going to do our rooms at your house?"

"We sure are. I hope y'all got all y'all ideas ready."

"We do! My Titi Lea helped us write a list last night!"

"Y'all saw Talea last night?" He asked. His spirits lifted because if they saw her that meant some form of peace had been made with his sisters and Star.

"Yea! We FaceTimed her on the iPad you bought us."

"Oh okay," he replied, attempting to mask his disappointment. "Star, I'm about to cash app you."

"Tahj I still have the money you gave me before you left."

He'd asked for her account and routing number before dropping her off after they left the courthouse on Tuesday. When she got inside she worked a little before taking a nap. When she woke up she had $100,000 in her back account. She almost passed out. Tahj had sent her a text saying how there was more from where that came from and how he had to make up for the time he missed. She offered no complaints, but now he was trying to send more money and it was just excessive.

"Girl, nobody asked you that. I love you True. Tell your sister I love her too and don't be mad at me. Okay?"

"Okay, daddy. I love you too!" She blew a kiss into the camera, making Tahj's heart skip a beat. When she ran off, Tahj looked at Star.

"You love me too, baby mama?"

"Ugh," Star fake barfed before hanging up. That nigga was so cocky it literally digusted her.

Choc wasn't letting Star get past her today. They had some things to discuss, so as soon as she walked in the door with the twins Choc was standing right there waiting. The twins ran straight to her and gave her a big hug.

"Titi Choc I'm ready to dance today!" True shouted excitedly.

"That's what I like to hear, True," Choc laughed. "Go ahead and go to the studio. Me and y'all mommy need to talk."

When they ran away, Choc looked at Star.

"So what we gotta talk about?" Star pursed her lips.

Choc eyed her closely. "Really?"

"Really."

Choc shook her head. "Let's go to my office. There's too much traffic in this lobby for this type of conversation."

Star reluctantly followed her to the office. When she entered she wanted to dip right back out. All of Tahj's sisters minus Tamia were sitting on the couch in the huge office. If this was some sort of ambush then she was ready. She kept pepper spray and a taser on her.

"What is this?" Star came out and asked.

"Us having an adult conversation with you. Please sit." Talea pointed to a chair next to the couch.

"I'm good on sitting."

"Girl calm down. We really just wanna talk to you." Tati snapped.

"I would believe that if your attitude wasn't so strong right now." Star snapped back.

"Cause you acting like you can't sit down. Doing the most." Tati grumbled.

"Maybe because y'all was all dragging for me."

"Dragging for you?" They questioned in unison.

"Yea, Tamia told me how y'all don't wanna fuck with me because of how I did Tahj or whatever."

"Then you're mistaken." Choc shook her head. "Yea, we all were in agreement with the fact that it was fucked up that you didn't tell Tahj about the twins for six long years, but we didn't *drag* you for it."

"Yea, and we're entitled to feel like you were wrong for that. But as soon as I was informed I knew it was more to the story, so I was never holding this against you. I already told Tamia she can't be speaking for me." Talea said.

"And the reservations Tamia and I had over not getting to know you has nothing to do with how you did Tahj, because I'm sure he did a lot to you that made you do something so drastic." Tati added.

"Ok, so what was the reason?" Star questioned.

"Honestly we hate his other two baby mamas." She replied.

"Hate is a strong word." Talea muttered. "But we don't like them bitches."

"Same difference,"Tati waved her hand. "Tamia specifically has had run-ins with them because they were mad with Tahj and taking it out on her. By default we all got involved. So now we have sour tastes in our mouths where his baby mothers are concerned. When he told us about you we were thinking, ``Oh great, another one.'"

"But I'm nothing like them."

"We see that. Six years bitch?" Talea tittered. "You're definitely a different breed because Nikka or Lexi's ass would've called Tahj as soon as they pissed on the stick."

"And would've,"Tati co-signed. "But on behalf of Tamia we'd all like to apologize. If it's any consolation she didn't think you would hear anything she was saying. She thought she was having a *private* conversation with Tahj."

"She sure didn't back down when I made my presence known." Star responded, garnering laughter from them all.

"Hey, that's Tamia." Choc laughed. "She's feisty, but she loves hard. She feels bad about how the conversation went."

"Then why isn't she here?"

"She's in Atlanta with her man. She's stubborn so she won't admit she's wrong anytime soon. I'm just letting you know how she feels based on what she expressed to us."

"That's fine because I'm not apologizing either. Nothing that serious happened that warrants an apology. All I want is respect moving forward. I understand I did something wrong, but I don't wanna keep getting beat up over it."

"Fair enough," Talea said. "Now last night the girls were asking if we could have a play date on Saturday and I told them I'd take them to Build-A-Bear. Is it oka-"

"It's okay. It's always okay. Feel free to come get them whenever you want on the weekends."

"Well damn, I guess after six years of being a single parent you anxious as fuck to get rid of them babies,"Tati jested, making everybody holler. Even Star had to laugh at that one. Okay maybe she would continue to hear about how she kept the twins a secret, but she felt ten times better about Tahj's family after having that conversation. As tough as she tried to play, not being liked by people who shared a bloodline with her daughters bothered her. She still wasn't sure if they liked her, but at least they cared enough to clear the air.

The twins were in heaven as they played with their new toys in the living room. Star was at her kitchen table finishing the last few pages of her newest children's book. This particular book was about little black girls embracing their natural hair. It was titled "Nappy, Happy, & Sassy." The title was bold, but it was about taking the power back from a derogatory term.

"Mommy look at my dollie!" Tahiry stood up and held up her new Lol Surprise doll.

"She's beautiful, baby." Star said even though she didn't really look. She could never really work whenever they were home because they demanded attention. She would always try though. Just when she was getting back into the groove of writing, her phone rang, interrupting her flow yet again. It was Colley calling her.

"What girl? I'm working."

"What's new? Bitch you're 25 and be acting like an old ass grandma. Let's go out tonight!"

"Girl in case you forgot I'm at home with my kids. Where is your kid?"

"With my daddy."

"Now how you got that man to babysit?" Star giggled.

"He misses her. And you know my daddy loves me. He just be acting stupid sometimes."

"No, you be tryna send that man to an early grave with your shenanigans."

"Lies. I just be being myself and he can't take me. But look, I'm kid free and I'm tryna be outside! What we doing?"

"You can be outside all you want. I gotta be inside with my children, hoe."

Colley smacked her teeth. "Ugh, you make me sick. Where Tahj ass at?"

"Still outta town."

"Don't he got bukoo siblings? Ask one of their asses to babysit."

"Girl, I barely know them people to be asking shit like that."

"Star you don't miss going out?"

"I mean I never really did it. I can't miss what I never really did."

"Cousin, you don't know what you missing out on. The streets be fun."

Star laughed. "Girl, I really hate you."

"But I'm so serious. Revolution is supposed to be popping tonight and it's going to be 68 degrees outside."

"And?"

"And that means you can pull out a nice ass thot-fit because it won't be super cold!"

"I guess,"Star giggled. "I do have bukoo clothes in my closet that I never get to wear because all I do is stay home."

"Seeeee…"

"But Colley the fact of that matter is I have no babysitter so I can't co-"

Knock! Knock! Knock!

"Colley let me call you back, somebody's at my door."

"At 9 o'clock at night? You expecting somebody?"

"No."

"Then bitch stay on the phone."

Star kept her phone to her ear as she made her way to the door. When she looked out the peephole she smacked her teeth.

"Colley, I'll call you right back." She ended the call and opened the door.

"I thought you were in L.A until Monday?"

"Twinkie's tears pulled me back earlier than I expected,"he chuckled, before pulling something from behind his back. It was a small, light brown Maltipoo. As much as Star was anti-pet for the twins, she had to admit that the tiny puppy was adorable.

"They're gonna lose their minds." She said, as she stepped to the side to let Tahj in. When he walked down the hallway and entered the living room the girls jumped for joy.

"DADDYYYYYYY!"

"Is that a puppy? You got us a puppy?!" Tahiry screeched with her little arms wrapped around his neck.

"Yup. Y'all gotta take care of it though or else y'all can't keep it."

"We'll take great care of it daddy!" True held her hand to her heart.

"I can't wait to teach her tricks!" Tahiry expressed.

"How'd you know it was a girl, baby?" He chuckled.

"I don't know. She just looks like one. What's her name, daddy?"

"That's up to y'all."

They looked at each other and smiled.

"FRENCHY!" They blurted it out together before grabbing the dog from Tahj's hands.

"Frenchy?" He repeated.

"That's Fancy Nancy's dog name." Star said as she reentered the living room.

"Oh alright, that makes sense." Tahj chuckled. "You mind if I stay here tonight, Star?"

She started to scream hell no, until something dawned on her.

"Sure. I'm about to go to my room." She said before twisting off. Tahj watched her ass jiggle in her booty shorts. He couldn't wait to slide in that when the twins went to sleep. Ever since he hit it again he couldn't stop thinking about her. He tried to fuck one of his regulars in LA and shawty pussy felt trash because he was comparing her to Star. He was feigning for her and needed a hit ASAP.

An hour later the twins were getting themselves ready for bed. Star had already done their hair care routines so she didn't have to worry about that. When she walked into the living room after spending all that time in her bedroom, Tahj was in shock.

"Where you going?" He asked as he openly ogled her.

"I'm about to go out with Colley. You don't mind watching the girls since you're going to be here right?"

Tahj wanted to pull a hater move and say no so badly. She was dressed in a tiny red mini dress, thigh high red boots, and a small red clutch. She pulled her hair up into a puff, so her pretty and natural beat was exposed. She looked too damn fine to be going anywhere without him.

"Man when you decided you was going somewhere? You ain't even know I was coming here. Who was gon watch my daughters if I didn't pull up?"

"I would've had to stay home, but since you're here then it only makes sense that you babysit. I mean you asked to spend the night anyway." She looked down at the time on her phone. "I'm about to go. Colley needs me to curl her hair at her house. Don't let them girls bamboozle you into letting them stay up all night."

"Star!" Tahj stood up as she rushed for the door. She didn't look back when he called her name because it didn't matter what he wanted.

"Star! You don't need to be going no where bruh! They said it's supposed to storm later on tonight." He said the first thing that came to his mind. He didn't know what the fuck the weather would be like because he hadn't checked it.

"Boy shut up," she giggled. "Do me a favor and clean my kitchen for me. Bye!" She slipped out the door. Tahj stood there in disbelief. This girl had the audacity to leave him at her house to babysit and then told him to clean up. She had him fucked up. He was hoping she enjoyed tonight because this wasn't happening again.

"That's a real one in your reflection. Without a follow, without a mention. You really pipin' up on these niggas. You gotta be nice for what to these niggas? I understand, you got a hunnid bands. You got a baby

Benz, you got some bad friends. High school pics, you was even bad then. You ain't stressin' off no lover in the past tense. You already had them...."

Star stood on the couch of her brother's section at Revolution rocking her hips and snapping her fingers to the Drake song that was in rotation. She hated to admit it, but Colley was right. Outside was hella fun. They weren't expecting Diamond to be at Revolution with his knucklehead friends but it was a good thing they were. Diamond and his boys spared no expenses. They had bought the biggest section, so Star and Colley were beyond comfortable. They also ordered endless bottles of alcohol which meant free drinks all night long. If her brother did it like this every time he stepped out then she could see herself going out with him more in the future.

"Bitch Diamond friends is some fine." Colley raved. "Ou, there go his play brother. Throw me down, cousin. I know you know him."

Star's face balled up. "Girl you do not want no Zane."

"Bitch yes I do. That nigga trade."

There was no denying that. In New Orleans one of the meanings for the word trade was a guy that was extremely good looking, and Zane was definitely that. He was so handsome that he had an outstanding 500k followers on Instagram for his looks alone. Girls loved staring at his rock hard, 6'4 body, looking at his yummy peanut butter complexion, and peering into his dreamy bedroom eyes. Star could see him being Colley's speed, but she wasn't setting that shit up. She wanted no parts if that shit went left. If Colley was involved shit was bound to go wrong, and Zane was a notorious playboy.

"You got a mouth. Go use it on him."

Colley smirked. "I will. Just not in the way you're thinking of."

Star laughed. "Nasty ass."

"Guilty." She smiled. She was about to get up to go shoot her shot with Zane, but a girl walked up and stuck her tongue in his mouth. Just like that her little dream of hooking up with him died.

"Oop..." Star muttered.

"Now bitch why you ain't tell me that boy was taken?" Colley put her hands on her hips.

"Cause I ain't know. Bitch that's Diamond brother, not mine." Star responded dismissively as she observed the big booty, brown skin beauty. "She's fine too, cousin."

"And is,"Colley shamelessly agreed. "Oh well, there's more trades in this bitch to choose from. Ole girl lucky I'm tryna change because the old me would've still tried to fuck with his ass."

"You always bragging about how you used to fuck people's men." Star rolled her eyes.

"Not bragging. Just owning my truth." She smiled. "But Star…"

"What?"

"Don't look right away. The nigga to your left is all in your face and he's *hot*."

Star did the opposite of what Colley advised, and looked directly to her left. She immediately locked eyes with a handsome light skin guy. She usually didn't go for the high yellow brothers, but he was a looker. He looked like he would bury a block and that turned her on. What drew her in was his full beard, his bushy eyebrows, his big lips, and low eyes. He wasn't standing too far from Diamond and he towered over him. Diamond was 6'1, so that meant this mystery man had to be *really* tall. She could also see that he had some muscles under his True Religion fit. When he smiled and revealed a mouth full of gold teeth her heart momentarily stopped. Seeing that he had her full attention, he swaggered over to her.

"You beautiful, love." He spoke directly into her ear, with his accent in full effect. Star was from New Orleans but she never got tired of hearing the black men from her city speak.

"Thank you," she softly smiled.

"You Diamond sister, right?" He questioned.

"Yea. How did you know?"

"Cause that nigga told us to be on our best behavior with his sister and lil cousin around." He chuckled.

That didn't surprise Star. With the exception of Zane, they were surrounded by a bunch of street niggas. Her brother was knee deep into the drug game, and the company he kept reflected that. Diamond had started hitting the block when he was 15, and although Star hated that for him she had no control over what he did. She still didn't like the fact that her only sibling put his freedom on the line daily, but at least she could say he was good at what he did. He was also smart enough to put money up and invest into other things.

"Yea sometimes he thinks he's the oldest."

"Nah, that man is just looking out as he should. Shit if you was my woman you wouldn't even be here."

Star sucked her teeth. "Oh so you that type of nigga?"

He grinned. "What type of nigga?"

"The controlling type that wants to keep his woman at home while he runs the streets." Star responded with a stank face while thinking about Tahj. That nigga had the audacity to try to get her to stay home by lying about the weather. He was ridiculous. The worst part was that he wasn't even her man!

"No you got me all wrong, baby. I wouldn't have you out here around these vultures. When shit pop off these niggas forget who's around, and you too pretty to be in the mix like this. I'm not controlling, I'm protective of what's mine. Ya feel me?"

"Mhmm," she stifled a smile while rolling her eyes. "You're saying them like you're not a part of the group."

"Man, go ahead," he chuckled. He couldn't deny what she said because it was the truth. He automatically knew she didn't get out much. If she did then she'd know who he was. He was an infamous Jackboy and drug dealer. He did whatever made him the money that day, and he was going to get a bag by any means.

"Yea that's what I thought." She laughed.

"Fuck allat," he laughed. "I'm Isaiah."

"And I'm Star."

"You sure is. I swear my night brightened up when I first saw you."

Star exploded with laughter. She was used to corny pick up lines like that with a name like hers, but she thought it was cute coming from him.

"Now I've known Diamond since we were teenagers. Why is this my first time seeing you?"

"Probably because I moved away when I was 18. How old are you?" She asked, while silently praying he wasn't Diamond's age. She wasn't that much older than her brother, but everybody knew boys matured slower than girls. She didn't have time for anybody younger than her.

"I'm 26, love. Just turned 26 a few days ago actually."

"Happy belated birthday," she smiled, while silently rejoicing. She would be 26 later that year, so they were the same age. She could live with that.

"Appreciate it, love. How old are you?"

"25."

"Perfect. So when are you free for a date?"

Her head jerked back, as she fought to hold back a smile. "Boy you barely know me."

"Duh. That's what the date is for." He chuckled.

"I guess you got me there."

"I know I do, so wassup?"

"I have kids, so I'll have to keep you posted."

"Oh forreal? So do I."

"How many?" She asked flatly.

"Damn," he chuckled. "You sounding like you ready to turn a nigga down if I say the wrong thing."

"Shit I might." She admitted. All she could think about was Tahj and how he spread his sperm thin.

"That's fucked up though. I didn't do you like that when you said you had kids. What you not tryna combine your football team with somebody's else's?" He jested.

She laughed. "I don't have a football team. I have twins."

"Then we a perfect match because I only have two kids myself."

"And how many baby mama's?"

"Damn what nigga with bukoo kids and babaymama's hurt you? Cause you on me right now." He laughed. "I only got one babymama girl. And I have two sons. One is 8 and one is 7."

"Oh okay, well I guess we can work something out."

"So you just gon dodge my question?"

"In the middle of this club? Hell yea."

"Bet. You can tell me on our first date next Saturday."

"I told you I have to keep you poste-"

"You're out right now which means you have access to a babysitter. Next Saturday should give you enough time to ask the same person to keep them, don't you think?"

"You're making a lot of assumptions."

"But am I wrong?" He posed.

"No," she giggled. "You're not. I'll work something out."

"Give me your number, cause if you capping I'ma blow that bitch up."

She didn't hesitate to put her number into his phone when he gave it to her. She wouldn't mind his fine ass blowing up her line. She was looking forward to it.

For the next hour, Isaiah stayed by Star's side. They talked about everything under the sun from being parents, to their favorite tv shows, and other random things. She eventually got really tipsy and started dancing on him. She noticed her brother shooting her several disapproving looks but she wasn't worrying about him. She was enjoying herself. Colley had even linked up with the cutie that Isaiah had come with. His name was Donovan and he was a tall drink of water.

"Come home with me." Isaiah whispered in her ear as she popped her ass in his lap to a throwback Travis Porter song.

She pretended to be offended. She'd felt his hard dick against her ass several times and her coochie was throbbing. Going home with him didn't sound half bad, but she was hesitant. She'd never done this sort of thing…but maybe it was time she lived a little. She'd been so consumed with working and being a mother that she never enjoyed her youth. It wasn't like she was getting any younger. Now that she had more help with the twins it was time to live her best life. Perhaps she could start here with Isaiah.

"Go home with you for what?" She fronted.

"Yo fine ass know." He smacked her ass.

"C5 what you doing nigga?" Diamond questioned as he entered their personal space.

Star didn't know who the hell he was talking to until Isaiah's hands went up in surrender.

"We just kicking it, my nigga. That's all."

"You couldn't find another bitch to kick it with?" Diamond questioned.

"Diamond, go away!" Star snapped. "I'm grown, yea! Older than your ass."

"Man, I came over here because your baby daddy dming me on Instagram saying you better have your ass back to the house by 2am. What you want me to tell this nigga?"

Star was mortified for two reasons. Tahj reaching out to her brother when he didn't even know him personally was the first reason. Her phone had died an hour ago, so he couldn't reach her, but that didn't give him a right to contact her family! The second reason was Diamond saying this shit in front of Isaiah. He'd just made her look problematic as fuck. That was probably his goal.

"Don't say shit! Block his ass!"

"I'm saying though, that's the twins' daddy. He might need to get in touch with me for something serious one day. I think I'ma just give him my number so he won't have to DM me through IG."

"Do what you want, Dime. This doesn't have to be a conversation right now though."

"So you not gonna call him and update him about your whereabouts?"

"Fuck no! Why would I do that?"

"Because he's at home with y'all kids."

"Okay. Which means they're safe. My whereabouts are none of his concern. That ain't my man."

"Whew. Women." Diamond huffed before walking off.

"How old are your twins?" Isaiah asked.

"Six."

"You still messing with they daddy, huh?"

"What?! No!"

He laughed. "Why else would that nigga be doing the most right now?"

"Because he's an entitled ass nigga. Fuck him though. Where you live at?"

"Shit I could show you. You leaving with me tonight?"

"Yea. I'm rolling with you."

Tahj had pushed her to do something she normally wouldn't have done. Him telling her to be home at a certain time just made her want to go against the grain. This wasn't Burger King and he wasn't having shit his way.

"Hmmmm, oh my God." Star moaned, as Isaiah worked two fingers in and out of her wet snatch. She told him she wasn't comfortable with having sex just yet, but that only made him resort to other forms of foreplay to make her cum. She was coming up on her third orgasm. If he still wanted to fuck she'd be open to it now.

"You so fucking fine," he spoke with a low gruff before wrapping his lips around her hard nipples. He bit it with just enough pressure before circling his tongue around it. With females he always had to choose when it came to bodies. If a chick had big breasts she usually lacked in the ass area. Or if she was dragging a wagon then she was flat chested. Star had more than a healthy helping of both. He was like a kid in a candy store as he explored her body. When she expressed that she wasn't sure about sex he swore he'd chill and just lay up with her, but he was a man first. It made it no better that her body was responding in a way that made him want to keep making her cum.

"Let me taste this pussy."

"Okay," she bit her lip before pushing his head down between her thighs. He went straight for the kill and latched on to her clit. "Fuck yea, Isaiah! Right thereeeeee!"

She raised her hips off the bed and humped his face like a maniac but he took it all in stride. Soon her legs were shaking like a tree in the fall.

"Three for three." Isaiah boasted as he came up for air. He crept back up her body and pressed his lips into hers. She eagerly accepted his tongue and tasted herself. He began pressing his hard dick into her pussy, creating friction against her clit. She pulled away from his lips.

"Fuck me," she demanded.

"You sure? Cause ain't not coming back from that."

"I'm positive. C'mon…"

He pulled down his Versace boxers and his dick sprung out, slapping Star's coochie. He started to line his pipe up with her entrance, but she quickly stopped him.

"Woahhh, condom."

"Awwww c'mon Sta-"

"Condom." She blinked her eyes, not budging. She didn't know this nigga to be fucking him unprotected. It was bad enough she let her baby daddy run up in her raw.

Seeing that she wasn't bending on the issue, he reached over to his nightstand and got a magnum. He seemed like the type to keep condoms nearby in his room. He stayed in a modest one bedroom apartment off Bullard in the East. When Star saw where he was pulling up to she seriously thought about telling him nevermind about their little sleepover. This part of the East used to be nice and it still looked nice, but it was definitely the jungle. She was no stranger to the hood, so she brushed it off. She was happy she had because the dick she was currently receiving made it worth it.

"This pussy so juicy….and tight," he expressed as he long dicked her.

"Ouuuu,"Star tooted her lips up as he fucked her deeper. Yea, she hadn't been living at all, but this was the start of something great.

Chapter 7

January 25, 2020

"Yayyy! Pancakes!" True clapped her hands excitedly as Tahj set plates in front of her and her sister. Their existence was the only thing holding him together that morning because he was a ticking time bomb.

"Daddy you not hungry?" Tahiry asked with a mouth full of pancakes.

"No, baby girl."

"That's too bad, this is good." True uttered through bites.

Tahj had to be in some alternate universe. He was cooking breakfast for his kids while waiting for his baby mama to come home from the night before. He was convinced that Star had done this just to get under his skin and it was working.

"I'ma be in the living room y'all." He said to the twins before exiting the kitchen. While walking his phone rang. It was Star's brother.

"Yo, you got in touch with your sister?!"

"Nah, her phone is still going to voicemail so I'm assuming it's dead. But I know she's on her way home."

"How would you know that if you haven't spoken to her?" He couldn't put his finger on it, but something in the water wasn't clean.

"Say what's up with y'all? Cause I know y'all *just* got back in contact. Last night she said she's single, so why you asking so many questions?"

"Whatchu mean what's up with us? She dropped off the face of the earth last night and I'm tryna make sure her ass is good."

"She straight, big dog,"he chuckled. "She should be walking through the door at any second."

"Nigga where she was at?"

"Aye, that's up to her if she wants to tell you. My name is Paul and that's on y'all. Bye." He ended the call. On que, he heard a car pulling in the driveway. He looked out the window and saw Star's car. He barged out the front door to greet her trifling ass.

Star didn't know what to expect upon returning home. She knew she'd hear Tahj's mouth about staying out all night or her phone being dead, but she didn't expect him to be charging towards her full force like a Buffalo. She slammed her car door and ran around it.

"COME HERE BITCH!" He ran around the car as she jetted to the other side. She didn't even know she could move that fast, but him chasing her was lighting a fire under her.

"What is your problem?!" She screamed vehemently.

"Really bitch?! You standing in front of me with the next nigga's clothes on and you got the nerve to ask me that?!"

"Yea! You not my man! You coming at me like we agreed to be in a relationship!"

"It's about respect!"

"I haven't disrespected your psychotic ass!"

He banged his fist on the top of her car, making her jump. "You don't think staying out all night while I'm here with our kids isn't disrespectful? You gotta be playing!"

"Nigga you agreed to babysit! It sounds like you mad I was with the next nigga, and I don't know why! I don't belong to you!"

"I'ma kill you!!!" He ran after her again. This time she barely dodged his ass as she ran around her car *again.*

"Tahj stop! My neighbors gon call the police!"

"Good! They can call your ass an ambulance too!"

Her heart dropped as he threatened her. She didn't know if he meant it, but she wasn't going to give him a chance to make good on it. She needed to get far away from his crazy ass. Instead of running around the car again, she made a mad dash for her house. She was able to slip inside as soon as he reached the door. She hurried up and locked it. Tahj began banging on the door, making the girls run to the front.

"Mommy why did you lock daddy out?" Tahiry asked with a sad face. Star felt bad, but she had to put her safety first. Tahj was so mad that he had totally forgotten about his daughters being in the house as he banged on the door and cursed. The twins had never witnessed this type of chaos and it infuriated her that they were experiencing it now.

"Go back to the kitchen now." She instructed forcefully. They listened right away and walked off briskly.

"Tahj you scaring the twins! Leave!"

"You wasn't worrying about my daughters when you was getting slutted out last night!!! Anything could've happened!" He kicked the door. "Open this fucking door!"

"You gon kick my door down, Tahj! Stop!" She screamed as her eyes grew wet. Calling the police crossed her mind, but that was the last thing she wanted to do. Calling Diamond was her next thought but things would go from bad to worse if she did that. She wanted Tahj to leave, not die. Suddenly it hit her. She knew exactly who to call.

"Hello?" Choc answered the phone as Tahj continued to bang on the door.

"You need to come get your brother or send somebody to come get his ass before I call the police! He's at my house acting like a fool!"

"Wait, what's going on?!"

"He's mad because I went out last night and slept out."

"Girllll," Choc drawled. She could sense that her brother still had a thing for Star and this only confirmed it. "He's too old for this shit. My brothers stay on the Westbank. Ima send them over there."

They must've been right around the corner, because ten minutes later they pulled up. Tarik and Tavior were shocked as they walked up Star's walkway. Their brother who never sweated much was practically foaming at the mouth in anger.

"Nigga your kids are inside! Are you crazy?!" Tarik pulled him away from the door.

"Man fuck that hoe! I'm good on her! I just want my shit outta her house so I can leave!"

That was partially true. His phone and briefcase were inside, but he was also going to use that opportunity to get to Star's ass.

"Alright, I'll get it." Tavior said, seeing right through his bullshit. "Step back, Tahj."

Tahj smacked his teeth as he walked down the porch and stood on the walkway. His brothers weren't going to let him get to Star. They may have been younger than him by a few years but they were the same size as his ass. Both of them could successfully hold him back if need be. Now that they were here he was thinking more clearly. He didn't need to be cutting up with Star while the twins were close by. He wasn't about to create an unhealthy environment for them.

When Tavior knocked on the door calmly and made his identity known, Star was still skeptical. She answered the door with the security chain still intact. When she peeped the scene, she opened the door quickly to let Tavior in. She quickly gave him Tahj's things, and he made a quick exit without asking her anything. Whatever took place wasn't his business. He just needed to get his brother's things so they could leave.

"I want my fucking kids, too!" Tahj shouted as Star went to close her door. Seeing another glimpse of her disheveled hair enraged him. He wanted to hurt her like she was trying to hurt him. Since he couldn't get to her he went for the next best thing.

Tarik knew what he was trying to do, and he wasn't having it. "Nigga let's just g-"

"No, it's fine. He can have them for the rest of the weekend." Star said, while looking over her shoulders. "Girls, put on your shoes and grab that dog so you can leave with your daddy!"

Disappointment washed over Tahj. He was expecting her to put up a fight.

She looked back towards Tahj. "You need me to pack them a bag?"

"Bitch I don't need shit from you."

"Tahj, c'mon man…"Tavior scolded. "You don't gotta call that girl out her name."

"Fuck his stupid ass,"she hissed. "Have my kids back by Sunday night."

"I'm keeping them for as long as I want." He snapped.

Star started to go off, but she realized the longer he kept them the more alone time she'd have to do whatever the hell she wanted. A break would be nice. He was trying to get under her skin, but he was actually helping her out a lot. She needed to finish her book anyway.

"Yea, alright Tahj." She mumbled.

Tahj could see that she didn't believe him, so he couldn't wait to show her. He was going to keep the twins for a few days and there wasn't shit she would be able to do about it.

Chapter 8

January 30, 2020

"It hurts Titiiii,"True whined as Talea braided her hair.

"I'm almost done, baby." She cooed as she finished off the braid. She was doing a simple style of braids up into two ponytails. It was age appropriate and it would last for about two weeks if managed properly.

"Maybe you gripping her hair too tight." Tahj said.

"Boy, I know how to do kids' hair." Talea snapped. She'd been a licensed cosmetologist since she was 19 and she was going to turn 30 in February, so it was safe to say she was quite experienced in her profession.

"I'm just saying. My baby can't be complaining for no reason."

"Tahj leave me alone before this be the last house call I do for you." She warned playfully. She usually worked out of her salon, but she came to Tahj's house to do the girls hair after school.

"Daddy I'ma miss dance practice." True whimpered. She was saying anything that came to her mind to get out of that chair.

"Baby dance class is only on Monday, Wednesdays, and Friday's for your age group now."

As Talea was gripping the final braid, her phone started ringing.

"Tahj, answer that for me."

Tahj picked up her phone. She had an incoming FaceTime call from Tavior. When he answered, Tavior shook his head at the sight of his face.

"Nigga you been shaking your head at me all week. What's good?" Tahj questioned.

"I just can't believe my big brother going on out sad over some cooch-"

"Son, my daughter right here." He cut him off abrasively.

"Shit, my b. Wassup Uncle baby?"

"Hey Uncle,"True replied, not even knowing which uncle it was.

"She don't even know which uncle she talking to." Tavior chuckled.

"And you don't know which twin you're talking to,"she rebutted, making them all erupt with laughter.

"Nah I know who you are, *True*." He laughed. Only she would have a smart comeback like that. Tahiry would never. "Your daddy's been crying, huh baby?"

Talea laughed so hard that her shoulders shook. Tarik and Tavior wasted no time telling them all what had taken place at Star's house and they found it hilarious. Tahj was always the man who had the women in his life under control and it boggled their minds. They would always wonder what kind of spells he put on his baby mama's to make them settle for whatever he gave. To say that things had flipped was an understatement. He couldn't control his new baby mama to save his life and she was way younger than his ass. They still found Star shady for hiding the twins for so long, but they also had a newfound respect for her. She was humbling the fuck out of their arrogant ass brother.

"No, but he was mad last weekend because my mommy wouldn't let him in the house." True replied innocently. Talea and Tavior laughed even harder.

"Alright nigga, what you want?" Tahj snapped.

"Hold on,"he got his last few laughs out. "You coming with us this weekend to our Vibe magazine photoshoot, right?"

"That's this weekend?"

Tavior frowned. "Bro you slipping."

"Never that. My job is to book the gigs, not keep up with the schedule. That's what your assistant is for."

"And nigga your job is to accompany us to the gigs too."

Tahj sucked his teeth. "Tav you talking like I go with y'all everywhere."

"I never said that, but you usually come with us to the big stuff to make sure everything goes smoothly."

"And I'll be there this weekend nigga."

"Oh so you gon finally bring that girl her kids back?"

"Man these my kids. Ain't like she worrying about em anyway." Tahj said bitterly. Star hadn't contacted him once since he saw her last weekend. He thought she would've broken by now and been blowing his line up. He'd been looking forward to ignoring her, but he never got the satisfaction.

"Tahj." Talea eyed him before looking back down at True. That was her way of reminding him to watch what he said about Star in her presence. He got up and exited the kitchen. On his way up to his room he poked his head in the twins room to check on Tahiry. She was watching TV while eating hot Cheetos. That was his favorite snack too when he was a kid.

"When y'all leaving?" Tahj asked Tavior as he entered his bedroom.

"Tomorrow night."

"Alright, bet." He said, before hanging up. He went to call Star next, but he was interrupted by an incoming call. He was immediately annoyed, but he answered anyway.

"Wassup Nika?" He greeted her as cordially as possible.

"So you ain't get my text?!"

"Yea I got that shit. I just ain't feel the need to respond." He replied easily.

"Wow. The fact that you can say that is fucked up."

"How? I don't like to dignify bullshit with answers."

"It's not bullshit! You playing favorites and everyone can see that!"

"Man you really bouta piss me off. I'm flawed as fuck. We all know that. But the one thing I'm good at is being a daddy and giving my kids equal attention. Stop fucking playing with me. I had all my kids from Monday to Wednesday."

"And yet it's Thursday and them lil girls still at your house! Then you getting their hair done! Tazzy needs her hair done too!"

He started to question how the fuck she knew any of that until he remembered that he'd posted a video of Talea braiding Tahiry's hair on his ig story. It was time to block Nikka's ass.

"For one, you said you don't like braids in Tazzy's hair. For two, when you speaking of my fucking children say they names," he spat. Then he thought about it. "Actually, don't even speak on the twins no more. It's obvious you got hate in your heart for them and that's sad as fuck, bruh.

He'd known Nikka since highschool, and he'd never been more turned off by her until now. Anybody who spoke ill of his children was an enemy of his. He couldn't carry

Nikka how he'd carry anybody else he wasn't fucking with due to the kids they shared, but what he could do would hurt her so much more. He wasn't being cocky, he just knew what it was on her end. She wanted him in any capacity she could have him in and that's exactly why he was revoking her access to him.

"Ain't no hate in my heart. I'm just calling a spade in spa-"

"Keep talking and you gon be homeless."

There was silence on Nikka's end for a few seconds.

"Ever since that bitch popped up outta nowhere with her kids you've been threatening to put me out of my house. I don't think that's a coincidence. If ole girl needs somewhere to stay just say that."

Tahj laughed. "Nah, ole girl got a career of her own and a three bedroom house that she purchased herself. Maybe you should take notes."

"TAHJ FUCK YOU! You must be fucking that bitch again! I'll fuck both of y'all u-"

He ended the call, and blocked her number. It wouldn't be permanent. It would just be until she stopped aggravating him. At this point his head was hurting but he still had to make one more call.

"Wassup? You forgot my kids existed? You haven't called me about them since I left last weekend. What type of shit you on?!" He questioned back to back, angrily.

"Shit you just said they're your kids, so what I gotta call you about them for?" Star tittered.

"Yo, you really patheti-"

"Tahj you can say whatever about me but I swear I don't give a fuck. I have been a full time mama since 2013. This week off was very much needed, so thanks."

"And who's fault is it that you were a full time mom?! That was you who decided to be stupid and keep me in the dark!"

"Ok. That's me, Mrs. Stupid," she laughed. When he heard a deeper laugh in the background, he paused. This bitch was actually with another nigga. Suddenly he regretted keeping the twins so long because his plan had terribly backfired. She'd probably been sucking dick all week. He wanted to go off, but he was starting to see that was pointless. Star was going to do what she wanted to do. He couldn't control her. That was a hard pill to swallow. It was also hard to contain his jealousy when he didn't even know why he was so damn jealous. He and Star hadn't been a thing since 2012, and even then it wasn't official. Yet here he was in his feelings about her giving somebody else her time and Lord knows what else.

"Who you with?" He asked calmly.

"A friend."

"Alright, well when you're not with that friend, hit me up. I'm going out of town this weekend, so it's time for the girls to come back to you."

"You can just drop them off tonight."

"What time?"

"It needs to be before 7. I already know I'ma have to do their hair."

"Nah, they hair straight."

"How? I mean the ponytails they was rocking when I FaceTimed them yesterday looked decent bu-"

"You FaceTimed them?"

"Actually they've been FaceTiming me since they left. I know you didn't think I went this long without talking to my children."

"Shit I don't know what to think about you right now."

"Good. I never did like being predictable. So what's going on with their hair?"

"They got some braids," he took the phone from his ear and sent a quick picture of Tahiry's hair that was already finished to Star. "I just sent you a picture."

Star checked her messages and quickly decided she liked the braids. They were neat, the perfect length, and super cute. They even had blue beads at the ends to match their school uniforms, adding to the cuteness.

"I like them…but Tahj, when it comes to their hair I don't like too many hands in it. Especially hands I don't know."

"Yea well I know the stylist and she killed it, so you're welcome."

"Nigga I didn't thank you! And I'll slap the fuck out of you letting some bitch I don't know do my daughters hair. Did you watch her do it?!"

"Say don't call my sister a bitch."

"Your sister?"

"Yea. Talea did the braids and she asked me if you were cool with it first."

"But you never asked me anything."

"Because I didn't want to bruh. Now go back to your nigga. He can't be feeling this back and forth between me and you."

"He's good." Star claimed as she looked over at Isaiah. He was all in her grill. They were sitting outside Morrows waiting for their table to be ready. She'd been on a date everyday with him that week and each one had been better the last. She liked his personality and the sex was superb. She couldn't ask for anything better.

"Ion want nothing else, Star. I just wanted to tell you the girls are coming back to you today, so enjoy being a hoe."

Star's mouth dropped as the call came to an end. Just when she thought the call would end on a positive note, he surprised her. Despite being cursed out, she started laughing.

"What's funny?" Isaiah asked.

"Nothing, that nigga just crazy."

"You laughing though. You must like it."

"You want me to cry?" She giggled.

"I just wanna know if there's anything still lingering between y'all? Cause I'm really feeling you and I don't want to waste my time. You feel me?"

"I do, and I would never waste your time. I was honestly just laughing because he cussed me out. There's nothing going on between us."

"But why would he cuss you out if there's nothing going on between y'all?"

"I don't know. He probably *wants* something to go on between us, but that doesn't have shit to do with me."

"So when y'all broke up?"

Star laughed. "We were never together. We had a little fling. That's all."

He smacked his teeth. "Then his ass needs to give it up."

"He ain't gon' have no choice but to do that."

Chapter 9

February 14th, 2020

"Happy Valentine's Day, mommy!" Tahiry shouted as she and True ran up the walkway towards the door. When they reached her they gave her two heart shaped cards that they'd made in class. Handmade cards from her babies were her favorite part of Valentine's Day.

"We made these for you in school, mommy! And we went to the store with daddy and got you something else!" True eagerly volunteered.

She looked up at Tahj who had a big Chanel shopping bag in his hand and her heart pounded. She only fucked with affordable designers so Chanel never made the cut. She could buy herself anything but as a single mom she prided herself in making responsible decisions.

"Can I come in and give it to you?" Tahj asked.

"Yea..." she stepped to the side to let him into her house for the first time in weeks. The last time he came in was the night he'd watched the twins while she went out and that ended badly. After that he just didn't come in anymore. She didn't verbalize that he couldn't, it was just like an invisible line had been drawn and they had boundaries. If she ever went to his house to pick the twins up she didn't go inside of his shit either.

Although Tahj was still in his feelings about her seeing someone else he realized things were better this way. Spending nights at each other's houses and being in eachother's faces only complicated things. At least on his end. It made him yearn for something more that he was probably never going to get out of Star. Yea, he'd been able to fuck but evidently it wasn't that deep to her. He'd broken her virginity but she'd probably been with plenty of other niggas over the years, making sex more of a casual thing for her. Sex was definitely a casual thing to him and he absolutely did not catch feelings for every broad he slid in. Star on the other hand was a different story, and that's why it was best that he kept his distance in every way possible. Of course they had to communicate about the kids and things of that nature. Anything extra was sure to cause confusion again.

"Oh my God!" Star gasped as she pulled a black boy Chanel bag from the box it was packaged in.

"I'm guessing you like it." Tahj chuckled.

"I love it!" She exclaimed. Then a thought ran through her brain. "But Tahj I can't accept this…this is a five thousand dollar bag and you're giving it to me as a

Valentine's Day gift. Maybe if it was Mother's Day I could get with it bu-"

"Man chill," he laughed. "It's really not that deep. My daughters got this bag for you. Not me."

She gazed up at him. "Tahj these lil girls are broke."

"Hey!" True exclaimed in offense.

"They could never be broke with me as their daddy." Tahj laughed. "Forreal though, take the gift. Despite what you think, this is the perfect occasion to accept it. Today's about love."

"So what you love me now?" She tittered.

"I mean I love my daughters and you're an extension of them. It's good for them to see me giving you nice things on holidays or any time for that matter."

The twins had checked out of the conversation that they were barely paying attention to anyway and ran to the kitchen for a snack.

"So the other bm's got Chanel bags too?" She questioned.

He smacked his teeth. "All these questions, Star. Damn."

She giggled hysterically. "That's cause you full of shit. Take this bag back because I know you gon want something in return. You not about to hold shit over my head."

He was immediately offended.

"Yo, you think I would hold a *Chanel* bag over your head? What type of broke nigga do you take me for?"

"The same nigga who held a house over his other baby mama head."

"In *your* defense. She was threatening to press charges against you for whooping her ass, yea."

"Don't be blaming me for that."

"It's the truth though. I've never been an Indian giver. But if somebody is attempting to complicate my life when I'm making life easy for them then I will use the leverage that I have. A Chanel bag doesn't have shit to do with none of that though."

"Okay, so why didn't Nikka and Lexi get one?"

"Lexi is married and I have the utmost respect for that. Buying her something this extravagant would be out of line. And with Nikka…" he thought about it. "I'm just not feeling her right now."

"Hmmp," she muttered. "You'll be back in her face and bed soon."

"If that's what you think." He shrugged, seeing no need to convince her otherwise. He wasn't sticking his dick in no bitch who couldn't respect his seeds. Yea, he was supposed to be in a relationship with Nikka when the twins were made. But in the present day they were no longer an item and she'd fully accepted his kids with Lexi a long time ago. He didn't understand where all the animosity was coming from when it came to the twins, but he was good on that bitch. Contrary to his threats when it came to the house, he'd never put her out on the street. She was the mother to two of his kids, so that meant she was good for life by default. But she wasn't getting anything extra out of him like luxury gifts. He had allowed Baby Tahj to get her some flowers and Godiva chocolate, and that was only because he asked if he could get his mom something for Valentine's Day. He wasn't going to deny his son of that no matter the circumstances.

"So who planted a garden in this bitch?" Tahj asked as he looked around at the red Roses that seemed to be everywhere. He'd been holding that question in but it finally slipped out.

Star laughed. "Wouldn't you like to know."

Isaiah had come to her house with the flowers and a chef to cook them brunch hours ago while they twins were in school. He even got her a Celine charm bracelet. It was super cute and she was happy that he'd done it early because Tahj couldn't keep the girls tonight.

"So you not gon tell me this nigga name, Star?"

"Why would I do that? I'm just dating. It's nothing serious."

"If that nigga going through all this trouble then it must be serious for him. You be sucking his dick huh?"

"Tahj!"

"Keep it a buck." He demanded. "I bet y'all be fucking raw, too. That nigga better not be around my kids."

"Tahj, get out of my house." She laughed while pointing to the door.

"Wait, hold up. You got anything planned with the girls tonight or for this weekend?"

"We're just going to chill. I have to work."

"I thought you finished your book?"

"I did, but now I'm working on the illustrations."

"You do all that by yourself?"

"I majored in illustration at SU, so hell yea I do all that myself."

"Damn. That's what's up baby mama."

Instead of getting mad, she laughed.

"Appreciate it baby daddy. But why do you wanna know what we're doing?"

"Because I wanna take them with me to LA. I have a business meeting tomorrow for a new shoe for one of my clients with Nike, but I want to take the kids to DisneyLand. Well really the twins since they've never been, but I gotta include everybody or else I'm never going to hear the end of it."

"Whew, you think you can handle all of the kids by yourself while traveling?" Her eyes widened. Really it was scary for her girls to be on the other side of the country without her. She didn't mind when they went on the other side of the Westbank to their daddy's house because she could still reach them quickly if something happened.

"I've done it before,"he chuckled. "Without the twins of course, but what's two more?"

"It makes a difference."

"It might,"he admitted with laughter. "But they're well behaved. I got it. Are you cool with it?"

She hesitated.

"Uh-oh…"he uttered.

"It's nothing personal, I've just never been that far apart from my babies." She said with a long face. "But I guess I gotta share now. You can take them."

The look on her face hit him like ten bricks.

"Just come with us, Star. I could use the extra help."

"I thought you said you had it?"

"I do. But I don't want to see you looking all sad and shit. I don't want you worrying either. You can see up close how I handle the kids out of town. That way you'll be more comfortable with sending them alone with me for future trips."

"Okay. I'll come." She agreed. She would feel much better if she was there for this trip because sending her babies off scared her.

"Alright. Our plane is going to be ready at 7, so go hurry up and pack. I'm about to go round up the troops and I'll come back for y'all."

"Our plane?"

"Yea. We only fly private around here, baby mama."

She smirked. "Okay baby daddy. Sounds like a plan."

"Your job has obviously been great to you." Star voiced to Tahj. They'd been in the air for an hour and it just hit her that she was on a private plane when she looked back at the kids laying down on the bed sleeping.

He smiled. "You just noticed that?"

"No, this is just the first time I'm saying it. I remember when you had one client."

"Shit, me too. Life was way easier back then."

"I bet. You only had one kid too…one you didn't tell me about," she shamelessly jabbed.

"Yea. I used to be off the hook."

"You not anymore?" She giggled.

"Man, I haven't made a baby in four years. I think that shows growth. Enough about me though, tell me more about what I missed in your life. I'm curious."

"Okay. Ask me anything."

"Alright. Let's start with where did you go when you left my house after Christmas?"

"I went to my apartment."

"You had an apartment?"

"Sure did. A girl my old friend knew signed her lease over to me. Do you remember when I went missing one day after school? I was looking at that apartment. That's the first place I brought the twins home to."

"I knew you was up to no good that day."

"Yea but not the no good you were accusing me of. You had a lot of nerve accusing me of anything actually." She laughed.

"I was projecting." He confessed. "So you did your last year of highschool with the twins being newborns?"

"Nope. I finished my junior year and then went and got my ged. It was hard enough trying to complete that year pregnant, so I said fuck my senior year. I also didn't like the fact that I would be older than my classmates due to being held back in elementary school. And on top of that I was going to have newborns. Honestly I was ashamed."

Tahj shook his head. "For no damn reason. Star it wasn't your fault you got held back, no. That's on your sick ass auntie's head. Wasn't it that bitch who didn't bring you to school for like three months because she claimed it was too far from where she stayed?"

"Yup." Star nodded, as traumatic memories of her childhood came back to her. Her Auntie Fee would constantly berate her and call her stupid because she'd gotten held back over something that was beyond her control.

"So you had no reason to be ashamed. And plenty of people have kids in their teens."

"I know that now, Tahj. But that's how I felt then."

"So when did you start at SU?"

"In the spring semester of 2013."

"Who helped out with the twins?"

"Nobody. Well, they went to daycare. Other than that it was just me and them."

Tahj sighed heavily. "I commend you for that, Star, but you really made life ten times harder than it had to be. I would've helped out a lot, bruh."

"Yea, sadly I did…but going through the ringer with you and the two other women you had pregnant at the same time as me wouldn't have been a walk in the park either. I would've been equally, if not more stressed."

"Damn..."

That was all Tahj could say. Her words made him understand that he didn't make her feel secure enough to come to him, and that fucked him up.

"Don't take it wron-"

"No," he cut her off. "This whole time I've been blaming you for being selfish, but my selfishness led to you doing what you did. I was just doing whatever made me feel good and disregarding other people's feelings. For the first time I can see that you did the same exact thing. I'm sorry, Star."

Her heart instantly felt ten times lighter.

"Apology accepted, baby daddy."

"Back to your family. I know you're still close with Colley and your brother, but the rest of them people cut off right?"

"I haven't spoken to any of them since you came and got me from Fee's house in 2012. Fee has tried to reach out to me a few times, but I just ignore her. I was forced to see them in 2015 though."

"Forced huh?" He frowned. In his opinion there was no reason good enough for Star to subject herself to that sick ass family of hers. Star had to leave Fee's house because her older cousin pulled his dick out in front of her and asked her to suck it. She ended up whooping his ass with a nearby weapon, and Fee stumbled upon the scene. Instead of calling the situation out for what it was and siding with her niece who had been assaulted, she put 100% of the blame on Star. She then told her she had until the end of Christmas break to find someone else to stay. Star had too much pride to accept that pathetic offer. Nor did she feel safe in that house anymore. An enabled abuser was dangerous. So she called Tahj even though they had just exchanged numbers and asked him to come get her. He was the one who said she could call him if she needed anything. She needed him that night and he came through. He even knocked her nasty ass cousin out and spit in Fee's face. Even though he went on to hurt her she'd never forget how he was there for her when she needed him the most.

"Yea...that's what happens when there's a death in the family." She divulged, while fighting to control her emotions. This was still a sore topic and her way of coping was pretending like it never even happened. Tricking herself into thinking that had allowed her to navigate through life normally.

"Who died?" He asked in concern. As soon as he asked, the answer came to him. She hadn't brought her mom up once since they'd gotten back in touch. Last he heard she was in jail, but Star hadn't said anything about her or the twins visiting.

"It's your mom isn't it?"

She nodded, as she teared up. She was happy he was able to figure it out on his own because the shit was too hard for her to say. Her mom passed away from AIDS while in jail. What tore Star up about it was that she or nobody else knew she was battling that. Apparently she'd been diagnosed the month she got locked up in 2004. Her mother had beaten the odds and lived a year longer than the survival rate, but it still broke Star's heart that she had to die in jail alone. She wouldn't have even been in jail if it weren't for her. Her mom would always tell her that it wasn't her fault, but she still felt like she was to blame. Her father had already passed away a year before that in prison due to a fight that went left, leaving him stabbed to death. Her heart was already heavy due to that situation, yet she was able to push through it because her memories of her dad were vague. But when her mom died she almost lost it and fell apart.

"Shit…I'm sorry to hear that Star. She was still in jail when she passed?"

Star nodded her head yes. She wanted to open up and explain how she died. She even wanted to tell him why her mom was in jail in the first place because she'd never discussed that with him. She just couldn't bring herself to do it. Crying in front of him was hard enough. Tahj took it all in, and he wasn't going to push her. She'd tell him on her terms. If that was never then he was cool with that. He wrapped his arms around her and pulled her into his lap so he could hug her tightly. When he kissed her forehead and said it would be okay she really felt like it would be.

    She hadn't been able to be this vulnerable about her mom in front of anyone. She couldn't do it in front of the twins because they didn't need to see her like that. She would've liked to confide in her brother but he was so shut off emotionally that he didn't even cry once when their mom died. He was even late for the funeral. That's where she and Diamond differed. While Star sympathized with their mom's situation and all of her bad decisions, Diamond just felt like she should've done better and he didn't make any excuses for her. He had a lot of resentment in his heart for their mother. It was evident that he didn't want to talk about it, and Star took heed. She was on her own with the mourning process. Until now of course. She still wouldn't be 100% okay after this, but it just felt good to have somebody hug her while she cried.

February 15th, 2020

"Mommy look at Minnie!" Tahiry smiled while pointing at the parade they were watching. They'd been at Disneyland for a few hours and while it was obvious the kids were having the time of their lives, and so was she. She'd never been here before and like most kids she was a Disney fanatic growing up. Her inner child was *living*.

"I see, baby." Star giggled as she filmed the kids watching the parade and dancing. Baby Tahj was the only one standing off to the side.

"What's wrong?" Star asked him after ending the video.

"We've been doing girly stuff all day. I want to ride some rides." He pouted. He was trying to control his jealousy but seeing his dad dote on all the girls irritated him. He was outnumbered so whenever they did something as a family he'd have to suck it up. His dad also always told him to put his sisters first, so he never felt comfortable complaining.

"Yea, we have been," she laughed. "After this parade we can probably ride a few rides."

"No we can't because Tahja wants to go to Cinderella's castle."

"Well *they* can do that. Me and you can go get on rides."

His face brightened up. "Really?! Any rides I want?"

"Any rides you want." She giggled. "Ask your dad if it's okay first."

"Daddy!" He ran to his dad who was preoccupied with wiping ice cream off of Jari's face. Seeing him in daddy mode was precious and Star constantly felt silly for ever doubting him.

"Wassup man?" Tahj looked up.

"Can I go with Star to ride some rides while y'all go to Cinderella's castle?"

He looked over at Star. "You cool with that?"

"It was my idea. I just told him to ask for your permission first."

Star had only been around his kids a few times but she made sure to never overstep when it came to them.

Tahj laughed. "What I'ma say, no? Yea, you can go, man. And listen to Star."

"Yes sir," Baby Tahj said, before running back to Star and grabbing her hand to pull her away.

An hour later Tahj was leaving Cinderella's castle with the girls and about to call Star so they could meet up with her and Baby Tahj. As he was going to his call log, he got an incoming call from Nikka. He had long ago unblocked her because he had to communicate with her about their kids. That was the only reason he wasn't going to ignore her call at that very moment. He had their kids in another state, so she deserved to call whenever she wanted to.

"Wass-"

"WHY THE FUCK IS THAT BITCH IN CALI WITH YOU AND MY KIDS?!"

She was screaming so loud that he had to pull the phone away from his ear for a second.

"Man what?" He questioned although he'd heard her clearly. He was more so confused on why this was a question and how she even found out. He hadn't posted anything that would show Star was there and Star only had social media for her books.

"Baby Tahj posting selfies and shit with this hoe on his Instagram! What the fuck, Tahj?! You condoning that shit?! Why the fuck is she there anyway?! I never said my kids could be around her!"

"Man these are my kids too and she's the mother to two of my kids, so she's going to be around. Just like you and Lexi gotta be around sometimes. And I don't know nothin bout no selfie. You the one who told a seven year old he could have an Instagram, so that's on you."

"If that's the case then me and Lexi should've been invited on the trip too!"

"For what? I just wanted it to be and my kids. She's here because she's never been away from the twins."

"Then her and her children should've stayed home!"

Tahj laughed despite being aggravated. "Staying home is no fun. I'm sure you can attest to that right now."

"BITCH FU-"

He ended the call. Right after that he went to Baby Tahj's Instagram. He'd posted a picture of him and Star smiling before the ride they were on started five minutes ago. The caption read "Me and my twin sister's mama. Isn't she pretty?" The entire post made Tahj smile, while Nikka was at home losing her mind. She'd even commented on the post telling Baby Tahj to delete that shit. He couldn't believe how immature she was being. If it truly bothered her that much all she had to do was reach out to Tahj and ask for the picture to be taken down. As Baby Tahj's mother, he would've let her have that. But with the approach she took he was going to let that picture sit there and not say a word about it. Hell Baby Tahj could post all the pictures of Star he wanted on his Instagram for the remainder of the trip if he wanted to.

"Brown skin girl, ya skin just like pearls. Your back against the world. I never trade you for anybody *else, say. Brown skin girl, ya skin just like pearls. The best thing about the world. I never trade you for anybody else, say. Oh, have you looked in the mirror lately? Wish you could trade eyes with me. There's complexities in complexion. But your skin, it glow like diamonds."*

Tahj wasn't expecting to see a full on concert in the living room of their vacation home after getting out of the shower, but it instantly brought a smile to his face. Star and all of his daughters were singing and dancing to Beyoncé's song, Brown Skin Girl. It was a very appropriate and fitting song choice.

"And you over here recording them," Tahj chuckled as he sat next to Baby Tahj on the large sofa.

"I'm on Instagram live, daddy."

Nikka was probably at home watching with a red face. He was mentally prepared to hear her mouth about this shit for the next few weeks. Baby Tahj had given her plenty of content to react to. He'd even posted a group photo of all of them that a stranger had offered to take after raving about how beautiful their family was. As soon as Star got her phone back from the stranger Baby Tahj was insisting that she send it to him. Then he made her lock his number in her phone. It was to say that he found a new friend.

"You can't be letting people know our every move, son." Tahj laughed. This was exactly why Tahj told Nikka's ass that no child needed an Instagram. They didn't know how to act with that shit. She insisted that it wasn't that big of a deal, and that's why it was backfiring on her now.

"Daddy come dance with us!" True ran over to the couch and pulled Tahj up. Now Baby Tahj was recording all of them together.

Towards the end of the song, Star plopped down onto the sofa. She was exhausted and laughing hysterically. She was having so much fun with the kids. She would always tell herself that she was through with having babies, but now she could see herself popping out at least two more. Seeing how the twins interacted with their siblings was enamoring.

"Now you then started some shit," Tahj laughed as he sat next to her. Another Beyoncé song came on and the girls continued to dance.

"That wasn't me. Your daughters started that." She laughed, as her phone started ringing.

"Who's that?" Tahj asked.

"My brother." She said as she answered the phone. "Yea Diamond?"

"I passed by your house and you wasn't home. Where you at?"

"See," she laughed. "That's why you don't pass by without calling first. I'm way in Los Angeles."

"Why? How you leave the state and don't inform your only blood relative?"

"For starters, you're not my only blood relative." She giggled. "And secondly, I didn't tell you because it was a last minute thing. Tahj wanted to take the kids to Disneyland and I tagged along."

"Okay. Cut up."

She cracked up with laughter. "Stop it, Dime."

"Nah, forreal," he chuckled. "That's where you *need* to be. I don't know Tahj that well, but I'm sure he's the man for you."

"Boy where is all this coming from?"

"Look, you're grown, so I can't control you. I just feel like you don't need to be with a wild ass, street nigga like C5. You need a legit nigga like Tahj. Especially with my nieces in the picture. And that's their father anyway. You might as well make it work."

Star smacked her teeth. "That's a horrible reason to make something work, Diamond. And you got the nerve to talk about somebody being wild."

She noticed Tahj was all in her mouth trying to figure the conversation out, so she stood up and went to her room in the huge mansion. Clearly Tahj did everything big. Even last minute trips.

"Why do you think I'm telling you? I know first hand how it is. I had to let somebody go that I really loved because I'm outchea living reckless and she got caught in the crossfire. Shit learn from my mistakes, sis."

"Look Diamond, I'm just having fun with Isaiah. Ain't nobody falling in love."

"Yea aight," he sucked his teeth. "I can't believe that nigga told you his name is *Isaiah*. Don't nobody call him that weak shit."

Star laughed. "But that is his real name. Why you mad?"

"I'm mad because it's evident he was tryna hide the real him from you. Everybody calls that man C5 because he causes mayhem everywhere he goes like a category 5 hurricane."

Star rolled her eyes, thinking he was just being dramatic. She'd never seen anything like that from Isaiah. He was always sweet and calm with her. "And yet he's your friend."

"Because I like hanging with niggas that shoot first and ask questions later. That doesn't mean I gotta be an advocate for you dating him."

"Okay Diamond. I'll keep in mind that you don't approve. Anything else?"

"Nope. Nothing else, hard headed ass. I love you. Kiss my nieces for me."

"Will do, and I love you too."

While the entire house slept soundly, Tahj walked downstairs to the kitchen to get something to drink and a midnight snack. When he entered the kitchen it was dark, but there was light coming from the table. Star was sitting there with her laptop.

"What you doing up?" He asked as he turned on the light, and went straight for the refrigerator.

"Can't sleep so I decided to work."

"Yea I can't sleep either, but I gotta question," he said before taking a swig of water.

She looked at him, signaling that it was okay to ask whatever was on his mind.

"Where do you sell your books at? Are they in stores?"

"A few books are in select stores, but the main platform I use is amazon and my own website."

"How much money do you usually make with every release?"

The corners of her mouth turned up. "I think that's my business. Get me a water bottle please?"

"Nah, get it yourself since it's your business."

"So childish," she laughed as she stood up and attempted to pull her shorts down. She thought she would be downstairs alone so she didn't bother covering up more. She wore a pink cotton sports bra with matching booty shorts.

"Fine ass," Tahj smacked her booty as she walked past him.

"Nigga don't touch me!"

"Oh yea, I forgot you got a lil boyfriend. My bad." He smirked.

"For one, I don't have a boyfriend. Secondly, you don't need to be touching me because you don't need to be touching me. It don't have nothing to do with the next nigga."

"Oh yea? That nigga must not be fucking you right then." He said as gripped her ass.

Instead of talking, she swung on him this time. He caught her arm and pulled her into him, giving him full access to her ass and lips. He leaned down and kissed her deeply. She forgot that she was supposed to be demanding respect and gave in. He backed her into the countertop as his hands fondled her ass like he was kneading dough.

"No! Wait! Wait!" She breathed heavily with her hand against his chest when he lifted her onto the countertop.

"What man?" He grumbled. He'd already pulled his dick out and it was as hard as a rock. If she was setting him up to leave him hanging he was going to be pissed. "You want this dick and I want this pussy. Don't even start."

"I don't think we should do this Tahj…shit,"she moaned as his mouth came into contact with her neck. His wet and warm kisses were making her heart and pussy tremble.

"Why not?" He asked while attempting to pull her shorts down. "Raise up."

She shook her head no.

He sighed heavily. "C'mon Star. Just let me put the tip in."

"Boy, what kind of high school shit is that?"

"Why would you do me this, Star?"

"Because I know how you're going to act afterwards! We've been doing great. Bringing sex into the picture is going to complicate things again."

"I'm not gon' trip this time. I promise." He claimed. He would've said anything for her to shut up and pop that pussy.

"You're just saying that."

"No I'm not," he said while gazing into her eyes. "I don't like the way you had me acting last month, either. This time I'ma check my emotions. Real shit."

"So you not gon act crazy?" She questioned. She wasn't fully convinced, but she wanted the dick. She'd pretend to believe anything that came out of his mouth.

"No Star. I promise." He licked her lips before kissing her deeply. "Lift up, baby."

She raised her ass off the counter top, and he was able to pull her shorts down her thighs. She kicked them on to the floor.

"OHHHH!" She moaned loudly when he rammed himself inside of her. She'd been getting consistent dick from Isaiah so she didn't understand why it still hurt when Tahj entered her. He must've been a different type of horse.

"You clamming up already," he groaned as he worked his hips in and out of her at a fast pace. He wanted to blow her back out, and he was succeeding. She couldn't even fuck him back or see straight because her eyes were tearing up. His dick was unbelievable.

"W-waittttt," she put her hand to his chest. She needed a second to get it together.

"Ain't no wait." He kissed her nastily. "Put that fucking hand down and take this dick."

She dropped her hand and threw her head back in ecstasy when his dick reached her favorite spot. He grabbed her ass cheeks with his hands and started drilling her shit. She lost all her composure and started screaming.

"TAHJJJJ! OH MY GOD! I'MA CUM! I'MA CUM!"

"Go ahead,"he urged. "Make that pretty pussy cum all over my dick."

His words went straight to her pussy and she made it rain on him. In that type of gushy his dick folded under pressure.

"FUCKKKKKK!" He roared as his back went stiff and his dick started twitching inside of her. "With pussy like this you must want a nigga to go crazy. Come here."

He grabbed her neck forcefully with his hand and tongued her down. "I fucking love you."

She caught chills. He'd told her he loved her before but it was back in 2012. After everything that transpired she felt like there was no way he could still feel the same. She was so taken aback that she didn't even respond. She just pulled him back in for a kiss while praying she hadn't awakened the crazy in him again.

Chapter 10

February 23, 2020

"Long time, no see. What kind of relationship is this?" Isaiah smiled, as Star slid into his car.

"A non-existent one." She laughed.

"Awww, you really be tryna fuck over a nigga." He chuckled.

"Boy you don't care. If you did then you would've tried to see me."

"Me?" He pointed at himself in disbelief. "I've been tryna get up with you since you got back from your lil family vacation." He said. The saltiness in his tone didn't go missed. When Diamond told him where Star was that weekend he was immediately in his feelings. Although she told him otherwise, something was telling him she was still screwing her baby daddy.

"Lies," she scoffed. "You texted me trying to question me about why I was somewhere with my kids. I didn't appreciate that so I ignored you. After that it was crickets from your end. That's why I was surprised to hear from your ass today."

"You heard from me today because I missed your fine self. I was mad because you ignored me when I was asking a real question."

"I'm just trying to see why it was a question, though. My baby daddy just came into our kids' lives, so I wasn't comfortable with him taking them to another state without my supervision. That's all there was to it. You acting like he took me somewhere with just us two. That trip had six kids on it. The focus was not on him and I."

That was partially the truth. She just left out how she and Tahj still found a way to fuck multiple times before the trip came to an end. They even had sex on the plane coming back. She felt like a new bitch after joining the mile high club.

He stayed true to his word and didn't start acting crazy once they touched down in New Orleans. It was just weird because she was now in her feelings over that. He hadn't even attempted to hit it again. She didn't know how to put it into words, but being desired by Tahj felt good.

"Okay so why not explain that when I texted you and asked about it? I can't ask a question now?"

Star thought about it. Maybe she was being kind of hard on him. To make the situation worse she'd just blatantly lied to his face. She could definitely cut him some slack. This was a guy she actually liked after all. Not some bug a boo.

"I guess you're right."

"It's cool. Consider it water under the bridge. Bring your ass here." He gripped her throat and kissed her. When he pulled away from her, he backed out of her driveway.

"Anything in particular you wanna do, love?"

"I want to eat."

"Yea, me too. Where you wanna go?"

"You pick."

"Cool. Let me surprise you."

"Whatever it is, it better be good."

"C'mon now. I always take you to the best spots and your fork always finds its way into my plate. You know I got good taste, girl."

"We'll see today," she laughed. "So what are you doing for Mardi Gras?"

"I'ma be with my family."

"Your family?"

"Yea. My boys, my mom, cousins, aunties, uncles, and siblings. My family." He chuckled. Star's stomach tightened because outside of her kids, she couldn't relate. Diamond would probably be with his people, and she could probably go with him, but unless he invited her she was cool on that. Then she'd already told Tahj he could have the girls, so it wasn't like they could do their own things. At this point she'd probably have to settle for spending Mardi Gras with rowdy ass Colley. She wanted to have fun on Mardi Gras, but not Colley's type of fun.

"What you gon get into for Mardi Gras?"

She shrugged. "I'll probably go to Zulu with my cousin and then I might go to Masquerade that night with her. You should come to the club at night."

He hesitated. "I don't know, Star. I be with my kids on holidays."

She raised an eyebrow. "Even at night when they would be asleep?"

"Well they'll probably spend the night at my house."

"Your house? You have a one bedroom apartment to my knowledge."

Before he could answer or she could dig into him about how suspect he was being, her phone rang, saving him. It was Diamond, so she answered. She fully planned on getting back to Isaiah because they needed to have that conversation. She'd been so wrapped up into having fun with him that she hadn't been asking important questions.

"Where you at, Star?!" Diamond asked urgently. She could hear a lot going on in the background.

"I'm riding in the car. Why? What's wrong?" She questioned.

"Alright, listen. If that nigga C5 try to link with you tell him hell no! He did some fuck shit and the streets talking. He's hot right now and you don't need to be nowhere near him."

Diamond had just got the news that C5 was supposed to do a job with another notorious robber. They had made plans to hit up a jewelry store together and split everything 50/50. Somewhere along the lines C5 felt like it would be more beneficial to do the job alone. So he went over his partner's head and did it by himself. Now his partner wanted *his* head and he was letting everybody know it. He'd even put a bounty on him.

Star's heart dropped. "I'm in the car with him now."

"Man who the fuck is that?!" Isaiah snapped. There was no reason she needed to be telling anyone she was with him in the car. That was some set up shit.

"What?! Man tell that nigga drop you off somewhere! Don't even let him bring you back to your hous-"

POW! POW! POW!

"AHHHHHHH!" Star screamed as glass shattered everywhere. She instantly felt severe pain to her arm and shoulder.

"STAR?!" Diamond shouted in horror as she dropped her phone on the floor.

"FUCK!" Isaiah vented as he reached for his gun in panic mode. After what felt like forever, he located the gun underneath his seat.

"GET DOWN STAR!" He demanded, as he prepared to start busting back. The bullet that just wheezed past his head was a clear sign that somebody was trying to kill him. He'd been in this type of situation before, but he was usually the initiator.

Star was so hysterical that his demands went through one ear and out the other. Her body was aching and there was blood everywhere. Her entire life was flashing by, so her emotions were all over the place. The last thing she was worried about was getting down so Isaiah could shoot back at the perpetrators.

Seeing that she wasn't listening to him, he was about to let the choppa sing past her head. If she got caught in the crossfire it would be her fault for ignoring his instructions.

"Waaaaaahhhhhhh!"

"Shit!" He hissed. Police lights damn near blinded him. Considering they'd just saved his life, he should've been grateful. Maybe he would've been if he didn't have an illegal and hot firearm on him.

The two shooters tried to make a quick getaway, but three more police cars surrounded them. It was over for them and they knew it. The only thing they could do was hold their "L." Isaiah on the other hand wasn't trying to go down for this shit. Especially since he hadn't even gotten the chance to shoot back. This wasn't worth doing time for, so he thought fast. He didn't even process his thoughts. He just dropped his gun into Star's big Coach purse. Her eyes were shut tight and she was screaming out in pain, so she didn't see a thing.

A few short seconds later, his door was being ripped open and he was being forced out of the car and thrown on the ground. Star's door was opened with the same force, but the cop's attitude changed when he saw she was injured. He got on his radio and called for an ambulance.

Diamond pulled up to the scene at the worst timing. He was going crazy trying to call Star's phone until he realized he had her location. They'd been sharing their locations with each other since 2017, so it had slipped his mind. For the first time since sharing locations, it finally came in handy today.

"Back up sir," the police tried to block Diamond off as paramedics pushed Star away on a stretcher. All he saw was her eyes closed and blood. He naturally assumed the worst.

"NIGGA THATS MY FUCKING SISTER! MOVE!" He shouted in the white officer's face.

Hearing Diamond's voice made Star open her eyes. She'd had them closed to cope with the immense level of pain she was experiencing. It seriously felt worse than childbirth.

"That's my brother," Star cried to the paramedics. "Please tell them to let my brother through."

One of the paramedics relayed the message to the officer, and he let Diamond through. Once he was at Star's side he was able to see everything up close. It appeared that she'd been shot in her right arm. She'd survive this.

Somebody else was going to die though. He looked around with a crazed look on his face.

"Diamond..."Star called out to him in a weak voice as they moved her into the ambulance. She could tell he was about to do something stupid, and she couldn't let him do that.

Star's voice was drowned out by Diamond's thoughts. He saw C5 being lifted off the ground with handcuffs on him and he ran up.

"BITCH!" He cold clocked C5 dead in the mouth. His front tooth loosened as a result of the vicious punch.

"HEY!" A female officer grabbed Diamond up.

"Nigga you dead! I put that on my mama!" Diamond vowed, with his hands behind his back.

"Boy fuck you and that prostitute with her dead ass," C5 growled with a bloody mouth.

Diamond's darkest memories about his mother were triggered. He tried to rush towards C5 again. He was going to off this nigga in front of everybody. He didn't give a fuck.

"Do you want to go to jail with him?! Because you're walking a fine line, buddy!" The female officer warned.

"I say read his black ass his Miranda Rights now. He just assaulted someone right in front of us." A white male officer said.

"Man just let me get back to my sister," Diamond grumbled. His heart was racing out of frustration that he couldn't hurt C5 like he wanted to. But Star needed him more.

"I'll walk you over there." The female officer said. As they started walking together, Diamond saw two other niggas getting put in the back of a police car. They had to be the shooters. He took a mental picture of their faces. He never forgot faces. Especially faces that violated him.

"Here's your sister's bag." The female officer held up Star's purse. When he reached for it, she pulled it back.

"You're lucky I was told to search the car. There's something very interesting in this purse. Something your sister can go to jail for I'm sure."

Diamond's eyes shifted. He didn't know where this was going, but he was all ears.

"I'm sure there's a reason you're telling me this."

"Of course there is." She smirked evilly. "If you give me your number and answer when I call, we'll pretend like this doesn't exist. Don't answer when I call, and I'll make your life a living hell."

"What the fuck do you want though?" He raised an eyebrow. If she was asking him to snitch about street shit or anything like that then she could have his ass to kiss. Hell he would take the wrap for whatever was in Star's bag before he went out like that.

When her eyes lowered to his crotch and then she looked back up at him with lust in her eyes, he quickly got the picture. This bitch was giving immunity in exchange for some dick. Her white ass could definitely get that. She was obviously older than him but she wasn't gross looking. She was actually kind of pretty and appeared to be in shape.

"I think we can work that out... Officer?" He looked down at her badge to get her name.

"Call me Karen." She insisted before patting his back and giving him Star's purse. "Go to your sister now. She's going to pull through."

He couldn't wait until she pulled through because they had a lot to talk about. The first thing he was going to ask her was why the fuck a gun was in her purse.

Chapter 11

"You like them, baby girl?"

"Yea," True nodded with a smile while looking down at her all white G-Nike's. She liked anything that was new, and the Air Force ones on her feet were just that.

"What about you, baby?" He asked Tahiry.

Her shoulders went up and down. "I guess they're nice."

"You guess?" He laughed.

"I wanted some sandals, daddy." She whined.

"Girl you can't wear no sandals in February. Especially on Mardi Gras at the parade. People gon' step all over your little feet." He chuckled while poking her chubby cheek.

"These are for boys." She whined.

"Nuh-uh!" Tahja exclaimed. "Because I have some!"

"Daddy, I want new shoes." Tazzy said with her face balled up.

"I bought y'all some G-Nikes in December and y'all haven't worn them yet. I'm only getting the twins some because they don't have any." Tahj explained. He was going to have all of his kids on Mardi Gras so it was his job to dress them. With the help of his sisters he'd already picked out the girls outfits. To make it easy, they were all wearing the same thing down to their shoes. Baby Tahj was never a hard task because he would dress just like him. Holidays were no exception.

"So we only came here to get the twins some shoes?" Tazzy asked.

"Yea. Why? Do you need something?" He asked in amusement.

"Yea. I want a Build-A-Bear." She grinned.

"Ughhh," Baby Tahj groaned. He just wanted to go home and play Fortnite.

"Ooouuu! Me too, daddy!" Jari shouted.

Tahj had nothing else to do, so Build-A-Bear workshop was definitely their next stop. After buying the twins' shoes, they began to make their way there. That was until they bumped into familiar faces.

"What y'all doing here?" Tahj asked as he hugged his sisters, Tati and Tamia.

"Last minute Mardi Gras shopping. You know how we do." Tati laughed.

"Wassup man?" Tahj poked Angel's cheek. He's stolen Tatiana's entire face.

"Hey Unkie," he uttered cutely, making Tahj's insides melt. He missed having kids that young.

"Where my niece at, girl?" He asked, referring to Noeva, Tamia's daughter.

"With her grandma." She rolled her eyes. She didn't like bringing her active two-year-old to the mall. All she would do is wreak havoc on those peoples' stores.

"Oh she's with mama?" He stifled a grin.

"This nigga got jokes, Mia." Tati laughed.

"I ain't laughing though." Tamia said with a blank face, making Tati and Tahj laugh harder.

"That's sad, sis. You could let your mom babysit." Tahj said just to get a reaction out of her.

"You let her babysit your kids first then come tell me that shit. Until then, stop playing with me." She snapped.

"Alright, you going hard." He chuckled. The reality of the situation was that he'd never let someone as mean spirited as his mother be around his kids alone. Her physically harming them wasn't his worry. It was more so the shit that she would pour into their impressionable minds. Porscha had let their dad's poor decisions turn her cold. Instead of taking that negative energy out on the person who rightfully deserved it, she took it out on his outside kids. As a result of Tahj and Tamia choosing to build relationships with the outside kids, Porscha was bitter towards her own flesh and blood as well. Tahj tried to be understanding because there was no telling how she felt after being betrayed by their dad time and time again. Tamia however, didn't have the same patience as him. She also had her own separate issues with their mom, so she had a shorter fuse when it came to dealing with her. These days their relationship was non-existent due to a physical fight they'd had when Tamia was pregnant. She wasn't open to rekindling the relationship after that, and Tahj didn't blame her. What their mom did and said to her was unforgivable.

"Sure is. Don't be trying me." She fluttered her eyelashes. "What y'all bouta get into?"

"We going to Build-A-Bear workshop, Titi Mia!" True volunteered eagerly. "You coming?!"

"I might. I was just saying how I need to get me a new bear." She said while patting her head.

"Really, Mia?" Tati giggled.

"We gotta get my cousin something too, Titi." Tahiry said.

Tamia whisked Tahiry up and kissed her cheek. "You so sweet, baby, but that cousin of yours don't need another damn thing."

"Don't do Noeva like that." Tahj chuckled.

"I said what I said. Her daddy just blew over ten thousand dollars on her at the American girl doll store. We gon need a bigger house soon for just her stuff." Tamia rambled as Tahj's phone started vibrating in his hand. Seeing Diamond's name on his screen made him answer right away. It had to be something serious if Star's brother was calling him.

"Wassup Diamond?"

"I need you to get to University Medical Center right now." He said urgently.

"Is Star okay?!" He clamored, fully alerting Tati and Tamia.

"No, man. I mean…she'll be okay if that's what you're asking. But you need to get her ASAP."

"I'm on my way now." He ended the call. He didn't even want to hear what happened over the phone because he wasn't sure if he could handle it.

"What's going on, bro?" Tati asked.

"I-I gotta get to the hospital."

"Well we're right behind you. Let's go." Tamia responded. She didn't know what was going on, but it sounded like an emergency. He didn't need to be by himself with all of his kids in the middle of an emergency.

Hours later

"Diamond you still not telling me what the fuck happened. I understand she was shot. I need answers as to why."

"Man...I told this hard headed ass girl she ain't have no business fucking with that nigga. He got too much shit going on, and he then got her caught up. But best believe I'ma handle his bitch ass when he hit the streets again."

"That nigga can be handled now! Where he at?!"

"He got arrested, but say, you need to focus on my sister and the twins. Let me handle C5."

"C5, huh? What's his government name?"

"I told you to let me worry about that. Star gon need you."

"Nigga she need you too! You her brother."

"Yea, maybe, but the difference between me and you is that I don't have shit to lose. I don't have kids and I already take penitentiary chances everyday. I need you here looking after Star and my nieces."

"I don't need nobody to look after me." Star finally found her voice and spoke up after playing possum for the last few minutes. She started coughing because her mouth was unexpectedly dry. When she attempted to raise her right arm to cover her cough she winced. "OWWW!"

"Uh-huh, finna talk all that shit for nothing." Tahj glared at her.

"My…my arm hurts." She teared up.

"Because you were shot in your shoulder and grazed with multiple bullets." Diamond divulged. "You should feel nothing right now though because they drugged you up when they took the bullet out of your shoulder."

"Wait what?"

"You don't remember what happened?"

"No…I…I remember being with Isaiah and them shooting bu-"

"Isaiah." Tahj nodded. "That's his name."

Diamond shook his head. "You don't remember getting shot, Star?"

"I remember my arm hurting a lot. I guess the confirmation just has me in shock."

"It was shocking for me to see that shit. I thought them niggas hit you multiple times in the arm because there was so much blood. You got lucky, sis."

"Lucky?! I don't feel lucky."

"Well you are,"Tahj grumbled. "You lucky my kids were nowhere around you while you kept that type of company. What the fuck is wrong with you, bruh?"

Disbelief washed over her face. "Are you seriously coming at me like this is my fault?!"

"You the one who chose to kick it with the nigga knowing he was in the streets!" He rebutted with no remorse.

"Diamond!" Star called her brother to come to her rescue, but he just looked at her with a straight face.

"I can't even defend you, sis."

"What?!"

"You holding niggas guns now?" He questioned.

Her heart dropped. "Come again?"

"That nigga's gun was in your purse. And before you try to lie I know it's not yours. I've been trying to convince you to get a gun for years now and you've been against it."

"Wow, so now you holding niggas guns? You...you love this nigga?!" Tahj asked with rage in his eyes that scared the shit out of Star.

"I swear, I didn't hold anything for anybody!" She started pleading her case. One side of her wanted to curse them out for coming at her like she was the problem, but the other side of her couldn't let them think she would be that stupid to hold someone's gun.

"You didn't answer my question though." Tahj said.

"Fuck that question!" She exploded. "I love my kids and myself! I wouldn't do anything to jeopardize them being taken away from me or my damn freedom! Y'all got me fucked up!"

Diamond nodded with an even face. "So he put it in your bag without you knowing."

"He had to!" She replied. It went over her head that Diamond wasn't asking her anything. He'd come to his own conclusion. He had suspected that from the beginning, but he had to hear it from the horse's mouth first.

"Okay. I believe you." Diamond responded while thinking of ways he could end C5's life.

"You better be done with this nigga or I'm taking my daught-"

"Tahj ain't nobody worrying about that man! He was just something to do!" She exploded.

"And look at you. All shot up over a nigga that was just something to do."

"Alright Tahj…"Diamond warned.

"'Nah, fuck that. She needs to know that this shit could've ended worse."

"I can't move my arm right now, Tahj! I realize that this shit is bad!" Her voice cracked. "You don't have to rub it in my face!"

"Calm down,"Diamond rubbed her head before kissing her forehead. "Everything is going to be alright. Tahj is saying all of this out of love, right?"

Tahj scoffed in disgust.

"Where's my daughters?" Star whimpered. Now she was thinking about how she almost came close to never seeing them again.

"I sent them home with Tamia. When you get out of here y'all gon come stay with me for a little while. Until I can find you another house."

"Excuse me?!"

"Star them niggas started busting at y'all a few minutes away from your house. They know where you stay which means you're not going back there."

"But that's *my* house. I own it. I put my blood, sweat, and te-"

"That's all fine and dandy, but are you tryna die there too? Because you can do what you want, but my daughters are going to stay with me."

"Are you really threatening to take my daughters from me right now?" She cried.

"No. I'm inviting you to stay with me until I put you in another house. That was you who went off on an independent woman rant when I'm trying to put your safety first."

"And even if safety wasn't a factor you're going to need someone to help with the twins while you recover from getting shot." Diamond offered.

"Whatever." She allowed tears to free fall as she realized she was public enemy number one and outnumbered. All of this because she gave a cute guy a fair chance. Never again.

Chapter 12

March 2, 2020

"Cousin, when are you coming home? I miss you." Colley whined.

"Bitch I keep telling you to just come to Tahj's house. You haven't seen me since I got out of the hospital last week, so you can't miss me too much."

Colley sucked her teeth and gave a dramatic eye roll. "Bitch your baby daddy lives deep on the Westbank. Nobody tryna drive all the way out there."

"Then I guess we just won't see each other because this is where I'm going to be for a while."

"And why is that? Didn't the doctor say you would make a full recovery by spring?"

"Yup."

Star couldn't believe how lucky she'd gotten. Only one bullet penetrated her shoulder and she had little to no nerve damage. She was definitely still experiencing discomfort in her arm and shoulder, but it was nothing pain medication couldn't fix. The down side to constantly taking medication was being tired 24/7.

Tahj had made resting a breeze for her though. He would have Talea comb the girl's hair for school. He also handled everything dealing with their schooling and extracurricular activities. He basically made sure she didn't have to do anything physical pertaining to the twins.

"Yo, you hungry?" Tahj poked his head into the door. He'd given her his master bedroom and he was now staying in the basement which wasn't bad since it was like a bachelor pad down there.

Star jumped. "I could've sworn I was here by myself. What the fuck?" She clutched her chest.

"You ain't been here by yourself for about two hours girl. You were asleep when we first got in. You hungry? I had Marshall whip up a few things. I can bring you something." He said.

"Who the hell is Marshall?" Colley asked.

"His chef." She smirked.

"Damn Tahj then got boujee." Colley cackled.

"That's why you don't want to come over here? You scared it's gon rub off on you?" Tahj teased after overhearing her.

"Boy I ain't scared of shit, and let me find out y'all over there discussing me."

"Bitch please,"Star laughed. "If anything he always hears us talking and he wants to know why you don't just come over here."

"Yea, you're family. You're always welcomed." Tahj co-signed, figuring she needed to hear that.

"I might come over there tomorrow after I drop Suga off by my daddy."

Star's face balled up. "What you dropping my baby off for? I want to see her too."

"Well her grandpa has been asking for her."

"Whatever hoe,"she rolled her eyes. "Tahj, where are my babies?"

"They downstairs doing their homework. You never answered my question about being hungry. I know your ass been sleep all day."

"I'm about to come downstairs Tahj."

"Why? You can lay down. I'll bring you the food."

"You know I didn't get shot in my legs right? I can walk. I want to come kiss my babies anyway."

"I can send them up here by you St-"

"Tahj I'm coming downstairs and that's that. Now go head so I can get up and put on some clothes."

"Girl you acting like that nigga never seen you naked before." Colley commented.

"I'm saying…"Tahj uttered.

"Both of y'all can go straight to hell. Bye Tahj."

"Alright,"he chuckled as he made his way to the door. "Stunt for your cousin."

As he exited, Star stifled a smile. Colley broke out into a giggle fit. "Y'all been over there fucking up a storm huh?"

"Eh, negative." She quickly denied, because it was true. They hadn't fucked once since she began staying with him.

"Wait so you mean to tell me he hasn't hit it once since y'all got back in contact?"

Star's eyes shifted, giving her away. Colley hollered with laughter.

"Relax," Star urged, as she climbed out of Tahj's king bed. "It was only once or twice."

"Once or twice my ass," Colley snickered. "He must be giving your pussy a break since you then fucked around and got shot."

"Oh so you blaming me for that now too?"

"I would never. You just gotta be mindful of the company you keep, cousin. Cause that could've ended badly and I would've lost my mind without you."

"Awwww," she gushed. "But I'm tired of hearing that shit too. It really kills me when Diamond says that shit like he's not into the same stuff. If that's the case I shouldn't hang out with him either."

"I mean, that's true, but Diamond's smart. Of course he's not invincible but he's one of the few street niggas who's actually mindful about the way he does his dirt."

"And Isaiah wasn't?"

"Girl I didn't know shit about Isaiah, but *clearly* homeboy wasn't living right."

"Yea, that much is true." Star sighed heavily. "But girl I'm bouta go downstairs. You better come see me soon."

"I will bitch. I promise."

"Okay. Love you."

"Love you too."

After the phone call ended, Star went to the bathroom to brush her teeth and wash her face. Then she slipped some booty shorts up over the panties she'd been rocking along with an oversized football shirt.

When she walked in the dining area of the kitchen the girls were at the table engrossed in their school work while Tahj watched silently. Star didn't know how he did it because she could never get them to sit still or be focused for long periods of time.

"Y'all working hard,huh?" Star made her presence known as she neared the table.

"Mommy!" They looked up with excitement before jumping up.

"Be careful," Tahj said sternly. "Don't be jumping on her."

"Mommy, you feel better?" Tahiry asked after kissing her cheek and pushing her hair out of her face.

"Yea baby. My hair looks a mess huh?" She smirked.

"No, you look pretty mommy." True said before hugging her neck and kissing her.

"Mommy we skipped three reading levels today!" Tahiry reported.

Star gasped. "Whattt? Y'all gotta read me a book tonight before bed then. I want to see the progress."

"Yayyyy!" True applauded. "Reading time in mommy's room!"

"Aye, that's my room." Tahj smirked. He felt immense pride in his chest. His daughters were perfect thanks to Star and her parenting.

"You can always have it back and I can go hom-"

"Chill out, this is home. You know I'm just messing with you. Let me go get you a plate of food."

Star would often throw out how she could go home if Tahj even breathed the wrong way just so he could ask her to stay. It inflated her ego and she wasn't ashamed to admit that to herself. A few minutes later Tahj emerged from the kitchen with two plates.

"I fixed you a lil bit of everything." He sat the plates in front of her.

"Whew, I could get used to Marshall," Star said as she eyed her lamb chops, seafood potatoes, shrimp pasta, and blackened salmon.

"Yea you getting used to my clothes too. That's my practice jersey from my senior year in highschool you got on."

She looked down as if she just noticed she was wearing it. "Oh it is? I just grabbed something out of the drawer. I ain't know it was for you."

"You didn't know the clothes in my drawer was for me?" He smirked in amusement. "Alright, Star. How you feeling today? You good?"

"I couldn't feel anything thanks to them percs."

A frown appeared on his face. "You need to slow down with those."

"Tahj, I'm fine. I took them because my shoulder hurt. Not because I'm addicted."

"Alright, I'm just saying…"

"Say less. I got this."

"If you say so. Is there anything I can do for you though?"

She eyed him skeptically. "Like what?"

"Girl, get your mind out of the gutter. I was just tryna see if you needed a favor or som-"

"No I don't need no damn favors."

"Alright Star," he shook his head while holding back laughter. Of course she'd think that his favors involved sex.

"Baby Tahj is calling me," Star tittered as she showed Tahj her phone screen. He'd been calling or texting her everyday since the twins reported back to all their siblings that she had gotten hurt.

"You better answer the phone for my boy. You know he don't play," Tahj chuckled. A few times Star missed his call because she was asleep, so he'd call his dad and urge him to check on her.

"My brotherrrr!" True jumped up and skipped over to the phone so she could talk to Baby Tahj too. It didn't matter to her that she'd already seen him a few hours ago.

Star answered the FaceTime with a smile on her face only for it to disappear within a few seconds.

"Why is my son's number in your phone and why are you in communication with him?"

"Man I know that ain't who I think it is." Tahj grumbled as he stood up and took the phone from Star's hand before she could curse Nikka's delusional ass out. Clearly the ass whooping she'd bestowed upon her hadn't been enough. This bitch still had pressure on her chest.

"Nikka what the fuck are you doing?" Tahj questioned as he walked out so the twins wouldn't have to hear this nonsense. Star was right on his tail. She was nosey and the issue was her, so she didn't feel like she was intruding.

"I'm tryna see why the fuck that ugly hoe is in constant contact with my child! Does that seem normal to you?"

"Bitch our kids are siblings! You should be happy your children likes me, dumb ass." Star lashed over Tahj's shoulder.

He spun around. "Star shut up. I got this."

"Shut up?! Nigga I don't need you to handle no bitch on my behalf. Especially this weak ass bitch!" She snatched her phone from him. "Gimme my shit!"

Tahj was stumped into silence. Maybe he'd fucked up by telling her to shut up, but when he took her phone he had every intention to deescalate the situation. Star was on 10, but she had a right to be.

"Girl who you calling wea-"

"You, hoe! Now look, if me talking to your son on his phone is an issue then just block my number. But that's only going to make him feel like he's doing something wrong when he's not. I'm also going to *always* see him in real life and I'll continue to treat him *and* your daughter like my own because that's just how my heart is set up. Stay mad, bitch, but you ain't stopping shit over here!"

"Tahj it's bad enough you got that bitch and her kids practically living with you, but you gon allow her to disrespect your other kids now?!" Nikka screamed.

Tahj's silence came to an end. "What? She didn't disrespect shit."

"She's disrespecting *me,* and I'm the mother of your kids so by default she's disrespecting them."

"If that's the case then you're disrespecting the twins. Nikka, give it a rest bruh. You just picking at this point." Tahj breathed in exhaustion.

"Picking?! Nigga I'll show you picking!" She ended the call.

Tahj just shook his head as he suddenly felt stressed. To say he loved Nikka's dirty drawers at one point he couldn't stand her disgusting ass now.

"You need to get control of that bitch before I fuck her and you up." Star pointed her finger in his face.

He calmly removed it. "Chill out, bruh. You know that shit wasn't my fault."

"The hell it ain't! She's comfortable doing that type of shit for a reason. You gave that bitch all that audacity and now it's time for you to take it away. Humble her, or me and you gon have a problem. Because I didn't make babies with the bitch. Me and my daughters shouldn't have to constantly be disrespected by her. Especially since we're over here minding our damn business. And if you ever tell me to shut up in another bitches presence again I'm drawing blood. On my mama!" With that Star stormed off, leaving Tahj with an even bigger headache.

Star's words kept replaying in Tahj's head over and over again, and each time they got louder. He wasn't going to get any sleep thanks to her ass, so he decided to go upstairs and talk to her. He wasn't sure what he could say, but he'd figure it out once he was in her face. What he couldn't do was let this fester all night.

The first thing he noticed when he stepped into his bedroom was the twins sprawled out on the bed with books beside them. Reading time had clearly been successful. Since he could hear the shower running he knew Star was in the bathroom. He was about to scoop the twins up and bring them to their room that was now decorated to their liking.

"No Tahj!" Star said in a hushed tone from the bathroom door. "Leave them."

"Why? They don't need to be sleeping with you."

"I know, but I want them too. One night won't hurt." Her eyes squinted as he swaggered towards the bathroom door. She hated how fine he looked in his basketball shorts and white beater. "What do you want?"

"To talk to you." He pushed his way into the bathroom where she was ass naked.

"Tahj!" She squealed before grabbing a large towel to cover herself.

"Girl cut it out. You doing the most over some shit I then seen on multiple occasions."

"What do you want?!"

"I wanted to apologize to you for the way Nikka came at you."

She raised an eyebrow as if she was gauging his sincerity. "Oh really?"

"Yea, man. Why you gotta do all that?"

"I don't know, maybe because you was just saying how her being a dumb ass had nothing to do with you."

"Yeah well you changed my mind, Star. I guess the way I've carried her since high school makes her think certain shit is okay. It might take her a minute to get adjusted, but I just want you to know that I will never tolerate her disrespecting you or my babies."

She stifled a smile. "The twins aint no damn babies."

"They are my babies. Shit the least your ass can do is let me make up for lost time."

Guilt immediately consumed her.

"Okay. You got that."

"I know I do."

"But it's something else you forgot to apologize for."

"Sorry for telling you to shut up. Now let's hug it out." He moved towards her with his arms out.

"Boy move!" She backed up.

"We can't hug?"

"While I'm naked? Hell no! This whole lil conversation could have waited until I got out of the bathroom, yea."

"I ain't know if you was gon start fussing or what, and since my kids are sleeping I figured coming in the bathroom would be best."

"I hear you, but Tahj?"

"Wassup?"

"Why you keep walking towards me?" She pushed his rock hard chest that was almost touching her.

"You backing away from me like you scared." He laughed.

"No I'm just not finna play with you."

"But I want to play with you."

Her face twisted in confusion. "Wha- AH!" She yelped when he lifted her up on the bathroom counter as if she weighed nothing.

"You so dramatic," he said huskily as his hand found it's way between her legs.

"Tahj, moveeee," she whined weakly as his finger came in contact with her clit.

He smirked when he applied pressure to her clit and her legs spread further. "You want me to move but your legs keep getting wider and this pussy soaking wet…it's not adding up, baby."

"I can't stand youuuu…ouuuu," her back arched. One minute he was playing in her pussy with his fingers and the next he was on his knees with his face between her thighs. She should've seen this coming from a mile away. She'd naively assumed since Tahj had made no moves to touch her since they returned from LA that sex between them was a wrap.

"Oh my God, Tahj," Star whimpered as she closed her eyes shut. That made him pull away.

She looked down at him in panic mode.

"What you doing?"

"What you doing? Keep them eyes on me."

"Okayyy," she whined before forcefully pushing his head back to her wet center.

"Pussy so sweet," he voiced before flickering his tongue across her slit.

"Yessss, right thereeee," she moaned when he started sucking on her pearl. She held his head and whined her hips to chase her orgasm that was vastly approaching. To her dismay, he said fuck her chase and stood up with his hard dick in his hand.

"Tahj stop playing," she groused.

"I'm definitely not playing with yo' ass."

He forced her up and bent her over on the sink before ramming his dick into her from behind. From there he propped one of his legs up on the toilet and commenced to long stroking her.

"I'm cumming! I'm cumming!" Star shouted.

"Fuck, I feel it." He gritted as he looked down at her secretions coating his dick. "I see it too. I love this fucking pussy." He slapped her ass roughly. "You like how this dick feel in you?"

"I love itttt!" She whimpered. "Tahjjjj!"

"I know, baby, I know." He got about four more pumps in before he blasted off deep inside of her. He'd tried, but that pussy was too good to stay out of.

March 8, 2020

"That's what I'm talking bout," Star raved as she looked at her book sales for the past week. "I'ma fuck around and buy me another house. Might even get myself a new car."

Her phone started ringing across the coffee table in the den, making her jump. She immediately started laughing afterwards because any little sound in Tahj's house had been making her jump all weekend. He had flown to Miami for a last minute business meeting with a client on Friday and the girls were spending the weekend with their Auntie Talea. Star had been by herself and she was ready for it to come to an end because she was extra paranoid.

Despite not recognizing the number that was calling, she answered her phone anyway.

"Hello?"

"Yo, where you at?"

She was quiet for a few seconds before responding. "Who's this?"

"Man you know who this is. I need to see you."

"And what reason do you need to see me, Isaiah?"

"Because you have something that belongs to me and I'd like it back."

"Nooo, I think you're mistaken."

"Say, I'm not finna play with yo' duck ass! I should pull up to your crib right now and fuck you up just for the way you got your brother coming at me, but im tryna spare you in all this."

"Spare me?!" She exploded with laughter while silently rejoicing in the fact that she wasn't home. Perhaps Tahj had hit the nail on the head with his reasoning for her not returning to her house. "You should've spared me before you put a gun in my purse, bitch! You should've spared me by keeping your distance when you knew you had beef in the streets! Me or my brother don't want shit to do with your stupid ass! Ain't nobody worrying about you!"

She knew that Diamond was probably somewhere trying to get at him but she wasn't about to say that over the phone.

"Bitch and I ain't worried about you! I just want my gun back!"

"Ion got it."

"Star. If you know what's best for you, you'd return my property effectively immediately."

"If you know what's best for you, you'd get the fuck off my line. Next time if you want something don't put it in somebody else's bag." She ended the call and then blocked the number he'd called from. As tough as she just played it on the phone, she was a little shaken up because this nigga was under the impression that she had his gun and refused to return it. That wasn't good, so she called her brother.

"Wassup, sis?" He answered her call right away. "You good?"

"No. Isaiah just called me, threatening me about that dumb ass gun."

"Threatening you?! Man, I know you lying!"

Diamond couldn't believe this nigga had the audacity to call his sister when he didn't even have the balls to hit the streets and face him like a man. C5 had been going out of his way to lay low. Maybe he realized that it wasn't wise for a gun that he'd made hot to not be in his possession and that's why he'd called Star to get it back. Either way, Diamond wasn't feeling it.

"Where you at?! You haven't left Tahj's house have you?"

"No, Diamond."

"Then you good. And you ain't gon have to worry about this nigga calling you either. But just in case, do me a favor and change your number."

"Ughhh," she groaned, hating how this was now inconveniencing her.

"I know. It's annoying. But just do that for me. Okay?"

"Whatever Diamond."

"Alright, love you. I'll call and check on you later."

"Okay. Love you too."

When she got off the phone with Diamond, Tahj's house phone started ringing. An eerie feeling crept up on Star, but it disappeared when she saw the caller ID. She was really spooking herself out for nothing. Although she had clarity on who was calling, she still didn't feel comfortable answering, so she let the phone ring. When they called right back she figured it had to be an emergency so she stopped being scared and picked up the phone.

"Hello?"

"Well about time! Did you not see me calling?!"

"Ummm, Tahj isn't home. Would you like to leave him a message?"

"You the maid or something?"

Star bit back a curse word that was on the tip of her tongue. This was this man's mother. She refused to go there with her.

"No. My name is Star."

"Ohhh, you his new baby mama. The one that hid kids from him for damn near seven years. He left you at his house by yourself? Hmmm, he better than me."

Star slid her tongue across her teeth. Tahj's mother or not, this lady was not about to disrespect her. Besides, it was obvious she and Tahj weren't close if he wasn't keeping her updated with his life. Hell, he hadn't even taken the twins to meet either of his parents yet. That said a lot.

"You don't talk to your own son?"

"Come again?"

"I'm just saying. Maybe if you guys communicated you'd know that I'm currently staying with him. It's a long story that I don't care to get into, but did you want something? Because I was working."

"You were working, huh? Well hopefully you're saving up to get yourself your own place because I can't see my son helping you out while you're down on hard times for long. He's generous but if your name's not Janikka you won't get much out of him."

Star laughed, even though this old bitch was crawling under her skin.

"Mrs.Bellamy, my name is Star and your son told me I can stay here even though I own my own home and can afford to put myself and *our* kids in another place."

"Then why the hell are you at his house answering his phone like you pay bills?!"

"Because I can. That's why. I'm guessing you don't want shit, so goodbye. Go call Janikka." Star hung up in her face, while loathing that she had to go there. She tried being nice but she wasn't about to let a bitch punk her.

She went right back to looking at her book sales just to be interrupted about five minutes later. Tahj was

FaceTiming her. She braced herself for an argument because she was certain he was about to go in for the way she'd just handled his mother. That's why she was shocked when the call connected and he was smiling.

"Man, what you told my mama?"

"I ain't tell her rude ass nothing." She rolled her eyes.

He chuckled. "She said you cursed her out."

"Honestly I don't remember what I said, but she was talking a lot of shit."

"Do you remember what she said?"

"She had an attitude from jump because I guess I didn't answer the phone quickly enough for her and then she got to saying that if she was you I wouldn't be staying in her house. Blah, blah, blah. Oh, and she said I better save my money for my own place because apparently Janikka is the only baby mama you would really help out. So yea, I told her ass bye and to go call Janikka."

Tahj looked mad for a second before bursting into hysterics. "Mannnn, I don't know if I should be mad or amused, but don't pay my mama no mind. I deal with her on my own terms for a reason. And you should know that shit she said about Janikka wasn't true."

"How would I know that?"

He tilted his head and squinted his eyes. "Who's in my house right now?"

"You say that as if she didn't live with you for years."

"So did Lexi."

"My point is proven." She laughed.

"And what's your point, Star?"

"That you having me here ain't nothing special. Not that I expected it to be, so we're cool."

"Oh we cool?" He smirked.

"Mhmmm." She held back a smile.

"Keep that same energy when I get back."

"When are you coming back exactly?"

He grinned. "Let me find out you miss a nigga."

"Boy, please."

He stared at her intently.

"Ok I wouldn't say I miss you. I'm just tired of being here by myself. I'm bouta tell your sister to bring my baby's back. It's getting late anyway and they have school tomorrow."

"I was gon tell her to just bring them."

"Excuse you?"

He laughed. "It ain't like you can drive and bring them."

"Why I can't?" She questioned with an attitude.

"Star, don't make me fuck you up. The doctor hasn't cleared you to drive yet."

"I feel fine though."

"You ain't gon feel fine if you get behind that wheel without clearance from a doctor because I'ma put my foot up your ass."

"Tahj go to hell." She tittered.

"You really scared over there?"

"Yes. I am. Every little noise got me jumping."

He laughed. "I'll be back tomorrow morning."

"Good. I have something to tell you when you get back."

"You pregnant?"

Her eyes ballooned. "Hell no! If I was, would you be that nonchalant?"

"Hell yea. I'm used to having kids. One more, preferably a boy, wouldn't hurt."

"Well you won't be having that boy with me, playboy."

"That's cold," he chuckled. "It's possible though. I been nutting in you all week."

Star inwardly cringed because she had been reckless with Tahj. Plan B's had been the only thing saving her. She vowed for her next doctor's visit that she was going on birth control. Sex with Tahj was the best but they did not need to complicate it with a new baby. It was bad enough that her feelings were already involved with how things were. Getting pregnant would amplify those feelings.

"I know you not tryna trap me."

"Trap you? How's that when I just straight up told you I want another son."

"Boy I'm finna hang up in your face."

"We live together, yea."

"Not for long. When are we going to look for my new house?"

"Whenever you fully heal."

"I smell bullshit. I'ma just go back to my house."

"Chill out, man. We can go look at houses next week since you so hard up."

"Ain't nobody hard up. I'm just holding you to your words. That's all."

"Hey, Papi…"

Star's stomach bubbled as she watched Tahj make eye contact with the lust filled voice that had just acknowledged him. She wanted to smack that smile right off his stupid ass face. Since she couldn't reach out and touch him, she ended the call.

"Dumb ass nigga."

Tahj called right back when he noticed she hung up, but she declined the call. He didn't let that deter him as he called again. She eventually answered.

"What?!" She snapped.

"What's wrong with you?"

"You seemed preoccupied."

He smiled at her apparent jealousy.

"You in your feelings over a random woman speaking to me?"

"So you mean to tell me a random bitch called you *papi*?"

"It be like that all the time with the niggas I represent, Star." He chuckled. "Groupies be saying whatever for attention."

"And you just be ignoring them?"

"For the most part,"he scratched his head.

Star smacked her teeth, seeing right through him. "Yea right, nigga. You probably be knocking all them hoes down."

"Nah that's just your imagination running wild." He fronted. In reality every time he traveled he fucked on women that threw themselves at him. Of course he had his picks and chooses, and he always had a field day with them. On this trip he'd fucked a hoe he'd been hitting consistently in Miami since last year. But Star didn't need to hear all that even if he was single and well within his rights to do what he wanted. If he was being honest with himself, doing what he wanted hadn't even felt as exhilarating as it usually did. All he could think about was getting home to his kids and Star. Something was happening to him and it was weird.

Chapter 13

March 9, 2020

"I'll meet y'all out in LA on Wednesday. I promise." Tahj said to Tariq over the phone as he stepped into his house for the first time in days. He was always away from his home but this was the first time he actually missed it.

"Nigga why not today?"

"What am I coming today for? Y'all ain't doing shit but working in the studio."

"Man this nigga Tavior over here in love and shit. He takes Jamaya everywhere with us now."

"Oh so you want me there to kick it and shoot the shit with you because your partner in crime switched up on you?" He quizzed.

"Something like that."

"Well I can't help you, lil bro. I have real responsibilities here at home, so unless there's business I need to tend to then I ain't coming."

"Mannn, don't tell me you switching up on me now too."

"What?" Tahj chuckled as he walked in his kitchen and saw multiple pots on the stove. He wasted no time checking them. There were red beans that were still cooking on a low fire, corn bread, and Turkey necks. He knew his chef hadn't done this because he'd been off since the weekend. This had to be all Star, and he couldn't wait to thank her. This was the way to come home on a Monday.

"Nigga you been having responsibilities since Baby Tahj was born but you always made time to play. I guess Star got the juice."

"Nigga," Tahj laughed. "Get the fuck. I haven't seen my kids in days. That's my number one priority right now."

"Blame the kids. That's convenient."

"Bye Tarik." He ended the call.

He was being partially honest. He couldn't wait to jump back into his daily routine with his children, but he was equally excited to be back under the same roof as Star. He jogged up the stairs to see what she was up to because the house was so quiet that it sounded like no one was home. It was almost 1pm which meant Star would usually be up and working. When he stepped into his room he saw why it was quiet. She was knocked out with her laptop next to her on the bed.

He walked over to the bed, climbed in, and snuggled up behind her. Star shifted in her sleep when she felt sweet kisses all over neck and face. Without even opening her eyes she knew Tahj was home. His presence was like no other and she could smell his Tom Ford cologne.

"I know you see me sleeping." She muttered.

"No shit. You forgot you was cooking?"

"No. That's why I put the fire on low. My arm started hurting right after I finished the corn bread, so I took a pain pill."

"See, you need to sit down somewhere and chill."

"And just starve in the process?"

"Kill the dramatics, Star. I had Marshall prep five days worth of food for you."

"I wanted something fresh today and I'm sure the kids will too when you pick them up from school."

"Yea Baby Tahj love him some red beans."

"And you do too." Star giggled.

"I do, and I appreciate it. But you gotta take it easy."

"I've been taking it too easy. I'm boreddd,"she whined.

"Let's get out and do something then."

"Like what?"

"Shit I don't know. Anything, since you so damn bored."

She let out a deep breath. "I don't know about that right now."

"You don't know about what?"

"Going places."

He looked at her strangely. "Star, you confusing me. One minute you bored, the next minute you don't want to do nothing. Which is it?"

"I would *like* to do something, but Diamond asked me to chill."

"Why?"

"Remember how I said I had to tell you something yesterday?"

He raised up. "What happened?"

"Lay back down, baby." She touched his chest.

Knowing he was being bullshitted he brushed her off. "Oh now I'm your baby? Star what the fuck happened? Tell me now!"

"Okay first of all, calm down. You don't have to talk to me like that."

"Don't make it seem like I'm directing my anger towards you. Tell me what happened."

"Long story short Isaiah called me yesterday demanding that I return his gun or else he was gonna pull up to my house. I cursed him out and then blocked the number he called me from."

"What?! This nigga got life fucked up!" Tahj exploded. "And Diamond said he was gon handle it?! He taking too long if the nigga calling your phone making threats!"

"Not too much on my brother. He said Isaiah's been hiding."

"That bitch would wanna hide! And I bet not hear you say shit else about going back to that house! Real shit, Starlah!"

"Starlah?" She tittered at him saying her full name that nobody ever used.

"This a laughing matter to you?!"

"No," she bit her lip. "Damn."

His anger was really turning her on but she'd never say that out loud because it would sound sick.

"Call that number back and tell that nigga pull up!"

Her head jerked back. "What?!"

"Tell him pull up here so I can bust a cap in his ass legally. Unlike him, my guns are registered."

"Okay, you're talking crazy Tahj."

"And he's not?!"

"But you're not him! You're smart! You wouldn't invite a deranged nigga to your house where your kids rest their heads."

"Yes I would. I'ma kill that nigga. Go to your block list and give me his number."

"No." She shook her head.

"Star, I'm not playing with you."

"And I'm not playing with you! Can I have a kiss?"

He started to lean in until he realized he was being played. Star never initiated any type of affection with him. It was always him making a move. But now she wanted to ask for kisses and shit.

"Man get the fuck, you full of shit."

"So you not gon kiss me?" She sat up and leaned in towards him.

"Move, Star." He said as she puckered up her lips and grabbed his jaw. She pecked his lips sensually.

"It's gonna be okay, baby daddy."

"I know it's going to be okay," he nodded before laughing. The wheels were spinning in his head but he realized it was in his best interest to not tell Star anything.

"Somethings vibrating," Star said in the midst of another kiss.

Tahj sighed in annoyance. "That's my phone."

"Answer it."

"We in the middle of something."

"And we can get back to it after you answer your phone."

He threw his head back in agony before retrieving his phone from his Gucci joggers. Worry washed over his handsome face when he saw who was calling.

"What's going on?" Star questioned.

"The girls' school is calling me." He responded while accepting the call and putting it on speaker. "Yea?"

"Mr. Bellamy? Good evening, we're calling about all four of your daughters. We figured it would be easier to just reach out to one parent instead of calling all the girls mothers indiv-"

"It's fine. What's going on?" He questioned hastily.

"Well there's no easy way to say this but the girls were just involved in a physical altercation at recess."

"Nooo, not my girls."

"I'm afraid so, Mr. Bellamy. All four of them jumped on one girl."

Star couldn't believe what she was hearing. The twins were only in first grade so they didn't get into this type of trouble ever.

"We're going to have to suspend them for two days. Typically we give week suspensions for fighting but multiple bystanders said that the young lady they had the altercation with had been picking on Tahiry since last week. This young lady also has a reputation for being a bully, so I think the punishment fits the crime here."

"Oh hell no," Star voiced. She wanted to go upside the little girl's head who'd been messing with her sweet baby.

"What was that Mr. Bellamy?" The dean asked.

"Nothing. I'm about to come pick them up now, Dean. Thanks."

Star had already gotten up and was slipping on jogging pants.

"What you doing?"

"Coming for the ride. What it look like?"

"It looks like you ready to fight."

"Maybe I am."

Tahj exploded into laughter. "Man, the lil girl already got jumped. Stand down, mama bear."

———————————

"So who wants to tell me what happened?" Tahj questioned after they'd been silently riding for a few minutes.

The girls were unusually quiet and it was probably because they thought they were in trouble for fighting.

"Emily was being mean to Tahiry!" Jari blurted out.

"Emily? Ain't that's your best friend?" Tahj asked. He could've sworn she and Tazzy had been over to that little girls house on numerous occasions.

"She's not my friend no more. Are you listening daddy? She was being mean to Tahiry!" Jari repeated passionately.

"Explain everything that happened."

"Last week she kept saying she didn't want to play with me because I think I'm better than everybody, but I don't think that!" Tahiry expressed with tears forming in her eyes. Tahj and Star wanted to jump to the back seat and hold her, but her sisters were quick to comfort her.

"Baby don't cry," Tahj coaxed. "It sounds like Emily has some insecurities of her own."

"What's that mean? Securities?" True attempted to say.

"Insecurities," Star clarified. "It means someone isn't happy with themselves so they attempt to bring others down."

"Well Emily must be really insecure. I told her last week if she doesn't want to play with my sister then we can't be friends anymore. Because daddy you told me it's me and my siblings against the world." Jari spoke confidently.

"I sure did, baby." Tahj smirked proudly. "What happened today that led to a fight?"

"Emily pushed Tahiry off the jungle gym." Tazzy answered.

"And I pushed her back." True said while rubbing her twins back.

"Then I kicked her in the back." Tazzy volunteered.

"And I just started punching her." Jari shrugged.

As much as Tahj and Star wanted to laugh they controlled themselves because they didn't need them thinking they were praising this type of thing.

"Alright, well look, y'all did nothing wrong. But next time you tell a teacher or us what's going on before it gets to a physical place. Okay?" Tahj looked back at them.

"Yes daddy,"they all replied together.

"I gotta call they mamas,"Tahj said to no one in particular. He wasn't stressing the conversations because he was sure they'd be on the same page as him. As if his mind was read, he received an incoming call from Lexi.

"Might as well get one call out the way," Star said. Lexi's call was coming through the Bluetooth in the car, so her name popped up on the radio. Tahj answered her call.

"Tahj what the fuck is going on?! Emily's mom called me and said that she got jumped because the twins were being mean to her!"

Star's neck snaked in disbelief. She could already see a narrative was about to be painted to make her girls the problem.

"That ain't want my daughters just told me. They all just sat up here and gave me the same story, so I don't give a fuck what that white bitch told you to paint her daughter as innocent. Even the Dean said she's a bully."

"Tahj. Language." Star chided as her eyes shifted to the back seat.

Tahj brushed her off because Lexi kept talking.

"Really? Emily's a bully? We've been knowing this little girl since the beginning of the school year and she's been nothing but nice to the girls. Now that those other two girls are in the picture my daughter is fighting and getting suspended from school. Use your brain, Tahj!"

Star opened her mouth to go in, but Tahj beat her to it. He was shouting so loud that she had chills all over her body.

"NO USE YOUR FUCKING BRAIN! I'm telling you what *our* daughter told the Dean and me, and Tahjaria ain't never been a liar! She said Emily was picking with her sister! I could've sworn we both taught her to stand up for siblings! I don't know what type of shit you on right now! It sounds like you more concerned about Emily and demonizing the twins than your own daughter's word."

"Excuse you?! I'm so concerned about my daughter that I don't want her getting suspended from school for fighting!"

"And neither do I, but I would've been more mad had she not done anything. I ain't raising no pushovers!"

"And I'm not raising no hood rats!"

"What are you trying to say, sweetie?" Star questioned with loads of animosity. She wanted to say so much more but she was trying to be mindful of the girls.

"What I just said has nothing to do with you hun, but if the shoe fits, wear it!"

"Baby I'm not Cinderella. I've been listening to this entire conversation which means I'm aware that you're trying to pin this whole ordeal on me and mine. I'm letting you know right now that this ain't what you want. The common denominator here is obviously an outsider. Go direct your energy to that little girl and her mama."

"Amen." Tahj co-signed.

"Tahj really?! I can't believe you're defending this."

"I can't believe you on my line going against our daughter's side of the story. I thought you were better than that. But I guess you bitter just like your sister wife. You just better at hiding at."

He knew he shouldn't have gone there especially in the presence of his daughters, but he was mad and his mouth was now running with no filter.

"WHA-"

Tahj ended the call and then blocked Lexi's number. He didn't want to talk about it anymore and she was sure to call him back.

"One down, another one to go." Star glared at him. At times like this she was reminded why it was best to not let things get out of hand with him. She couldn't see herself dealing with this dynamic forever. Co-Parenting was truly the only way.

March 21, 2020

"Daddy, Frenchy pooped on our bathroom floor!" True called herself snitching on the dog.

"Go get a trash bag and pick it up."

Her little face scrunched up in disgust. "Pick it up?"

"Yup. That's your dog isn't it?" Tahj questioned with a grin. "It's your responsibility, baby girl. Now get to it."

"But daddy it's Twinkie's dog tooooo…" she whined and stomped her feet.

"Didn't you discover the poo?"

"Yea bu-"

"Then it's your job to clean it up, True. I'm not gonna repeat myself."

"Ughhh!" True stomped off with a long face.

Star was entering the den at the same time True was exiting. She immediately noticed something was wrong with her and rubbed her head. Whatever it was she was certain it wasn't a big deal. True could be bratty at times.

"What's her problem?" Star asked Tahj as she flopped down on the couch far away from him.

He wasted no time calling her out.

"Man, why you all the way over there?"

She pretended to be confused. "I need a reason for sitting in this exact spot?"

"Alright Star, play dumb." He chuckled dryly. He was fed up with her hot and cold ass. Two weeks ago it was all love and they were sexing on a regular basis. Now she was back to giving him her ass to kiss. She hadn't been vocal about whatever her issue was, but her actions said everything. All of a sudden her body was hurting and she didn't want to have sex anymore. She was full of shit and he knew it, but he didn't press the issue. For starters, he'd never been denied sex in his life. He didn't know how to approach the situation without feeling like a lame. He just went along with her lie and acted like he believed her, but that shit was starting to make him feel lame too. He was coming closer and closer to swallowing his pride so he could see what the fuck was really going on. He was positive they'd been making progress.

"Boy what are yo- nevermind," she giggled. "What was my baby mad about?"

"I told her to pick up Frenchy's shit."

Star laughed. "That's exactly why I ain't want their asses with a dog. Poor babies probably thought it would be all fun and games."

"This is good then. The dog is teaching them responsibility and other life lessons."

"That's a fact." She readily agreed.

"I'm surprised you left the room."

"And why is that?"

"Because that's where you've been staying since last week. Everytime I'm home you be glued to that bitch."

"No, I told you my arm has been hurting badly."

"We need to get you back to the doctor, man."

"Not necessary. I have a scheduled check up next week and I'm feeling a lot better today. Colley's about to come over. I hope that's okay."

"You don't have to ask me if family can come over, Star. This is your home too." He replied, totally bypassing the bogus arm story. That was her intent.

Star cackled. "That's sweet, baby daddy, but this is *not* my home. My name is not on the deed. You can put me out anytime you feel like it."

"Why the fuck would I do some bitch shit like that?" He asked, feeling genuinely offended.

"The same reason why you had me thinking we were in love when I was 18, when you really had a whole family you neglected to tell me about. Baby I don't know or try to understand what goes on in that brain of yours." She laughed.

His heart dropped. She was still stuck on this? In his mind if he was willing to bypass her wrong doings then the least she could do was not throw old, ancient shit in his face.

"Man, you still on that bullshit?"

"Do you want me to forget?"

"Forget? Maybe not. But bringing that shit up to crucify me is wild coming from a bitch who hid my kids from me."

"A bitch?" She stood up like she was about to square up.

"Say you don't want it with me right now. You got a bum arm. I'll tear yo ass up."

"I don't give a fuck! I'll beat your ass with one arm! Don't call me out my name you dirty dick bastard!"

Tahj licked his lips after laughing. Okay, maybe that insult got to him a little. It was just odd because he'd been called a whore by women too many times to count and it *never* got under his skin.

"Then your pussy dirty, too. You let me hit that shit with no condom more times than I can count."

"Let's talk about now though. You ain't been hitting shit and you won't be. *Bitch.*" She spewed evilly. Yea, he had gotten to her. She had been being wildly stupid to let this man inside of her condomless after everything. She may as well have tattoo'd "weak bitch" across her forehead.

"That's fine. Been there. Had that. It was getting boring anyway." He fronted his ass off. It was convincing enough for Star though because he'd hurt her feelings.

"And I can say the same about your weak ass dick."

"Man you wish my shit was weak."

"Ion gotta wish. It's a reality."

"You talking all that shit and probably standing over there pregnant. Take your goofy ass on somewhere."

"Bitch you wish I was pregnant. Dumb ass."

Ding-Dong!

"Go get your company and leave me alone, Star. Real shit."

"Gladly. Ugly ass nigga gon call me goofy. Must got me confused with his funny looking ass mammy. Apple clearly don't feel too far from the tree." She ran off at the mouth as she twisted out of the room. Meanwhile Tahj paid no attention to how she'd just insulted the fuck out of of his mother. All he could do was watch that fat ass in her grey tights. He wanted to fuck her so bad.

"Bout time bi-" Star's words trailed off when she opened the door. She was expecting to see Colley but someone else was standing there. It was Tahj's sister that she'd had the least interaction with because the first one went terribly. She had her beautiful baby girl on her hip with Baby Tahj and Tazzy standing next to her.

Tamia smirked. "Still wanna whoop my ass?"

"Maybe." Star batted her eyelashes.

Tamia nodded and put her baby down. "Y'all go on inside." She said to the kids. They ran in the house right away.

Star was about to get ready, but Tamia caught her off guard by breaking out into laughter. Maybe Tahj's whole family was touched. Or maybe it was just the kids Tarell's wife had given birth to.

"Girl I come in peace," she held up a bottle of wine. "Consider this an apology."

"I don't know…I can't accept that unless you come in and drink a glass with me."

"Hey, I've never been one to turn down a drink." She accepted the offer while stepping inside.

Tahj was surprised to see his baby sister and Star enter the den laughing together like old friends. The last time he checked they had some unresolved issues.

"Girl I knew you looked familiar." Tamia giggled. "So how's that hoe little Freddy doing?"

"Freddy?" Star laughed so hard her stomach hurt. "Now that's petty. But I don't know how Frandesha is doing, we're not friends any more. I don't mess with any of my high school friends anymore actually."

"Hmmp, well ya better off without them weak ass hoes." Tamia replied carelessly.

From day one Star had recognized Tamia's face because her old friend had some serious beef with her behind the nigga that Tamia was currently married to. At the time Star didn't know that Tamia was Tahj's sister. Although now that she was looking at her up close she was wondering how she'd missed it. They looked a lot alike. Hell even her daughters resembled Tamia.

But just like Star was lowkey now, she was lowkey back then too. She wasn't wrapped into Frandesha's drama which meant she wasn't tuned in 24/7 on social media. She didn't stalk Tamia like Frandesha and her other ex-friend, Dontranique. She would simply listen to her friend vent and then try to offer sound advice. Because the advice didn't involve ass kissing and telling Fran she was 100% right, Star was written off as a hater and they would clash.

That wasn't the cause of the end of the friendship though. Star just outgrew them and fell back. Of course they took it personally but they couldn't whoop her ass for not wanting to be their friend anymore. Dropping them like a bad habit had been easy because Star lived in a different city at the time. She had no idea what Frandesha or Dontranique was up to these days and she could care less. Check for them for what?

"Mia why you talking to her? She was just talking about our mama." Tahj ratted, propelling Star's mouth to drop. She thought she was being thrown under the bus, but he knew what it really was. The last person Tamia would want smoke behind was their mother.

"I hope she said something horrible about the old skeezer. C'mon Star, let's go pop this bottle open." Tamia twisted off.

"Messy ass nigga." Star flipped him off as she walked past him.

"Girl, take yo ass on somewhere." He chuckled.

"Gladly."

About two hours later Tamia and Star were tipsy and on their second glass of wine while snacking on Rotel dip that Star had whipped up quickly. It was funny how Tamia had proclaimed that she wanted nothing to do with her but she was genuinely enjoying her energy. She could admit that Lexi and Nikka were nice and cool girls in the beginning but she never connected with them like she was currently with Star.

"I still can't believe you went to high school with Noel, Tati, and Antwan. That's so crazy."

"Not really, girl. New Orleans is small. I was in the same grade as Noel and of course he used to go with my friend at the time, so I was cool with him on some hi and bye shit. I didn't really know Tatiana at all, but her quiet self used to have the hoes mad because she had Ant's nose wide open." Star reminisced.

In high school she was to herself. She had a few friends of course, but her priorities were different. She always knew the time at her aunt's house would be limited.

"That's my sis." Tamia smiled proudly. "But shit, I didn't meet Tati until we both were 15."

"Wait, seriously? How can that be?"

"Girl my daddy is a rolling stone. That's how. I didn't even know of Tati's existence until she came to live with Talea. That's a whole 'nother story chile, but her living situation was a fool with her grandma. She's still dealing with that shit."

Star empathized right away.

"If nobody understands I do. I lost both of my parents to the system at a young age and I had to live with my mom's sister. That lady there…whew!" Star shook her head as memories came back to her.

"It was that bad, huh?"

"Worse than bad. She was verbally, emotionally, and physically abusive. Then her oldest son was a pervert. I got the fuck before he could really violate me if you know what I mean."

"I definitely know what you're getting at. That's so sad, bruh. You would think as a woman she would want to protect you no matter what. My own mama is a piece of work and yea, that hoe is verbally abusive for sure, but I always felt safe in my own home for the most part. She also never beat me. It's still fuck her though."

Star laughed. "Can I be real for a minute?"

"Please do."

"Alright whenever I hear people complaining about their mothers I be wanting to roll my eyes because I wish mine was still here."

Tamia gasped. "Your mom passed away?"

She nodded. "A few years ago. She died in prison."

"Damn. I'm so sorry, Star!"

"You good. I'm probably just over sharing right now."

"Sis, if you're oversharing then so am I. We're both getting all up in each other's business so it's cool."

"Well when you put it like that…" Star giggled.

"But back to the topic of my mom. I love her unconditionally. I always will. Sometimes I think about her dying while our relationship is in the place it is. That's why I gave her chance after chance in the past. I would always tell myself that's my mother and if something happened to her I'd be devastated. Yea, I used to be on that life's too short shit. But that's the thing, life *is* too short to give my good energy to someone who's not willing to change or see their faults. The same goes for my no good ass paw, but I tolerate him *sometimes* over a phone call or something. My mom though; it's curtains. Once she spoke on Noeva it was over for her."

"Damn. I can definitely understand because I don't play about the twins."

"That makes two of us." Tamia spoke with conviction.

"Star."

Star looked towards the entrance of the kitchen when she heard Tahj's deep voice calling out to her. He pointed to Colley who was behind him, and she was Suga-less. Star wasted no time voicing her disappointment.

"Bitch I was starting to think you was gon fake me out again. Where's my baby? I thought you was bringing her."

"Nope. Her grandpa wanted her."

"Colley, you full of shit. If you wanted to get rid of Suga then just say that."

"Girl *anyways*," she emphasized to get the topic of discussion off her daughter. She turned to Tamia. "Hey, how you doing? I'm Colley. Star's sister-cousin."

"She's the daughter of that auntie I was just telling you about." Star added.

Colley's head snapped back. "Girl, don't be telling people I'm related to that hoe!"

Tahj and Tamia bursted into laughter.

"Colley, that's your mama though." Tahj reasoned through laughter.

"Bull shit. I emancipated myself from her when I was like 16. Ion have no mama."

"Shit you speaking my language," Tamia tittered. "I'm Tam-"

"Tamia." Colley finished for her. "I know who you are, girl. I be seeing you on social media all the time."

That wasn't shocking to anyone considering Tamia had over a million followers. She'd always been well known locally but her popularity skyrocketed when the world found out she and Noel were expecting a child. All of a sudden everyone wanted to keep up with her and she capitalized off it. She had multiple businesses, she did paid promo, and she would even do YouTube videos from time to time. Most people knew her face because of that.

"I ain't gon stunt…you look familiar too."Tamia said while openly staring at her as if it would come to her any second.

"I danced at V-Live for a few nights back in 2015."

"Oh yeaaa, what was your stage name?"

Although Tamia came from a financially stable family and could've gone off to college for any career of her choice like her big brother, she and Tati went through a rebellious stage. Their reasons were different but they both started dancing for a living fresh out of high school and they made a lot of money doing it. So much money to where Tamia found it hard to walk away. Once she got pregnant she had no choice.

"I'm too embarrassed to say." Colley laughed as she sat down. "Ouuu, rotel."

"Excuse you!" Star exclaimed as she slapped Colley's hand that was inching towards her plate.

"Damn hoe, I can't have some?"

"Get your own. It's a big pot on the stove." Star replied.

"I can fix it for you, Colley." Tahj offered.

"She can fix it herself!"

Tamia and Colley looked at each other before breaking out into laughter.

"Girl I don't need your baby daddy making my food. I got it." Colley sassed before standing up and making her way over to the sink to wash her hands.

"So I can't fix your cousin a plate?" Tahj asked Star while leaning against the counter top.

"Let's get your brothers over here so I can cater to them."

Tahj's heart pounded.

"What?! My brothers?!"

"So Colley, you really not gon tell us your old stripper name?" Star purposely went back to the original conversation although she could really care less.

"Girl, I only danced for four business days. Let's leave the past in the past. And fix me a glass of whatever y'all drinking, or do I have to get that myself too?"

"No I got it," Star laughed while standing up. As usual Tahj watched her backside closely as she walked away. Tamia was looking at him with an amused grin but he was so into Star's ass that he didn't even notice.

Tamia's eyes shifted to Star who was moving around the kitchen like she was the woman of the house. It definitely appeared as if she was.

"So Star you staying here for good?" Tamia asked, already knowing she was starting shit.

"In New Orleans? Hell yea. This is my home."

"No, I mean in this house with Tahj. You look real comfortable, girl."

"I am, but I ain't staying here. I just got off the phone with a realtor before y'all got here." She divulged, knowingly dropping a bomb on Tahj. She took great joy in watching anger overcome his handsome face. She was still salty about their argument, so this was getback for her.

"Man get the fuck, Star." Tahj grumbled.

"Whatchu doing all that for? It was understood that this was temporary from the jump, silly."

"So where you moving to cousin?" Colley asked as she sat at the table with her rotel dip.

"I'm thinking somewhere deep into the Westbank actually." Star replied after sitting a wine glass in front of her.

Tahj was trying to contain himself in front of company but the more Star talked about moving the more infuriated he became. He didn't even know why she was exploring those options when she still had a crazy lunatic lurking around the city for her. Diamond had tried his hardest to locate C5 but the nigga had disappeared. It's like he knew Diamond would want to see him for how he came at Star. A few people had even told Diamond that C5 had bounced to another town in Louisiana. Diamond was now vowing that it was on site and everybody knew he meant business.

If Tahj was being real, C5 was the least of his concerns. He owned plenty of guns and he carried one everyday. He would go to the gun range for fun. If that nigga came near Star he wouldn't hesitate to put him out of his misery. But just because he wasn't worried about him didn't mean he wouldn't use him in his argument to get Star to stay here with him.

"What you doing with your other house?" Tamia asked. She was already in the know about what happened to Star thanks to Choc. They all knew she had been shot but they didn't have any details. Once Tahj gave Choc a full run down it was a wrap.

"I'ma just go ahead and sell it even though it breaks my heart to do so."

"Yea, that's gotta be devastating. But safety first, sis." Tamia affirmed before taking a sip of wine.

"This girl is full of shit."

They all looked at Tahj who had the nerve to pull up a chair to the table with them.

"Tahj what?" Tamia snickered.

"Star is full of shit. How the fuck is her rushing to leave this house to live on her own safe?"

"Probably because ole boy won't have any knowledge of her new home. Duh." Colley giggled. It was comical to her because it was evident that he wanted Star to stay right there with him. He was definitely sweet on her and even someone standing from a distance would be able to see it.

"Nigga if you love this girl and want her to stay here then just say that." Tamia instigated.

"I definitely ain't saying allat." He grumbled.

"And that's exactly why I'm getting the fuck."

"Wait so that's what you wanna hear?" Tahj questioned. He'd be ecstatic if that was the case because that meant there was hope for them. He knew Star loved fucking him and even though she'd never voice it, he knew she enjoyed his company too. But that didn't mean she wanted to be with him for the long haul. In fact he knew she wasn't having that. That's why she was so hard up to leave his house.

"Hell no," she cackled. "What I'm saying is nobody's trying to stay here and be your live in baby mama slash in house pussy. Maybe you've got it twisted and I definitely contributed to that so I'll take ownership for my part, but I'm not the bitch you finna be humping on and fucking over."

"Ouuuu, girl I really like you." Tamia smiled. This was all so entertaining to her. All she needed was popcorn, but her rotel dip would do the job.

"Really Mia?" He glared at her before looking back at Star. She'd just played him in front of company so he wasn't about to spare her. "Son, honestly you doing the most. I want you here because as the twins mother I'm concerned for you and my babies safety. I also feel the need to make up for lost time with my daughters. So I don't know what fuck you talking bout but you need to relax. Me and you was never that serious."

Star wasn't phased. Something was telling her he wanted to put on for their little audience.

"Exactly, so me leaving should be bout nothing to you. And as far as the girls go you can keep them whenever you want just like you've been doing before I even came to live in this house. The fuck? I ain't hard up, no."

"I know that's right. Cause I never heard a bitch complain about an eager babysitter." Colley co-signed.

"Man let me go upstairs." Tahj stood up to leave. He felt like he would explode.

"Yea go check on your kids and stay out of women's business." Tamia dismissed him.

Star laughed hysterically. All three of them had just tap danced all over Tahj's nerves and she now felt like a new woman.

"I want to go somewhere tonight." Colley suddenly expressed. "I'm child-less so I need to live it up.

Tamia sighed. "Same..minus the childless part. But it's nothing to call Noel's mama and drop Noeva off."

"What y'all tryna do?" Star asked.

"A hookah bar or something chill cause looka me." Colley pointed at her casual outfit of black latex pants, a white crop top, and blue and black Jordan ones. She was comfortable and cute.

"You look cute, but yea, I'm down to get into something slight. Shit I'll even do shamrock." Tamia said.

"Yea me too. What about you Star?"

"What about me?" She looked lost.

"You hear us talking about going out, bitch. You coming or what?" Colley quizzed.

She hesitated.

"Now you then talked all that shit to my brother just to let him pull your strings," Tamia shook her head in mock disappointment.

"Huh? I ain't even say shit," Star laughed. "Tahj ain't pulling shit over here. Y'all know my situation."

"And I don't go anywhere without my security guard so you gon be straight." Tamia vowed.

"Bitch you got a security guard?" Colley questioned in amazement.

"Sure do. I thought my man was tripping when he said he would get me one but I then had some run-ins with psycho people that proved him right."

"Whew, I guess me and my 25 thousand followers are oblivious to how the fame shit works." Colley said.

"It's a trip. But Star you rolling or you folding?"

She looked behind her as if someone was watching. "I'ma go grab some clothes and I'll get ready by Colley's house while you drop your baby off."

"Perfect." Mia smirked

Chapter 14

April 3, 2020

"They really look just like you." Porscha smiled at the twins as they ran around the park with the rest of their siblings. She couldn't believe that she was *just* meeting the twins even though Tahj had known about them since

January. She couldn't say she was completely shocked. She barely got to see the grandkids she'd been knowing about.

"I know, huh?" Tahj smiled proudly. "They got a little bit of their mom in them though."

"Hmmm, I've seen her on Instagram. I don't see it."

"You saw her on Instagram. How?" Tahj questioned. The last time he checked Star only had a business page that featured her work.

"That daughter of mine be posting her on her stories and tagging her. They seem to be close. Can't even fuck with her own mama but can deal with a whole stranger. Isn't that crazy?"

"Nah, not really."

"Really Tahj?"

"Really, ma. We not gonna sit up here and pretend like Mia doesn't have good reasons for cutting you off. On top of that, Star ain't no damn stranger. She's the twins' mom. Them being close is a no brainer."

"Well she ain't close to Nikka and Lexi like that."

"She tried to be for the sake of her nieces and nephew. She stopped fucking with them because of the drama."

"Yea and I'm sure you were the cause of it."

"I don't know about that. Nikka and Lexi had justified reasons to be mad at *me*, not my sisters."

"Well I'm not talking about those *other* girls. I'm talking about the one me and ya daddy made."

"Mama, I don't care what you talking about. Chill out before I take my kids and dip." He asserted. This is why he spent very little time around his mother. She was always so negative and it was draining.

"Boy you so damn sensitive. I don't know who you get that shit from. But back to Nikka…"

Tahj looked to the sky in agony because it was apparent she was about to beat a dead horse.

"She says you got that new baby mama of yours living with you. You and her together now?"

"Ma, you been knew Star was living with me because you called my house starting shit with her."

Porscha gasped and threw her hand over chest. "Lies! I did not! I was calling for you and she got smart."

"Whatever, mama. I'm not about to go back and forth about that. But nah, me and Star not together. We just cohabitating for now."

"Boy who you fooling? You *Tarrell's* son. Sometimes I feel like I should have gone ahead and made you a Junior."

"Glad you didn't," he muttered. "But I don't even know why you bringing him up. I can admit I have some of his ways, but I prefer not to be compared to that man."

"And why is that?"

"Because I actually take care of my kids."

"What?! Now your daddy may be a whore but he was a terrific provider and a great father to you and your sister."

Tahj released dry laughter. "So just fuck his other kids, right? As a matter of fact, don't answer that. Because I already know how you feel and you're entitled to that. The fact still remains that he was a deadbeat to the majority of his kids. That ain't me."

"Ok. It's not you. But I didn't hear you denying that he was a good father to *you*, either."

"Maybe because I'm still coming to terms with the fact that he wasn't as great to me as I once thought."

"What? Tahj, how can you say that? Don't be letting bitter folks get in your ea-"

"The last thing somebody can do is get in my ear. I'm a grown man thinking for myself and I think the nigga could've did better where *all* his kids were concerned. Including me and Tamia. But that's old news. We grown now."

"And y'all turned out fine. I think us as parents had something to do with that, so stop talking like that."

"How can you say that when y'all are barely a part of our adult lives? Tamia turns 23 this year and hasn't really fooled with you since she was a teenager."

"That's on y'all. We be trying but it's hard to be a part of someone's life when they clearly don't want you in it."

"Then maybe it's time to do some self reflection and change, mama. It's not too late."

"I ain't bouta kiss nobody's ass. Especially Tamia's."

"That's fine, mama. Just stop complaining about our boundaries because nothing will change unless you do."

"Granny, can you come push us on the swing?!" Tahiry ran up holding Tahja's hand.

"I sure can, baby." Porscha stood up and followed the girls over to the swings.

Now that Tahj was by himself he had time to go investigate what had been on his mind since his mom brought it up. He went straight to Tamia's Instagram. The very first picture on her page was a picture of her, Star, Tati, and Colley sitting at Morrow's with drinks in their hand. The picture had been posted 5 minutes ago and the caption read "Yes to day drinking with my bitches." He expected nothing less from Tamia's ratchet ass. He clicked on the picture to reveal the tags and there it was. Star had been tagged but it wasn't her author page. She had a new account called @SuperStar. If he had to guess he'd bet his messy ass sister was behind it. He could hear Tamia in her ear saying "bitch you need to get you an Instagram page and show off that nice ass body. You're gonna really come up. Watch."

He was happy to see Star's page was public and she surprisingly already had 10k followers. He bet they all came from Tamia tagging her. Star only had ten pictures so far and half of them were of the twins. She no longer had reservations about showing them off freely since they were not a secret to him anymore. The very first picture she'd posted had been at shamrock and it was captioned "here's to new beginnings." She was standing by a pool table and showing off her voluptuous curves. She had on a basic black athletic set with pumas and she still managed to stand out. Just looking at the pictures made him even more mad about her sneaking out of his house to go out with Colley and Tamia two weeks ago. All he knew was that he went upstairs to check on the kids and he played a game of call of duty with his son. When he came back down no more than 30 minutes later his kitchen was a mess and the women were gone. Including Star.

He called her going off but she just said she'd be back later and hung up. She came back to the house around 1am drunk. She literally laughed in his face when he called himself checking her. She passed out on the bed, refusing to let him ruin her good night. Ever since that day she'd been linking up with Tamia for any little thing like shopping or lunch and Tahj couldn't do much about it because she'd usually leave the house whenever he left for work. Through Tamia she'd gotten closer to Tati. One side of him loved it because he was a family man, but another side of him hated it. His sisters may have been settled down but they were still young which meant they spent a lot of time outside. He selfishly didn't want that for Star because it could lead to certain things. Like her dating again. But at this point it looked like his hands were tied. Once again, he had no control over Star.

———————————

"Daddy we hungry!" Tahja volunteered from the backseat.

"Didn't y'all have nachos right before the park?" Tahj asked.

"That was nothing but a snack." Baby Tahj mumbled. "We want real food."

"Yea, we want real food daddy!" True backed him up.

"Real food, huh? And what's that?"

"I want golden wings, daddy." Baby Tahj grinned.

"Ouuu!"

"Yea, me too!"

"Yea I want some shicken!"

Tahj laughed loudly at his daughters agreeing instantly to what Baby Tahj wanted because that's typically how it went. He was the leader of the pack. He was the oldest so it was only right.

"Alright golden wings it is."

About 15 minutes later Tahj was pulling into the golden wings parking lot and receiving an incoming call from Janikka. He braced himself before answering the phone. He made sure it wasn't on speaker because he never knew what would come out of her miserable mouth these days.

"Where you at?" She asked in a chill voice. He was surprised, yet grateful.

"About to get these children something to eat then I'ma finna do drop offs."

"Drop offs where?"

He knew it was too good to be true. The bullshit was coming.

"I'm dropping my kids off to their mothers so I can catch this flight to LA, Nikka. You know what it is because I always keep y'all in the loop with my schedule so there's no confusion when it comes to our kids."

"Well nobody don't gotta work around *your* schedule. I'm about to board this plane and go to Miami.

"Miami?!"

"Yea." She smirked, mistaking his reaction for jealousy. "I think I deserve a vacation."

"Nikka you doing this on purpose, bruh. I have to work to take care of us all and you being petty."

"I'm really not. Me and my friend bouta have a grand ole time. What you can do is cancel your little work trip, take your kids with you, or find a babysitter. Dont you got a live-in baby mama in your house? She can't watch the rest of your kids?"

"That ain't her job! That's like me attempting to throw all six of them off on you! I bet you wouldn't like that, so why try to put that off on the next woman?"

"Maybe her new best friends Tamia and Tatiana can stay at the house and help her then. They claim to love their niece and nephew so much. Regardless, it ain't my issue because I ain't there. Hope you figure it out. Bye." She ended the call.

"This girl here…"he mumbled.

While standing in the long line at Manchu he attempted to make some calls. Naturally he asked Lexi if she could watch Baby Tahj and Tazzy this weekend first. They'd all lived together before and she'd watched them plenty of times by herself. He was met by yet another surprise.

"What you mean you headed to Biloxi with your husband?!"

"Exactly what I said. We needed a get away."

"Son y'all childish as fuck plotting because y'all know I have somewhere to be. This shit don't get old to y'all?"

"Boy me and my man not thinking bout you."

"And I ain't thinking or talking about your man. I'm talking bout you and Nikka. It's no way y'all not in cahoots with each other."

"I have no idea what you're talking about." She lied. The truth was she and Nikka felt some type of way about how Tahj's family had embraced Star after being cool with them first. The shit was simply fake. They felt like it was Tahj's fault so they decided to take it out on his ass. He hated for somebody to come between him and his money.

"I'm sure you don't. Bye Lexi." He ended the call, already knowing he'd get nowhere with her. He called all his sisters but all of their weekends were full and they couldn't squeeze two kids into it. His brothers were out of the question because they were in Atlanta working. As he pulled up to his house he was starting to think he'd have no choice but to miss work. But that would look terrible. He couldn't let his client show up to a meeting for a sponsor alone. His job was to negotiate deals and protect all his clients. He couldn't do that effectively from his house.

While they were getting out of the car, Star was saying goodbye to Colley after being dropped off. She was tipsy and full after having lunch with the girls at Morrow's.

"Hey kiddos." She slurred as she twisted up. The kids swarmed her with hugs making her stumble.

Tahj looked over at her in disdain. He had no idea why she felt the need to go to lunch with his sisters dressed like a slut. She was all did up with a neat bun at the top of her head, a full face of makeup with a red lip at the center, skin tight, low rider denim jeans, a satin crop top that tied at the front revealing her stomach, tan red bottom pumps, and her signature Louis Vuitton tote.

"You drunk, Star?" He questioned because she was laughing like an idiot and stumbling over her feet.

"Boy no," she tittered before focusing on the children. "Y'all had fun with y'all grandma?"

"Yea! Mommy, she said we can go to her house whenever we like!" Tahiry said happily. She was just excited to finally have a grandma.

"Ion know about allat." Star said under her breath.

"Star, are we staying with you this weekend? My daddy gotta work and my mama then skipped town." Baby Tahj revealed.

"Boy," Tahj popped him upside the head. Evidently not putting the phone on speaker meant nothing around him because he still managed to catch the entire conversation *and* repeat it.

"Ow!" He howled.

"Tahj don't be hitting this baby!" She grabbed Baby Tahj and rubbed his head. " What, you mad because he exposed your tea?" She giggled.

"Mannn," Tahj dragged.

"Where's Lexi?" She asked.

"Apparently she decided to take a spur of the moment vacation with her husband."

Star bursted into laughter because she had a feeling those hoes did this on purpose to antagonize Tahj and it was working. He looked *stressed.*

"Man I'ma just take em with me."

"How are you gonna do that and work?"

"I'll figure it out."

"Tahj I'm here. Why not ask me?"

"Because I didn't think you would want to."

"You wouldn't know unless you ask. I don't mind. Now if you just assumed I would and threw them off on me that would be a problem."

"But all these kids by yourself? You sure."

"I'm a mother of twins. I'll be fine. Where are you going anyway?"

"LA."

"Yea, we can definitely call this even if you bring me back something nice."

"I'ma definitely look out. Thank you, forreal."

Star watched in amazement as Baby Tahj, Tazzy, and Tahjaria swam like pros in Tahj's luxurious pool that came with a waterfall, grotto, and long water slide. Her babies could swim but not as well as them. They needed floaties and they had no shame about it. It was Sunday and well into spring, which meant the weather was beautiful. The sun was shining, so Star decided to make it a pool day. She invited Colley over and they made burgers, barbecue chicken, macaroni, baked beans, and lamb chops. Star was currently working on her third plate and Tahja was in her lap helping her.

"It's good huh, mama?" Star asked as she watched Tahja scarf down a piece of chicken.

"Mhmm, I like shicken and yours good, Star."

"Awww," Star hugged her before looking over at Colley who was typing away on her phone while Suga dozed off on the beach chair next to her.

"Won't you take that baby inside and lay her down."

"For what? She good."

Star was still surprised that Suga was here today because lately it had always been an excuse. Star couldn't help but feel like it was no coincidence that Colley finally brought her baby here when she knew for a fact Tahj was gone and wouldn't be back until Monday. She had an eerie feeling that she tried her hardest to ignore. Her little cousin may have been flawed but she wouldn't…..

Then again, maybe she would. The moment Baby Tahj saw Suga he boldly asked Star if they had another sister they didn't know about. So it wasn't just her eyes seeing this. Even a *child* saw it. At that very second Star couldn't help but notice that Suga and Tahja looked like fraternal twins. It was scary. And the fact that Colley was acting oblivious to it was making Star sick to her stomach. She thought Colley was one of the few people in this world that she could trust, now she wasn't so sure.

Star felt the chair buzzing and looked down. It was Baby Tahj's phone and his mother was calling. She decided to answer the phone and tell her baby Tahj was in the pool. Or maybe she wanted to be petty.

With all the shade that had been thrown her way this weekend alone it was her right. The night before Star and the kids had a movie night. While they were making their own personal pizzas from scratch, Baby Tahj went live on Instagram. His mom joined while he was in the middle of giving Star a kiss on the cheek. The fool commented and said "I'm gonna have a talk with you about putting your lips on people that's not your blood, son." Thankfully Baby Tahj wasn't invested in reading the comments, but Star had seen it. That's what Nikka wanted.

Then this morning Star posted a picture of the elaborate breakfast she'd cooked on her page. Nikka commented and said "ok step mother of the year! @BigLex I see more trips in our future, girl. We got a full time babysitter on deck now." Lexi responded and said "yes ma'am! Cause this one gon do whatever Tahj says. Let me plan my trip to Tennessee next week. #iloveithere."

Knowing they were looking for drama, Star didn't engage. She screenshotted it and then blocked them both. It didn't even bother her because she knew those hoes were crying behind those comments. If they truly felt like Star was the duck to keep their kids while they ran wild they would've shut the fuck up to not ruin a good thing. But they were begging for attention which meant they were very bothered. That's why she planned on giving them more of a reason to be mad. She already knew she could beat both of their asses. No she'd never touched Lexi but she had a feeling that bitch was weak too.

"Hello Nikka," she smiled big, showing off her pearly whites. "Your son is in the pool. Want me to call him over here?"

Nika didn't find shit amusing. "You got a lot of nerve answering his phone."

She never dropped her smile. "Why wouldn't I? He's in my care and his phone is right next to me because he has enough sense not to get it wet. What's the problem?"

"The problem is I ain't leave him in your care!"

"Oh yea, you left him with his father whom you told to find a babysitter. Isn't that what you called me on Instagram?

I'm just doing my job, toots. What's the issue? I thought you loved it here." She said mockingly.

"First off, Lexi said that."

"Rightttt, you called me step mother of the year. That was so sweet of you, sis. Is it cool if the kids call me mommy since we're one big happy blended family now?" She cheesed hard. Now she was just antagonizing this bitch for the hell of it. It was easy and fun.

"Ouuuu, you lucky I'm in Miami. I swear!"

"Or what?" Star giggled. "You *know* what it is on my end, Miss Girl. But let me get back to *our* kids. See you around, stank."

"BIT-"

Star ended the call while Colley laughed her face off.

"Star, I think Nikka was mad. Her face turned red like a tomato!" Tahja said animatedly.

"Oh shit!" Colley held her stomach that was aching from laughing so hard. Star looked at her and Suga again. She couldn't ignore what her gut or common sense was telling her anymore.

"Tahja, go play with your brother and sisters, baby."

"Okay! But I'm coming right back for a piece of that cake you made!"

"Alright girl," Star laughed as she climbed off the chair and ran straight to the pool. She jumped in and landed on a floatie. She was an excellent swimmer as well.

"That lil one know she can eat." Colley commented.

"She sure can."

"What's up with you, bitch?"

Star faced her. "What do you mean?"

"Your energy…it's off."

"It sure is off."

"Okayyy, but why? What's the problem? Don't tell them bitter baby mamas getting to yo-"

"Nah, you just watched me handle one. They're lightweight. My issue is with you."

"Me?! The fuck I did you?" Her neck twisted.

"Colley I take issue with *anybody* playing in my face and you're no exception."

"Girl what? You gone have to tell me exactly what the problem is because I'm lost."

"Bitch *who* is Suga's daddy? It's time to give it up."

It looked like Colley saw a ghost.

"How is that your business?" She asked nervously.

"Bitch look at the pool and tell me why Suga resembles *all* those kids."

Colley let out a deep breath before saying fuck it. She asked so she was going to get the real. "Why you you think I didn't want to bring her over here?"

Star's heart stopped for a few seconds.

"S-so wh-when did yo-you and Tah-Tah- my baby daddy hook up? I want to know every damn thing before I drag you."

"You gon fight me over dick?" She asked in astonishment.

"No I'm fighting you for being a fake ass bitch! Imma have something for his ass when he returns too! Both of y'all muthafuckas been pulling the wool over my ey-"

"Star, shut the fuck up!" Colley cut her off, not being able to take it anymore. "I've *never* fucked Tahj, but Suga is related to him by blood."

Star's heart dropped. "Tarik or Tavior?"

"I wish," Colley laughed, despite herself. "At least my baby would have an active daddy, but no."

"Then who the he-" she gasped when it dawned on her. "Don't tell me you fucked these people daddy!"

"It's not my proudest moment, but it is what it is. Tarell's the papi. There. You happy now?"

Suddenly Star was wishing she had turned the other cheek. Because now she knew a secret that she didn't want to know. She wanted no parts of this shit. To make matters worse Colley had been smiling in Tarrell's daughters faces knowing that her child was their sibling. This shit was so grimy and right up Colley's alley.

Chapter 15

April 6, 2020

"Baby y'all have too much hair for me," Star breathed in exhaustion as she brushed Tahjaria's hair up into the last ponytail. She had washed and combed out the girl's hair last night, and that alone felt like running 20 miles. She decided to comb everybody's hair simply in two ponytails this morning but even that was time consuming and tiring when all of them had thick and long hair.

"I know. My daddy said we have beautiful hair." Jari said proudly.

"Yea, it's really beautiful."

"But my mommy said she gon perm it once I turn ten because it's too nappy. She said the perm gon makes my hair good like hers." She rambled.

As much as Star wanted to bite her tongue she wasn't built like that. Especially when she was dealing with a child and their self esteem.

"What your daddy told you?"

"That my hair is beautiful." Jari repeated.

"Then that's what it is. Your hair texture is perfect the way it is and there's no such thing as good hair. God gave you this and there's nothing wrong with your naps. I have them too, see?" She pulled at her huge puff ball that rested at the crown of her head.

"We both have brown skin too, Star."

"Yup, and that's beautiful too. Don't let anybody tell you otherwise."

"Mommy we put our uniforms on!" True waltzed into the bathroom fully dressed with Tahiry and Tazzy.

"Good girls. Where's Tahja and your brother?"

"He's downstairs eating cereal. Tahja is on the bed in the room."

"Okay," Star said while clamping the last bow on one of Jari's ponytails.

"What y'all in here doing?"

"Daddyyyyy!!!!!"

The girls rushed Tahj with hugs even though he had his hands full with Tahja. She was the only one without her uniform on because she needed help. Star observed Tahj in the most inconspicuous way possible. She didn't want to inflate his already huge ego but he was looking *good* to say that he was fresh off a flight. He was dressed down in army green Balmain Joggers, the matching sweatshirt, Yeezys on his feet, and he had a Diamond cross around his neck. As he talked Star realized he had gold teeth in his mouth and her pussy thumped. She found herself rolling her eyes because he'd probably done extra shit just to entice her.

"When did you get back? I did not hear you come in."

"About ten minutes ago."

"Well I'm glad you're here. You can dress your baby and take these kids to school."

"They wore you out, huh?" He smiled knowingly.

"Something like that but everybody was well behaved so it was cool."

"Good. Y'all there's donuts downstairs." He said to the girls.

"Yayyyyy!!!" They all celebrated before dashing out of the bathroom. She walked past Tahj so she could go lay back down, but he stopped her.

"Where you going?"

"To my room. Is that okay with you?"

It was funny how she now took complete ownership of Tahj's room and he didn't even correct it. He didn't even see anything wrong with what she'd said.

"Alright,"he stepped back.

She gave him a suspicious look, wondering what the hell he was up to.

"You're being weird." She finally said after he ignored the face she was making towards him. She left him in the twin's room and went to the master bedroom. When she walked in, her mouth hit the floor. His weirdness made sense now.

"Oh my Goddd,"she stressed as she walked over to the neatly made up bed. There were hundred dollar bills spread across the end of the bed. She didn't know how much money it was but it looked like thousands. As if that wasn't enough there were three designer bags lined up. They were sitting on top of their boxes neatly. She had a sky blue Lady Dior bag, a big pink Chanel boy bag, and a brown Louis Vuitton Damier Alma bag. She already owned two Louis bags and she treated herself to them after going back and forth in her head about it for months. Coming from nothing, she always thought twice about purchasing luxury items. That didn't mean she wasn't like every other woman who wished to own them. Now she had three bags that she didn't have to spend a penny on. She silently gave Tahj a round of applause. He'd done a good job on bringing her something back, alright.

Star was so happy with what she saw, she pulled her phone out and went to her Instagram story to record a video.

"So y'all I told my baby daddy to bring me back something from LA and look...this nigga did the absolute most." She giggled, as she ended the video.

"So you don't like it?"

Tahj's voice startled her.

"Actually I love it. Thank you." She wrapped an arm around him and gave him a half hug. It would've been a full hug if he wasn't still holding Tahja.

"That's all I get?"

She tilted her head. "Whatchu mean?"

He eyed her lustfully, making her stifle a grin and roll her eyes.

"I'm not bouta play with you, Tahj. Especially since you ain't did me no favors. I did you the favor and this was my reward. Remember?"

He shook his head while laughing. He couldn't even be mad like he wanted to be. This girl was something else.

"You a cold piece of work, baby mama."

"I said thank you! I'll definitely be willing to do business with you again if it's like *this*..." she looked back at the bed.

"Forreal? I can leave the kids with you anytime?"

She laughed out loud at the absurdity. "I think not! More like, we can work on a case by case basis. You can *ask* whenever you need help and I'll respond based on my availability. But please note that my free time does not mean I'm available."

"Don't take advantage of you. Got it."

"Great. Now let me count this money."

April 12, 2020

"This punch is Jesus on the main line." Tamia praised before taking a long sip of her Newyow's punch. The alcoholic beverage was fruity and strong; two of her favorite combinations.

"There goes Star," Tati said after glancing to her left.

Star had arrived at their lunch date a little later than them because she got into a small argument with Colley. After parking close to the restaurant Colley called her asking what she was getting into. She'd seen a picture Star posted on her Instagram story. It was a mirror picture but she could clearly see Star all done up with her natural curls hanging while rocking a pretty blue maxi dress that hugged her body like a second skin. She was sitting at home bored with Suga so she wanted in on the action.

"Bitch where you going and why wasn't I invited?" Colley questioned.

"How you know I'm going somewhere?" Star asked, being petty. She was still upset with her because now she felt like she was in the middle of some shit that had nothing to do with her. Telling Tahj or his siblings Colley's tea was something she obviously wasn't going to do because her loyalty was always with her cousin. But she couldn't help but feel fake because she was constantly around these people with this type of secret. It wasn't right. She almost canceled her lunch date with Tati and Tamia but she felt like that would make her look guilty of something. She was just paranoid about the whole situation now. Even being around Tahj now for a long time was the worst. Luckily he was always on the go or preoccupied with the kids.

"Cause bitch I saw you on Instagram and I know you don't get that dolled up to sit in the house. So what's tea? What we getting into?"

"Well *I'm* about to meet Tamia and Tati for lunch."

"Ohhh, so I guess me being invited out with your in-laws is a wrap now, huh?" She asked bitterly.

"Girl, do you hear yourself? You got a whole baby with these people daddy!"

"Didn't you hide the twins from Tahj though?" She countered. Deep down she knew it was a weak argument but it was all she had.

"Sure did. And I didn't hang out with his sisters while withholding that information. Let's not compare apples to oranges."

"No, let's! You acting like I'm this nasty ass bitch who can't be trusted or something! Well news flash, I didn't even know Tarell was Tahj's daddy until after I started fucking him!"

Star rolled her eyes because Colley had already run this story down to her. The closer Colley got to Tarell and the more he told her about his kids and personal life was when she was able to put two and two together. When she saw a picture of Tahj and Tarell on Tarrell's phone she got all the confirmation she needed. That wasn't Star's issue with Colley though, so it was irrelevant to her.

"Girl, I could care less about that. Keeping it real, Tahj's daddy is a pig for even fucking with you. You got pregnant with Suga when you were 18 and that man is in his 50's. He's a creep! If you think I'm mad with you over dealing with him then you're really simple minded."

"Bitch fuck you! Why are you mad? You not the one who got a baby with a married man who refuses to be in your child's life!" Her voice cracked.

"Colley, I'm mad because you never told me! You've always known who my baby daddy was so I think I deserved to know this shit. Especially after Tahj entered our lives! But to add insult to injury you've been smiling in his sisters faces like everything is gravy. You don't see how this will make me and you look once the truth comes out?"

"Once the truth comes out? So you gon expose me?!"

"No. You need to tell them."

"Pshhhh, girl you must be outta your rabbit ass mind. I'm not bouta fuck up my money."

Just when Star was about to ask her what she meant by that, Colley hung up. Now Star was in a pissy mood, as she sat at the table with Tamia and Tati but she tried to pull it together.

Tamia detected something was wrong immediately. "Girl, what's wrong with you? It's my brother, huh?"

That made Star laugh. "Chile, one thing Tahj not gon do is worry me. That boy ain't do me nothing."

"But somebody did. What's tea?" Tati pressed.

"Family bullshit." That was all Star could offer. She certainly couldn't go into full detail.

Tati nodded understandingly. "Hopefully it all works out. If not, just cut their asses off."

"Why would you tell her that?" Tamia laughed while picking up a crawfish ball.

"Shit I would think you would agree. You cut off yo mama *and* daddy." Tati rebutted.

"Girl fuck you." Tamia laughed. Star laughed nervously at the mention of Tarell. This shit was just as hard as she'd anticipated.

Chapter 16

April 17, 2020

Star smiled as the girls rushed out of dance class and ran to her as she sat in the lobby of Choc's dance school. This was her first time picking them up since she'd gotten shot. She got to see how much progress they'd made since January and they were killing it. She couldn't wait for the recital in June.

"Mommyyy!" Tahiry hugged her.

"I didn't know you was picking us up." True kissed her cheek, making her heart flutter. Being showered with love had to be the best part of being a parent for her.

"You picking us up too, Star?" Tahjaria asked with excitement in her eyes after hugging her. The look on her pretty little face made Star wish she *was* picking them up. Tahj hadn't asked her to, so that meant she wasn't.

"Yea, I want to go home with y'all too." Tazzy said.

"Um, Tahjaria and Tazzlyn! Come on!"

Star looked up and saw Nikka. She was decked out in Fendi prints and her hair was in a sleek high ponytail. She even had on a full face of makeup. She looked like a glamour Barbie. Even Star couldn't deny her beauty, but on the inside the bitch was ugly.

"Mommyyyy, can we go home with the twins?" Jari begged.

It looked like smoke was about to blow out of Nikka's ears, but instead of blacking out, she forced a smile.

"So y'all don't want to go to Build A Bear workshop and Chuck E. Cheese with y'all GG Porscha?" She asked.

"YAYYYYY!" The girls celebrated. Just that fast they'd forgotten about wanting to go to their dad's house with Star and the twins. Yea, they loved them and all but they loved Build A Bear, Chuck E. Cheese, and their grandma too.

"That's what I thought,"Nikka laughed. "Come on, let's get out of here. Y'all brother in the car."

As Nikka ushered them out of the building, the twins had sad faces making Star's blood boil.

"Mommy, GG don't want us to go?" Tahiry whimpered.

"I would've been good," True looked down.

"How about we have a full weekend of fun? We can have a movie night tonight, go to the Children's Museum tomorrow, and Sector 6 on Sunday."

What she really wanted to say was "fuck your ugly ass grandma. Y'all don't need her." Maybe she should've said it. Porscha had basically said fuck them when she decided to have a grandkids date and not include the twins. It would've been nothing for Porscha to go through her son and set something up so all the kids could be there. Even if Porscha asked Star to bring her kids she would've obliged. Yea she disliked Nikka but she would've tolerated her for the occasion. There were just too many ways to go about this and that led Star to believe her babies hadn't been included on purpose. Since it hurt their feelings it hurt her.

The girls agreed to Star's plans unenthusiastically. Everything their mom named was fun but they still weren't with the rest of their siblings and grandmother. Star was hoping Tahj was home so she could tell him this shit, but to her disappointment he wasn't. She was anxious to get everything off her chest so she decided to call him when the girls went upstairs. To her dismay he didn't answer. She normally wouldn't have done this but it was about his stupid ass mama playing with her babies so she called again. Still, there was no answer.

"That nigga better be busy," she mumbled to herself, as she opened the refrigerator searching for something quick to fix the girls for their movie night. While she was pulling out frozen pizzas, her phone rang.

"But couldn't answer the phone like a minute ago." She muttered as she watched Tahj's name flash across her screen. He was FaceTiming her. When she answered the call and saw him she couldn't help but wonder where the fuck he was going. He was in his Lambo truck looking fine as hell in a blue Balenciagia shirt, the matching baseball cap, and a Diamond chain that held a picture of all his kids. At the beginning of the month he'd set up a photoshoot with the kids and he wasted no time putting the pictures to use.

"Where you at?" Flew out of Star's mouth before she could catch herself.

He grinned, blinding Star with the diamonds in his mouth. Now she was really in her feelings. If he was looking this good then hoes were nearby. She was positive.

"Around. Wassup?"

"So that means you can't answer my calls? Got it." She replied dryly. She wasn't feeling his vague response. Now she was thinking a bitch was sitting next to him in the passenger seat.

"Never that, Star. You see I called you right back right?"

"After missing two calls in a row, but whatever. You can get back to whatever you was doing. I guess your kids don't matter."

Tahj had to laugh. She acted like she hated the idea of being with him but she had the nerve to be acting jealous. He really didn't understand her sometimes.

"Me and you know that's bull shit. Now tell me what's going on with the twins. I know it's important if you called me twice."

"Yea," she sighed. "So you know I picked them up from dance class right?"

"Right."

"Okay so Tazzy and Jari were asking me if I was picking them up too. Before I could answer Nikka walked up demanding that they come on."

"Oh Lawd," Tahj clutched his head when he heard Nikka's name. "Fuck she do now?"

"She was being her usual miserable self. Only this time your mama gave her the ammunition."

"My mama? Fuck she do?"

"Listen," Star urged. "When Nikka told the girls to come on they asked her if they could go home with the twins. So Nikka was like no, y'all going Build A Bear workshop and Chuck E. Cheese with GG Porscha. So of course that made the twins feel some type of way because they wanted to know why they weren't invited."

"And I want to know too. What the fuck? These bitches tripping." Tahj spat angrily.

"Right?! To be honest I could care less who wants to spend time with my babies. They'll never go without love and attention."

"Facts." Tahj concurred. "But it's still the principle. How the fuck my mama decide to spend time with *my* kids and leave two out? I'ma tell her ass to treat them all equally or say fuck em all. Keeping it all the way 100 ion even want her ass around none of my kids without *my* supervision. Nikka and Lexi's ass can't handle her."

"After today fuck her when it comes to True and Tahiry. They good. You should've seen their faces, Tahj. They was about to cry and everything. This shit got me heated based on that alone."

"You and me, both. But I'ma handle it. Trust me. Y'all in for the night?"

"Yea. We're about to watch some movies."

"The movie gon be watching y'all 40 minutes in." He chuckled.

"So," she giggled.

There was a knock on Tahj's glass. It was his date telling him that they were about to cut the cake at his client's birthday dinner. He'd stepped out to his car to call Star back, but now it was time to get back in. Antonio wasn't just a client, he was also his closest friend since college and they'd both started their careers together.

"I'm coming," Tahj said with a grin as he eyed Miani. She was a thick, brown skin beauty with a Naomi Campbell weave. She was a New Orleanian like him so he often took her to events and parties he attended in the city. She carried herself well and she was beautiful. She was the perfect arm candy and a good friend. He couldn't think of a better date. Well, actually he could. But he wouldn't even fix his mouth to ask Star to come somewhere like this with him. She barely liked chilling with him in the house.

He knew they both felt things for eachother but that meant nothing if one of them wasn't willing to dig deeper and explore those feelings. He was starting to accept that.

"You on a date, Tahj?" Star asked bluntly.

"Nah, I'm at my boy Tone's birthday dinner…but I got somebody with me." He replied honestly.

"Oh." Her heart dropped. She wanted to respect the fact that he'd kept it real but now she was wishing he'd lied. Regardless, she had no right to feel any type of way or go off about this. He was single and she'd been telling the man she didn't want him. "Well, have fun."

"I should be back soon to join y'all for movie night."

"There's no need for you to do that. Stay out and enjoy yourself."

"I'ma enjoy myself by coming home. I love you. Bye." He ended the call.

Star's mind was blown. He loved her but he had the next bitch at his best friend's birthday party with him? This was the exact reason why she couldn't take him seriously. He was a hot ass mess and she refused to be his fool.

As Tahj pulled into his driveway, his phone rang. His mom was finally returning his call. He'd called her right after he got off the phone with Star but she didn't answer. Since he had to get back to Tone's dinner he didn't press the issue. He knew she'd get back to him eventually and now she was.

Tahj accepted the call. "Hello?"

"Hey my baby. I'm sorry I missed your call earlier but I was spending some time with those kids of yours. I really wish you'd let us get them more often, Tahj. We're not getting any younger."

"Man fuck allat," he grumbled harshly.

"Come again?!"

"I was clear. I said fuck allat. You got a lot of nerve sitting up here acting like you give a fuck about spending time with my children when you left two out. If you ain't gon give them all the same treatment then just say fuck all of em as a collective."

"Wait, I know you're not disrespecting me because I rounded up the grandkids I'm actually familiar with?!"

"You disrespected my daughters today so I don't give two shits, real talk. And keeping it a buck you not really familiar with any of my kids like that. You don't have a strong presence in any of their lives to be playing favorites. You can count on one hand how many times you've seen them this year, so what the fuck you trying to do besides create division amongst my kids?!" He roared.

"Boy you really need to calm down before I slap the shit out of you! How the fuck I'm creating division amongst your kids?! You did that when you decided to have three different baby mama's! I don't know the newest one that well and from the one conversation we had I learned she was rude, and I don't like the skank ass company she keeps, so I don't have to deal with her if I don't want to! Nikka and Lexi respect me, so I went to them!"

Everything Porscha said rolled off of Tahj's back because it was irrelevant to the topic at hand.

"Man you don't gotta deal with *none* of my bm's. I'm your son and I'm 100% involved in all my kids' lives. Who you hit up the last time you wanted to see them? Me! Just admit that you, Nikka, and Lexi wanted to do some petty shit today and y'all used my kids as pawns. But it's cool, you think Tamia cut you off? You ain't seen shit yet."

"Alright Tahj, this is going a little too far no-"

Click. Tahj ended the call and proceeded to block her number. He couldn't say that he'd never speak to his mother again at that moment, but he was good on her for the time being.

Tahj was ready to share the conversation he just had with his mother word for word with Star, but when he walked into the den she was smiling at her phone. She was actually smiling *huge*. He'd certainly never seen her smile with him like that. His antennas immediately went up. He just stood back and watched her for a second because she still hadn't noticed him. He thought she was smiling at text messages or something, until she started talking.

"Boy you silly. I'm not that same girl I was in college, no."

He wanted desperately to hear what the mysterious lame ass nigga was saying on the other end of the call, but she had in her air pods. The twins were sleeping soundly on the couch next to her. Tahj couldn't help but feel disrespected. She was sitting in *his* house like a Queen with his kids next to her, yet she was kiking on the phone with a nigga. He started to go in until a rational voice of reason spoke to him. He'd just dropped a bitch off before coming home. A bitch that he'd told Star about.

He walked deeper into the room, finally making his presence known. Star looked like she'd seen a ghost before ending the call. She didn't even say goodbye to the person she was talking to. If anything she was just taken back. She hadn't heard him come into the house at all.

"You ain't have to get off the phone with your boyfriend." He jested bitterly.

"Tahj, please." She huffed. "When did you get here? I didn't hear you come in."

"I guess you didn't with those air pods in. That nigga must've been saying a bunch of bullshit in your ear and you was probably eating it up."

"Yea. Probably." She pursed his lips, refusing to give him any clarity. He'd led her right into that phone call and she wasn't offering any explanations.

"Just make sure you're more alert when you here by yourself with my babies. That could've been anybody walking in here on yo ass and you got your head in the clouds."

"And if that happened you would've been just as responsible. Wasn't you somewhere with a hoe when you could've been here with us?"

"Mannn, I was at my friend's birthday celebration. I would've been there regardless of me having a date or not. And we both know I be away a lot for work too, so you better listen to what the fuck I'm saying."

"Tahj go ahead somewhere. Ain't nobody who doesn't live here getting in this bitch with the way you got it locked down. You just tripping about me being on the phone with somebody." She hissed.

"Whatever, Star. You heard me, man. What we watching though?"

"We? Your kids sleep, yea."

"But we not. Put something on for us to watch."

Star wanted to protest, but it wasn't like she was doing anything else. Why not watch movies with her baby daddy that she just so happened to live with? It wouldn't hurt.

Chapter 17

April 23, 2020

"Smile girls," Star instructed while holding her camera up. The twins looked up at their mom and posed. They felt super pretty in one of their recital costumes. The recital wasn't until June, but they had a photoshoot today for the recital book. Talea had done the girls' hair in pretty buns and Star had even put some makeup on them. It was just some pink eye shadow and lip gloss, but you couldn't tell them shit. They were feeling themselves and Star loved to see it.

"Look just like their daddy," Tahj boasted, mainly to get a reaction out of Star. When she cut her eyes at him he snickered. "Don't hate, girl."

"There's nothing to hate on, baby. Twins tell your daddy who ya momma is."

Tahj sucked his teeth. "I know you they mama. That's why I know it gotta hurt you to look at them and see me. You must've been mad at me for your entire pregnancy, huh?" He jested.

Star glared at him. "Tahj, get out my face."

"Sisterrr!" True exclaimed as Tahjaria walked in the dance school with Lexi. A few seconds later Nikka entered with Tazzy. The girls had on the same costumes as the twins with similar buns. Star felt like she was in the twilight zone because Tahj had really made the same child four times.

In a perfect world Star would've loved to be cool with Nikka and Lexi because their daughters were literally attached at the hip. In reality she could never see it happening. Not at this point. Too much had been said and done in regards to her babies. Even now, those bitches couldn't even *speak* to her kids. Their daughters siblings at that. Meanwhile Star hugged and kissed their daughters like it was nothing. They didn't like it one bit but now they knew that Tahj would dig in their ass behind Star. Nobody felt like dealing with his wraith.

"Where's my baby?" Tahj asked Lexi, referring to Tahja.

"With my mama." She answered. "Speaking of mama's, yours is on the way."

His face tightened. "For what?"

Lexi's eyes bounced around in confusion. Star quickly decided that she was being phony. "Because I invited her. She said she wanted to see her grand daughters take their dance pictures."

Tahj looked at Nikka. "What I told you, son?"

"Huh? I didn't invite her, so why are you addressing me?" Nikka retorted.

"Because I know y'all talk. But my mama ain't coming up in here. If I was y'all I'd call her and tell her don't even make a blank trip."

Lexi looked at him in astonishment. "Tahj, this is your *mother* we're talking about. You don't need to be letting *nobody* come between y'all."

The slug she shot at Star flew right over her head because she was busy taking selfies with all of their daughters. The irony.

"Man, I don't care what you talkin bout. What I said is clear and I'ma stand on it. My mom is not coming in here."

Choc just so happened to be walking by and overheard them. She'd been running around like a mad woman all morning making sure everything was in order for the full day photoshoot. If their conversation had been about anything else she would've missed it.

"She's surely not." Choc wasted no time jumping in and backing her brother up. "I don't know why y'all would invite her up here knowing I don't fool with her."

Choc used to try and stay neutral when it came to Porscha. After all, that was her big brother and little sister's mom. But the disrespect that Porscha would spew via social media in recent years made that very hard. She talked cash money shit about *all* of Tarell's kids. This was Choc's business and if she didn't want someone to come in they weren't coming in. Period.

"I figured it wouldn't be an issue, sis." Lexi coaxed. "I mean today is about the kids."

"Exactly, so Porscha's presence isn't needed. She can come here if she wants but security won't be letting her ass in."

With that, Choc twisted away leaving Lexi and Nikka looking dumb. Star who caught the tail end of the conversation was trying her hardest not to break into laughter, but she lost the battle with herself and laughed out loud.

May 1, 2020

"Beautiful just like their mom. Makes me think about what our child would've looked like."

Star read the DM and rolled her eyes while holding back a smirk. Ever since she'd responded to this nigga at the beginning of last month he responded to *everything*. It reminded her of how he used to apply pressure back in college.

Brock was one of the first people she'd met at Southern due to them being paired together for a group project. Unlike everybody else, he learned about her baggage quickly. Group projects required fitting people into your schedule and spending a lot of time. With him being a student athlete his free time was limited, but so was hers because she was a mother. There was no way he couldn't find out about the twins. Prior to him finding out he was constantly shooting his shot only to be rejected. Star figured once he found out about her babies he'd fall back. That didn't happen. He only went harder.

When the project came to an end the time they spent together didn't. He would chill at her apartment 24/7 and that resulted in him being around her kids a whole lot. He was a natural with them but that didn't come as a shock considering he was the oldest of ten siblings.

She and Brock had undeniably became close friends but he wanted more, and he never hesitated to ask for what he wanted. He started wearing Star down and their relationship took a turn from friends to friends with benefits.

As soon as he got a whiff of the cooch he became adamant about them putting a title on what they were doing. But after Tahj, Star was scared and holding back. Since she didn't want to lead Brock on she planned on breaking their situationship off before it got too heavy. A wrench was thrown in her plans when she learned she was pregnant.

Initially she wasn't going to tell Brock. She was going to go to the clinic and handle it. But he discovered the pregnancy test box while he was over. Shockingly he was excited and immediately started making plans for their future. She snapped him out of it by telling him that she was going to get an abortion. Devastation washed over his handsome face. Right there he promised to never speak to her again if she did such a thing. He'd kept his promise until now.

@Brock34: Let me take you out, Star. Please.

Star thought about it. She was older now and more mature. She was single and in a better headspace as well. Back then her mental was all fucked up and that's why she couldn't handle a man actually trying to do right by her. She could definitely handle it now.

@SuperStar: Ok. Where are we going?

May 7, 2020

"Alright...I let you slide during the week. It's the weekend now, so nothing should be holding you back from spending the night."

"Actually I gotta go get my kids from their dad because he has something to do."

Brock shook his while wearing a grin. "Same ole Star."

"Excuse you?"

"Excuse *you,*" he chuckled. "You know what I'm talking bout man. Anytime you not feeling something it's always an excuse instead of being straight up."

Star burst into giggles. This was her and Brock's third date this week. He'd been asking her to spend the night since the first one. She knew how he could get carried away and she was attempting to take things slow. He was somewhat right though. She was making excuses. Her kids weren't even with their father. They were with their Auntie Talea.

"And that's where you are wrong. I have no problem with flat out saying no. I have a problem saying flat out no to *you*."

"Can't tell." He smirked. Star would've gone weak at the knees if she wasn't already sitting. It was weird how every guy she entertained after Tahj was the opposite of him looks wise. She hadn't put much thought into it then but maybe it was something she did subconsciously.

Brock had warm and toasty light brown skin, waves for days, pretty lips that did great things, a full sized beard, and a fade full of soft waves. Star could agree with him on one thing; their baby would've been gorgeous.

"Look, I'm just trying to take things slow. We just started talking again."

"Yea," he sighed. "I guess I gotta respect that shit. Now that I'm thinking about it I should be the one trying to take it slow. You had my head gone and then broke my heart."

"Brock, I did you a favor."

"A favor?! A favor how?!"

"Neither of us could handle the burden of a child. I already had two and I was struggling."

"I thought I was helping you with that."

"You were,"she admitted. "But that wasn't reality. The twins weren't your babies so you had no real responsibility for them. I knew you could get up and leave as soon as you got tired of me and that's what you did."

"Star, tell that bullshit to somebody else. I didn't walk away from you because I was bored and I damn sure didn't walk away from the twins. You killed my baby…and I'm still not okay with that."

"So why did you hit me up?"

"Because I can't get your ass out of my head no matter how much time goes by. And although I don't agree with what you did, I can somewhat understand your reasoning now."

Star's heart skipped a beat as she peered into his pretty brown eyes. She definitely wouldn't be able to hold back with him for too much longer.

"Yea right Mr. big time basketball star. You ain't been worrying about lil ole me."

He laughed because he'd been playing with the Golden State Warriors since he graduated college back in 2014.

"Fuck the hype. I'm telling you what it is. Now if you just let me *show* you we could really be great."

Involuntary chills ran up Star's spine. Yea, Brock was dangerous.

"Fuck." Tahj grunted as he watched Miani suck the skin off his dick. She was a certified headhunter.

Miani looked up at him and got off on how much she was bringing him pleasure. He couldn't get enough of her oral skills and that gave her immense pride. He'd keep coming back for this if nothing else.

Tahj grabbed her by her Brazilian bundles and started fucking her face. His dick was touching the back of her throat, but like always she handled it like a champ. She only gagged once or twice for dramatic effect, and it always got him off even though he knew she was pretending. Her ass didn't have a gag reflex.

"Shittttt," he stressed as he nutted in her mouth and watched her swallow. "That's what I'm talking bout, Miani."

"Fuck me now, daddy." She purred while standing up anxiously.

He was about to give her what she wanted when his phone rang. He smacked his teeth before answering. This was her third time calling him since Miani had his dick down her throat.

"Yo."

"You don't get tired of being so mean to me?" Nikka asked softly. She *almost* made him feel bad. Almost wasn't good enough though.

"I'm in the middle of something, bruh. Wassup? The kids good?"

"Always. I just saw something alarming in your son's phone. But since you're busy I'll hit you up lat-"

"Man, what's going on with Tahj?!" He cut her off.

"Keep it real Tahj, do you have another child that we were in the dark about?"

"What?" His face twisted up. He should've known Nikka was calling with some bullshit.

"I'm not trying to start anything. I'm just asking a real question. Because our son has pictures in his camera roll from last month with a little girl who looks just like the rest of your daughters."

"Nikka, maybe it's one of his cousins."

"Negative. I know all of your siblings' kids. I asked our son who it was and he claimed the little girl belongs to Star's cousin. You fucking cousins now?"

"Nikka I'm finna hang up on your weird ass. I don't know what type of wild scenario you've created in your head but I've *never* touched Star's cousin."

Nikka smiled to herself because she already knew that. Before calling Tahj with this she'd already gotten the tea from somebody else.

"Well maybe she belongs to someone in your family. I'll send you the pictures."

"Whatever bruh." He breathed before ending the call. He wasn't taking shit she just said seriously because he felt as though she was being dramatic. Colley's daughter resembling the twins was likely because they were related. But her daughter resembling all of his kids had to be a reach. Nikka was the queen of reaching.

"What the fuck…"he muttered when he saw the pictures of Suga pop up on his phone. She'd taken selfies with Baby Tahj as well as his other kids and the resemblance was frightening. To make matters worse he got the same feeling in his chest that he felt whenever he looked at his blood. A male in his family had definitely fucked Colley and there was no way Star's ass didn't know. This was his *first* time seeing this little girl and he knew. He had to get home and figure some shit out ASAP.

"I gotta go, Miani." He stood up while buckling up his pants.

As Star walked up to the door Tahj stared at her intently. She was coming from somewhere in a body hugging pink dress, strappy gold heels, and a Dior Handbag he'd purchased for her. He could tell she'd just left from entertaining a nigga and he couldn't shake the jealousy if he wanted to. He felt what he felt. But that wasn't something he was about to press her for. Especially with the shit that was on his mind.

"The kids inside?" Star asked, feeling a little annoyed. She was in the middle of following Brock to his place when Tahj called her telling her he needed her to get home and be with the kids because he has business to fly out for.

"Come inside." He stepped aside, allowing her to walk in. Feeling how dead the house was was alarming.

"Tahj, are my kids here?" She crossed her arms over her chest.

"Nah."

"Nah? What you mean? You made me come here for nothing?"

"I wouldn't say that. You had fun tonight?"

"Yup." She answered proudly.

He nodded as if everything was everything, confusing the hell out of Star. She wasn't messing with Brock specifically to make Tahj mad. If that was the case she would be using every opportunity she had to throw him in his face. But to see him act all nonchalant when he didn't know where she'd been going for the past few days made her feel some type of way. Did he not care anymore?

"That's what's up. I hate I had to interrupt your date night but it's some shit we need to talk about."

Here it comes, she thought to herself. He was about to find some bullshit reason to complain about her dealing with another man. She was preparing herself to combat anything he threw her way.

"What Tahj?"

"Who the fuck is Colley's baby daddy?" He blurted out. He saw no reason to beat around the bush any longer.

Star's heartbeat stopped for a moment.

"W-w-what?" She stuttered.

"Don't play with me right now, bruh. With how close y'all is I know you know. If that lil girl is my family I think I deserve to know."

Star was at a loss for words. How did he find out? She fully planned on keeping her mouth shut until Colley womanned up and told the truth for herself. Now what she feared was coming into fruition. She was being backed into a corner and forced to reveal a secret that wasn't hers.

"You know." Tahj voiced in disbelief. "You know and you ain't said shit."

"Tahj, that's Colley's business. It's not my right to say anythi-"

"Star, I ain't trying to hear that. Maybe I could fuck with that point of view if you hadn't gotten close with my family. How do you feel comfortable being around us and keeping this type of secret? Come to think of it, that same question applies to Colley because she's been in my sister's face's right with you. That's what y'all do in y'all family, huh? Y'all hide babies?"

Shots were fired and it hit Star right in her chest. She felt that one. He was *pissed*, and she couldn't even blame him. This was grimy, but he needed to understand how she was put in a fucked up situation too.

"First off, Colley didn't do what I did. I didn't tell you about the twins. Colley told her baby's father about Suga. He just decided not to be in her life."

"So Suga is my dad's child." He stated confidently. Before getting that last piece of information he figured Sugar could've been for one of his brothers. But there was no way Tarik or Tavior would have abandoned a child they knew about. That was right up Tarell's alley.

"Unfortunately." Star sighed.

Tahj just shook his head, before grabbing his car keys off the table in the foyer.

"Wait, where are you going?"

"Away from you."

"What?! Tahj," she touched his shoulder. He jerked away from her with quickness.

"Move, bruh. I don't know how the fuck you could be around me and my people for this long and not say shit. You fake as fuck, Star."

"Fake?! Tahj I just found out myself! And Colley is my cousin!"

"Yea, I understand you were stuck in the middle but right is right and wrong is wrong. You should've told Colley she was dead wrong to be around us with that type of information. And do you really expect me to believe that you just found out about this shit?"

"I did!" She beseeched.

"I saw *one* picture of the lil girl and knew what it was. You didn't see it all these years?! Man, I gotta get away from you right now."

"So you gon really leave?"

"Fucking right! It's either me or you, and I'm never gon put your stupid ass out!" He shouted angrily before leaving.

Once he was gone Star let out a loud scream. This shit was a hot ass mess.

Chapter 18

Tahj sat outside of his parents house waiting for his dad. Tarell seemed thrilled when he got a call from Tahj saying that he was stopping by. He hadn't seen his son in person in months. He didn't know why he was getting a random visit out of nowhere on a Friday night, but he was excited nonetheless.

That excitement was evident as he strolled out of the house smiling. He stopped in confusion because Tahj was just sitting in his truck instead of getting out. After thinking on it for a second, Tahj decided to get out of his truck.

"You not coming in, son?" Tarell asked as he ambled over to him.

"No. I see mama is home." He said while nodding to Porscha's Honda in the driveway. He remembered a time when his parents only drove luxury vehicles. Thanks to his fathers bad decisions those days were long gone. To make a long story short he'd drowned himself in child support debt, he would trick his money with young women, and he was trying to live like Hugh Hefner at home with Porscha. Before he knew it his money was running low and they had to downgrade. A few years ago he'd been reduced to getting an apartment because his finances were so bad. It took a lot of hard work and willpower, but he was finally able to purchase a two bedroom house a few months ago.

"Yea,"Tarell sighed. "She told me what happened. I don't think she meant no harm, Tahj. She's just more familiar with your kids from Nikka and Lex-"

Tahj waved him off rudely. "I ain't come here to talk about that shit."

"So what the fuck did you come here for?" Tarell questioned, feeling severely disrespected. It was a shame really. None of his kids showed any respect to him as the parent.

"I got another little sister, huh?"

Tarell's eyes widened and he swallowed what felt like a lump in his throat.

"Who told you that shit?"

"Just answer the question, man. You be going out of your way to keep secrets."

"Shit I ain't think it was your business. I know you be trying to play best big brother of all time but me and Lanae have an understand-"

"Lanae?" Tahj's face balled up. "Nigga who is that?"

Tarell immediately came to the realization that he'd jumped the gun. Tahj could see the regret on his face.

"Dad….how many kids you got? Real shit."

Tarell let out a deep breath as he prepared himself to be honest for once. Hell he was already caught.

"Ten, including the ones you already know about."

"So you have three new children?"

"Yea, I guess you can say that. But who are you talking about?"

"The name Colley rang a bell?"

Tarell threw his head back. "I knew that bitch would start talking eventually. She was so mad when I broke things off with he-"

"Man, that girl ain't tell me shit. Star is her cousin. My kids then been all around my little sister and I had no idea. I mean that lil girl looks just like us."

"Hey, I got strong genes." Tarell laughed.

Tahj pushed him roughly. "This shit funny to you?!"

"Woah! What the fuck is wrong with you?!"

"What's wrong with me?! Nigga that's a question for your sick ass!"

"What? Nigga you lost your mind?!"

"I would ask you that but that would be a dumb ass question! Colley had to be 17 or 18 when you started fucking with her!"

"And?" He looked perplexed.

"Are you serious? Nigga you 54!"

"I know how old I am. Colley and any other woman I fuck with know what they want. You acting like she was 7, nigga. And you have no room to talk!"

"What?! I don't fuck with kids!!!!"

"Yes but when *you* were 16 you was fucking on a grown ass woman. You forgot I brought you to the doctor to get rid of that chlamydia she gave your ass?"

The words leaving his fathers mouth were extremely triggering, but he wasn't backing down. This talk needed to happen. He needed to get the shit he'd been scared to say as a boy off his chest as a man.

"Yea, I remember that. I also remember telling you about the first time that pedophile came on to me when I was 12. You praised me and gave me condoms."

"A pedophile, Tahj? Really? Obviously you enjoyed it if you kept fucking her. I don't know why you're trying to put the shit off on me now and play victim. You never told me that you told her to stop."

"It doesn't matter!" He exploded. "You knew I was a kid and she was an adult! I didn't know what the fuck I wanted!!!!"

Tahj had finally come to terms with what happened to him as a child by none other than Star's Auntie Fee. When she first gave him head when he was only 12 he knew it felt good, but it was also weird. After he busted a nut he recalled feeling guilty. That's why he went straight to the person who always protected him; his father. He was dumbfounded when his dad patted him on the back and said "my boy!!!" He then proceeded to give him sex advice and condoms. Shortly after that, Fee took his virginity. Deep down Tahj always felt the situation was twisted but Fee and his dad made him feel like it was okay, and that's why he never went out of his way to protest. That was until he got an STD and his dad said he couldn't fuck with the older woman anymore. His dad only knew Fee as "the older woman" his son was knocking down. He had no idea that he now had a child by the older woman's daughter. This was a prime example of how small New Orleans was.

"Look, what's done is done. You want me to apologize for being proud of my son for getting some pussy?"

"Nigga fuck you. After today you forever on my shit list."

Not being able to take the blatant disrespect Tarell swung on Tahj. He had attempted to pop him in the mouth, but Tahj dodged his fist and threw a mean right of his own. Tarell stumbled back, but Tahj didn't let up. He followed through with several more lethal blows to his dad's face. Soon Tarell was on his back as Tahj kicked him.

"I should kill your weak ass!!!"

"Tahj! What are you doing?!" Porscha ran outside and attempted to push away from Tarell, but he was too big and too strong.

"I'ma call the police if you don't stop!" She threatened.

Tahj hit his dad in the face two more times and blood splattered everywhere. He finally stopped.

"Alright. I'm done."

He turned to leave.

"You fighting your own daddy now?!" Porscha screamed.

"Man *you* need to fight this nigga for once. He keeps having babies on your weak ass."

"Hmmm, so the cats out of the bag about Star's cousin, huh? Well I hope you can see now that that girl ain't shit. Just like your daddy she kept a secret from you."

"Ma, real shit. I hope you learn to love yourself one day because you lost."

Porscha smiled wickedly. "That makes two of us, son."

Before going to sleep last night Star had decided that she wasn't going to let anybody make her feel bad about this entire fiasco. It wasn't her fault. Plain and simple. She was an innocent bystander just like Tahj and his siblings, and if they couldn't understand that then it would be nothing to say fuck them again.

Yea, that's what she'd convinced herself of last night. When she woke up the next morning she felt sick to her stomach yet again. She smelled breakfast downstairs and loud recognizable voices. This nigga had his entire family over, ready to pounce on her. Before she could think of her next move, the door opened.

"Goodmorning."

Star looked at him strangely. He wasn't mad anymore?

"What you looking at me like that for?"

"I...well, maybe because you left last night like you weren't coming back."

He chuckled lightly. "I just needed space. I also needed to get answers."

"F-from who?"

She was hoping this nigga didn't go confront her little cousin on no crazy shit. Then they'd *really* have issues.

"My paw. Who else?"

"Oh." She muttered feeling silly.

"Yea, oh." He mocked before sitting on the edge of the bed. "After driving around for a while I realized my anger may have been misplaced."

"May have?"

"Yea. Because I still feel like you were wrong for not telling me, but I get it, your bond with Colley is stronger than the one you have with my family."

Although that was nothing but the truth, Star still felt some type of way about his delivery.

"I mean, yea," she admitted. "But it wasn't even like that, Tahj. I *literally* just found out the truth myself and I wanted to say something but I felt like it wasn't my place. I even distanced myself from Colley because I was annoyed about the position she put me in. Anytime we would talk I would tell her to just tell y'all, but she said that was never happening. I think y'all dad told her he would stop giving her money if she was loud about their baby."

"Yea. More than likely with his grimy ass. But you didn't see the resemblance between that baby and your own daughters?" He quizzed.

"Definitely. And it had me suspicious as hell from day one. I was so suspicious that I asked Colley some questions that made us have a little falling out."

"What you asked her?"

"I asked her did y'all fuck and make Suga."

All Tahj could do was laugh.

"Now that's fucked up. I wouldn't even do that. I still see Colley as a child. Like Mia and Tati. That's why it got me fucked up that my dad was even fucking with her. That nigga on some R.Kelly shit, and nobody has ever held him accountable. Nigga should've been locked up."

"That's a black family for you. They'll let predators get away with murder. Just look at my Auntie Fee's son Devlin."

Tahj's head snapped up. "That nigga never actually touched you did he?"

"Nope, his nasty ass just pulled his penis out in front of me. But I wasn't the first person he tried in that hou-"

Star abruptly stopped herself when she realized she was talking too much. That wasn't her story to tell.

"Just know he was a serial predator." Star continued. "And his maw never held him accountable. She just played dumb like she ain't know what the fuck was going on."

"That's because she's just like his ass." He said before thinking.

Star's heart skipped a beat. She remembered trying to touch on this topic with him in 2012 but he brushed her off. She wanted answers today.

"Tahj what did my aunt do to you?"

"Some shit she had no business doing with a child at her big ass age. But it's all good. Water on the bridge."

"No it's not *all good*. You know that shit wasn't right, correct?"

"Hell yea."

"You know it was sick, right?"

"Absolutely."

"So what makes you think that shit has zero impact on you and how you've carried yourself since it happened? We're all products of our childhood."

"So what you tryna say Star?"

"I don't know…maybe talking to somebody about what happened wouldn't hurt."

"Nah because the first time I tried doing that since it happened didn't go well. I ended up beating Tarell's ass yesterday."

"Probably because he said some ignorant shit. You can't talk to a predator about a predator and expect good results, Tahj. I was thinking about something like therapy."

Tahj thought it over for a few seconds. "I've thought about it before. A lot of my clients do it and some of my sisters too. The thought of telling a stranger shit that I pushed to the back of my own mind used to be crazy to me."

"Well it's not at the back of your mind anymore."

"Yea I guess that's true. But say, my brothers and sisters downstairs and they'd like to meet their little sister. Call Colley."

"Alright," she breathed nervously. "Are they mad with me?"

"Nah...I told them that you and I found out at the same time." He smirked. "This shit already chaotic, we don't need no added drama. Now call Colley so we can get our story together about how we found out."

"She wears a 3T, right?" Tati asked as she pulled adorable Juicy Couture Spring outfits out of a big bag. "We went shopping early this morning and got all this stuff so I hope it's the right size. We got some stuff in size fours too."

"Yea those sizes are good, but she has *a lot* of clothes y'all." Colley said, feeling overwhelmed.

"We see she's well taken care of." Tarik said. "We just wanna spoil her too, so if you need something don't be scared to use our numbers."

"Yup. Because Tarell's money is not guaranteed." Choc disclosed.

Colley knew that already. Just last night Tarell called her shouting about how he wasn't giving her another cent since she wanted to run her mouth. She hadn't felt the burn of his threat yet because her bank account was sitting pretty. She barely had to touch the money he gave her monthly because she was well taken care of by the niggas she fucked with.

"Yea he told me last night that I'm not getting nothing else out of him, but that's fine. I've never depended on him anyway."

"Regardless, we're here to help." Tahj professed. "And don't do that nigga no favors. Caidence's last name is Bellmany so put his duck ass on child support."

Star looked over at Suga and determined she didn't need to be in here for this conversation. "Suga go upstairs and play with your cousins...I mean your nieces...girl, this is a mess."

Tamia exploded with laughter because Star really appeared to be uncomfortable with the entire situation. It was weird for her as well as her siblings too. To know their dad was still out here making babies while they were having kids of their own was disgusting, but it was their reality. The only reason they were trying to do the most was because they knew their father wasn't making any effort to be a part of the little girl's life. They were also big on family in general.

Once Suga was gone, Tamia looked at Colley. "So let's address the elephant in the room. Why didn't you tell us what it was when we started hanging out Colley? We wouldn't have been upset with you."

"Honestly, I had no way of knowing that and I was embarrassed. Then to make matters worse I was taken money in exchange for my silence."

"Which confuses me," Choc voiced. "This nigga paying you to be silent like it's a secret that he's a serial cheater and makes outside kids religiously."

"Well I think around the time I got pregnant his wife was threatening to divorce him and take whatever he had left. As time went on she didn't leave him, but our arrangement didn't change…until now."

"Look, we not here to nail you to the cross for this. You're young and my father knew what he was doing. As long as you don't keep us from Suga we good." Talea winked with a smile.

"Then we'll be good." Colley giggled while thinking about how she had bukoo new baby sitters at her disposal now.

"So what about these other two siblings we have?" Tavior questioned. "Should we try to find them?"

"Shit we might as well." Tahj said. "Colley, do you know anything about them?"

"Well there's Taina and she probably just made three. I only know about her because her raggedy ass mama, Lanae, went out of her way to be seen by me and all his other young hoes. We had several fights while she was pregnant. I didn't want to beat a pregnant bitches ass but she was straight disrespectful."

Star's mouth gaped. "Why is this the first time I'm hearing this?"

"Bitch I couldn't tell you all this when you didn't even know who my baby daddy was at the time."

Tamia squinted while thinking hard. "Does this Lanae chick have pink hair?"

"Yea. You know her?"

"No, but my mama fought her because she showed up to their apartment a few years ago."

"Yep. That sounds like that rat. And I *think* the other baby mama is this girl named Amil. I wouldn't have known about her either if it wasn't for Lanae. I never saw her at all myself. All I know is that she's younger than me. I don't know anything about her kid."

Tahj's stomach twisted. "Man y'all paw is sick."

"Shitttt, I don't claim his ass. They need to lock him the fuck up." Tarik spat.

In that moment they all silently understood that their father was dead to them all forever. They didn't even want to associate with someone like him.

Chapter 19

May 15, 2020

"School's out! School's out!" IT'S SUMMER BREAK!" True sang loudly as she skipped in the house while swinging her empty backpack around.

"Girl calm down." Tahj laughed while watching her cut up. She threw her bag down and started doing a happy dance that consisted of shaking her legs.

"Ou, get it sister!" Tazzy shouted before joining her.

"Y'all silly,"Tahj shook his head with laughter before answering his vibrating phone. "Wassup?"

"Hey, so is everything set for tomorrow?" Lexi asked.

"Yea,"Tahj said as he stepped through the house. Star was in the kitchen cooking and it smelled like home.

"Cool. You ordered the cake I sent you, right?"

"Yep."

"Perfect. I spoke with the decorator and she'll be arriving at your house around 10 am. Is that cool?"

"I have a meeting in the morning. But someone will be here to let her in."

"I can come over and let her in. It'll also make it easier so I can get my girls ready."

"I thought Talea was doing their hair tomorrow morning. Isn't that why they're sleeping here?" He questioned. He knew she was trying to be slick but he wasn't having it. The only reason he agreed to throw Tahja's 5th birthday party at his house was on the strength of his baby. Lexi lived in a nice and spacious home that came with a pool but her back yard was tiny. His backyard was huge and perfect for a party. They'd thrown this party together last minute but there'd been no drama so far. He should've known better.

"She is, but I have Tahja's custom swimsuit."

"Ok. I should be home by 12. You can come dress her then. The party starts at 3."

"You really treat me like a stranger. What I can't be in your house without you all of a sudden when we used to live together? I'm not gon bother your ugly ass baby mama. I just want to make sure everything is straight for my baby party."

There was silence from the other end.

"HELLO?....bitch I know this nigga aint hang up on me.

"What you cooking?"Tahj asked Star as he walked in the kitchen.

"Pork and beans and wieners. Then ima fry some pork chops."

"Ghetto ass meal." He joked.

"And it's gon hit the spot too." She giggled

"It sure will. My babies gon tear that shit up."

"And nigga you will too," she laughed. "Where are my babies anyway?"

"In the front having a dance party. But I need to start back hitting the gym because you don't be playing fair with the shit you be cooking."

"I might need to come with you."

"Shit let's go Monday."

"Alright, but don't be doing the most and acting like my trainer."

He laughed because he knew he would do the most. When he hit the gym he didn't fuck around.

"Imma be chilling."

"Yea right," she laughed. "I got Tahja's birthday gift today."

"Oh yea?" He smiled. "What did you get her?"

"A LOL Surprise doll house, a couple of LOL dolls, and the American Doll I ordered for her came in with the book."

"She gon scream her head off. I know you can't wait to see that reaction."

"Yea, about that," Star scratched her head. "Could you record her reaction for me?"

"What?" His face screwed up. "Why would I do that when you gon be here?"

"Actually I'm not going to be here. I just don't have time for drama. The twins will be here though. I've already spoken with Talea and she's going to keep an eye out to make sure Lexi and Nikka don't pinch my daughters."

"Wait. Do you seriously think I would let somebody mistreat them?!"

"Absolutely not. One thing you always do is check your baby mamas. I can give you that, but you're one person. You won't see everything with a party going on at your house."

"Okay. I get that. But why are *you* not coming? It's like you missing your own child shit."

Star stifled a smile. "See. That's why them hoes hate me now. They think I'm tryna take their spot. Tahja only has one mama, Tahj. Yea I love her, but she's not my child and I know when to take a back seat."

"You can take a backseat and still come, Star."

"Not when Lexi texted me today talking about how I should sit this one out of respect for her."

"Man fuck Lexi! She has no right to say who should sit out of shit at *my* house. Especially when I'm welcoming her pale ass husband with open arms!"

Star cackled. "But still Tahj, anytime me and your other baby mama's are in the same space it's nothing but drama. Tahja deserves a drama free birthday, so if I have to remove myself then I'm willing. And if I'm being honest I don't want them hoes at nothing we throw for the twins. So I'll give Lexi this."

"You don't gotta give her shit! They have no right to show up to the twins' birthday parties because they have no relationship or bond with them. Tahja loves you."

Star hated to admit it but he had a point. She still wasn't willing to deal with the bullshit though.

"Tahj I'm just trying to choose peace. Everybody Tahja needs here tomorrow we will be here. Her birthday will be just fine without me."

Tahj shook his head in disappointment, but he was done convincing her. He couldn't even blame her for choosing not to deal with his worrisome bm's. If he had a choice he'd dodge them too.

"I can't even be mad. Do what's best for you."

May 16, 2020

"How you gon agree to spend the day with me but be on your phone the entire time?"

Star looked up from her phone at a shirtless Brock who was watching her closely. It was almost 6 pm and she'd been with him since 1. They started their day off with brunch at Monty's on a Square, after that they took a stroll on the RiverWalk, and then went to Canal Place where he'd spoiled her rotten. After shopping they went back to his place where she finally let him feel the pussy again. His dick was just the way she remembered it...mediocre. It wasn't bad, it just wasn't mind blowing the way she knew sex could be thanks to somebody. She still reached her peak from head and she had a nice day with him, so she had no complaints.

"Boy you had my attention all day and I can't scroll through Instagram?" She giggled.

"You've been getting calls and scrolling through Instagram all day, Star. What's up with you and your baby daddy?"

"Huh? Where that come from?"

"I'm just trying to see why *his* daughter would call you about her birthday party earlier."

When Star received a FaceTime call from Suga's phone she naturally answered thinking it was her. But Tahja's face appeared in the camera. Star's heart melted because she looked so darn cute with the top of her hair up in a bun and the back hanging. Her birthday theme was the Little Mermaid so she was wearing a purple metallic bathing suit top with "birthday girl" embroidered on it in gold.

"Hey birthday girl! You enjoying your party?" Star asked.

"Yea. When you coming back Star?"

That morning Star made her a big birthday breakfast and she gave her her gifts. When Talea arrived to do the girls' hair, Star bounced. Tahja was an hour into her party when she realized Star wasn't there and that confused her. True and Tahiry were there.

"I'm coming back tonight, baby."

Her face fell. "You gon miss my party?"

Star didn't know what to say. It was easy to tell Tahj she wasn't coming. But she felt awful saying it to Tahja's face.

"Yea, Tahja. I'm sorry but I can do something with you during the week."

"Okay..."she pouted before ending the call. After that Star had been watching Tahj and his siblings' Instagram stories all day. She couldn't help but feel like she should've been right at the party.

"Maybe because *his* daughter is the little sister to our daughters. We're family."

"So you and that nigga family?" He scowled.

Star laughed at his jealousy.

"Unfortunately, yea. That nigga is my family by default, but we have nothing going on. I've just built relationships with his kids in a short amount of time."

"That's cool, and I can kind of relate. I fell in love with the twins at first sight. Let's do something fun with them during the week."

"Uhhhh,"Star stalled while thinking of a nice way to say no. Having him around the twins when they were babies and Tahj wasn't in the picture was one thing, but now? Let's just say she wasn't trying to have it out with Tahj's crazy ass. Lord knows she'd kill him if he tried bringing one of his hoes around the twins. Granted, Brock meant much more to her than a random hoe, but she didn't know if they were in this for the long haul. They were just learning eachother again.

"That's a no,"Brock laughed. "I guess you gotta respect your baby daddy."

"Definitely. Only because I want the same in return from him."

"It's cool, Star."

He was definitely in his feelings, but Star didn't know what to say to soothe those feelings. Thankfully she received a text message that served as the perfect distraction.

Baby Tahj: Lexi over here talking about you to her people. I don't like that.

Star had been back and forth in her head all day. But that messy text from Baby Tahj pulled her to make a final decision.

"Brock I gotta head out. Somethings going on with my kids."

She had no plans to go to Tahja's party to confront Lexi over something Baby Tahj said. She did however plan on making her presence felt. Hell she'd tried bowing out gracefully and the bitch was *still* talking shit. Now she was going to give her a reason to talk.

"Y'all gathered everybody up?" Lexi asked no one in particular as she held Tahja while standing next to Tahj. They were getting ready to sing happy birthday and she felt so good inside. The day had been perfect and Star-less just like she wanted. Her husband was here but he knew how to fall back and let her and Tahj have their moment as Tahja's parents. Star would've been doing the most.

Tahj scanned the cake table area. "Yea, everybody's he-"

"Oh shit! There goes my sis!" Tamia screamed as Star walked through clad in a mock Ariel bikini that she'd been having for years, and it was perfect for this occasion. She kind of matched Tahja, which immediately pissed Lexi off. Here this bitch was, doing the most.

"Mommy!!!" The twins screamed while wrapping their arms around her. Right then Lexi's family that she'd been talking shit to knew that this was the infamous Star. They were just a tad bit confused. They'd been told by Lexi that Star was ugly, fat, and bald headed. She was none of those things. The girl had a body women paid for, her hair was beautiful and thick, and she had a pretty face. Based on the way Tahj was looking at her they quickly put two and two together about why Lexi was *really* mad.

"I hope I'm not too late."

"Nope! You're just in time!" Tahja exclaimed before trying to jump over the cake table and into Star's arms for a hug. Her mom snatched her back.

"Really Lexi?" Tahj frowned.

"Yea. We're about to sing happy birthday." She snapped.

"Girl nah," Tati tittered, making everybody laugh. Lexi was burnt up like a teapot on the inside as everybody shared a laugh at her expense. This wasn't over.

After singing happy birthday and eating cake, Star took a swim in the pool with Tahja and the rest of the kids. Lexi and Nikka sat poolside and looked on in disdain.

"Tahja seems to like Tahj's girlfriend." Lexi's mom, Ana, said while sitting by them. She knew Star wasn't his girlfriend, she just wanted to get a rise out of her daughter. She'd been the main one to tell her it would never work with

Tahj and she could do better. In return Lexi would tell her she didn't know what she was talking about because she was in her late 50's and had never been married. Ana knew that was the only reason she'd married that white man that she didn't love. Not only did she fuck around and get pregnant for him but she just wanted to say she had somebody. For some reason her daughter was desperate like that.

"That ain't his damn girlfriend." Lexi snapped.

"Well either way, it seems like my grand babies adore her and that's beautiful. It takes a village to raise children and you have a good one, daughter. Two moms means twice the love."

"Oh hell no!" Lexi hopped up and marched over to the pool. "Star, I need to talk to you right now!"

Star looked up at Lexi before looking over at Tati and Tamia who were on the edge of the pool. "Is she serious?" She laughed.

"I'm dead serious! Come on before I drag you out of this pool." She threatened.

Tamia looked on in shock because Lexi never got this hyped up. It was usually Nikka. However, Star didn't seem phased. She just smiled as if she were amused before sauntering out of the pool like a high paid supermodel.

"Let's go to the front of the house to talk." Star said indifferently before strutting off.

Tamia and Tati jumped up too. They weren't missing this. "Ana watch these kids, please."

Ana smirked because she knew her daughter was about to be humbled for once. "Gladly, baby."

"Where y'all going?" Tahj asked, fully alert as the girls walked past them to get to the back door. He was chopping it up by the cabanas with his brothers and some of his athlete clients who had daughters so they attended today. Even Lexi's husband was in the mix with them. Tahj could admit that he was a cool guy and he couldn't help but think that he deserved better than his baby mama. Not that Lexi wasn't a catch, it was just obvious she didn't really love ole Channing.

"Lexi wants to talk so we're stepping outside to the front of the house." Star answered simply before walking inside.

"Tahj if you know like I know, you'd follow us." Tamia urged.

Tahj and Channing took heed. Soon Tahj and all his siblings were outside. The only person who was in Lexi's corner was Channing and he was very confused about all this nonsense. Nikka was right there as well but she already decided this wasn't her fight. She'd fought Star before and lost, so her only hope was that Lexi could drag this bitch for the both of them.

"So what's the issue?" Star asked calmly. She paid their little audience no mind.

"You're my issue! I asked you not to come today out of respect for me and here you are!" Lexi yelled. She didn't care about the audience either because she was heated.

"Lexi this is me and Star's house, yea. How you gon say she can't be here?" Tahj asked while looking at her as if she were an idiot.

"Oop..."Choc instigated with light laughter. Meanwhile Nikka felt a dagger go through her heart. Apparently this living situation wasn't temporary or light like Tahj had made it seem in the past.

"But this is our daughter's party!" Lexi clamored.

"Okay and I'm very familiar with your daughter. She even called me earlier to ask where I was at. If we all love Tahja and want her to be happy then what's your problem?" Star questioned as if she were oblivious. She knew exactly what the problem was. She just wanted this bitch to say it in front of everybody, including her husband.

"Yea babe," Channing sighed. "This is all so unnecessary. I'm here and I'm not Tahja's biological father."

"But you're my husband!"

"Exactly. You have a whole fucking husband. So why are you so hard up to have a dry issue with me if you're so happy! One thing I can respect about Nikka is that she doesn't fake the funk. We all know she wants Tahj, but you are a different type of weird ass bitch. I'm not even fucking this man and you hoes stay in y'all feelings. You have an issue with what? Me treating your children with love and care?!" Star finally went off. "Bitch grow the fuck up. Aint you thirty something?!"

That right there hit a nerve. Lexi didn't even have a valid comeback because she'd just been read like a book, so she attempted to swing. She failed, but she did manage to get a good grip on Star's hair. That didn't derail Star because her hands were as free as a bird, so she put them to use.

"Damn!" Tarik gawked as Star pummeled into Lexi's face with skill and ease.

"Nah," Tahj pulled Channing back when he tried to break it up. "Let them rock for a minute."

Lexi couldn't believe her ears. He wanted them to fight even though she was getting beat up?! She didn't have long to ponder on her thoughts because Star body-slammed her into the ground, knocking all the wind out of her body.

"Bitch. Stop. Playing. With. Me. I. Tried. To.Be.Nice!" Star shouted like she was talking to one of her kids while still punching her in the face and across her dome.

"Alright. You got it." Tahj said once he saw blood being drawn from Lexi's mouth. He lifted Star off of her with ease and carried her into the house kicking and screaming.

"Oh God." Channing shook his head in embarrassment while standing over Lexi who just laid there like a dead body.

"Say, y'all not gon call them people, huh?" Tavior questioned. Channing was white after all and they were notorious cop callers.

"No. Lexi tried to hit her first." Channing knelt down to check on her forreal. "Well fuck me. I think she's unconscious."

"She alright," Tati rolled her eyes before pouring water on Lexi's face. She popped up quickly from playing possum. She was hoping someone would feel bad for her and call an ambulance. Then that bitch Star would go to jail. That didn't work out too well. Nikka looked on at the scene and knew from this day on trying Star would be good for neither of them. It was officially time to fall back.

Chapter 20

July 31, 2020

Star unboxed her new books with excitement. This summer she'd been in grind mode and she put out yet another successful children's book in June. After releasing that book she didn't take a break like she usually did. She went right back to work on a book geared to a new audience. Middle School and high school girls. The book was titled "Shoot for the Stars" and it was loosely based on her life. The book was going to be an ongoing series that guided girls through young womanhood. She basically wanted to show them through her writing that they could achieve anything despite their circumstances.

"Daddy can we order pizza?!" Star heard from the foyer.

Tahj had been gone for an entire week. She wasn't the only one who'd been working her ass off during the summer. With the kids out of school he had enough room to stick and move so he took advantage of that. With the NBA and NFL draft he picked up three new clients, so he was busy and the price was definitely going up. Everytime he was away he'd bring Star an extravagant gift back and she had started looking forward to them. Sometimes she questioned whether she was becoming a materialistic airhead, but she knew that wasn't the case. She was just falling in love with luxury and there was nothing wrong with that. After struggling for most of her life she deserved it.

She and Tahj weren't the only ones who'd been busy this summer. The kids had also been on the go. They were all in summer camp and the girls now had dance practice on Tuesdays and Thursdays. Tahja could go now too because she was five. Baby Tahj had started playing park football, so he had a hobby as well. Star was enjoying her alone time. Especially that day in particular. She was able to tie up a lot of loose ends for her upcoming birthday party slash book signing.

Star headed to the foyer to greet everybody. Tahj had picked up all the kids from summer camp after flying in. He had also picked up Suga from Colley's house. She called him during the week and he promised to get her when he got back to New Orleans.

After Star told them she cooked baked chicken and white beans with brownies for dessert, pizza was no longer in the discussion. They ran to the kitchen and Star followed to fix their plates. After they were all seated Star looked over at Tahj who was oddly quiet. Lately a sense of calmness surrounded him and it made her wonder what the hell he had going on. They had become close friends over the summer and it was able to stay in that space because they never spent too much time around each other. Star was grateful for that because she actually started to like and respect him again. Stil, she didn't know what was up with him. She wanted to ask but she didn't want to be intrusive.

"You hungry, Tahj?"

"Yea, but let me talk to you first."

"Okay." She replied, suddenly feeling nervous. She couldn't read him and that was unsettling.

They went to the den and sat on the couch.

"So where's my gift?" Star jested to make the atmosphere less tense.

Tahj cracked a smile, quickly letting her know that he wasn't upset about anything.

"Your birthday is in a few days. I'm saving the gifts until then."

"The gifts?" She repeated with a grin. "Okay then. I can definitely wait."

"Good, so what have you been up to this week?" The question felt loaded, but his delivery was chill.

"Nothing much. Just working and getting my shit together for my birthday."

"Yea I see your books came in." He looked at the boxes on the floor. "I gotta question though."

"Okay…"

"Who did you have here on Wednesday?"

Her heart dropped. She'd gone out for drinks with Brock on Wednesday and she got so twisted that he had to bring her home. He tried to come in, but even though she was drunk, she hadn't lost her mind. Brock wanted to fuck and usually she would've been down, drunk or not. But not at Tahj's house and in his bed. Yea it was practically her bed now but it was once his and they'd sexed in it more than once. Fucking another man in it would just be low. She allowed Brock to walk her to the door and she sent him on his way.

Unbeknownst to her Tahj saw this all on a camera he had installed on the side of his house to view the driveway. He wasn't able to see the man up close, but he saw a body leading Star up the walkway and then leaving.

"That was my friend and the only reason he brought me home was because I got drunk."

Tahj took a moment to think.

"Star I'm not mad or nothing, but I don't want no niggas coming to this house."

She frowned. "Isn't this *my* house too? I mean you always say that."

"I do. And because this is your house I would never bring another bitch here...Nikka and Lexi don't count." He added at the end already knowing she'd try to be smart and bring them up.

"I hear you, Tahj."

"Do you really?"

"Yea," she snapped.

"Don't catch an attitude with me, bruh. Especially when I'm not even doing the most. Keeping it all the way real, I don't like the fact that you dealing with somebody else. Then when I take in account of how your last situation with a nigga ended I really get drove. But you grown and single. I guess I gotta trust that you'll make better decisions this time around. All I ask is that you don't let niggas know where we stay, but I guess it's too late for that."

"Yea, my bad." She apologized. Now that he expressed himself further she realized that letting a man know where she stayed was a huge no-no after the C5 drama. Brock wasn't even that type of guy though, so everything would be fine.

"Just a heads up though, Tahj. I invited him to my party."

Tahj looked at her blankly before just laughing. "Man, we some dysfunctional ass people."

"Why you say that?"

"Because to the naked eye we're shaking up. Yet you invited your lil boyfriend to the same party my kids and family gone be at. That don't seem odd to you?"

"In hindsight, yea. But we know what it is, Tahj. I do my thing. You do yours. And before you say anything, yea, you don't bring girls around me, but I'm not stupid. I just feel like why be fake about it when everybody who's in our lives knows that we're not together like *that*."

"All that may be true, Star, but they know how we feel about each other."

"And how is that?" She laughed.

"Man look,"he dodged her question. "I don't have any problem with ole boy coming. You just make sure he doesn't have an issue with me attending either. I'll stay in my lane as long as he stays in his. I was just saying it might be a lil awkward. That's all."

"He's a chill guy. He won't be a problem."

"Cool,"he replied. "But I got another question."

"Yea?"

"How would you feel if I brought another woman around you?"

"I'll answer that when you tell me what it is you *think* we feel for each other."

"I don't think shit. I know we love each other."

"Okay so what was your question? How would I feel if you brought somebody else around me?"

She didn't acknowledge his response to her question because his answer was straight facts. He noticed how she ignore that but he let it slide.

"Yea."

"Okay I would probably be jealous, but there's nothing I would be able to do."

"This shit makes no sense."

"Huh?"

"You heard me, girl. If we both don't want to see eachother with the next muthafucker and we love eachother, then what are we doing?"

"I don't think love is enough."

Tahj felt like someone kneed him in the gut. She was straight up saying she loved him but a relationship with him wasn't something she wanted to explore. He could always count on Star to humble his ass.

"Can I ask why not?"

"Tahj do you really think you can be in a monogamous relationship?"

"I mean…I can try." He said, sounding unsure. He was willing to be all about Star. He just wasn't confident about relationships because he'd always sucked at them. He was second guessing himself for sure but he knew that he wanted to be with her.

She giggled. "When you can say that with confidence I'll consider it. Actually saying it will never be enough. You gotta *show* me."

"Show you how?"

"If I tell you it won't be genuine."

"Alright, Star," he shook his head. This girl was too much of a challenge, but he could handle it. "Last question."

"Damn nigga…"

"I know," he chuckled. "But this one is serious."

"Let's hear it."

"Alright, you know how we talked about me talking to somebody?"

"Yea."

"Well I've been going to therapy for about two months now and I think it's really helping. No cap."

Star smiled brightly before standing up to hug him. "That's great, Tahj. Forreal. I'm so happy for you."

"Thank you, but my question is can you come to one of my sessions with me? If you don't want to I understand, but my therapist said it'll help if somebody I trust sits in with me. I would ask one of my siblings but they don't know about me and your Aunti-"

"Shhhh," she put her finger to his lips. "Just tell me a date and I'm there."

August 3, 2020

"That food was good." Brock voiced as he opened Star's door for her.

"It always is."

Katie's was a small, uptown restaurant but the food was undeniable. Her shrimp po boy with oysters on the side had hit the spot, and now she was ready to go home and take a nap.

"You ain't never lied, so you excited for your party this weekend?"

Star's actual birthday was on August 5th and that day fell on a Wednesday, so she was having her party the following Saturday. She wasn't planning on doing anything special on her birthday beyond self care.

"Of course. I think the kids are more excited than me though," she laughed as she thought about how Baby Tahj had sent her options of what he should wear. She didn't have a hard core theme but her decor was going to be her favorite colors; yellow and orange. She'd hired a decorator to bring her vision to life so she knew it would be great. She wasn't expecting anything less due to the fact that she never had birthday parties.

"That's cool that you're allowing them to come. Most adults don't allow kids to come to their parties."

"I know," she giggled. "I just can't imagine not spending my birthday with my babies though."

"What about they daddy?"

"What about him?"

"Is he going to be there?"

"I told you he might come a while back, Brock. He's definitely coming though."

"But why?"

"Why not? We have no beef."

"Do you hear yourself? Do you really think I'm about to be in the same room as your baby daddy? What makes you think he'll be cool with being in the same room as me?"

"Look I already told him you're coming and he's cool with it. I'm not with Tahj and we don't have anything going on. It shouldn't be awkward at all. And if you really want to be with me then there'll be a time where you have to be in the same room as my kid's father. Hell, I gotta be around his baby mama's all the time."

"Yea, and that's clearly clouded your judgment. Got you thinking that certain shit is normal when it's really just a ratchet ass mess. This nigga got *three* baby mamas and y'all gotta co-exist for the sake of him."

Star was officially turned off. What the fuck was this fool talking about?

"We don't do *shit* for him. Our kids are family and they deserve to grow up together. And I don't play nice with anybody. I'm cordial at best but it's really no reason for me to be beefed out with his other two baby mama's. None of us are dealing with him."

"And you crazy if you think that."

"Okay, Brock. I'll be crazy but I really don't care. Tahj is going to be at my party and that's final."

"That's final, huh? Bet." He nodded with a hard scowl, looking like a little boy. She was starting to remember why she never gave this nigga her all back then. He could be the sweetest and nicest guy ever until she didn't give him his way. It was sickening.

Star began scrolling through her phone when Don't Make it Harder on Me by Chloe X Halle started playing from her phone, notifying her that she had an incoming call from Tahj. It wasn't really an appropriate time to answer considering she and Brock just had a small argument with him at the center, but this call could've been about her kids. That took precedence over a nigga's hurt feelings.

"Yea?"

"Where you at?"

"Ummm, just leaving Katie's."

There was a pause on the other end. If she didn't volunteer the information about who she was with then it was obvious it was that nigga. That nigga he still didn't have a name or face for. He would find out soon though.

"You still coming with me today to my session? It starts in an hour."

Star had totally spaced out and forgot.

"Of course I'm coming," she played it off. "I'm about to get dropped off to my car now."

"Okay, see you in a few. Love you."

"Love you too." She ended the call.

"BITCH IS YOU SERIOUS?!" Brock shouted. It was so abrupt that she jumped in her seat. "You so fucking disrespectful!"

Star could admit that she was out of line although that wasn't her intention. While speaking with Tahj she forgot Brock was there even though she was riding shotgun in his ride. Maybe Tahj was right. Seeing other people made no sense for either of them. She was stringing this man along. It didn't start that way at all, but it gradually grew into that. She liked him but she didn't have a strong desire to be with him. He was just cool and that would never be enough. Now with that being said she still wasn't going to tolerate being called out of her name.

"Who the fuck are you talking to?"

"The bitch who just answered a phone for another nigga in my ride! And what the fuck is that ringtone you have set for him?!"

"Okay, this is my phone, and my baby daddy called. I'ma always answer for him no matter where I'm at because it could be about my kids. You don't have children so you don't understa-"

"Fuck allat! You want be with that nigga! The only reason you entertaining me is because he don't want you!"

Star laughed obnoxiously at that absurd statement. "Brock you really don't know the half. I've been living with this man for months and he's begged for us to wor-"

"Wait, what? You live with that nigga?! Why is this the first time I'm hearing of this?"

"Maybe you don't pay attention because it's never been a secret."

Brock pulled over on the side of the road and unlocked the car. "Get out."

"What?" She asked in disbelief.

"You heard me, man. Get out my shit. I never want to hear from your hoe ass again."

Star thought about screaming obscenities or whooping his ass, but it simply wasn't that deep.

"Ya know what, baby? Gladly." She laughed before sliding out of his car while looking like a million bucks. She was dressed from head to toe in a casual Chanel ensemble that Tahj bought her.

Brock drove off like a bat out of hell. He was pissed off that she didn't put up more of a fight. He'd always thought she cared about them.

"Hello?" Tahj answered his phone on the first few rings for Star.

"Come get me, please."

"I thought you was getting dropped off to your car? Where you at?"

"I was. The nigga I was with got mad and threw me out. I'm in the Magnolia but I'm walking towards Claiborne Avenue. I'm sharing my location with you now."

"Man, are you serious?! Say Star, if that nigga come to your party I'm whooping his ass. I put that on my kids!"

"Tahj that nigga can choke for all I care. He showed his true colors today."

Star could say *a lot* about Tahj because he was flawed as fuck, but he'd never leave her stranded in the projects or anywhere for that matter. She guessed the "nice guy" wasn't so nice after all.

"I'm on my way to you now. Stay on the phone."

"O…kay."

Star thought she was seeing things when C5 stepped in front of her with a sinister smile. But he was right there in the flesh. Unbeknownst to her he'd just gotten out of jail after being there since the spring for battery charges brought onto him by his baby mama. Now he was back and with a vengeance. He hadn't forgotten how this bitch Star played him. With her heavy social media presence he knew it would be a matter of time before he ran into her. He definitely wasn't expecting it to be a sheer coincidence. He had been in the Magnolia visiting one of his hoes and he saw her walking down the street. This was just too good.

"Star, what's wrong with you?" Tahj questioned when he heard her voice change.

"Tah-"

"Tell Tahj it's finally time for you to answer to me!" He said before he grabbed her phone and threw it. Several people were outside but C5 didn't care. He was hyped up off of pills and alcohol. This bitch would die today if it was up to him. Hell his baby mama had already died this morning.

"Ahhhh!" Star screamed as he grabbed her by her hair. People saw what was happening but getting involved wasn't something they were going to do. It appeared to be a domestic dispute and people around here stayed out of those.

Tahj was already uptown when Star first called, so he pulled up to the scene as C5 was about to start wailing into Star's face.

He threw his car into park and hopped out with his gun cocked. Beating this niggas ass until he died crossed his mind, but it would be harder to plead self defense if he did that. So he was shooting.

Lucky for him he had the perfect shot because Star's head was down. He fired his gun and the bullet went straight between C5's eyes. Blood splattered everywhere, most of it landing on Star. She screamed as C5 hit the ground with a loud thud before running straight into Tahj's arms. This couldn't be life.

Chapter 21

August 5, 2020

Year 26. Star thought it would be the best one yet, but the days leading up to it had her thinking she was in over her head. After killing C5, Tahj was arrested, despite Star hysterically explaining that he was only protecting her. She was crying so hard that the police just assumed that she was an upset girlfriend crying about her man going down for murder in broad daylight.

That was until the people who sat back and watched the scene bravely came forward as witnesses. They backed up Star's story and some young kid had even recorded how C5 had been manhandling Star prior to Tahj pulling up. The witnesses' testimonies were written down and taken into account, but they still had to question Tahj. So Star pulled herself together and called his family. She felt a large sum of guilt for getting him into this mess when he'd never had a run in with the law to this magnitude. She thought his family would look at her sideways but they rushed to her side for support. Tarik called his lawyer ASAP.

With the evidence and one look at C5's criminal history his lawyer already knew Tahj would walk freely. However, he didn't see another victory falling into his lap. In the midst of the interrogation they were interrupted with news about how C5 had killed his babymama that morning. That was further confirmation that Tahj had only been defending Star from a lunatic. A few hours later they finally released him with no charges. Everyone was relieved and happy. Star was as well, but she still felt pretty shitty about the whole ordeal. Now it was her birthday and she was in the same funk. When she turned on the bright lamp that rested on the nightstand in the pitch black dark room, her heart swelled up.

Gold and red balloons were all over the ceiling and red roses covered every inch of the room in pretty gold vases. The door squeaked open.

"You decent?" Tahj asked.

She nodded through tearful eyes, and before she knew it the whole damn world was entering the room. Tahj held a delicious breakfast on a tray, Diamond carried a small rosette birthday cake that was lit up, and Tahj's sisters, Colley, and the kids sang happy birthday. Star couldn't contain herself as she cried tears of joy.

"Mommy what's wrong? You're not that old," Tahiry rubbed her shoulder, making everybody laugh. Even Star.

"She's crying tears of joy. Right?" Tahj asked.

She sniffled while nodding. "I really love y'all. Thank you so much. I feel like I don't even need a party after all this."

"Girl, don't be silly," Choc laughed. "There's no such thing as celebrating too much."

"Yea because the whole month of June belongs to me and Mia." Tati giggled while slapping hands with Tamia.

"Make your first wish, sis." Diamond urged while holding the cake out in front of her. He felt like shit for not being there to protect Star when it mattered the most, but he had unlocked a new level of respect for Tahj. He didn't hesitate to bust his gun for Star. Despite all the shit his sister had talked, Tahj was definitely a real ass nigga. Diamond was just happy that somebody had off'd C5 even though it wasn't him. He had enough shit on his plate anyway, so a murder case was the last thing he needed. Tahj was clean as a whistle down to the weapon he used, so he was able to kill the nigga and get off scotch free.

When Star blew out her candles all she wished for was love, peace, and happiness. She already had some of that in her life but she needed it in abundance now.

"What you wished for Star?" Tahja asked.

"Her can't tell you," Suga uttered.

"Alright, y'all come on and get out Star's face so she can get up and get her day started." Talea laughed while escorting the babies out. Everybody else left the room as well except Tahj. He sat Star's breakfast on her lap.

"The chef came over this morning?" She asked while eyeing her chocolate chip pancakes.

"No. I whipped that up myself."

"Really?" She laughed.

"Yea, really. I can cook, yea." He chuckled. "You feeling better today?"

"Now I am."

He smiled. "That was our collective goal. To make you smile."

"Y'all succeeded."

"Just know you ain't seen nothing yet."

"Tahj are you okay?" She asked while looking into his eyes.

He appeared confused. "I'm straight. Why wouldn't I be?"

"C'mon…do I have to spell it out?"

"Oh you talking about me popping that nigga?" He asked with zero remorse. "Because I'd do it a million times for you. I'm not sorry about shit."

"I don't expect you to be sorry, but damn. You took a whole life. It doesn't make you feel any type of way?"

"I mean, it's a wild thing. I ain't no cold hearted killer. But the only way I would feel fucked up on the inside right now is if something happened to you."

Goosebumps formed all over her body.

"I just feel bad that all this happened because of me and my choi-"

"Star this shit is not your fault. I've fucked with my fair share of crazy bitches too and it could've gone left at any time. I know you never wanted none of this shit to happen. But it's over now, and we can move on." He stood up, bent down, and pecked her lips lovingly. "Eat your breakfast and then get dressed. We got a full day ahead of us."

All of that was music to Star's ears. It was over and she was ready to move on. Happiness, peace, and love was the only thing she was accepting for year 26.

———————————

August 8, 2020

Tahj was right. Star hadn't seen anything yet. Her actual birthday had been great by itself. She had a spa day right in Tahj's basement with all the ladies and then she had dinner at the house that looked like a real party. Tahj had hired a professional decorator to transform his dining room and it was almost unrecognizable. After dinner he presented her with an icy Diamond charm bracelet that was extremely personal to her. Her favorite charm on the bracelet was a heart shaped picture of her mom. He also got her a brown Birkin bag. She had to twerk in excitement after opening that Hermès box. She never even thought of owning one because they weren't accessible to the average person. It was safe to say that after Wednesday she was *good* and didn't need shit else.

Choc's theory was accurate though. There was no such thing as too much celebrating. Her party was showing her that. She did an hour of signing books and she wanted to cry. Readers came from all over to celebrate her. She'd done book events before but they always included other authors. This was the first major thing she'd done on her own, so she had been nervous. It was safe to say that the turnout had exceeded her expectations.

Now the party was in full swing and she'd been dancing all night. She was on Dussé so she was lit and she couldn't see anything bringing her down. Everything today had worked in her favor from the actual party down to her look. The yellow two piece skirt set that she got custom made consisted of an asymmetrical crop top with a mini skirt and long train that fit her like a glove. She topped the look off with gold Gianvito Rossi heels and the charm bracelet Tahj got her. Talea had blown her hair out and gave her a gorgeous updo. The bun was sleek and the two pieces of hair left out framed her face perfectly. Sometimes professional makeup scared her because it had the potential to be clown-like but her glamorous gold and yellow beat was beautiful.

"*I'm a pretty pretty black b-tch with a bad -ss demeanor. Pockets on fat; p-ssy on aquafina. I make it floody call me hurricane katrina. We get along like we Martin and Gina. We forever y'all could never come between us. Past b-tches hating you know hoes love to team up...*"

The DJ blasted the clean version of Reedy's "Get Use to This" but it didn't stop Star from cursing like a sailor. She'd ask the kids for forgiveness tomorrow, but she wasn't censoring herself for the remainder of the night. When the beat dropped she bent over and shook her rump in a circle.

"Let's go cousinnnn!!!" Colley screamed while recording her on Instagram live.

Tamia ran up out of nowhere with a fresh strawberry Long Island in her hand and she bent over next to Star and started going to town. As small as she was in comparison to Star she had no problem keeping up with her booty work.

"Tamia your daughter here!" Noel tried to pull her up. Beyond tipsy, she turned around and started shaking her ass on him. He couldn't do anything but laugh.

Tahj stood back and shook his head as Star continued to cut up. She was now squating and riding an imaginary dick to another explicit bounce song. Sure, the dj was playing the clean version to everything but bounce music was so raunchy bleeping out the curse words didn't help much. It was a good thing that the kids were having a grand ole time in the kiddy section that Star insisted on. There was a ball bit, a space walk, and slides. The kids weren't the only ones enjoying that area. About thirty minutes ago Star had climbed her drunk ass in the ball pit. Tahj knew she was past her limit when she started screaming she was drowning.

"Oh shit! Star, you gotta teach me that!" Tavior's girlfriend Jamaya hollered as she watched Star roll her hips and then bounce one ass cheek at a time to "No Guidance."

Tahj scowl hardened at the sexual moves she was putting on display. He wanted her to have fun, but damn.

"Man, you just had Tavior Junior this summer. You don't need to learn any more tricks." Tarik jested.

"Bae your brother hating on us," Jamaya snitched to Tavior as he walked up with two drinks. He handed her one.

"What's new? That nigga always hating." Tavior laughed. He had a nice buzz going from the liquor and an edible.

It seemed like everybody was under the influence except Tahj. He'd indulged in a little alcohol but he wanted to be the sober one if everybody else was going to be fucked up.

"Freaky...I can learn a lot from you, gotta come teach me. You a lil' hot girl, you a lil' sweetie. Sweet like Pearland, sweet like Peachtree. I can tell you crazy, but shit kind of intrigue me. Seen it on the 'Gram, I'm tryna see that shit in 3D, mami. I know I get around 'cause I like to move freely. But you could lock it down, I could tell by how you treat me....."

Star ticked her waistline to the beat as it slowed down with her eyes closed. Yea, she definitely needed more nights like this before the summer officially ended.

"Aye!"

Star stopped twerking right in her tracks because it sounded like God was calling out to her. When she looked up she saw it was just Tahj's ass standing over her. He forcefully pulled her up.

"I could see your fucking underwear. Relax." He gritted into her ear. His anger combined with his warm breath in her ear made her coochie tingle. If she were sober she would've cursed him out, but she was drunk and very much horny. Or maybe the liquor was giving her the balls to do what she always wanted to do; fuck on him.

She wrapped her arms around his neck. "Let's get out of here so I can ride that dick until I fall asleep."

"Mannn…"he laughed. "Calm your drunk ass down. You ain't even cut your cake yet."

"Fuck that cake."

"So you want to leave right now?"

"You don't?" She shot back a lust filled stare.

"No."

Her heart dropped when he removed her arms from around him.

"No?!" She questioned with her hand on her hip. She knew damn well this nigga wasn't denying her.

"Not until you get your gift."

"Tahj what are you tal-"

Tahj looked over at the DJ and gave him the signal. Star grew nervous when the music got lower and the DJ asked everyone to make their way outside.

"You good sis?" Diamond laughed as Star stumbled for the umpteenth time while walking to the door.

"Hell no she not good. Take them damn shoes off before you break your ankle." Tahj ordered.

"My mama always said a lady never takes her heels off in public." She slurred, resulting in everybody within an earshot to laugh. Tahj shook his head and swooped her up bridal style as if she were light as a feather. Star wrapped her arms around his neck and rested her head on his shoulder. Admittedly she enjoyed being babied.

"Is mommy okay?" Tahiry asked as she and the rest of her siblings caught up with the adults.

"See, now you got my kids worrying." Tahj chuckled.

"Mama alright, baby." Star voiced, but she didn't even know who she was talking to.

"Aw shit, cousin. I think you might want to lift your head up and see this shit." Cordell urged. He was Colley's older brother. They were the only two of Fee's kids who had the same father and it showed. They were cut from a completely different cloth than their mom and other brothers. Cordell now lived in Houston Texas with his wife and two kids where he was a dentist. He absolutely hated New Orleans but he'd always make a trip for his father, Colley, or Star.

Star's head sprung up and she immediately jumped out of Tahj's arms. Suddenly she was stable. The scenery had undoubtedly sobered her up just a tad. *Two* of the cars that were on her vision board at home sat outside the Nola skyline building. A midnight blue Tesla and a black Rolls-Royce Wraith.

She turned to Tahj with her heart beating so fast she thought she'd pass out. "I gotta pick between these two?"

"Pick?!" He repeated incredulously. "Girl, stop playing with me."

He handed her both sets of key fobs. That resulted in her screaming and jumping over to her cars. As she looked at the inside of both cars for the first time all the kids were right on her trail.

"I'm so glad we got this car, Star. Look, it's stars in the ceiling." Baby Tahj pointed up.

"I know. It's nice." Tahja said.

"Yea. But daddy we need a big truck so everybody can fit!" True hollered from the back seat. Everybody shared a laugh because she sounded very serious.

"You right, baby girl. We need another family car." Tahj said, feeding into her foolishness.

Talea and Choc locked eyes with knowing smirks. Their brother's nose was wide open in a way they'd never seen before. They'd seen him be in relationships with Nikka and Lexi, so they knew he had a giving heart, but it had *never* been this excessive. Between the diamond charm bracelet, the Birkin bag, the two uber expensive cars, *and* the gift he'd yet to present her with he had to spend more than half a mil. He had that and then some to spare, but it was still surreal to witness. In their opinion Star deserved it. They didn't know everything but they could see a big difference in their brother since she'd been around. He seemed a lot calmer and settled down in life.

"What's this?" Star asked as Tahj handed her an envelope.

"I don't know. Open it and see."

She stared at him long and hard. Her heart couldn't take anymore damn gifts.

"Open it mommy!!!" Tahiry begged.

"Yea let's see what we got." Jari added.

"No this one is just for Star, y'all." Tahj chuckled.

"No fair." True crossed her arms.

Star decided to stop driving herself crazy and tore the envelope open. She pulled out two plane tickets and quickly scanned them. She looked back up at Tahj in shock. This was a complete surprise.

"We leave for Dubai on Monday?!"

Brock had a feeling he should've stayed away, but his guilty conscience wouldn't let him. He'd been trying to contact Star since the day after he left her stranded but he was blocked. His next step was hitting her up through social media but she'd blocked him on that too. So now he was taking a big risk by showing up to her birthday party. His plan was to sneak in with his gift and talk to her privately. He wasn't trying to be seen for one major reason alone. It was the reason why that dumbass argument in his car had started in the first place. Tahj.

"Who's that?" Diamond asked as he saw a body walking towards them from a distance. Him, Tahj, Tarik, and Tavior had stayed outside to smoke after everyone went back in after Star got her gifts.

"I don't know but they look scared." Tavior acknowledged when he saw the nigga stop dead in his tracks. It appeared as if he were hesitant about walking towards the entrance since people were standing there.

Tahj stuck his neck out to make sure his eyes were seeing correctly.

"Brock?!" He walked forward.

Realizing that laying low was no longer an option, Brock ambled forward as well. Now that Tahj could see him clearly, he was bewildered. The fuck was this nigga doing here?

"What's up, Tahj?" Brock held his hand out.

Tahj looked down at it, refusing to hide his disdain. Something fishy was going on here. He hesitantly dapped Brock off.

"The fuck you doing here, nigga?" He questioned.

"Ummm," he scratched his head. "I'm a friend of Star's."

"A friend? Nigga you know this my baby mama right? Instagram could tell you that much."

Star was featured regularly on Tahj's story and Brock was always in his views.

"Yea, I know. I met her way back in college though."

Tahj relaxed a little. "Oh so y'all really just friends?"

"I meannnn…"

Just as he was about to cut the bullshit and just keep it all the way real, Star stepped outside with Tati on her heels. They were giggling hysterically about something that wasn't even that funny.

"Can y'all come on?! We ready to sing happy birthda-"

Star's smile dropped when she saw Brock. He told her to stay away from *him*, so why would he think it was okay to show his face at her party? Especially after he left her stranded.

"Sis, you know this nigga? He claims y'all friends?" Tarik questioned. To him this shit was shady. Brock was someone who damn near begged Tahj to represent him years back. Tahj turned it down because his load was too big at the time to take on an average baller like Brock.

"We ain't no fucking friends! I don't know why his bitch ass is here!" She went in. The alcohol had her more turnt up then she would have normally been, but the way she felt was real.

"My bitch ass?!" Brock repeated in embarrassment. If this was how it was going to be he could play the same game. "No I'm not that, I'm your other baby daddy."

Tahj's breath left his body as he felt like someone had cut off his circulation.

"You pregnant for this nigga?!" He howled at Star.

Star smacked her teeth, showing she didn't care about what Brock had just blurted out.

"Tahj I've been drinking all night," she reminded him. He immediately felt silly. "Now I *was* pregnant for him in college, but I was at the clinic so fast to get rid of that baby. This nigga aint shit to me but a waste of time with weak ass dick."

"But you been taking this dick all summer, bitch!"

BAM!

Tahj punched Brock right in the jaw. Blood went everywhere and a tooth flew from his mouth making Star grimace in pain as if he'd punched her.

"This the nigga that left you stranded in the Nolia?" Diamond asked.

"Yup."

Diamond ran up and started punching on Brock too. He tried fighting back but he couldn't take Tahj and Diamond by themselves let alone together. When Tahj clocked him in the nose and his vision went blurry, he knew it was time to get the fuck. He backed up before literally sprinting across the parking lot to get to his car and away from them. It was time to leave Star's ass in the past. He couldn't take anymore ass whoopings like that.

"Weak ass nigga,"Tahj muttered. He looked over at Star. Her heart skipped a beat because she didn't know what he was going to say to her.

"Let's go sing happy birthday." He grabbed her arm and pulled her inside, shocking the hell out of her.

Chapter 22

August 11, 2020

Star turned away from the light that was shining brightly in her face. They'd gotten to Dubai yesterday and the jet lag was *real*. Tahj was handling it like a beast because he was used to major time differences with all the traveling he did. He allowed Star to sleep in last night and most of that day, but now it was time for her to get up. She couldn't sleep the entire trip away. He had great things planned for her.

He shook her body after turning on all the lights. "Come on and wake up. You promised to suck my dick."

Star's eyes flew open. "Boy don't fucking play with me!"

"Glad you're up." He laughed. She fell for his little trick just like he knew she would.

She smacked her teeth. "You play too much."

"Nah, that's you. You don't remember begging to suck my dick?"

"Tahj I'm about two seconds away from slapping you." She warned.

"Slap me for what? It's not my fault you got faded on your birthday and made promises you didn't follow through on."

Tahj thought for sure he was getting some pussy on the night of Star's party, but the more she drank led him to dead that notion. When the party was over he had to carry her out. She was whispering shit in his ear about how she wanted to suck the skin off his dick and ride his face, but he knew it was all cap. Yea, she may have wanted to do all that but she was in no shape to do it. His point was proven when she passed on the backseat of his car two minutes into the ride home. She had blacked out.

That Sunday they spent all day packing and Tahj presented her with more gifts. This time it was outfits for the trip and she was shocked at how good he did. That's when he admitted that his sisters had actually done the shopping. She still appreciated the gesture.

"Don't use the fact that I was drunk to your advantage by making shit up." She stifled a grin. She remembered talking freaky to him, but she wanted to let his mind wander a bit. As soon as she recharged her energy she was hoping right on his dick and showing out. With the way he came through for her he deserved it. She also deserved some birthday sex.

"Girl get your lying ass up and get ready so we can start our day." He laughed before pulling the covers back. She wore nothing but a plain white t-shirt and boy shorts. Tahj had half a mind to pin her to the bed and fuck her silly right then, but then the rest of the day would be down the drain. Sex could wait. They were in Dubai until Saturday.

"What should I put on?" She asked as she watched him ogle her booty.

"Swimwear." He slapped her ass before wiggling it with his hand. "Why you so fine?"

"Boy, move." She laughed as she climbed out the bed.

About an hour later Star was ready and feeling cute as hell. She donned a basic pink two piece bikini with a sheer, polka dot cardigan, a big cream Chanel straw bag with the matching slippers, and a floppy cream hat. Since she was going to be near water she opted for a natural beat. On Sunday night Talea gave her passion twists that reached the top of her butt, so her hair was ready for the water too.

She couldn't resist snapping pictures of herself in the huge mirror that covered the wall in the master bathroom. Tahj walked in to see if she was almost done, but when he saw her taking pictures he slid right in. He coordinated perfectly with her by wearing brown Gucci swim trunks, a brown and white logo tee, and matching slides. He rocked his signature Diamond chain that featured the kids and a flooded out AP watch.

"You better post the ones with me in them too." Tahj ordered as they exited the bathroom.

"I'll think about it." She giggled.

"You look good." Tahj voiced, not being able to keep his eyes off of her.

She turned around and flashed a smile. "Thank youuu. You like the bag? This trick ass nigga got it for me. His old ass loves spoiling me."

"Alright," he licked his lips. "Now I see you wanna get slapped."

"What's the issue?" She laughed hysterically. "You do love spoiling me."

"But it ain't trickin 'because I got it. And I ain't old, either."

"Nigga please. Ain't you knocking on forty?"

He laughed. "Nah, but you definitely knocking on thirty."

She gasped before rushing to him and swinging.

"So now you don't want to play, grandma?"

"Go to hell," she giggled before knocking him upside his head playfully.

"Girl bring your ass on." He said as he pulled her towards the back of the house.

"Tahj we really should've brought the family with us. This is too much house for just us two."

There were no words to describe the upscale mansion that sat on the beach. Star was just happy to call this place home for a week, but she really wished their kids could experience this too.

"I thought I was giving you a break by leaving the kids out." He chuckled.

"Well it has been nice to just sleep." She admitted. "But they would've loved this."

"Yea." Tahj agreed. "We should take them to Disney World before they go back to school."

"They would love that." She smiled.

When they exited through the back door, Tahj led her past the pool and down to the beach. Star's heart almost popped out of her chest when she saw what he was bringing her to. A beautiful lunch had been set up on the beach on a platform in the water.

"This is sooo nice," she gushed as she stepped up on the platform. She politely greeted the servers who stood close by as Tahj pulled out her chair for her. An elaborate spread of Arabian food was already on the table, but the servers came and poured them drinks of their choice and they fixed their plates. When they were done, they stepped off the platform to give them some privacy.

"Hmmmm, this is so good. I wonder what this is." Star expressed as she dug into her food.

"Don't ask. Just enjoy it." Tahj chuckled.

"Shit you might be right," she laughed. "You ever been here?"

"Yea, just once with Tarik and Tavior. It was Tav's 22nd birthday."

"Oh so it was a thot trip." She concluded.

Tahj laughed before shrugging. "Yea, I guess you could say that. You ever had a thot trip?"

"You think I had time for thot trips with two daughters?" She questioned.

"Shit you was pregnant with another nigga baby with two daughters. Clearly my babies ain't stop you from living."

"That was nothing." She rolled her eyes.

"You call letting a nigga skeet in you nothing?"

"You've skeeted in a lot of bitches to know, huh?"

He sucked his teeth. "Alright, flip it on me."

"Ya damn right I will. Cause you can't ask me about that when you was fucking three bitches raw at the same time. Nasty ass."

"I was young and dumb. And in my mind I was gonna stick around to take care of my responsibilities so it was okay. Doesn't that sound crazy?"

"Entirely."

"So you was in love with Brock?"

He knew it wasn't his business and he had no right to ask her about that time in her life. He just wanted to know though. His mind couldn't rest until he got answers.

Star laughed because he obviously wasn't letting this go.

"He was what I needed at that time in my life and I grew to love him…"

His heart plummeted.

"As a friend," she continued, bringing him instant relief.

"So you was letting a friend hit it raw, huh?"

"I was young and dumb," she smirked, throwing his line back in his face.

"Ok, you got that." He chuckled.

"I know I do, witcha mad ass."

"Girl I ain't mad. I'm just jealous. I'll get over it though."

"Please do because at the end of the day I only carried your big headed ass babies. Shit if anybody has the right to be jealous it's me. I was never your only baby mama."

"Being somebody's baby mama holds no weight anyway. Neither does being a baby daddy."

"Oh yea?" She asked. "Then why are you so pressed about another nigga getting me pregnant?

"Girl I'm pressed about the thought of another nigga touching you, period. That don't have shit to do with the twins and everything to do with how I feel about you."

"So you think we would still be here today if the twins didn't exist?"

He chuckled. "Probably not, and that's only because you would have no ties to me. You would've been able to say fuck me and my bullshit with no strings attached. So I guess I better thank God for the twins bringing you back into my life."

She gave him her middle finger, making him laugh harder.

"Forreal though, if the twins didn't exist I'm sure life would've brought us back together somehow. What's meant to be will always be no matter the circumstances."

"And what's meant to be, Tahj?"

"Us being together."

"Are you ready for that? For me, I mean."

"I been ready for you."

She scoffed. "I beg to fucking differ."

He laughed. "My heart been ready, man. I just never knew how to say it and I wa-"

"You were wilding," she finished for her. "I'm never going to tolerate fuck shit. If it's me and you then it's just me and you. They'll be no outsiders."

"That's perfectly fine with me. Fuck everybody. It's me and you."

"And you're sure you can handle that?"

The third degree was a given. Tahj's whorish ways had broken Star's heart years ago. She had a right to question if he could really be faithful.

"I'm almost 32, Star. I've been around enough to know that I've had enough. What about you? Are you ready to settle down with me?"

"It's not a question of if I'm ready. It's a question of if I can trust you with my heart."

"So let's work on building trust." He suggested. He was prepared to have a solution for anything she threw at him.

"We can work on that."

"Seriously?"

"Seriously." She giggled.

"Come here." He lifted from his seat and grabbed her by the throat from across the table. He kissed her deeply. He wasn't fucking this up this time and that was on everything he loved.

After lunch they went for a walk on the beach and then played around in the water for a little while. The next thing on Tahj's itinerary was a popular hookah spot that night, so they had plenty of free time. They headed back to the house where they could chill poolside for more privacy. It had been Tahj's suggestion and Star could immediately see why. They had been laying on the pool day bed for all of ten seconds and his tongue was already down her throat.

"Damn I missed this." He expressed huskily while gripping on her ass. Her cheeky swimsuit had turned into a thong with the way he was playing with her booty.

"Show me how much you missed it." She challenged before biting his bottom lip.

That was all he needed to hear. Seconds later she was on all fours while he licked her feverishly from the back. Star moaned as loudly as she wanted to because Tahj had music playing loudly from his phone. Her moans blended in perfectly with the melodic sounds of Dvsn. She arched her back and squealed as Tahj ran his firm tongue up her ass crack. He could get so nasty and she loved it.

"Just keeps us apart when we should be starting to keep our promises, we could be promisin'. You say I'm closed off. Let's open up and take our clothes off. I don't want nothing in between us. Nothing there to stop the feeling. I don't want nothing in between us. Got me thinking this might be love...."

Nothing was between them, alright. They were skin to skin as he slid into her. There was no barrier to hold them back. This was the real thing.

"Yesss, fuck me just like that." Star moaned while clutching his back.

He was stroking her so long and hard that he was touching her soul. This was exactly why she could never just have sex with him casually with no strings attached. Their souls were already tied. Casual sex between them was dangerous. But this type of love making? It was perfect. There was nothing else better out there for either of them and they were finally accepting that.

"*Just keep it honest, we made some promises. They got opinions, but that won't change a thing. We got each other, let's shut the world up and take our clothes off, baby, yeah. I don't want nothing in between us. Nothing there to stop the feeling....*" Snoh Aalegra crooned as Tahj struggled to hold on.

"I'm finna bust, baby. Where you want me to bust at?"

Star knew what he wanted her to say, so she went for the opposite.

"Down my throat. Let me swallow it, daddy." She begged.

He wanted to let loose deep in that pussy, but she had never given him head. He wasn't about to let this sweet opportunity pass him by. When she took him into her pretty mouth he was satisfied with the decision he'd made. She was slurping him up sloppily but with precision. She was determined.

"Fuckkkk!" He stressed as she played with his balls resulting in his toes curling.

"Shit Star!" He groaned as her head started moving at a rapid pace up and down his dick. He was almost there.

"What are you doing?!" Star asked after he ripped her mouth off his dick. She didn't have to wait for an answer because he showed her by sitting her body on his rock hard dick. Before she could attempt riding him, he gripped her cheeks firmly and pummeled into her.

"YESSSSS!" She screamed as she came on his dick.

"That's right, cum on this dick!" He encouraged as his back went stiff. "Aw shit, Star! Damn I fucking love you."

Star couldn't do anything but sit there and take all the nut he was skeeting into her. Normally she would've been worried, but the plan b's she'd tucked in her suitcase had her at ease. He could fill her up for the rest of the trip if he wanted to.

Chapter 23

September 19, 2020

Star was truly amazed at how great the twins' 7th birthday party had come together. Right after she and Tahj got back from Dubai they started planning it. The girls had their very own theme park called "Twin World" in a huge empty lot that Tahj owned.

Star had gotten the idea to do an amusement park party from Kylie Jenner and her daughter, Stormi. Of course she figured they'd do a downsized version of the party at city park or something, but Tahj was quick to tell her that he only did it big. She could see that, but she also felt like he was over doing it because it was the first birthday he was experiencing with the twins. Out of guilt she was allowing him to do the most with no back talk, and boy did he take full advantage of that. It was safe to say that the twins' party could go head to head with Stormi's and come out on top. Just like hers theirs was under a gigantic tent that was separated into three sections; Fancy Nancy World, Lol Surprise World, and Twin World. Each section had games, rides, and gift shops. Everything was also super detailed from the labels on the food boxes down to pictures of the twins all over the floors. Star's mind was reeling at how much all of this cost and she didn't spend a dime. She tried to pitch in but Tahj wasn't having it. She thought she'd gotten away with buying the girls custom made pink Dior outfits, but Tahj ended up reimbursing her for that too. She just gave up and let him have it.

"You saw this?" Colley smirked while showing Star her phone. They were standing in the gift shop of Fancy

Nancy World while the twins took pictures with Suga for a personalized hoodie.

"Girllll, that hoe is so fake," Star rolled her eyes and let out a small laugh. Nikka had posted a long and drawn out birthday message to the twins as if she had a real relationship with them. It didn't bother Star. It just made her think that bitch was more weirder than she already thought. "She's on Instagram talking about how she loves my daughters like they're her own but their birthday is tomorrow. Make it make sense."

"Bitch you can't make it make sense," Colley laughed. "From the looks of it I think she wants back into the family."

Star had already come to that conclusion on her own. Both Nikka and Lexi had been trying to play nice with her but she wasn't falling for the okey doke. She was cordial for the kids sake and kept it pushing. They didn't have anything extra to talk about because they weren't friends. After the way those hoes had talked about her kids in the past and treated them like outsiders they'd *never* be friends. Their true colors had already been exposed so it was too late to back track.

"My babies won't be her way back in. She should've had this energy from the jump."

"Facts but while we're on this topic, guess who called me the other day?"

"Who, bitch?"

"My sad ass mama."

Star's stomach turned. She already strongly disliked Fee for the way she'd mistreated her when she was her guardian. Now that she was aware of the way she did Tahj she really hated her. She'd attended a few of Tahj's therapy sessions with him and she heard a lot of the inappropriate shit Fee did to him in great detail. If she saw that bitch ever again she'd seriously beat her ass for being a vile ass person.

"What did she want?" Star asked, even though she didn't care.

"She started off acting like she wanted to see me and fix our relationship. Then she went on a dramatic rant about needing to meet her granddaughter and how life's too short."

"Don't tell me you bought into that nonsense."

Colley gave her a look. "Fuck no. I knew she was full of shit from the jump and she confirmed my suspicions when she asked me for five thousand dollars. I told that hoe I ain't have it, right? Why she gon tell me she knows I'm lying because she be seeing me on Instagram with Chanel bags? Girl I cursed her out so bad then hung up."

Star laughed. "It's sad that I'm not shocked by any of that. The fact that she can fix her mouth to ask you for anything is crazy. She shouldn't even feel comfortable talking to you, period…unless she's ready to talk about that shit she allowed her son to do to you in her ho-"

"Star," Colley chastised with warning eyes. "Nobody's trying to get into that old shit."

"Then don't bring that lady up around me because I can't forget certain shit happened."

"Things happened to me, not you. If I can get over it then so can you." She snapped.

"Excuse me?" Star scoffed. "Let's not act like I don't have my own reasons for not fucking with your mama. And yea, I feel some type of way about what happened to *you* on her watch. I'm sorry if you feel like you've gotten over it."

"Whatchu mean if I feel like I got over it? I am over it!"

"If you say so." Star's eyes rolled.

"Star fuck you. Ever since you've been talking to that shrink you've been talking down on me like I have a problem. I might not be squeaky clean with a perfect life like you, but I'm making it!"

"Fuck me?! Bit-"

"Star! Come over here and help me with something,"Tahj stepped in and pulled her away. He immediately led her out of the gift shop. He didn't know what was going on but he knew what she looked like when she was about to rip somebody's head off. He'd been on the receiving end quite a few times to know.

"Why you fussing with your cousin?"

"I'm so done with her, Tahj."

Tahj's eyes unintentionally went up to the sky. He wasn't buying what she was selling. Maybe because she claimed she was cutting Colley off every other week.

"I'm serious, Tahj!" She defended weakly.

"Look I'm sure y'all will get over whatever it is. You know you love your cousin."

"We can't get over what she's not willing to discuss, Tahj. And I'm tired of her projecting her shit onto me."

"Either way, today's about the twins. Let's focus on them."

"You're right," she sighed. "That girl just got a way of getting under my skin."

He cupped her face and kissed her before chuckling.

"What's so funny?"

"I'm just laughing because anybody else would've gotten slapped, but not Colley. You got a weak spot for her."

"Fuck that little bitch." She spat, evilly. Tahj laughed harder.

"Calm your ass down, and let's go ride some of these expensive ass rides I paid for."

As they walked into the main area dubbed as "Twin World," Star spotted Talea standing with Baby Tahj and a familiar looking boy who was about the same age as him.

"Tahj, whose son is that?" Star asked.

"Oh that's Tone's oldest son, AJ."

"I knew he looked familiar. That's his twin."

"So are the other two,"Tahj chuckled, referring to his other two sons. His boy having all sons was fitting.

Just as he said that, Antonio walked up to Talea and handed her a drink and a hamburger box. She was all smiles and Star could've sworn she saw her blushing.

"You seeing what I'm seeing?" Star asked.

Tahj was confused until it hit him where she was trying to get at.

"Oh no, Tone cool with my whole family. I doubt it's like that."

"What if it *is* like that? Would that be an issue for you?" She quizzed just to pick his brain.

"I mean they grown, so what I feel wouldn't matter." He replied, giving the pc answer. In reality he would feel like his sister could do better than a nigga who was stuck in some weird limbo with his baby mama. Most people would feel like he had no room to talk considering he once was in some sort of polygamous relationship with both of his baby mamas, but he did that for the convenience of having all his his kids under one roof. It wasn't because he was attached to Nikka or Lexi. At one point he had a lot of love for both women, but it was never a situation where he couldn't live without them or something. He wasn't sure if he could say the same about Tone. So for Talea's sake he hoped that they were just making casual conversation.

"Star!"

Both Tahj and Star turned around as Diamond approached them. On his arm was a slender dark skin girl and her face was striking. She reminded Star of a Bratz doll named Sasha she owned as a child.

"I see you, bro." Tahj smirked.

"Chill,"Diamond laughed. "I want y'all to meet my girlfriend, Chasmine. Chasmine, this is my sister and her boyfriend, Tahj."

"Hiii,"she smiled before sticking her hand out.

"No girl, I gotta hug you to see if this is real,"Star said before embracing her. "My brother finally has a girlfriend and I'm getting to meet her."

"Stop doing the most, bruh." Diamond said, feeling embarrassed. "We actually have something to tell you."

"You're pregnant?!" Star's mouth dropped before touching Chasmine's belly. She felt a small bump beneath her cute graphic t-shirt. "Oh my God! How far along are you?"

"How did you guess that? She's barely showing?" Diamond asked in disbelief.

"I ain't gon lie,"Tahj laughed. "I saw her glowing when y'all was walking up. I was like either this nigga making her really happy or she pregnant."

"It's both,"Chasmine giggled. "I'm almost five months along."

"You're so littleeee," Star gushed. "I can't believe my baby brother is having a baby. I'ma be an auntie. Chasmine I apologize in advance because I'm about to be all up in your mix."

"That's perfectly fine with me." She laughed.

"What are y'all having?" Tahj asked.

"We're waiting until the birth to find out." Diamond answered.

"Forreal? Y'all better than me. I was tweaking with all my kids to find out the gender." Tahj laughed. Of course he hadn't been that way with the twins because he didn't know about them until this year. It was crazy when he really thought about it. It really just made him want to shoot for a do over with Star. He always thought he was done having kids until she entered his life again. He could've knocked her up again by now since they were back together. She had started taking birth control pills, but he could get around that if he really wanted to. He wanted more kids with her and all, but for once he was going to do things right.

October 3, 2020

"Fuckkk, this dick not normal!" Star screeched as she hopped all over Tahj's dick. "It's tooo big!"

"Yet you taking it so well," he uttered as he stroked her at a quick pace from the bottom. "That's right, ride that dick just like that. This shit was made just for you."

"Don't ruin this moment with lies," she moaned as he hammered away at her g-spot. She was so close.

"Lies? Stop playing with me." He gritted as he yanked her head back and flickered his tongue all over her neck.

"Uhhhh," she moaned as he sucked her neck. She planted her feet firmly on both sides of him as she proceeded to bounce her ass. The Pretty Ricky strategically playing in the background gave her a smooth rhythm to work with and it sound proofed the room so they could fuck in peace while kids ran all around the house.

"I'm tasting every drop. Like at the candy shop. I'll lick your lollipop. I'll put that thing on lock. I'll let you

climb on top and let that nookie pop. I'm in the cookie jar. I ain't no rookie girl..."

"I'm not playing," she said, continuing to talk her shit. "How many bitches then had this dick? Is it really mine?"

"Who's getting it right now?" He asked after biting her neck.

"Meeee!" She squealed as she arched her back.

"There's the answer to your question." He popped her ass. "Now shut the fuck up and ride this dick so I can drop this load in you."

"Okayyy, daddy! Shitttt!" She screamed as her pussy convulsed. "I'm finna cum!"

"I feel you, baby. I feel you." Tahj breathed as he reached down and played with her creamy pussy.

"Uhhhhh!" She moaned as an orgasm ripped through her like a powerful tornado.

"Fuckkk," Tahj groaned while busting inside of her. He'd been holding on, but seeing and feeling her cum did it for him. "At the same damn time."

She laughed. "Now I gotta take a bath before I go downstairs to check on my damn food thanks to your horny ass."

"Me?! Girl that's your nasty ass, walking around in nothing."

"Tahj please," she scoffed as she climbed off his dick that was still semi-hard. He literally never got tired. "I had on tights and a t-shirt."

"Tights with no underwear. You know what the fuck you be doing."

"Yea, I be minding my business and then here you come."

"Alright, keep acting like you don't be wanting this dick and I'ma bend you over. Have you in here screaming again." He grinned.

Her pussy tingled.

"As tempting as that sounds, we do have company downstairs and I have food on the stove and in the oven." She said as she walked to the bathroom. He watched her naked body in all its glory as she twisted away. It made no sense for one person to be so damn perfect.

"Man, my family ain't no damn company, and I'm sure my sisters are watching the food. Come here." He grabbed her arm and tongued her down after following her into the bathroom. Soon they were going for round two in the shower. Although this round was quicker than the last, they still spent another hour in their room. By the time they made it downstairs everyone knew what they'd been up to.

"About time!" Tati called them out when they tried to enter the kitchen normally. They had a house full. All of Tahj's sisters were present with their significant others and their kids. The kids ran amuck through the house, the men were in the den watching tv, and the ladies were in the kitchen.

Star looked at the stove and noticed it was off. The big pot of shrimp pasta she was cooking appeared to be finished. The baked chicken she left in the oven was sitting in a serving dish and the chicken she was supposed to fry was right next to it in a matching dish.

"I finished your food for you." Talea said. "Hope you don't mind."

"Told you,"Tahj said to Star.

"Thank you, Lea." Star said, ignoring Tahj.

"Y'all lucky we didn't start carving pumpkins without y'all. We had to wait for this hoe who's always late,"Tamia pointed to Choc.

"This *hoe* got three kids and runs a business. Fall back!" Choc pointed back while twisting her neck.

"Bitch you say that like it means something. Nobody told you to have all them kids and I run *three* businesses so what's tea?" Tamia rebutted. Star laughed because to someone who wasn't familiar with their relationship they'd think it was real beef, but this was nothing more than silly banter amongst siblings.

"Girl, the only business you really run yourself is your heels classes. You got other people running your hair store and your exotic dance line."

"So, get like me and maybe you'll be on time for things." Tamia rolled her eyes.

"Bloop!" Tati instigated while slapping palms with Tamia.

"How about I whoop both of y'all asses?" Choc proposed, sounding rather serious. That alone made everyone erupt with laughter.

"But forreal, how y'all invite us over for family time and then disappear?" Talea asked Star and Tahj through laughter.

"That's a question for y'all brother." Star replied as she gathered up everything they'd need for pumpkin carving and decorating. With all these kids around she had no choice but to get into the Halloween spirit. At that very moment she rocked a cute Halloween graphic t-shirt, black tights, brown uggs, and a Halloween headband with pumpkins. She'd gotten a whole pack of Halloween headbands and Tahj's sisters along with some of the kids had already put them on.

"Star, when can we start our pumpkins! And can I have cookies while I do mine?" Jari ran up to Star and asked. She made sure to wrap her arms around her legs and throw on her best puppy dog face. She looked just like the twins when they were trying to game her.

"You can have cookies after you eat, pretty girl." Star leaned down and kissed her forehead.

"Starrrrr," Jari whined.

"Girl go head with all that. I said what I said. Now are you ready to eat or what?" Star questioned.

Jari turned to Tahj. "Dadddyyy!"

"Nope. Don't even try it." Tahj shook his head.

"Okay, I guess I'll eat. But I don't like pasta, Star."

"I know. I made corn and ricetoo. You want that with some baked chicken?"

"Yes!" She said cheerfully before skipping out the kitchen.

"That girl is a mess,"Choc tittered.

"*All* of Tahj's girls are a mess,"Star said as if two of his girls weren't hers too. "The only one with some chill is Baby Tahj."

"I guess he gotta be sane with all these girls around him. Star and Tahj give my nephew a little brother,"Tati smirked, being messy.

"Girl, he got Choc's twins, Tavior Junior, Tarik Junior, and Angel. With all those boy cousins what does he need a lil brother for?" Star sassed.

"Having a cousin isn't the same as a sibling though. I mean in this family it's pretty close, but it's still not the same." Choc offered her two cents. "You don't want to have any more kids, Star?"

"Sure. When I'm married."

"Hmmm,"Talea grinned while looking over at her brother. "How do you feel about that, bro?"

"I mean, it's understandable. I think I want my next child when I'm married too."

Tati choked on her water. "Did you just say the 'm' word?"

Star was just as shocked. She threw the word marriage out there to make the conversation end. She also wanted to kill any thoughts Tahj may have had about knocking her up any time soon. She would've never imagined him agreeing with her. She was stunned into silence.

"Really Tati?" Tahj tilted his head. "You doing the most."

"She not doing the most, nothing! You used to hard up say you don't believe in marriage! Am I lying?" Tamia looked at Choc and Talea for back up.

"These are facts." Choc said.

"Yup. He used to say marriage really meant nothing and was nothing more than a piece of paper that allowed the government to know who you're shaking up with." Talea carried on.

"*Used* to." Tahj repeated their words. "I can't grow and change my mind about certain topics? Shit at one point I used to say I was never having kids."

"Yea, but we been realized you was full of shit when it came to that. Marriage was something we truly never thought you'd come around to wanting, though."

"Yea, well things change and people change." Tahj shrugged before exiting the kitchen. He was about to go by the fellas because they were doing entirely too much by bringing up his old mindset.

"Star you the goat, bitch." Tamia blurted out once he was gone.

"Huh?" Star looked up from the plates she was making.

"Don't play dumb,"Choc laughed. "What you over here doing to my brother? Got him talking about marriage and shit."

"Chile honestly I'm just as surprised as y'all are. We've never talked about marriage. When I brought that up I expected him to say nothing or leave."

"Welp, guess he showed yo ass." Tati tittered.

"Miss girl, what are you smiling at?" Choc asked Talea when she noticed her smiling and blushing at the phone.

"What?" Talea clicked her phone off and looked up like she'd been caught red handed.

"I know this hoe not keeping secrets,"Tamia said. "Who is he? Tell us now before we jump you."

"Girl please," Talea scoffed. "Star, be grateful you don't have sisters. They always in your damn business."

"Talea, your business is our business. Now come on. Let us have it. Who is he?" Choc pushed.

"Star, let me help you with these plates girl,"Talea stood up and switched over to the Island.

"This bitch don't know how to be sisters,"Tati shook her head as if she were disappointed. "Star, do you want a sister? Because we finna give one up."

"Sure. We can do a family member swap. I'll take Talea and y'all can have Colley." She offered. They laughed but she was half way serious.

"Wait so y'all really beefing?" Talea snickered. "Because when I picked Suga up last weekend from her house I told her how I was linking with you to go to Sector 6 and she rolled her eyes. I asked her why she reacted that way and she just said nothing."

Star shook her head and as silly as it was, her feelings were hurt. She'd tried reaching out to Colley after the twins' birthday but she'd get dry responses or no response at all. The biggest thing that bothered Star was that Tahj and his siblings could still reach out to her for Suga and they'd get an immediate response. This wasn't the first time she and Colley argued or didn't speak for weeks, but this time bothered her more than others for some reason. She just felt like there was no need for them to be beefing over their childhood trauma. All she wanted to do was help her through it. But maybe that was it. Colley didn't want help nor did she want to deal with it. If falling back from certain topics was needed to keep the peace then Star was willing to do that. She couldn't force anyone to heal. Colley had to do that on her own time and terms.

"I wouldn't call it beef." Star answered after hesitating. "I guess she's just mad at me."

"About what?" Tamia asked.

"I don't know. Maybe I was doing too much," she admitted. "But let me ask y'all something…"

They all gave her their undivided attention, giving her the green light to continue.

"How would you feel if you knew something happened to somebody you loved as a child and you knew it still affected them currently? Could you just turn the other cheek and watch them slowly self-destruct?"

"Whew, that sounds familiar doesn't it?" Tati turned to Tamia.

"Sure does." Tamia agreed. "Can I go into detail, sis?"

"There's no need for you to go into detail. I will." Tati asserted.

"Oh shit, well excuse me," Tamia giggled. She was really proud of how her sister was so open to sharing her story because there was once a time when only she knew. Looking back, that was a hell of burden for them to carry alone when they were only kids.

"I was raped when I was 15 by my grandma's boyfriend." Tati divulged transparently. What she just revealed was heavy but there was an unmissable strength in her eyes.

"Oh my God," Star gasped. "Tati I'm sorry!"

"Yea, me too," she nodded. "I didn't tell anyone when it happened. My grandma's reaction had me thinking everyone would blame me or see me as a hoe. My mind was all fucked up. I moved in with Talea and I told Tamia shortly after. I don't know what it was about her because I didn't even know her like that at the time."

"Bitch we had an undeniable connection," Tamia interrupted.

"Okay, I guess we did." Tati smirked. "I was also drunk as fuck when I told her. That's what I did for the longest to cope with my pain. I would drink like a fish and get high off of weed and pills. The fact that I'm 100% sober now is a blessing. I guess I can thank rehab for that."

Star's eyes shifted to the wine bottles she'd set out. She thought it would be a good idea for them to sip wine while the kids did their pumpkins. She wasn't so sure now. She was actually thinking about all the times she'd been around Tati, a recovering addict, drinking recklessly.

"Don't do that, Star," Tati laughed. "My last experience with alcohol scared me straight. I could've lost Angel. Nothing, not even seeing other people drink, makes me want to indulge. I'm good. Trust me. And if an environment was ever too much for me I'd dismissed myself. Now back to the topic at hand, there's nothing you can really do for a person if they don't want help. I had my epiphany on my own. Of course my family was there to help me understand the gravity of the situation, but I also wanted to get better for myself because of my son."

"But Colley has Suga." Star said.

Tati shook her head. "Me and Colley are not the same. I don't know what she's going through specifically, but everyone deals with shit differently. Ya know?"

"Yea, I guess that's true. Because some things happened to my mom as a child and she was overprotective of me and my brother because of it. My auntie on the other hand, who's also Colley's mother…let's just say she might as well be the devil."

"Well there you have it. Consider it a blessing that Colley's not the devil like her maw. I notice that she's a little troubled and I think that's because I'm seeing the old me in her. But I think she'll be okay, Star." Tati assured.

"Yea, and don't worry yourself too much." Choc chimed in. "If you've spoken your peace about it already then leave it alone until she comes around. You don't want to push her away or make her feel pressured into dealing with something she's not ready for."

"And that's probably hard, too. I know it was hard for me to watch Tati deal with shit the wrong way but no matter how much I complained she was going to do her regardless." Tamia said.

"Yea, y'all might be right." Star sighed.

"Say, these kids are hungry! What's the hold up?" Supreme stepped in the kitchen with one of he and Choc's identical twins in his arms. Star didn't know which one it was. They looked a lot like their handsome father with their moms' pretty skin complexion. Seeing them made Star think about what it would be like to have boy twins.

"Nigga you hungry. Don't be blaming it on these kids." Choc laughed.

"What difference does it make? At the end of the day somebody's hungry." He said, making them all laugh.

"You can tell everybody to come get a plate, Supreme." Star said.

"Say no more." He exited the kitchen. No more than 30 seconds later everyone was running to the kitchen.

After everyone ate they migrated to the backyard where the kids and adults had fun with pumpkin carving and decorating. This was exactly the evening Star had in mind when she invited them over. She would hate it if she and Tahj didn't work out for multiple reasons. One of the main reasons being his family and how she was now attached to them.

"Somebody has a birthday coming up, right?" Star smirked when she overheard Baby Tahj dropping hints about toys and games he wanted. It was already established that he was having a Halloween carnival birthday party because he did that every year. It was a tradition he looked forward to and Star couldn't wait to experience it with him for the first time. Baby Tahj wasn't the only one with a birthday this month though. Somebody was actually before him.

"Me! My birthday, Star!" Baby Tahj exclaimed, garnering some laughter.

"I know your birthday is coming up, Tahj." Star giggled.

"Because I'm your favorite boy right?"

"That's right." She laughed,

"Daddy's birthday is coming up first, mommy!" True shouted.

"Thank you, baby." Tahj said as if he were upset, but it was really comical to him. When Baby Tahj entered the world the same month as him his birthday no longer mattered. It was now all about his son, and he was cool with that. "I'm glad somebody remembered me."

"How old are you making, Uncle Tahj?" Tarik Junior asked. His father was out of town working, but his aunties still made sure he was present.

"I'm turning 32, man." He answered.

"Wowwww," his eyes widened in astonishment.

"Daddy, was slavery really bad?" Baby Tahj asked.

Everyone paused before breaking out into hysterical laughter.

"Star, get your favorite boy before I hurt him." Tahj chuckled. Now he officially felt ancient thanks to his only son,

"Kids really be coming for ya head, bruh." Tamia's man, Noel, shook his head while laughing. "The other day Noeva asked me why her mama hair be coming off at the end of the day."

"And I told you to tell her ass to stay out my business." Tamia said as everyone laughed at her expense. It was no secret she rocked the wigs that she sold.

"No, remember when Angel told them people at his day care that he heard us exercising all night?" Tati's fiancé, Antwan, asked her.

Tahj's nose scrunched up in disgust while everyone else hollered. He could never casually talk about his sisters having sex. It would forever be weird to him.

"And you want another one. Tuah!" Tati scoffed.

"Fucking right I want a daughter."

"Girl, go ahead and give Angel a little sister." Star tittered. She was getting her back for her comments earlier about her having a son.

"Star I always did say you had a good head on your shoulders. Listen to your sister in law, Ta." Ant nudged Tati, increasing the laughs.

"Both of y'all can go to hell as far as I'm concerned." Tati muttered.

"So we meeting here for Tahj's birthday?" Talea asked, changing the subject.

"Yup." Star smiled. She was in charge of his birthday plans and she was super excited. Thanks to the party planner she'd hired, everything was running smoothly.

"What's the plans Star?"

"It's a surprise. Just show up and dress casually."

Tahj felt silly because he was actually excited for this birthday surprise shindig. He'd told Star he wasn't trying to do the most and he meant that, so he was appreciative of the fact that he could stay home. He was just anxious to see what she had planned.

Star knew Tahj had a love for horror movies, so they were going to have a lavish movie night outside. She drew her ideas out for the party planner and everything was coming into fruition. There was going to be a giant projector, plush life size bean bag chairs, and junk food galore. She'd let him pick the scary movie they were going to watch on his birthday, which was October 11th. It fell on a Sunday, so it would be perfect.

"Okay, Star, now tell them about my party." Baby Tahj insisted.

"This lil nigga," Tahj mumbled. Everyone shared a laugh once again.

"It's really back to back birthdays around here,"Supreme chuckled.

"It really is,"Tati said as if she were just realizing it. "Star is in August, the twins are in September, Tahj and Baby Tahj are in October, Jari is in November, and Tazzy is in December. Tahja's the only one who's spaced out from y'all."

"Yup, y'all daddy was *busy*." Tamia snickered, referring to Tahj.

"Tell me about it." Star uttered.

"Don't do me like that,"Tahj wrapped his arm around her waist. "I've been chilling for years now."

"You sure you don't have any more kids out there that we don't know about?" Star asked just to mess with him."

"Nah, you the only one who was ever bold enough to do me like that." Tahj laughed. Star couldn't do anything but laugh with everyone else because she'd walked herself into that joke. She also liked how she and Tahj could now laugh about things that used to be sore topics for them. They'd come a long way and she could only pray that they stayed on track.

Chapter 24

October 31st, 2020

"Can you make some rotel dip for us tonight, Star?" Baby Tahj asked as he walked on the side of the grocery basket. Star was throwing a Halloween party for the family that night so she was doing some last minute grocery shopping. She had half the mind to tell Tahj to get the chef to come through but she actually enjoyed cooking for her family. She'd already made a countless number of Halloween themed treats and desserts. The party had pretty much been set up since early this morning, but then she realized hot dogs and nachos weren't going to satisfy the adults' taste buds. Since Tahj's birthday party went off without a hitch she found a knack for party planning and she was already thinking about the thanksgiving and Christmas gatherings she was going to host at the house.

"We're already going to have nachos, boy."

"Nachos not the same as rotel dip though."

"Alright I guess I can make some." She quickly gave in. Just recently Tahjaria had accused her of never saying no to Baby Tahj. She denied it but she was starting to think that baby may have been on to something.

"Let me seee,"Star pulled up her grocery list on the notes app on her iPhone. "I got the chicken for the hot wings, the steak and shrimp for the kabobs, ground meat for sliders…and now Rotel, baked beans,and crab meat for the macaroni."

"We bouta eat good. I wish my mama cooked like you." Baby Tahj said.

"Boy, hush." Star said while holding back laughter.

"Forreal. Can you cook for my birthday next year?" He asked seriously. His birthday party was perfect like always but some of the food was ruined thanks to his mom who suddenly wanted to cook. Usually Nikka would just have the kids' parties catered because she couldn't cook to save her life. But when she saw Tahj's birthday party through her burner account on Instagram she felt challenged. Star threw one hell of a party and she didn't miss a chance to brag about all the food she'd cooked. Since Baby Tahj's birthday party was being thrown at Tahj's house Nikka figured it would be a perfect time to show Star that she wasn't the only woman who could work the kitchen. Unfortunately her competitive spirit mixed with her new found ambition ruined several dishes. Thankfully her mom had made half of the food, or no one would've eaten anything.

"Do you want Doritos for your rotel dip or do you want to use the regular nacho chips?"

"Doritos!"

"Alright let's go get them so we can get out of here."

When they were nearing the chip aisle, somebody bumped into Star. The woman said sorry, and Star simply replied by saying it was okay. It wasn't that serious. What made her stop dead in her tracks was when the woman said something to Baby Tahj.

"Boy you look just like your daddy. Tell him Miani said hi."

"Excuse you?" Star put her hand on her hip.

"Oh, I'm sorry! I just know his daddy s-"

"But do you know *him* to be addressing him? He's a child, sweetie." Star spoke to her as if she were slow. That infuriated her even more.

She was already upset that this bitch had come out of nowhere with kids for Tahj and he didn't hesitate to start kissing her ass. She thought she started making progress with Tahj over the summer because he would drop by her house often and he'd invite her out sometimes. That came to an end out of nowhere in August because he claimed he was going to make it work with Star. She got to see first hand how they were making it work through Instagram. Something had to be wrong with both of their asses because they posted each other a little too much. And from what she could see Star did *the most* when it came to his other kids. Take now for example, she had Baby Tahj with her at the store instead of her own daughters. Miani didn't know how Nikka did it because she would've put her foot down a long time ago.

"I know he's a child and like I said I'm familiar with hi-"

"Baby do you know this lady?" Star looked down at Baby Tahj.

"Nope. Never seen her in my 8 years of life." He responded.

"Thought so. Go get the chips and whatever snacks you want, Tahj. I need to talk to Miss Miani."

"Okay!" He ran off excitedly. He planned on getting as much stuff as he could carry.

"Who the hell are you?" Star cut straight to it.

"I'm a friend of Tahj. And you are?" She attempted to ruffle her feathers.

Star saw right through it and giggled. "Baby if you're Tahj's so called friend then I'm positive you know exactly who I am, so I won't even entertain your sad attempt at being petty. But that's why you spoke to a child who doesn't even know you, right? To be petty?"

"Hunny, if I wanted to be petty I could've stopped you and said I used to fuck the shit out of your nigga. But I wasn't even on that type of time."

Star cackled. "Oh wow. *Another* sad attempt at being petty. You're on a roll, baby! You think I give a fuck about how you *used* to fuck Tahj? A million hoes have that to their credit. I don't give two fucks about that. Unless you've fucked him recently of course…"

"No, I haven't because I'm not worried about him."

"Then why the fuck would you tell his son to tell him you said hey? Your dumb ass should've kept walking."

Miani could see this was going all the way left and she wanted out. She could get mouthy all day and she lived for throwing shade, but fighting was something she never did. She could tell Star was ready for that type of action. It was time for her to make a speedy exit.

"Ya know what, this is getting out of hand and I'm too classy to be fighting in the store. Goodbye," she turned to walk away.

"But you not too classy to announce your sexual history?!" Star blurted out to her back. "Weird ass hoe."

———————————————

"So she really stopped and spoke to my son?" Tahj asked in disbelief.

From the moment he went outside to help Star and Baby Tahj with the grocery's he could tell something had happened. When his son announced to him that somebody named Miani said hey he could've died. The moment Star told him she was willing to work on their relationship he cut off all the meaningless flings in his life. He was hoping that Miani hadn't thrown salt in the game and told lies. Yea he and Star were in a great place but his past alone gave her plenty reason to doubt him. He was ready to plead his case if he needed to,

However, there was no need for that. As soon as they were alone in the kitchen Star broke out in laughter before running down the story to him. If anything he was mad now. Miani had a lot of audacity for someone who used to suck his dick from time to time. She was also the occasional arm candy, but that's as deep as their situation went.

"I swear, Tahj! I could tell by how he was looking that he didn't know that hoe. Then when she mentioned you I automatically knew it was one of your old hoes."

"Of course that hoe don't know my son! I ain't never brought no woman I was just smashing around my kids. Bruh, I would've never expected this out of Miani."

"Why? Because she claims to be classy?"

"How you know what she claims?"

"Because when I started going off on her dumb ass she got scared and walked off fast while claiming she was too classy to be fighting in the store. She's lucky I had Tahj with me because I probably would've slapped her for fun."

"Man you don't need to be fighting. Fuck that hoe and anybody else that's hating."

"Speaking of haters, are your baby mama's joining us tonight?"

Lately things had been copacetic with Nikka and Lexi as far as coparenting. Star still felt how she felt about them. She knew deep down they didn't like her either and were in some weird competition with her that they'd made up in their heads. As long as those bitches stayed in line and respected her to her face she was good.

"Hell no. Especially not Nikka's ass. She asked me for money yesterday."

"Well that's not surprising. She doesn't work. How much she asked for?"

"$10,000! I automatically said no because like you said, she don't work and I'm already paying all her bills and putting money in her hand every mon-"

He stopped talking when he noticed Star had a look on her face.

"What's wrong?"

"Nothing." She pursed her lips.

"No, somethings wrong. We said we would always be honest with each other from now on about how we're feeling. So come on. Tell me." He pushed.

"Alright...I just think some boundaries need to be set with you and Nikka when it comes to money. That's the reason she feels comfortable asking you for money. Now I'm aware that she's going to benefit from you doing your part for y'all kids, regardless. I have no issue with you helping with bills in a house your kids live in. I don't mind you helping her out when she needs something that your kids also need. But her depending on you financially for all her needs in life? That's gotta come to an end, baby. Doesn't she have a business degree? I'm sure she can get a job."

"It's funny you say that because that's why she claimed she wanted the money. She said she wants to start her own business, but I know Nikka. She's been stashing the money I give her since Baby Tahj was born. She's sitting on a nice chunk of change. I think she just wants bragging rights to say I invested in her business."

"That may be true, but I think it's about that time y'all had a talk about what's acceptable and what's not when it comes to money."

"Yea, I feel you." He nodded. He wasn't rattled about anything she just said because he'd been thinking this for the longest. He would forever make sure Nikka was good on the strength of Baby Tahj and Tazzy, but by no means was he required to take care of her like she was his woman. He only had one woman and her name was Starlah.

"That's right, babies! Do the monster mash!" Choc egged the kids on. They were dancing to Halloween music while she recorded them on her video camera.

"That hoe really getting old. Recording shit on a video camera like it's the 90's." Talea mumbled, making Star giggle.

Choc's head spun around. "I heard that, heffa! For your information this camera takes great pictures and videos. Ask Star!"

"Yea, she did get some nice shots of me, Tahj, and the kids." Star laughed, feeding into their silly argument.

In the Halloween and football season spirit, Star had dressed the girls up as Saints cheerleaders and Baby Tahj was a Saints football player. To keep the theme going she and Tahj were dressed as referees. She had bought a sexy goddess costume just in case she planned on going out once the party was over, but after successfully throwing this party together and actively playing hostess, she was slumped. At this rate she was going straight to bed the moment everyone left. She'd clean up in the morning.

"You coming out with us tonight, huh sis?" Tamia asked. She'd asked before but she never got a straight answer. "We got a section at Bar 91."

"Mia, go head with that shit." Tahj butted in. Star wasn't even sure how he heard the conversation when he was at another table chatting with his brothers and Supreme. The only two people who weren't able to make it to the party were Antwan and Noel because they were working. That was a major reason Tamia and Tati were pushing so hard to go out. They didn't have shit else to do and their babies had grandparents who were eager to babysit any day of the week.

"What is she doing, Tahj?" Star asked. She was definitely playing dumb just to push his buttons.

"Exactly, what am I doing?" Tamia repeated innocently when she was anything but that.

"You being a shit starter as usual. I keep telling you Star not your turn up buddy."

"He speaks for you, Star?" Tati asked in an instigating manner.

"Girl, Tahj knows damn well I'ma do what I want. I don't know why he playing with me." Star giggled.

"So you going out with them?" He made eye contact with her. Her coochie tingled.

"I'ma do what I want," she sassed. Right after saying that a loud yawn escaped from her mouth.

"Then I guess you going straight to bed. Tired ass. Over there tryna talk shit about going out and can't even keep your eyes open." He snickered before returning to his conversation.

"That nigga thinks he's the boss of everything," Tamia complained. "You gon let him run you like that, Star?"

"Girl please," Star chortled. She was not about to succumb to peer pressure when she wasn't even hard up to go out in the first place.

"Tamia hush," Talea laughed. "That girl doesn't want to go out and it's obvious. Tahj don't have anything to do with it. And if your nigga was in New Orleans you wouldn't be going no where either."

"Whatever hoe," Tamia grumbled, conveniently ignoring her comment about Noel. "You just better not fake us out."

"Girl I told you I'm coming with y'all and I mean it." Talea claimed.

"Titi Star, my crown broke!"

Star looked down at Suga who was dressed in the cutest Princess Jasmine costume. She'd come to the party with Choc and her family, so Star still hadn't seen Colley. If she had to guess Colley was probably somewhere getting ready to go out tonight. Her cousin loved a slutty Halloween costume and she would always go all out. She was probably happy she could be child free while she got herself together.

"It's not broken, Suga," Star said after examining it. She snapped the crown back together within seconds and then put it back on Suga's head. "See? Pretty as ever."

Star puckered her lips and Suga kissed her before running off.

"It amazes me how much that baby looks just like me." Talea sighed. "She's just gorgeous."

Tati and Tamia smacked their teeth in unison, while Star and Jamaya laughed. She, Tavior, and Tavior Junior were bringing it as the Incredibles. Star had a hearty laugh at the sight of Tavior dressed as Mr. Incredible. She thought he was too macho to indulge in something like that, but he was a man in love. They would do anything shamelessly. Tahj showed her that every single day.

"Girl, that baby don't look nothing like you." Tati poked her lips out.

"You should be tired of hating, little sis." Talea flipped her natural long hair over her shoulder. From the moment Star laid eyes on Talea she said she reminded her of a black pocahontas. When Tahj told her that Talea's mom was actually Native American it all made sense. The Egyptian Queen costume she was wearing made her look even more exotic. Star could definitely see the resemblance to Suga.

But she honestly thought Suga looked like *all* her siblings who were all disgustingly good looking. God had definitely taken his time making the Bellamy's.

"Hey Colley!" Jamaya waved with a smile.

Star's heart dropped and her head turned in the direction Jamaya was speaking in. Colley was there alright in the flesh. She appeared to have her makeup professionally done and it was giving Star a mermaid or a fairy with the pink highlight on her cheeks. Her hair was styled in fresh long curls and she donned a brown tracksuit that hugged her slim but shapely body. Star's predictions had been correct. Colley had been out getting ready for tonight.

"Hey everybody! I had to stop by and see my baby." Colley smiled as she looked over at Suga who was now jamming to a Beyoncé song while eating a Halloween cake pop. "I see she's having a good time and not worrying about me."

"Girl, none of them children worrying about us with a party like this." Jamaya laughed. "I like your hair, Colley. How many inches is that?"

"40," she swung her hair across her back.

A skeptical look crossed Talea's face. "Bitch, that's about 26 inches at the most."

Colley sucked her teeth. "It's an invisible 40. I can see it but y'all can't."

Everybody hollered at Colley's silliness. Even Star almost let laughter slip until it dawned on her that her cousin was in her house and hadn't even acknowledged her.

"Bitch you don't see me?" Star snapped.

"Oop," Jamaya's eyes shifted.

"Of course I see you. Hey, cousin. Thanks for inviting me to your party."

"Really? Are you throwing sarcasm my way when you haven't been answering my calls or texts for a month? How would I invite you anywhere?"

Colley opened her mouth to respond but nothing came out. Star had her there.

"Exactly." Star maintained.

"Okay. You got that. But I didn't come here to fuss with you. Do you still feel like talking to me?"

Star *almost* snapped on her again but she caught herself. She wanted peace with Colley. If she came on to her harshly in front of all these people more drama would ensue.

"Yea, let's go inside." She stood up and led the way.

"I'm definitely taking a to go plate." Colley said when they entered the kitchen and she got a glimpse of the elaborate spread of party food.

"Please do. Now let's get to the real shit. Why haven't you been talking to me? What did I do to you that was that bad?"

"You didn't do anything to me, Star. You just always bring up stuff that I'm not ready to talk about. I have the right to deal with shit in my own way, yea."

"You do,"Star threw her hands up. "But when you bring up certain people to me it's hard to stay away from those things you don't want to talk about. I can't forget that your mo- nevermind.

"No, it's okay. Go ahead and say it. I told my mom that my brother Devlin was touching me and she called me a liar."

"Colley you don't have to say it. I'm sorr-"

"Don't apologize. I swear it's okay. Your pushy ass made me realize that it's okay to think about these things and even say it out loud. It's okay for me to go through the motions and feel hurt," her voice cracked. "Because for the longest time I didn't feel at all. I'm starting to understand that's not normal."

"Aw Colley," Star teared up before wrapping her arms around her. "You don't have to go through the motions alone. I'm always here. And you can't go weeks without speaking to me. We're better than that."

"Yea, we are," she sniffled. "I just wanted to get my mind right before I reached out to you. I know I'm always making my mess your mess and your life is so together now. I didn't want to interfe-"

"Stop it," Star shook her head. "There's no one in this world that understands you better than me. I don't care if it's my wedding day. You don't have to go through anything by yourself as long as I'm here. Your mess *is* my mess."

Colley nodded as tears fell from her eyes. She felt silly for ever doubting Star. They'd been thick as thieves through it all, and it wasn't changing anytime soon.

Chapter 25

December 11, 2020

"When December comes, I bet you want to wrap me all up and take me home with you. See what I look like under them lights. We'll keep it quiet, whatever we do. I'm just tryna keep my baby warm through the wintertime ...."

Star hummed the Ariana Grande original Christmas song as she focused on decorating her gingerbread house. Tonight it was just her and her girls decorating gingerbread houses. This had been a tradition of theirs for the past three years, and Star had looked forward to making the other kids a part of the tradition. Unfortunately their mothers wanted their own kids this weekend while Tahj was away on business.

"Mommy look at mine!" True exclaimed after successfully putting the pieces of her house together.

"I see, baby. It's looking good. How are you going to decorate it this year?"

"It's a surprise,"Tahiry whispered.

True gasped. "How do you know it's a surprise?"

"I heard you say it in your head." Tahiry shrugged before going back to her gingerbread house while Star looked on in amazement. Having twins was a beautiful thing to watch. They were so in tune with each other to the point they could read each other's minds and finish each other's sentences. It was kinda scary at times.

"Ding-Dong!"

"That probably y'all Auntie Colley and Suga with the food." Star said while standing up.

"Yayyy!" The twins celebrated. They knew Colley was bringing pizza so they were ecstatic.

"About ti- oh! Hey Chasmine!" Star hugged her quickly and stepped to the side to urgently let her in the house. It was freezing cold outside and her round belly was a reminder of the bun she had baking in her oven.

"Damn, you only see her, sis?" Diamond asked as he entered right behind her.

"Depends. What you got there in that bag?"

"Strawberry Cheesecake for my favorite girls."

"I better be included in that."

"Now you know I was talking bout the twins, but I guess you could have a piece. Now where these ginger bread houses at? Cause I'm ready to get my decorating on." Diamond uttered, looking rather serious. That alone made Star and Chasmine laugh.

"Boy you need to stop,"Chasmine tittered. In the middle of laughing her stomach growled loudly.

"Oh no, girl you need to feed my nephew." Star said with concern.

Chasmine grinned. "Your nephew?"

"You heard her, man. Your stomach growling like you haven't eaten all day. What's up with that?" Diamond spat.

"Nigga I told your ass I was hungry when we was on the way over here! You swore your sister always has food!"

Star was stunned by Chasmine's comeback. Thus far she'd only seen the girl be sweet as pie. That compared with her angelic face and presence led Star to believe her brother had snagged a goody two shoes. Maybe she had it all wrong and there was still a lot more she needed to learn about Chasmine. Funny enough, her snappy response to Diamond made Star love her even more. Her brother would walk all over a square. He needed somebody with a backbone.

"Because she does always cook." Diamond replied. "I ain't want to stop for nothing."

"I didn't cook anything today, bro. But Colley is bringing pizza."

"Ding-Dong!"

"That's probably her now." Star stepped back over to the door and opened it. Suga jetted inside right away.

"Uncle Diamond!!!" She sang cutely as he threw her up in the air.

"Hey beautiful!" He kissed her cheek.

"Girl, you got a lot of pizza for us." Star said as she took a few boxes out of Colley's hand. If she had to guess it looked like seven boxes of pizza. On top of that she had Buffalo wings and chicken Alfredo pasta.

"You always have a house full, so I wanted to be prepared just in case."

"Girl it's just us, the twins, and Suga."

"Where your other kids at?" Colley asked.

"With their moms."

"Damn, I guess I did overdo it."

"No you did the right thing." Chasmine grabbed two boxes of pizza. "Let me help you with that, cousin."

They all laughed as they walked to the kitchen. Before indulging in gingerbread house making, everybody went straight for the food, including the twins. After eating, they sat around the table working on their houses, talking, and singing Christmas music. The only thing that could've possibly made the setting better was Tahj and the rest of the kids.

"Cordell coming out here for Christmas, Colley?" Star asked.

"I wish. He talking bout some his wife's family is coming to Houston to spend the holidays with them and that I'm more than welcome to come."

"You should go, Colley. He was nice enough to invite you." Star said.

"I think not! I'm not tryna spend my Christmas with his bougie wife."

Star laughed. "Shanise is a little bougie but she's also really nice."

"Too nice,"Colley fake gagged.

"Colley you something else,"Diamond chuckled. "Ain't nothing wrong with that man's wife. You just don't see eye to eye with her because she not a ratchet rat like you."

"Ya fake mama's a ratchet rat." Colley poked her tongue out childishly, making everyone laugh.

"Zora is a ratchet rat,"he admitted, referring to the woman who took him in when his mom went away. "That's why I can recognize them easily. And you? You definitely one."

"Diamond, I don't care what you talking bout. I ain't going to no Texas. I really wish Cordell would move back home already." She whined.

"I was just telling that nigga to move back but he said there's more opportunities in Texas. He might be right about that, too." Diamond admitted.

"But there's still no place like home,"Star commented before taking a sip of her wine.

"I don't know about all that. You couldn't pay me to move back to my hometown." Chasmine said.

"Where you from?" Colley asked.

"Technically here, but after Hurricane Katrina my family relocated to Alexandria, Louisiana and that's where we've stayed since. So that's home and I hate it. It's so boring out there."

Star laughed. "So you don't ever see yourself moving back?"

"Hell no," Diamond answered the question for her. "We ain't raising our kids in the country."

"Yea, it's a no for me." Chasmine laughed. "I'm trying to get my family to move back out here. Or at least to Kenner or something. I just knew that when I left for college in 2015 there was no turning back."

"I thought the same when I went to college in BR, but New Orleans has a hold on me."

"And now it has a hold on me," Chasmine giggled.

"Our city tends to do that to people," Colley boasted. "So Chasmine, how did a nice woman like yourself meet my hooligan ass cousin?"

"Keep playing with me, Colley." Diamond warned playfully.

Chasmine laughed. "We met after the Classic in 2018."

"And she was not trying to fuck with me at first."

Star smiled. "Why not, Chas?"

"Like Colley said, he looked like a hooligan." She replied evenly.

They all shared a heavy laugh.

"In other words she was used to fucking with squares and lames." Diamond said.

"Whatever," Chasmine rolled her eyes with a small smile.

"Ding-Dong!"

"You expecting somebody, sis?" Diamond stood up, going into full alert mode.

"No," Star shook her head while thinking about who that could be. Only family and close friends knew where they stayed, and even they would call before coming over.

Diamond felt for his gun before walking off briskly.

"That nigga…" Chasmine muttered as if she were used to him being on go mode.

"STAR! Tahj baby mama out here!" Diamond shouted about twenty seconds later

Star immediately got up and walked to the front of the house. Janikka was there with Baby Tahj and Tazzlyn. They both had overnight bags even though it wasn't needed. They had everything they needed already at this house.

"Hey babies," Star greeted them with warm hugs. She then sent them to the kitchen so she could talk to their mom. Diamond had exited as well.

"What's up?"

"I'm dropping them off. I have something to do tonight."

"Girl, what?" Star tilted her head.

"I said I have something to d-"

"I heard what the hell you said, but you got me fucked up. I don't mind keeping the kids but I'm not your designated babysitter. I'm not obligated to do *anything*."

"Yet you're always bragging about how you treat all the kids the sam-"

"And I do! That'll never change, either! But let's not be purposely dense here. The twins are the *only* kids I'm stuck with when their daddy is not around. If you ever want me to keep your kids when Tahj is not here you better ask me or we're going to have problems. You already know how I give it up, miss mamas."

"Look Star, I honestly didn't think you keeping the kids would be a problem." She backpedaled. In her mind she thought she'd just drop the kids off and go about her business. After observing Star for months she thought she had her figured out. The girl was like an old lady. She didn't do anything but stay home. When she did "fun stuff" it always surrounded the kids. She would even push for them to go on vacation with her and Tahj. In Nikka's mind she made the perfect sucker.

"The only way it's going to be a problem is if you don't ask me ahead of time. The next time I'ma send them right back out the door with your ass. Got it?"

"Got it," she nodded obediently. "But uh, there's something else I think we need to talk about."

"Okay. Talk." Star demanded impatiently. She was ready to get back to her gingerbread house.

"How is Tahj's career going?"

Her face twisted up. "What?"

"No, not like that! It's just he's been giving me less money lately. And when I ask for more he'll just say no. I'm assuming you're having the same issues with him. So I figured maybe his job has taken a hit or something."

Star broke out in giggles. This chick was something else.

"Nikka, he has bukoo clients under his belt that are constantly working. Why would you think he's having career problems?"

"Dang, you might be right. So maybe he's not budgeting properly and spending money frivolously."

"Nikka, did Tahj not talk to you about money?"

"No! I mean, he did say it's time I get a job and provide for myself. But that's what led me to believe his money must be running low or something."

Star shook her head. Leave it to Tahj to not explain to this bird in depth why he was no longer funding her lifestyle.

"Well, did you ask him about that?" Star asked, deciding to entertain her stupidity. She was getting a kick out of it actually.

"I sure did. He has a lot of pride so of course he denied it. So I told him if he didn't give me more money I was gonna put him on child support. Guess what he told me?"

"What he told you, girl?"

"He said go ahead and do it and that it would make his life easier. What do you think that meant?"

"I can't call it, Nikka. But do what you gotta do for you and your kids, girl."

"Girl at this point I'ma just go ahead and start my own business because I don't have time to play with Tahj's stingy ass. Yea the house is paid off and he pays all the bills, but he's only giving me $3000 for both kids each month. So basically each kid gets $1500. The fuck is that?"

More than enough for them kids, bitch. It ain't like you're a single parent. He has the kids just as much as you do. You just can't buy your Chanel and Louis bags anymore, Star thought to herself. She wasn't going to say it out loud because she was done with this conversation. Tahj had set boundaries like he said he would, so she had no issues.

"I don't know, but I hope you figure it out. Bye girl."

"Bye. Oh, and thanks for keeping the kids."

"Uh-huh, you just remember what I said. I don't want to have to go upside your head again." Star threatened seriously.

"Girl, you silly!" Nikka laughed out loud while walking out the door. Star couldn't believe how dumb that girl was, but she was nothing crucial that could stop her happiness or peace. She was just a minor nuisance that came with Tahj and two of his kids. She could deal with that.

December 18, 2020

Star laid on Tahj's chest while staring up at him lovingly because he'd just finished fucking the shit out of her. She was now thinking of baby names and if he would cry at the sight of her in a wedding dress. His dick did that to her.

"Girl, you all in my face." He grinned before kissing her lips. "You love me, huh?"

"With all my heart."

Involuntary chills ran throughout his body. Yea, he was definitely making this as official as possible. It got no better than this. He'd never felt this strongly for anybody before.

"I bet not more than I love you."

She lifted up on his chest a little to stare deeper into his eyes. "How you figure?"

"Who fought for us?"

Star smacked her teeth before hollering.

"What's funny, man?"

"You, boy. Talking bout you fought for us. Nigga that's what you was supposed to do when you went out of your way to ruin us in the first place," she tittered.

"Now why you gotta go there?" He asked as if his feelings were hurt.

"Because you play too much. Wasn't you the nigga that didn't even tell me about your child when we first met?"

"Nah, that wasn't me."

"Really, Tahj?"

"Yes, really," he mocked her voice, propelling her to giggle.

"So we lying now?"

"Ain't nobody lying. We met each other when we were kids. I ain't have no damn children then." He chuckled.

"Now Tahj you know what I was talking about! You didn't tell me about Baby Tahj when we first started talking."

"Alright, I was also dumb and childish. If I could go back I would definitely lay all the cards out on the table for you."

"Wait if you could go back you'd still want to fuck with me?"

His head jerked back. "Hell yea! What kinda question is that?"

"I don't know. I just thought with your growth and all you would've made the choice to not cheat on your woman at the time."

He sucked his teeth. "With my *growth* I would've never been with Janikka for the sake of a child."

"So that's the only reason you were with her?" She questioned as if she didn't fully believe it.

"I'm not denying the fact that I had strong feelings for her at one point. When she had Baby Tahj I really put her on a pedestal because the fact that she had my first child was major to me. But I can't say that I was *in* love with her at the time. Not enough to ruin what I was trying to build with you."

"Tahj you barely knew me at the time." She rolled her eyes.

"But I know you *now.* Knowing what I feel now is enough for me to say I would've moved differently in the past just so I could've gotten this sooner. You feel me?"

"Yea," she sighed. "But I think everything needed to happen the way it did. It makes us appreciate what we have now more."

When she said "us" she really meant him but she didn't want to single him out.

"That's true…except you hiding a nigga's kids. That didn't need to happen."

"Lord, I'm never going to hear the end of that, huh?" She laughed.

"As long as you know what it's hitting for," he chuckled. "But how you feeling about us right now?"

"What do you mean?"

"I mean what I just asked. Can you see yourself being with me when we're old and grey?"

Her heart skipped a beat.

"Yes I can see it and I want it, but it's not that simple."

"Why's that?"

"Because us growing old together depends on if you act right."

"I'm the only one in this relationship capable of messing up?"

"Okay," Star breathed. "I guess it depends on *us*. But let's not pretend like you're not the one who struggled with faithfulness in previous relationships."

"*Previous relationships,*" he emphasized. "We talking about this relationship in the present day with me and you. I feel you though, Star. You're basically saying cheating is non negotiable in this relationship and you'll leave if I do it. Right?"

"Pretty much," she confirmed. "Other than that I'm aware things won't be perfect all the time. But why are you asking me this?"

"I'm just trying to see if we're on the same page. Nothing more, nothing less."

"Oh so you want to grow old with me?"

"Have you not gathered that from this conversation so far?" He countered.

"Maybe, but I still want to hear you say it."

"Alright, Star. I love you to death and I want to grow old with you."

Her heart pounded furiously as if it would burst out of her chest. Only he could make her feel like this. She kissed him passionately to convey how he made her feel. He thought they were about to go for round two when she pulled away laughing.

"What's funny?" He frowned.

"Us," she snickered. "I'm thinking about the last Christmas we spent together versus now."

"Mannnn," he threw his head back. "Don't remind me. I'ma make up for that. I promise."

"You promise, huh?" She smiled. "I sure will hold you to it."

December 19, 2020

"Daddy, snap me up," Baby Tahj stopped walking after they exited the barbershop. Any time Tahj went for a haircut, so did Baby Tahj. It was one of the few times they got to spend quality time together alone.

Tahj stopped and looked at his mini me in amusement. "Snap you up?" He chuckled. "Who you think you is, Junior?"

"A king like you said. Remember?"

"No man, I said you were a prince. I'm the king."

"I think it's about time I be upgraded to king status."

Tahj laughed so hard his stomach started hurting. His kids had to have been comedians in another life.

"You can be whatever you want to be, son. Give me your phone so I can take the picture."

"I want to take it in front of your car!" Baby Tahj sped off.

"Boy, slow down!" Tahj roared. He was too late because Baby Tahj ran directly into an old lady pushing someone's wheelchair. Tahj hurried over.

"I'm so sorry about tha-"

His words trailed off when he recognized who was speaking to. The one thing about life that always amazed him was karma and how it worked. It wasn't always immediate but it always came.

Fee was standing there with gray and thin hair, wrinkled, acne filled skin that she had the nerve to cover in clown-like makeup, and she looked thin and scrawny. Most people would naturally assume she was on drugs but Tahj didn't think so. It really just looked like she was in a fight with life and she was getting her ass whooped. She had on a maid uniform so she had to have just come from work. He would've been confused about why she was at the barbershop if she weren't pushing Devlin in a wheelchair. He'd gotten shot in December of 2012 shortly after Star left Fee's house and he was left paralyzed from the waist down. His karma came quickly and Tahj was glad to see it.

"Tahj, is that you?" Fee smiled softly. Tahj was surprised her teeth weren't rotten with the way she'd let herself go. "And this must be your son. Hey cutie! Damn, your genes are strong."

"Let's go, son." Tahj said to Baby Tahj as he put his hand on his back to lead him to his car.

"Wait! Tahj, can I talk to you about something?!" Fee asked to his back.

Tahj thought about ignoring the bitch or cursing her out, but maybe it would do him some good to speak directly to the person who'd been the topic in some of his toughest therapy sessions.

"Get in the car, Tahj." He instructed his son. Once he was in the car safely he turned back to Fee. "Wassup?"

"Ummm, one second," she looked down at Devlin who was avoiding eye contact with Tahj.

For Devlin to see somebody from his childhood who was up in life while he'd been at his lowest for years wasn't a good feeling. He didn't feel like a man so he didn't want Tahj to speak to him. Lucky for him, Tahj had no plans to do that.

That ass whooping he'd given Devlin in 2012 for fucking with Star was his final time acknowledging him.

"Here baby,"Fee handed Devlin money. "Go ahead and go inside. I made your appointment already."

Tahj found it odd that Fee was treating a grown man in his 30's like a child. Handicapped or not, that shit was ridiculous and even odd.

As Devlin wheeled away, Fee walked over to Tahj. "How are you doing?"

"Look man, cut straight to the point. I don't got all day. What the fuck do you want?" He questioned harshly.

"Wow. Is that the way you speak to your little girlfriend's auntie?"

"My little girlfriend?" He repeated in disbelief. "Bitch, don't even speak on Star because you failed her as a gurdian. The same way you failed your other kids."

"What?! I have great relationships with my kids who weren't brainwashed by Star! But I see she's brainwashed you, too."

"Son, you're really sick in the head! You're determined to make Star your scapegoat when you really just have issues!"

"I don't got no damn issues and this is going all wrong. I'm not trying to fuss with you about my niece."

"Then spit out your reason for wanting to talk to me!" He demanded impatiently.

"I need you to get Colley or Cordell to help me out financially. I'm about to lose my house and I'm already working three jobs. For some reason my calls don't go through to Colley's phone anymore and I don't even have Cordell's number. I see through Instagram that my grand baby is your sister. Whew, that daughter of mine has always been a big hoe! I admire how y'all embrace little Caiyenne though."

"First off, her name is Caidence you dumb hoe. Secondly, I don't blame Colley and Cordell for cutting you off. Thirdly, if Colley has always been wild then it's probably due to something that happened while she was in *your* house. Not too much on her, forreal."

"Aw lawd, you must be fucking her too."

Tahj's face tightened. "Nah, but I'm not shocked that your mind would conjure up some weird shit like that. Why would you even fix your mouth to ask them for money? Shit what makes you think I'm the one to make this happen for you? Now I'm positive you need help!"

"Oh, you're going to make this happen for me." She said confidently while crossing her arms over her breast.

"And what makes you think that?"

"You're going to help me or I'm going to tell Star how you used fuck the shit out of me. Or did you forget?"

"How could I ever forget a pedophile like you?" He asked her calmly. Months ago her question would've triggered him, but he was past that place. Most importantly, Star was already aware of what she was trying to blackmail him with. In fact she looked rather pathetic throwing statutory rape in his face as if they had some sort of a situationship.

"A what?!" She hollered in shock.

"You heard me loud and clear. You're a pedophile and what you did to me was sick. Everything that's happened to you in life, you deserve it. You and your son."

"My son? Whatever Star and Colley told you is a lie!"

Tahj quickly put two and two together from her outburst.

"Colley ain't told me shit, but I guess your guilty conscience is eating at you."

"I'm not guilty and I'm not a pedophile either! You used to love having sex with me!"

"Bitch I was a child. I didn't know shit and you took advantage of that. You even gave me a whole STD. I didn't like or want that shit."

"I couldn't tell by the way I used to have your dick squirting," she rolled her eyes.

Tahj's stomach churned in disgust as he fought off the urge to slap this lady. She wasn't worth sitting in jail over, so he would keep his hands to himself.

"I even have some old vhs tapes at my house proving how much you liked it." She bragged. "Now it'll be a shame if somebody sends that off to Star. Wouldn't it?"

"Videos? You recorded us?!"

"A couple of times." She grinned. "I started at the very beginning so you can't deny shit."

"I tell you what Fee, do what you want. You don't have no power over me." He asserted before walking off.

When he drove off he was on a mission. He had to tell Baby Tahj to be quiet so he could concentrate. After thinking about it for a second, he went with his move and called Star.

"Hey baby, what's up?" Star greeted him. "You and my favorite boy got y'all hair cuts?"

"Yea, we just left."

"Daddy can I talk to Star? I gotta tell her something!" Baby Tahj shouted anxiously when he really had nothing important to say. He just wanted to talk to her.

"Not right now, man."

"Tahj, why you told him no? Give him the phone."

"Where you at?" He questioned, ignoring everything she just said.

"At the grocery store getting some stuff for Tazzy's party."

Tazzy was having a Polar Express themed birthday party tomorrow. Everyone was going to meet up at Tahj's house for food and cake, then they were going to take a party bus to Christmas in the Oaks to see the lights. Nikka had let the pettiness go and asked Star if she could cook the food for the party. Star graciously accepted the request because she was territorial over her kitchen these days anyway.

"Oh okay. What's your Auntie Fee's old address?"

"Whyyy?" She asked as her mind started to race. Just why did he need to know that?

"I was looking at properties online and I'm tryna make sure I'm not tripping because I think I saw her house on the market." He lied. He didn't want to but he couldn't reveal his hand yet. He also didn't want her getting worked up about him running into her aunt. He needed to do what he needed to do first.

"Oh. It's 3500 Amelia and Saratoga."

"Gotcha. That wasn't the house I saw then. See you in a few. I love you."

"I love you too." She replied and he hung up immediately after. Something was up for sure and she planned on pressing him about it later.

Meanwhile Tahj was making his next call. He tried his best to stay clear of these people, but in this situation he was making an exception.

"911, what's your emergency?"

"Hello, I'd like to report a woman named Fetima Jackson for filming and participating in child pornography. It's located in her home. Her address is…"

"You making your chocolate cupcakes tomorrow, sis?" Tamia asked Star as they chatted over FaceTime. Star was still in the store and she was starting to think that she was taking a long time to shop because people kept calling her phone. First Tahj, then the twins who were getting their hair done by Talea, and now Tamia.

"No. Nikka's in charge of deserts."

"Bitch I know you lying! She ain't learned her lesson from Baby Tahj birthday party?!"

Star giggled hysterically. "Girl no, she's ordering the treats from this girl I referred her to. I think she's done playing around in the kitchen."

"Whew, thank God!" Tamia praised. "But let me find out you and Nikka besties now."

"Girl, go to hell." Star huffed, propelling Tamia to crack up.

"Forreal though, what's the tea?"

"There's no tea. Nikka as well as Lexi just knows their place now. As long as they're cool and respectful I'll reciprocate their energy. Especially when it's about the kids."

"I feel you on that," Tamia nodded in understanding. "But you know what I think got them hoes in line?"

"What?"

"Them ass whoopings you gave them. That'll get the most hard headed bitch's mind right."

"You might be right,"Star tittered.

"On top of that I think Nikka is finally learning how to live without Tahj and realizing she's better off." Tamia continued.

"Forreal? What you know that I don't?" Star questioned.

"Her social media presence tells it all. She's been going out more and enjoying her life instead of worrying about a man that doesn't want her,"she rolled her eyes. "And she's been calling me asking about vendors. She's starting a kids clothing boutique."

"Well the girl does have an eye for style and fashion. I wish her the best," Star stated genuinely. She wanted nothing more than for Tahj's baby mama's to legitimately move on. It would make everybody's lives easier, including theirs.

"Yea, that's what I said. And she always has Baby Tahj and Tazzy dressed to the nines."

Star checked out of the conversation when she felt someone tap her shoulder. She turned around and was met by a face she hadn't seen a while.

"Long time no see, Star! How have you been, girl?!"

Star offered a polite smile. "I've been fine. What about you Frandesha?"

"Frandesha?! Sis, flip the camera so I can see that hoe!" Tamia cackled at the fact that her old enemy was in Star's face. Really, she would've never had a problem with the girl had she not come for her jugular on multiple occasions over Noel. It was all water under the bridge now on Tamia's end because she was truly happy with her family, relationship, and life. This was nothing more but entertainment for her. She wanted to see how the bitch who used to say awful things about her was holding up in life.

Star had been talking on the phone with her air pods connected, so Frandesha couldn't hear a thing. She smoothly turned her camera to Frandesha who was still pretty but the difference was clear. She used to be more polished while simultaneously dripping in designer labels that she never missed a chance to brag about. Any time Star used to step out with her former "friend" she'd receive underhanded comments about her affordable attire. It got so bad to the point where Star didn't even want to go anywhere with her any more because she had gotten so materialistic. From the looks of her now, life had humbled her. She didn't look terrible, but she definitely had this dusty vibe about her. Her wig looked very stiff and her baby bangs were forced. The long lashes on her face reminded Star of spiders that would crawl away at any minute because they were crooked. She had on a basic ensemble of faded Juicy Couture tights with a matching logo top. It was obviously an outfit she owned from her previous life because it was worn down.

"I'm just maintaining. I see you doing it big now." Frandesha forced a smile.

Frandesha was a girl who used to be spoiled rotten and would pay top dollar to upkeep her appearance, but now she had been reduced to doing everything for herself. She was a single mother with no help from her baby's father, so her money was limited even though she worked like a dog waitressing and bartending. She made good money, but not nearly enough to fund the lifestyle she once had when she dated Noel. When they were together she had the world at her fingertips, and she never hesitated to throw it in anyone's face.

Now she was green with envy at Star's life because it was like they'd switched places. Star was now the kept bitch with a rich man. Her outfit alone said "I can buy your broke ass life." Star was dressed down in a black off white tracksuit with black Uggs, a matte black Chanel bag, and a small Diamond cross rested around her neck. She had a light beat that consisted of lashes, concealer, filled in brows, brown lip liner, and lip gloss. Her curly hair was in a sleek bun showing off her pretty face and happy glow. Yea, the sight of this bitch had Frandesha *sick.*

"Doing it big? I don't know about all that," Star giggled. "But I'm happy."

"Sis, now ain't the time to be humble. Tell that hoe you doing it bigger and better than she could've ever done it." Tamia urged in her ear, increasing Star's laughter.

"That's what's up," Frandesha nodded when suddenly Star's hand glimmered. The icy rock on her finger had caught her attention. "Congratulations."

"Huh?" Star asked in bewilderment before she noticed what Fran was eyeing. She released light laughter. "Oh girl, this is not an engagement ring. My step son got this for me for my birthday."

Although Tahj's money paid for the gift, Star found it heartwarming that Baby Tahj had picked out something this nice for her. He was undoubtedly her dream son.

"That's amazing. You're lil blended family is so cute. I be seeing y'all on the gram, flexing. You need to go ahead and follow me back, bitch. Don't be acting all Hollywood."

"Is that bitch serious?" Tamia questioned. "That hoe is still as desperate as ever.

Star laughed again at Tamia because she was really getting a front row seat to this conversation and offering petty commentary unbeknownst to Frandesha.

"I have so many followers thanks to my sisters-in-laws constantly tagging me in shit. I ain't even noticed you follow me. I would *never* let my position in life go to my head."

That felt like shade, but Fran let it roll off her back. It bothered her much more that she had the audacity to bring up her sisters in laws knowing the history she shared with Tamia. Now she felt like Star was trying to be messy when she wasn't even on that. She could play that game too.

"Hmmm, well girl I suggest making your man put a ring on it before he jumps to the next thing."

Star's head tilted. "Excuse me?"

"I'm just saying from experience, don't be playing house with nothing to show for it. Sure, y'all have kids but he then already jumped ship with his other two baby mama's. So we know that's not gonna keep the nigga. At least if y'all get married he can't put you out on your ass. Take it from me , girl, starting over ain't no joke."

Star's eyes danced around in disbelief for several seconds before she and Tamia bursted into hysterics.

"What's funny?" Fran's eyes fluttered with her hands on her hips.

"Whew!" Star caught her breath from laughter. " Bitch *you're* funny if you think you can give me *any* advice. You been really studying my life, huh?!"

"Drag her!" Tamia instigated.

"Let me enlighten you since you're tuned in! Tahj can leave me today or tomorrow and it won't matter! Me and mine gone be straight because mama got her own bread! I been having my own and I never depended on a nigga. That's something my maw taught me early and I took heed. I'm far from a kept bitch like you used to be. I see you struggling in life since Noel dropped you on your head. That Tyler Perry ass wig on your head and them old ass clothes is a dead give away. Don't ever think you and me are the same. I'm a hustler with an actual career. Unlike you I can maintain the life I'm living now on my own *if* I want to."

"Tell that hoe she don't even know who her baby daddy is to be speaking on yours!" Tamia hollered. Star decided it was time to disconnect her AirPods and let her do the honors.

"Repeat that, Mia." Star instructed. Frandesha's eyes grew to the size of watermelons.

"Bitch don't speak on my brother when you don't even know who your baby daddy is!"

"Actually I know exactly who he is!" Fran argued, refusing to be lil girled.

"So you mean to tell me you could have spared yourself that embarrassment with Noel years ago and you didn't? That's pathetic," Tamia tittered.

"Ya know what, I've come too far to be discussing old shit. Fuck y'all hoes!" Frandesha went off before storming off with a red face.

"Fuck like us, hoe, and maybe you can get another nigga to take care of you!" Tamia shouted.

"She gone, sis." Star tittered.

"Chile I don't see how you were friends with her."

"Me either, but I'm glad she's able to witness me live my best life with her mad ass." Star laughed.

After cooking for the majority of the day, Star was exhausted. The bubble bath she'd just taken was working it's magic and sending her fast to sleep. She was almost to the finish line but her ringing phone interrupted her. She looked at her screen in aggravation. It was Colley.

"The fuck she want?" She mumbled, but answered anyway. Colley had been going through a lot mentally lately with facing her past, so Star never felt comfortable ignoring her calls.

"Yea?" She yawned into the phone.

"You was sleep?" Colley asked, with urgency dripping from her voice. That alerted Star a tad.

"Just about," she responded groggily. "What's going on?"

"Bitchhhh, I'm bouta text you something right now. Check your messages!"

Star went to their text messages just as the screenshot Colley sent her popped up. Her heart dropped in shock as she clicked on it. Star immediately put her phone on speaker so she could talk and further inspect the mug shot she was looking at.

"Wait! Bitch I was not expecting to see this! Multiple child pornography charges?! Oh, she's going down!"

"Yea Fee bouta be in jail for the rest of her miserable ass life. I never knew she was a pedophile but looking back at the way she reacted when I told her my own brother was violating me it makes perfect sense."

"This shit is crazy." Star replied, trying her best to sound surprised. Maybe she would've been if she wasn't already privy to Fee and Tahj. Still, she was definitely shocked to find out that the bitch had allegedly recorded herself with little boys. She would stay tuned in when it came to this story and she was hoping they threw her aunts ass under the jail.

"Who you telling?! Multiple counts of child porn?! That means it was more than one boy. Star, my mom has sons so my mind is automatically going to some disgusting places."

"Hey, I wouldn't put the shit past her. Maybe Devlin is the way he is for a reason. I mean, our grandpa used to touch our mothers. That shit must've been a generational curse."

"The hell it is. It wasn't passed down to us. Thank God Devlin never had kids of his own."

"Yea, that is a blessing because ain't no telling…"

She lost her train of thought when Tahj entered the room. He had hit her up after she left the grocery store to tell her he wouldn't be home until late that night because something came up with work. His schedule could be unconventional and work could pull him away at any second, so she had no reason to doubt him. But for some reason when she laid eyes on him she just knew his ass hadn't been working. His eyes were giving him away.

"Let me talk to you, Star." He demanded as he sat on the edge of the bed.

"Where were you?" She questioned. "Guess who done got herself locked up?"

She wanted to know where he'd really been, but she also had this burning desire to tell him about Fee.

"Your Auntie Fee."

"You saw the mug shot on nola dot com already?" She guessed.

"Star, hang up the phone and I'll tell you how I know."

She sucked her teeth and then told Colley goodbye before ending the call.

"Okay. How do you know?"

"Because I called the police on her duck ass."

"Wait, what?"

"I ran into her right after I left the barbershop. She thought it was a good idea to black mail me with videos she secretly recorded of us when I was a child in exchange for money. I wanted to kill that hoe but I got her locked up instead."

Star gasped. "That's why you asked me for her address?! Why didn't you just tell me what was happening from the beginning?"

"I just felt like I wanted to handle it on my own. I didn't need you getting all excited because then I would've been tripping out too."

Star wanted to go off but she quickly realized she'd prove his point by doing that. She could also admit that she would've popped off had Tahj called her and said Fee was trying to black mail him with child porn. She could actually see herself pulling up to that lady's house to beat her ass. Then she would've been in jail too. Tahj had handled it right all on his own.

"So where have you been for all these hours?"

"At the police station. They wanted me to come down and view the tapes. I confirmed my identity in a few of them. I have no clue who the other three boys were, but they definitely looked like they were around my age at the time."

Her jaw dropped. "Wow."

"My sentiments exactly. I ain't know I was opening up a can of worms or that your auntie was a repeat offender."

"That bitch ain't no auntie of mine,"she sneered. "So are they giving her bail?"

"I don't know all that yet, but if they do, her ass won't be able to pay it. One of the detectives told me that her dumb ass was in there telling on herself. She was saying shit like she ain't forced nobody to do shit. She was just the hottest mama on the block and everybody wanted a piece of her."

"Oh her ass is getting football numbers."

"Huh, bruh? It's sounding like an open and shut case to me. But I let them know that I'll cooperate 100% and even testify *if* it goes to trial."

Star scooted closer to him and grabbed his hand. "I'm proud of you, forreal. You're doing the right thing."

"I know. Let's just hope it pays off."

"It will. I know it will."

December 25, 2020

Star was going to need stitches because her stomach was sure to explode from laughter as she watched Tahj and his brothers perform to Forever My Lady by Jodeci for the Bellamy family talent show. Tahj was as serious as ever making intense eye contact with Star, while Tavior and Tarik moved in perfect sync behind him. They also didn't sound half bad harmonizing; showing off just how musically inclined they really were. Tahj however was extremely tone def, but he was still winning Star over. She was thinking about making the lyrics come to life and giving him another baby.

"Alright, I think it's unanimous. We won that." Tavior bragged while popping his Ralph Lauren pajama collar. Everyone had on pajamas this year for the get together per Star's request, but everybody was on board. The thought of staying in pajamas all day was comforting. All the males had on red and black Ralph Lauren plaid pajamas and all the females rocked red bodysuit onesies with merry Christmas across the butt courtesy of Tamia's pajama line. They were all able to let loose, drink,and eat all that they wanted without worrying about their appearance. This was definitely the best Christmas yet.

"Y'all wonnnnn?!" Ant questioned dramatically. "Lies. Me and my bro killed that shit."

He and Noel had indeed killed it singing Let it Snow by Boys II Men. Everybody had gotten their life and all, but it was no way anybody could seriously beat that.

"Boy y'all sing for a profession. Y'all do not count!" Tati laughed, resulting in Angel laughing too. That made everybody else holler.

"So these fools not in the music industry too?" Supreme pointed to Tavior and Tarik.

"Aht-aht, they *producers*,"Tahj said.

"Them reference tracks they be making say otherwise,"Noel butted in.

"Okay, but at the end of the day singing is not their job description." Tahj argued.

"Shit, it obviously ain't in yours either." Choc tittered, making everyone laugh harder.

"My turn, mommy!" One of Choc's twins, Siraj, tapped her leg.

"Put on my boy favorite song, Tahj." Supreme laughed.

Just like that, the argument about them winning came to a halt as Siraj danced and rapped his two year old heart out to Rody Rich's High Fashion. Everybody recorded and bucked him up to no end. After Siraj performed for them, the adults took a backseat and let the kids do their thing. When all of Tahj's daughters danced to Ballerina Girl by Lionel Richie he thought his heart would explode from love and adoration. They were redoing the choreography they did for Choc's dance school recital in the spring. Choc was so proud that they remembered the entire thing that she had tears in her eyes.

"Where's Suga, Titi Star?" Noeva asked. "Her gotta dance with me."

"She should be on her way soon, baby." Star answered. The thing about holidays with large families was that everybody had other people they had to see. Like Tavior and Jamaya had been with Jamaya's people all morning and evening before finally coming to Star and Tahj house around 6pm.

Colley, on the other hand, was still with her dad. He had gotten married a few years ago and had adult step kids. Colley loved spending time with them on holidays. They always got her and Suga nice gifts. She did promise to end her day with Star and the Bellamy's though.

"Cookies!" Angel shouted.

"Here," Star handed him the entire plate of freshly baked Christmas cookies.

"Girl he gon eat them all and be hyper as fuck." Tati complained.

"And? Not too much on my youngin." Ant asserted.

Tati flipped him off quickly before any of the little ones could see, making everyone laugh.

"Our other little sister coming?" Tarik questioned with laughter in his voice. Everybody gave him a look because they knew his ass was trying to be funny.

They were able to track Lanae down via social media about their little sister, Taina. Lanae had positive DNA results for Tarell and Taina, so paternity wasn't in question. It was a good thing she had it in black and white because Taina looked like them the least. She mostly looked like her mom but she was a pretty little girl, and if she had their blood flowing through her veins then they wanted to be a part of her life. Well, Lanae wasn't exactly making that easy for them. Quite frankly, she had them fucked up.

She was attempting to treat them like they were the baby daddy that left her ass high and dry. The last time they tried to get the baby was Thanksgiving day. She had the audacity to tell them that they weren't seeing her child until they coughed up some cash to put her daughter in the same type of living situations they all had. She also let them know that they weren't getting Taina if they didn't take her big sister too because they were a package deal. After that situation they were feeling like fuck it. They weren't about to kiss anybody's ass over their child. At the end of the day Lanae was making her own daughter miss out by acting entitled. The Bellamy's would give to their family automatically, but they weren't about to get suckered.

They were also still struggling to find the other mystery child their dad had. All they knew was that the baby mama's name was Amil, so their information was limited. They actually considered reaching out to their dad for answers, but they weren't that desperate yet.

"I was really hoping that Colley was over exaggerating about that child's mama," Talea sighed. "But one thing about it, I ain't about to make Tarell's problem mine. If that baby wants a relationship with us when she's older and can speak for herself then I'll be here."

"I second that,"Choc raised her hand.

"Yea, I don't need baby mama drama from a chick that ain't even my baby mama,"Tahj declared. Things were finally smooth sailing with his own baby mama's, so he wasn't jumping head first into a messy situation with his fathers bm.

"Daddy can we finally open gifts?" True ran up and asked. They'd already exchanged gifts as a household that morning, but now everybody had to exchange gifts as a family. The huge Christmas tree decorated in red and gold ornaments was overflowing with gifts. They were trying to wait for Colley because Suga had a bunch of gifts under the tree as well, but she had already told Star it was cool if they started without them.

"They have been waiting for hours now." Star said.

"Alright y'all, go for it." Tahj announced. The kids immediately went berserk and ran for the tree.

Star was already satisfied with her Christmas gifts. Tahj had let it be known before she started opening gifts that morning that the year's theme was diamonds. He'd gotten her so much jewelry she could've opened up her own jewelry store or start a snow storm. She got him quite a few things as well, including another Diamond chain dedicated to all of his kids. He loved showing them off in any way possible.

After spoiling each other rotten this morning, she wasn't expecting to get it ten times again from his family. This was one of the many Bellamy traditions she could get used to. Her in-laws didn't play at all. She damn near cried when she unwrapped a vintage gold metallic Louis Vuitton bag that Paris Hilton had popularized in the early 2000's. Tamia had gotten her that, and she made her feel like the Gucci boots she'd gotten her wasn't enough. But Tamia loved them and swore she'd been wanting them for some time now.

"Alright, I got one more gift for you, bae." Tahj smiled as he pulled Star into his embrace.

"Here you go," Star threw her head back in agony. Tahj was about to show out and her heart already couldn't take it. But she loved that he was a gift giver because she loved receiving.

"Yea. Here I go," he chuckled, as his brothers gave him a knowing smile. Star looked around and suddenly felt like everybody knew something she didn't. Even her own kids who were smiling all goofy.

"Let's head to the back yard, y'all." Tahj ordered while grabbing Star's hand and leading the way.

The backyard was decorated just as elaborately as the rest of the house for the holiday season, but Star didn't recall the projector being set up. Tahj had the remote in his hand and pressed play once everyone was as quiet and calm as possible.

"Baby while we're young. I think we should do something crazy Like say, "Fuck everyone." And just run away from the daily routine. Yeah you know what I mean. I'm tellin' everybody you're mine and I like it. And I really hope you don't mind, I can't fight it. No, you

know I cannot hide it 'cause I am so excited. That I finally decided on you...." Star got chills all over her body as Jhene Aiko provided the perfect soundtrack to the slide show that was playing. Every picture or video they'd taken together or with the kids since they reunited in January was showing up on the projector. Although Tahj had laced her in diamonds already, this gift was her favorite because it was the most meaningful. By the time the slide show was coming to an end she was in tears. Tahj still had his arm around her for comfort and Baby Tahj had his arms wrapped around her waist for additional comfort. She felt so much love around her. She was getting ready to thank Tahj but to her surprise, it wasn't over yet. Final words popped up on the screen, making her heart stop.

"I told you the theme was diamonds this year so it would be a shame if I didn't put a Diamond engagement ring on your finger. Will you marry me?"

Star literally screamed, startling everyone except Tahj who just laughed while pulling a box from his pajama pocket. He opened it up, before getting on one knee.

"Will you marry me, Star?" He asked out loud.

"Yes! Yes!" She nodded vehemently. He didn't hesitate to slide that enormous rock on her finger where it belonged. Tahj kept his word. He made up for the last Christmas they spent together.

Chapter 26

Colley looked at the time on her phone and the last bit of her patience chipped away. She'd been waiting outside of her dad's house for Tarell for about twenty minutes and she was over it. If she had followed her first mind she would've already been at Tahj and Star's house. She'd let Tarell convince her to wait for his ass when he was anything but reliable. She was about to go. She didn't need a damn thing from him.

Just as she started her car up, someone's headlights shined from behind her. She looked in her rear view mirror and saw Tarell's car. When he got out and approached her, she got out of her car.

"About time. I was about to leave."

"Yea right. I know you wasn't passing up no money. Here." He handed her an envelope before peaking into the back seat where Suga slept peacefully. "Can I hold and kiss my baby?"

Colley frowned. "Ion know about allat."

"What you mean you don't know about all that? I can't kiss my child now?"

"Can you? Shit you've only done that once or twice since she's been born."

"Look, I know I've dropped the ball but I want to do better now."

Colley laughed in amusement. "I won't hold my breath, but I'll tell you this here, don't bring that inconsistent shit my child's way. She's better off without you."

"That's a hell of a thing to say after you done took my damn money!"

"And I'll always take it whenever you offer. I didn't make her alone so the least you can do is contribute financially. Instead of meeting up with me to give me money you could just pay your child support."

He smacked his teeth. "That's what I wanted to talk to you about. Can you take me off of that shit? You see, I'm more than capable of giving you money. We don't need them crackers in our business."

"Tarell go feed that shit to the next dumb bitch. I'm not buying what you're trying to sell me right now."

He stepped closer to her. "Let's go somewhere and talk."

She backed up in disgust. She couldn't believe she used to be head over heels for this old bastard.

"Nigga, you have issues if you think I'm going anywhere with you. Goodni-"

"**BANG! BANG! BANG!**"

All the wind was knocked out of Colley's body as she felt something sharp penetrate her stomach. She looked at Tarell in disbelief before passing out on to the ground. Tarell was just as shocked as she was as he looked at Porscha in horror.

"PORSCHA, WHAT THE FUCK ARE YOU DOIN-"

"BANG! BANG!"

She shot Tarell twice in his stomach, making him double over.

"Bitch I'm tired of you playing with me! This shit ends today!"

"I-I'm s-s-so-sor…"Tarell struggled to say as he struggled to breathe.

"Yea, you a sorry muthafucker! You promise to do right over and over again and my dumb ass believes it. If you can't do right by me, then ain't no sense of you being here, bitch!" She pointed the gun at his head and then she blew his lights out. As she looked at the love of her life dead on the ground next to his mistress, she didn't know how to feel. She couldn't even hear herself think because his bastard child was in the car screaming at the top of her lungs. When evil thoughts started coming to Porscha about the child she knew what she had to do. This man had ruined her and there was no coming back from it. It was time to end this shit for good. She held her gun up and pulled the trigger, offing herself.

"You never try me. Always stood right by me. Make living lively. Highly spoken of. My only love, the only one.You're my wifey," Tahj sang to Star as the entire family stepped to Wifey by Next. The night was winding down, but everyone was still going strong and partying. The adults were dancing and getting more drunk, while the kids played with the new toys they'd just opened. Everyone was lit.

"You ready to be my wife?" Tahj whispered in Star's ear.

"Yes indeed," she smiled. "You ready to be my husband?"

"Hell yea, and I can't wait to knock you up again. Baby Tahj wants a lil brother, something serious."

"I'm sure we can work something out for him," Star giggled.

"Mommy, since you and daddy are getting married does that mean you'll have our last name now?" Tahiry asked.

"That's exactly what that means, baby girl." Tahj chuckled.

"See! Told you," Baby Tahj teased before poking his sister and running off.

"The whole world gon know we getting married tomorrow. Baby Tahj gon make sure of it. Watch."

Star shoulders shook as she laughed. "Boy, stop."

"I'm serious. I already know he gon tell his whole school when they go back in January."

"I know you gon let my baby be."

"I am. We just gotta teach about discretion."

"Discretion? Is this coming from the man who already posted about it on Instagram?" She tittered. "Maybe Baby Tahj gets his big mouth from you."

Tahj laughed in response because he had been eager as fuck to let the world know the great news. He couldn't fault his baby boy for feeling the same way.

"Mommy your phone is ringing!" True ran up with Star's phone in her hand. Her heart skipped a beat.

"What's wrong?" Tahj questioned. He immediately noticed the troubled look on her face.

"Colley's dad is calling me."

Star loved her Uncle Cordell but it was rare that he called her phone ever. Then the fact that Colley hadn't shown up yet gave her an unsettling feeling. She answered the FaceTime call with no hesitance. As soon as the call connected it felt like someone snatched the soul out of her body. Colley's dad was crying hysterically with blood all over him as police lights flashed in the background.

"Star! They got my baby! They fucking got her!"

Star dropped her phone and hit the ground. She instantly started crying as she asked God why he could never spare her. First her daddy, then her mom, and now her little cousin. Not even just her cousin, Colley was her sister. This shit didn't feel real.

Chapter 27

November 28, 2021

"Tryna rewind 'til we're back where we started. Yeah that's all I want. Night after night after night I'm still haunted...I'm haunted baby...I'm haunted by you, you, fall asleep and dream of you, you. Late at night I scream for you, you, waiting on a deja-vu. But until then I live with Hallucinations."

Star wiped a tear away as she became emotional on the happiest day of her life. Thus far, her day had been beautiful but her heart was still heavy for her loved ones that couldn't be here. It was bittersweet.

"Can I ask you a question, most beautiful bride in the world?" Tamia asked as she appeared behind her in the mirror. Star just looked up because she felt like she'd burst into tears at any moment.

"This song is beautiful, but it's sad as fuck. Why have you been playing it in here all day?" She asked, referring to the dressing room.

Star didn't have words because the song reminded her of a person she missed deeply. The question just triggered something inside of her, making her cry. Before she knew it, multiple people in her bridal party surrounded her and led her over to a couch as she broke down. She could hear Tamia apologizing but she had already zoned out to simpler times.

September 5, 2003

"Titi, can I come live with you? You gotta nice house!" Colley voiced loudly as she ran in the kitchen with Star right on her trail. They'd been playing with her many Bratz dolls while watching The Cheetah Girls. They were undoubtedly having the time of their life. To top it off, Teione, Star's mom, was cooking white beans, fried chicken, and baking chocolate cake for dessert. This place was much better than Colley's house and she loved coming over every other weekend.

Although Teione wasn't on the best terms with Fee, they could be cordial for the most part.

"Your maw have a nice house too, niecey pooh." Tee Tee laughed while pinching Colley's cheek and kissing it. "Y'all girls hungry?"

"Yes mama! Can I have two pieces of chicken?" Star asked.

"You can have whatever you want, baby. Ou shit! This my jam!" Tee Tee exclaimed before turning up the volume on her radio.

"I'm wishing on a star. To follow where you are. I'm wishing on a dream. To follow what it means…" Rose Royce sang, but Tee Tee sure was helping them out.

"Baby, you hear this?" She looked at Star. "This was me and your daddy song. This is how you got your name."

Star smiled, despite already knowing that information. Anytime the song came on her mom would repeat this story and she loved hearing it everytime. Mainly because her dad wasn't around due to him being locked up. Tee Tee would always say that she made it hard for Star's dad to love her because she had problems, but he never let it deter him. Apparently this song was always his go to whenever they *had a falling out and it worked like a charm every time. When Tee Tee got pregnant and they learned they were having a girl, Star's dad declared that they were finally getting their own little Star.*

"Super Star you will always be blessed and highly favored because you were made from love." She kissed Star's forehead. Colley looked at them longingly. She wished her mom showed her that type of affection or said sweet things like that, period.

"What about me, Titi? Was I made from love?" Colley questioned.

Tee Tee's heart swelled. Something about Colley reminded her of herself when she was a little girl.

"I tell you what, niece, you are very loved by me, Star, Diamond, and your entire family. We're gonna always be here for you and you can come to my house anytime." She kissed her.

"Star! Star!"

Star looked up, finally snapping out of her gut wrenching cry.

"What's wrong? Why are you crying?"

"I-I miss herrrrr." She sniffled.

Colley wrapped her arms around Star and hugged her tightly. "I know you miss your mama. She's looking down right now and she's so proud of you. Bitch I'm proud of you. You have no idea. Now stop messing up your makeup."

Small laughter released from Star's mouth, while she silently thanked God for sparring Colley's life. After being shot in the stomach twice it was a close call, and everyone thought she wouldn't make it. Even Star. For a moment everyone thought she'd really died because of how her dad worded things on Christmas night.

Colley showed everybody just how much of a fighter she was because she pulled through. She had to undergo intense therapy but with her family by her side she felt invincible. Colley as well as Star felt like there would be a rift in their relationship with the Bellamy family because of this tragic situation. Porscha and Tarell were *dead*. Of course they knew that none of the Bellamy's were fans of their dad or Porscha, but death was death. Nobody wanted to see their family die.

They were right about that too. Tahj nor his siblings were jumping for joy when they learned their father died at the hands of his wife, and that she had tragically taken her own life too. There was this dark cloud over the family and quite a few tears were shed. However, that had no bearing on how the Bellamy's treated Star and Colley. In fact, the situation brought them closer. No one was making excuses for Porsche's vile actions either. She was wrong and had gone off the deep end. Everyone saw that and wasn't afraid to voice it. Then there was Tarell. All his kids knew he'd get his one day because he wasn't living right. They figured he'd get a life sentence in jail like Fee or something to that extent. They would've never predicted that Porscha would be the one to take him out of his glory. The situation was sad and still weighed heavy on their hearts, but they had come to terms with it and made strides towards moving forward as a family.

"Let me touch up your makeup, girl." Jamaya giggled while blinking back tears. "You got me in here bouta cry."

"Same," Tamia wiped away a tear. "I feel so bad for asking you that dumb ass question."

"Mia, that wasn't your fault," she laughed. "I've been crying all damn week. Ask your brother."

"I will as soon as we get back out there to him. Fix her up, Ja." Tamia instructed.

This was Star's third and final dress change for the day. The first dress she wore was an extravagant Givenvy white dress with a long veil and train. It was perfect for the wedding ceremony. For the reception she changed into a sleek and classy Vera Wang dress with less fabric so she could move around easily. Now she was putting on a white, bedazzled jumpsuit that came with a detachable train. The number had been custom made for her by a famous black designer named Daisie Martelle. She was ecstatic to end her night off wearing this because she looked like a bad bitch. She made a mental note to stop crying because it didn't go with the look.

"You wearing slippers out there? Or do you want your heels?" Colley asked.

"Heels so I can take pictures, but I need my slippers on standby."

"Gotcha," Colley bent down with Star's sparkly red bottoms to put them on her feet. Making Colley her maid of honor was a no brainer, but she was really taking her job seriously. That made Star be super proud of her decision.

Thirty minutes had gone by since Star had left Tahj's side and he was growing worried. He looked around at all their guests enjoying themselves while doing the bunny hop. He would've loved to join them but he wasn't about to without his wife. He got chills just calling her that. His wife. That shit had a nice ring to it.

"Ayeee!!! I'm so glad I got my own! I ain't worried bout Josephine! In my life it's a natural high! Come and bunny hop with me!" Star shouted at the top of her lungs while jumping into formation with everybody else. Tahj had to laugh because she'd seemingly popped up out of nowhere.

"Man, where did she come from?" Tarik questioned, while laughing at the same thing.

"I don't know, but let me go join her. Auntie Holly, are my boys good?"

"Boy, don't ask me that again. I keep telling you I got these babies. Go enjoy your wife." She encouraged him.

Auntie Holly had been an Angel to him and his family through a very tough year. She'd always been his favorite aunt growing up and well into his adulthood. Their relationship just kind of fell off when she got married and moved with her husband to Atlanta. They still talked every now and then, but it hadn't been the same as when she stayed in New Orleans. Sometimes he was tempted to beg her to come back but he saw she was happier.

She was his mom's sister and an outcast in their family. Porscha was the Golden child because she did everything "perfectly." She went to college, graduated, got married, and then had kids. Holly had been a teen mother and went straight to work to provide for her kids. She never had time for college and finding a husband. As the years went on, Porscha got snobbish and felt like she was too good for her sister who still stayed in the hood. They hadn't been close as sisters at all, but hearing about the tragedy still pulled Holly back home to New Orleans.

It was a blessing she did come, too, because the rest of Porscha's family were finding fault within Tahj and Tamia for the unfortunate events. According to them this would've never happened if they'd been there for their mother instead of entertaining their fathers outside kids and side hoes. Holly cussed them all out on behalf of her nephew and niece. She now resided in a home down the street from Tahj with her husband and she was their unofficial nanny. She was a much needed help with the newest addition to their family; Tyree and Tylen Bellamy.

When Star and Tahj found out she was pregnant at a doctor's visit in March they were shocked because they hadn't seen any of the common signs. At the same time they were both really happy about the news. Her pregnancy brought them the light they needed at such a dark time. When they welcomed their babies on October 25,2021 the world suddenly felt like a better place. All of the kids were equally, if not more excited than them. Baby Tahj was especially happy about not being the only boy anymore. He also couldn't stop smiling about his baby twin brother's birthdays being so close to his.

"You alright?" Tahj asked Star as he popped up behind her while she was dancing.

"I had a little breakdown, but I'm cool now."

"You say that shit like it's nothing."

"Crying is good for the soul. You asked me if I was good and I am. It's our wedding day and we're surrounded by people we love. Of course I'm good. Shit, with you I'm forever good."

He smiled proudly as his eyes beamed. "That's what I like to hear, baby. But our official wedding day was on February 13th. Don't you forget."

"How could I? You woke me up out of my sleep and dragged me to the courthouse. Damn near held a gun to my head." She laughed.

"Star please, it didn't take much convincing. You were eager to become my wife."

They had set a wedding date right after getting engaged, but as time passed Tahj felt he didn't want to wait. Life was too short to prolong what they could do now. So he decided to take the initiative and speed things along. Although she liked to stunt when it came to the details, she was with it. They'd been married about nine months now and they had zero regrets about how they did it.

"No, I think you were eager to be my husband."

"Okay. We were both eager. How about that?" He posed.

"I can live with that," she turned around and kissed him.

"Mommy!!! Daddy! Look at us!!!"

Tahj and Star looked up at their kids doing the bunny hop. They had all been a part of the wedding today. The girls had all served as flower girls and Baby Tahj had been the ring bearer. Like Star and Tahj, they wore Givenchy for the ceremony.

"Y'all better get it!" Star egged them on as she rocked in Tahj's arms.

"I can't wait to make more with you." Tahj whispered in Star's ear.

She smirked. "Nigga we gotta get your fertile ass neutered."

"Don't do me that, bae. I think I want shoot for ten now. What you think?"

"I think you should go to hell."

He laughed because it had been his goal to get that type of reaction out of her. He thought he was good on having more kids until they'd been blessed with more twins.

"Please. We'll name the next one after you."

"We was doing that anyway. It's only so many T's I can take." She rolled her eyes while stifling a smile.

"Okay, so you do want more kids. Noted."

"Yea maybe when Tyree and Tylin are like 4."

Tahj sucked his teeth. "Whatever, bruh."

After Bunny Hop went off, the DJ switched it up with a slow, love song by Dvsn called For Us. This was almost the song they chose for their first dance, but they opted for Corinne Bailey Rae's Like A Star. Well actually Tahj was hard up about that being the song for their first dance. After paying attention to the lyrics Star just let him have it. Just knowing he felt that way about her made her want to give him whatever he wanted. But this Dvsn song really hit the spot for Star and it was making her emotional again as she slowly danced in his arms.

"*I don't wanna waste a minute of my life without you in it. And I don't wanna act like you ain't been the one from the beginning. I don't wanna lose another battle to my pride when I know that I love you. And there's enough to last, yeah. Forever and for after.*"

"You crying?" Tahj chuckled, even though he had wet eyes himself. He'd cried more this year than he ever had. He shed tears over his parents, he cried when the twins were born, and he cried today when he saw Star walking down the aisle. Now he was tearing up because he was fucking happy all around for once. He couldn't see life getting better than this.

"Yea, and you are too." She tittered. "We probably look like fools."

"Yep, two fools in love, Mrs. Bellamy." He professed before kissing her deeply.

The end!!!!

For updates, visuals, and sneak peeks join my reading group on Facebook, "That's All Cee Reading Group."

Made in the USA
Middletown, DE
05 May 2023